Thursday's Child

. . . a pride and prejudice journey of love

Pat Santarsiero

Thursday's Child is a work of fiction. The characters depicted are either from the author's imagination or from Jane Austen's novel, *Pride and Prejudice*.

© Copyright September 2, 2011 by Pat Santarsiero

First drafts were written in 2009 and 2010 and posted serially beginning September 2, 2011 and ending October 20, 2011.

Cover art digitally enhanced by Angel Lugo

ISBN-13:978-1484054833

Dedicated with sincere appreciation

To all the readers at AustenUnderground who supported and encouraged me, and especially to

Gayle Mills, Katie Baxley, & Wendi Sotis

whose invaluable support, suggestions and editing made this book possible.

I am eternally grateful.

Monday's child is fair of face,
Tuesday's child is full of grace,
Wednesday's child is full of woe,
Thursday's child has far to go.

LORD, WHAT FOOLS THESE MORTALS BE

PROLOGUE

A relentless August sun was making the long journey most uncomfortable. She had been riding in the hired carriage for well over an hour, her destination unknown to her. She truly hoped the driver was more enlightened than she. Her only companion was the steady cadence of the carriage, thus allowing her far too much time to think. *This is only going to be an interview*, she told herself. Certainly she was not committing to anything yet. Indeed, *both* parties needed to be in agreement.

She sighed deeply. She could not believe that events had led her to this point in her life.

In the year since Elizabeth's beloved father had died, her life had changed dramatically. Her carefree days at Longbourn seemed so long ago. Her leisurely rambles through the woods, her lively and challenging conversations with her father, and her shared intimacies with her dear sister Jane were all just memories now. As she stood on the brink of a decision that would forever change her life, she wondered at the circumstances that had brought about her present situation. Certainly twelve months ago she would never have even considered the decision she was about to face.

Pat Santarsiero

The shock of losing her father so suddenly to a heart attack had been further exacerbated when a very eager Mr. Collins announced he would be immediately taking possession of Longbourn.

Mrs. Bennet had tried to persuade Mr. Collins to delay fulfilling the provisions of the entailment until she and her five daughters could make other living arrangements but was granted a mere se'ennight to accomplish this task.

On the grey, bleak day that Elizabeth had stood at her father's grave, she knew that her life and the lives of all her sisters would be irrevocably changed. They were no longer the gentlemen's daughters they had been just days before. They would now have to make their own way in the world. The brunt of that task would fall to Jane and herself, as they were the eldest.

As she watched the scenery outside the carriage move past her, she remembered how the events of that week before her father's death had been filled with such hope....

Her mother and two youngest sisters, Kitty and Lydia, were beside themselves with joy over the prospect of seeing Mr. Bingley (and his £5,000 a year) at the Meryton Assembly on Saturday and could speak of little else. As unaffected as Jane had seemed by the news of Mr. Bingley's attendance, Elizabeth knew her beautiful, serene sister to be every bit the romantic. For herself, Elizabeth knew that only the deepest love could ever induce her to marry. Of course she *was* curious to see just who would turn up at the Meryton Assembly. Mary was the only sister who truly had no interest in the dance or in Mr. Bingley.

All of these musings were brought about by the fact that Mr. Bennet, after vexing his wife for several days, had finally done what any father of five unmarried daughters should. He had visited Mr. Bingley at Netherfield, told him of his five daughters, and welcomed him to the neighbourhood.

Thursday's Child

On Tuesday, to Mrs. Bennet's surprise and delight, Mr. Bingley returned Mr. Bennet's visit and arrived at Longbourn mid-morning. He was indeed anxious to meet the five daughters on which Mr. Bennet had expounded.

"Why, Mr. Bingley! How very good of you to call!" exclaimed Mrs. Bennet. "Girls! Girls! Come meet Mr. Bingley!" As the five daughters gathered into the parlour from every direction of the house, Mr. Bingley was enraptured. The sounds of giggling and petticoats swishing wafted around him. As if in synchronized time, all five Bennet daughters stopped before Mr. Bingley and made ready to curtsey.

"This is my eldest daughter, Jane," said Mrs. Bennet. Mr. Bingley lowered his head in a deep bow. As his eyes looked upward in greeting to Miss Bennet, he stopped all movement. Their eyes met, and, as they did, both parties immediately blushed. Mr. Bingley quickly regained his composure.

"It is a pleasure to make your acquaintance, Miss Bennet."

Jane, not recovering from her embarrassment as promptly as he, merely nodded and smiled in response.

Mr. Bingley was then introduced, in order, to Miss Elizabeth, Miss Mary, Miss Katherine and Miss Lydia. All curtsied and exchanged greetings. However, Mr. Bingley would later have little memory of any of them, except Jane; indeed, she was a perfect angel.

According to Charlotte Lucas, Elizabeth's best friend and closest neighbour, rumour had it that Mr. Bingley would be attending the Assembly with at least five ladies and eight gentlemen. The Bennet household was all anticipation for Saturday.

On Wednesday evening, as Mr. Bennet sat in his library, sipping his port and going over the estate books for the month, he felt a gripping pain in his chest.

Saturday morning, Mr. Bennet was laid to rest. That evening, the dance at the Meryton Assembly proceeded without the five Bennet sisters.

~*~

Charles Bingley paced the foyer at Netherfield Park, impatiently waiting for his two sisters, Caroline and Louisa, to finish dressing. Louisa's husband, Mr. Hurst, and Bingley's best friend, Mr. Fitzwilliam Darcy, had decided to wait in the library so that they might at least enjoy a glass of port whilst awaiting Bingley's sisters.

From the foyer they could hear Bingley inquire, "What can be taking them so long?" This entreaty was directed to no one; hence, no one replied. Still he continued, "I do not want to arrive too late! Sir William said the Assembly is to begin at eight o'clock, and it's already quarter past!" His natural enthusiasm was heightened considerably by the knowledge that the angelic Miss Bennet would also be attending the dance this evening.

Darcy and Mr. Hurst made their way from the library towards the foyer where Bingley was still muttering to himself. Darcy tried to conceal a smirk as he watched his friend's nervous agitation. Although Darcy insisted on being punctual, he had to admit he was in no great hurry to attend a country dance, nor any dance for that matter. He disliked social occasions and never felt at ease amongst strangers.

Darcy would have preferred a quiet evening enjoying the library at Netherfield, but memories of previous evenings in the company of Caroline Bingley reminded him that this would not be possible. He knew whatever decision he made with regard to tonight's festivities, Caroline's decision would mirror his own. The thought of spending an entire evening alone with Caroline Bingley made the decision to attend a country dance amongst strangers the more appealing choice.

Thursday's Child

He had hoped accompanying Bingley to Hertfordshire would help take his mind off of his obligations and familial duties. On his last visit to Rosings Park, his Aunt Catherine had again brought up the subject of his betrothal to his cousin Anne. As vehemently as he had argued against such a union, he knew that he either had to find someone suitable on his own (and soon) or marry his cousin. The Darcy name must persevere.

His many seasons in London had accomplished nothing other than convincing him that there was no one of his acquaintance for whom he held any tender feelings. The thought of meeting more conniving mothers and mercenary daughters was so abhorrent to him that he was beginning to wonder whether he might just as well marry Anne as face another season of the same.

As Caroline and Louisa finally made their way down the staircase, Caroline slipped her hand under Darcy's arm. "Shall we get this over with?" she asked with her usual look of superiority.

Yes, this was going to be a very long evening. Indeed, for both Darcy (who had no expectations to the contrary) and Bingley (who had the highest expectations of seeing his angel), the evening was a dismal disappointment.

CHAPTER ONE

"I think I will take the children out to the park today," said Jane as James Morgan sipped his tea.

"That's a fine idea. The weather certainly has been agreeable of late."

"Oh, Jane, while you're out, would you mind stopping off at my dressmakers? Could you find out if the fabric I ordered has arrived yet?" asked his wife, Emily.

"Of course, it shall be no trouble at all."

Jane Bennet had been in London since her father's death. She had immediately accompanied her Aunt and Uncle Gardiner following the funeral, staying with them in their London townhouse at Cheapside while her Aunt Gardiner made inquiries to find a suitable position for her beloved niece.

Within a few weeks she had heard that a prominent family, who resided at Grosvenor Street, was looking for a new governess for their three children. Jane had many qualities to recommend her for such a position, her sweet nature and unlimited patience making her the perfect candidate. The family immediately fell in love with Jane, and Jane immediately fell in love with the family.

"Jaime! Sarah!" Jane called to the two eldest children from the bottom of the stairs. She then went to the nursery and lifted Caleb, age two, from his bed. As she waited for James (or Jaime as he was called), age eight, and Sarah, age six, to reach the bottom of the stairs, she gathered up their coats, hats, and gloves. "Come on, you two. If we hurry, we might catch a glimpse of that family of ducks again this morning."

Sarah jumped at Jane's words. "Can we bring some bread to feed them?" she asked.

"I believe I just might have some pieces wrapped in my pocket," said Jane, much to Sarah's delight.

Mr. James Morgan and his wife, Emily, were not part of the hierarchy of London society. Mr. Morgan had made most of his fortune from the shipbuilding business his father had started years before. As it turned out, the business had proved to be highly lucrative, thereby affording the Morgans their current comfortable life style. Considering all that had happened, Jane was indeed quite content with her present situation, caring for their three delightful, well-behaved children. Jane's mind only occasionally wandered back to that very amiable and handsome gentleman who had once visited Longbourn.

The weather was indeed delightful for March. As they approached the park, Jane watched whilst the two older children ran to play. She held Caleb on her lap as she took a seat on a park bench and pulled Lizzy's latest letter from her pocket. Although she had read it several times already, it gave her comfort to read it again. She missed her sister dearly. Until their father's death, they had never been more than a bedroom wall away from each other, sharing every thought, every secret hope, and every fear. Now, she was in London, and Lizzy was wherever Mrs. Worthington happened to be travelling at any particular time.

Elizabeth Bennet had secured a position as a lady's companion not long after her father's death. Her knowledge of books and her easy conversation were all the qualifications Mrs. Worthington required. Having been a widow for several years, Mrs. Worthington could no longer stand the uninterrupted peace and stifling quiet of her home. She longed for companionship and conversation. Her son, John, lived in Oxford with his wife and family. She visited them once or twice a year but did not want to be a burden to them. Fortunately, her husband had left her enough money to live comfortably, and so she decided she would travel when her health permitted. She sought a companion with wit and intelligence to accompany her. She had found just that in Elizabeth Bennet.

Jane unfolded Lizzy's letter and read again:

March 23, 1812

Dearest Jane,

I was pleased to receive your last letter and to hear that you are getting on so well in London. I miss you so much, my dear sister. It is my sincerest hope that I shall be able to visit you in London soon. Mrs. Worthington and I have just arrived at Bath. We will be here for about a fortnight before travelling back to Mrs. Worthington's home where we will stay until July. At that time Mrs. Worthington is planning to visit her son and has given me leave to take a holiday if I wish. If all goes well, I shall visit you in London then.

Your news regarding Charlotte and Mr. Collins was quite shocking. I suppose with their being neighbours, it was inevitable that Mr. Collins would get around to making her an offer. That she accepted him, however, is what is most surprising. Our mother's nerves must be quite unsettled knowing that Charlotte Lucas is now the Mistress of Longbourn.

What news from Meryton? You know I must rely on you, dear Jane, to keep me informed of our family. Our mother has held fast to her vow to never speak to me again since my refusal of Mr. Collins, and it seems our younger sisters do not have any desire to displease her by writing to me themselves.

Jane, I know we have never talked about Mr. Collins's proposal, and because of your generous nature, you have never admonished me for my selfish behaviour. However, I find it rather hard to forgive myself. I realize now that I could have saved our family from all of the unpleasantness that has occurred since our departure from Longbourn. I have lived with that guilt and regret ever since, but I swear to you, my dear Jane, that if I ever have the opportunity to redeem myself, I will sacrifice anything to make it up to all my family.

I fear your opinion is right that our sister Lydia has grown wilder since our father's death. The situation with the Militia being in town disturbs me greatly. We both know how flighty Lydia can be, and where Lydia goes, Kitty shall surely follow. I sincerely hope our mother will take the trouble to check her unbridled behaviour before she is beyond amendment.

I must close for now, Jane. Mrs. Worthington and I have yet to unpack before dinner. Please give my love to our Aunt and Uncle Gardiner. Write me soon, dear Jane. With love from

Your affectionate sister,

Lizzy

Jane returned Lizzy's letter to her pocket, turning her attention to the Morgan children at play, as she looked around the park. She really liked this place. It wasn't so big that she worried the children would run off, but it was still large enough to require a good deal of exercise to walk its circumference. However, rather than walk around it, she much more enjoyed simply sitting on this bench and watching the other people as they came and went. She liked to see the other children at play and watched to see who had brought them there. Since this was an affluent area, it was usually a governess, such as herself.

She also liked to watch the young couples taking romantic strolls, deep in quiet conversation. Again, that amiable and handsome gentleman from Netherfield crept into her thoughts. She shook her head, as if ridding her mind of his image.

Jane shivered, becoming aware of the chill in the air, and she had yet to stop by Mrs. Morgan's dressmaker. She gathered up Caleb in her arms and walked towards the pond. Sarah had just finished scattering the last of the bread. The ducks squawked loudly to show their appreciation.

"Well, Sarah, I believe you have made friends for life."

Sarah graced her with her widest grin.

"We really should be going. Jaime, take your sister's hand. We still have an errand to run."

That evening Jane was to dine at the home of her Aunt and Uncle Gardiner. One of the advantages of her employment with the Morgans was their proximity to Gracechurch Street. Her aunt and uncle would often invite her to dine with them and would send their carriage round for her.

Jane climbed the steps to the entrance of the townhouse at Cheapside, a smile gracing her beautiful face. She was always so happy to be in company with her aunt and uncle for they were the finest people she knew.

As they gathered around the dinner table, Uncle Gardiner smiled at Jane. "One of the reasons your Aunt Madeline and I have invited you this evening is to inform you of an extended trip we are planning to take this summer. Another gentleman and I have recently invested in a company that is based in America. Since my partner cannot spare much time away from his other businesses, he has asked if I would go and check on its progress. Your aunt and I thought it would be a wonderful opportunity to make a real holiday of it. After concluding my business, we plan to travel about the country and do some sightseeing. I've been told there are many places of great interest to visit there."

"That does sound most exciting," said Jane. "When have you planned to depart?"

"Well," said her Aunt Madeline, "we plan to leave London sometime in June and return by Christmas."

"Yes," her uncle continued, "I'll have time to get my business in order by then. I have already written your mother to let her know of our plans. I will try to keep her regularly informed of our whereabouts."

They spent the next hour discussing her aunt and uncle's travel plans, and soon it was time to leave. Jane knew she would miss them, but she did have the hope that Lizzy would visit her during the summer to help fill the void.

CHAPTER TWO

Ever since the disastrous events surrounding Ramsgate, Darcy had been reluctant to leave Georgiana for any long period of time. He had been most anxious to see her again, and so upon his departure from Netherfield, he had returned to her in London.

Hertfordshire had been a quiet diversion from the hectic pace of the city. The people were pleasant enough, but he certainly didn't want to spend more time in their company than necessary. He hadn't met anyone who had held his interest for anything longer than a brief conversation.

Bingley, as was his custom, had found some delight in a young lady he had met at the small country estate of Longbourn but was disappointed when the family's situation had suddenly changed, forcing her to leave for London. Bingley hadn't gone into much detail about the family, and Darcy was somewhat relieved that he would not have to live through another one of his friend's infatuations.

Darcy was looking forward to spending Christmas with Georgiana at Pemberley. He would stay with her until Easter, when he would then travel with his cousin Richard for their annual trip to Kent to visit his Aunt Catherine and cousin Anne at Rosings. His guilt over Georgiana haunted him constantly. He wanted to provide his sister a more stable life than he had given her in the past. He knew the best way to accomplish that would be for him to marry. She would then have a sister who could be her friend and confidant, someone who would help her rebuild her self-esteem.

After many sleepless nights, Darcy had come to a decision. On this trip to Rosings, he would propose to his cousin Anne.

It had always been his Aunt Catherine's greatest wish that they would marry. This alliance was desired, not for any romantic notion, but to unite the two vast estates of Pemberley and Rosings. He and Anne had always been fond of each other, but there was never a great attraction between them. He had affection for her, but only as a cousin. If she felt more, she never betrayed those feelings. However, Darcy did truly respect and care for Anne. Perhaps this was enough of a foundation on which to build a marriage.

He was certainly a man who knew his responsibilities to his tenants and his family. For both, he would need to produce an heir to guarantee that another generation of tenants would make their livelihood on Pemberley soil and inspire confidence that not only would the estate flourish under his reign as Master of Pemberley, but for generations to come.

Of course, his duty to family was apparent. His estate would be handed down to his progeny. Pemberley's estate was set up similarly to Rosings with an added exception: if no male heir was produced, the estate would then be settled on the first female child born; but, contrary to tradition, should that female child marry, the estate would still remain in the Darcy family. Pemberley was not hindered by any sort of entailment.

Anne would not be denied Rosings Park upon her mother's death; however, should she marry, all her property would automatically become her husband's, hence, his aunt's obsession.

Of course, Darcy would love to have a son to whom he could leave Pemberley, but a daughter would inherit just the same. His desire to someday produce an offspring was not tainted by a fixation to produce a male heir.

Even though they were almost the same age, Anne knew very little of the world. Her health had always been poor, and she rarely travelled beyond the gates of Rosings. She seemed to take her ill health in stride and seldom complained. She was pleasant and good natured and, on many occasions, rather witty. She usually did not display that side of her personality in her mother's company, as the great Lady Catherine de Bourgh would not be amused at what she considered unladylike behaviour. However, Darcy and Richard had often been witness to many of her jokes and teases. Darcy was confident that a marriage between the two of them could be, at the very least, tolerable, and at the very best, agreeable.

With his decision to marry Anne, came the unsettling admission that he was giving up on making a match based on love. As often as he had scoffed at Bingley for falling in and out of love regularly, he knew deep down in his heart that he would have liked nothing better than to find someone with whom he could share his life.

As the years passed, his hope of finding that special someone had dwindled considerably. Although many a young lady had professed affection for him, he had doubted their sincerity; not one had taken the time nor trouble to discover anything about him beyond his position in society and his yearly income.

Despite the many eager attentions offered to him by the ladies of the ton, he would never allow his ardour to overrule propriety. Beauty and charm were certainly not uncommon amongst his acquaintances, and had he wanted nothing more than an ornament to adorn his arm, he could have had his choice of any number of young ladies. However, he had found that the more eager the young lady, the less interested he was. And to single out any one woman with his attentions would draw such scrutiny from his family that it hardly seemed worth the effort.

Of course, any woman of his choosing would have to be of quality and substance, someone he would be proud to stand up with and one of unquestionable reputation. Perhaps his standards had been too high. Perhaps he had been pursuing a dream. As unlikely as it was that the woman he had invented in his imagination truly existed, it would still be a difficult task to abandon such hopes.

Nonetheless, he knew what was required of him and that he must marry soon. He must choose a wife worthy of the Darcy name. If he had not found her by now, then she truly must not exist. With no expectations of his finding the *one,* he was now resigned to at least forming an appropriate and advantageous alliance that would please his family and conform to the dictates of his position in society.

If he had to choose a wife from the "suitable" ladies of his acquaintance, he might as well choose Anne. Why not choose the path of least resistance?

He knew many men in his position married for reasons other than love. Until now, he had believed he would not be one of them. He had truly wanted to follow the example set by his own beloved mother and father. George and Lady Anne Darcy had shared a deep love and respect for each other. Though George Darcy had come from a wealthy, influential family with ancient credentials, they were not a titled family. Lady Anne had cared little. She would marry the man she loved.

Darcy had heard his Aunt Catherine allude many times to the fact that she and her sister had enjoyed countless titled admirers calling upon them, vying for their hands. Obviously, his aunt had not been a proponent of his parents' union.

After Lady Anne's death, shortly after Georgiana was born, George Darcy was never the same. Darcy had often witnessed the vacant look in his father's eyes, for George blamed himself for her death. When Lady Anne had become ill after Darcy was born, her doctor had expressed his fear that another child would weaken her further and the likelihood of both mother and child surviving would be slim.

The thought of bringing harm to Lady Anne had been so abhorrent to George Darcy that he denied himself the pleasure of her in his bed for many years. But as her health had steadily improved, Lady

Anne had insisted that she was now well enough to survive the birth of another child, should they again be blessed with such a gift.

Longing to be intimate with his wife once more, George Darcy had acquiesced to her entreaties. When both mother and child had survived Georgiana's birth, the happy couple's joy was great indeed. However, within weeks, her health had begun to fail, and six months later, Lady Anne died. The elder Mr. Darcy had lived with that guilt for the rest of his days.

~*~

Easter would arrive early this year. It was March, and there was still evidence of winter upon the ground. Colonel Richard Fitzwilliam placed his bags in the boot of the carriage and opened the door. Slipping into the seat, he shivered slightly from the cold. "It's good to see you again, Cousin," he said as he greeted a smiling Darcy.

After spending the next half hour catching up with family news regarding Georgiana and Richard's parents, Lord and Lady Matlock, Richard asked, "Are you ready to face another delightful fortnight in our dear aunt's company?"

"You may be pleasantly surprised this year, Richard. For once, I do not think she will be giving us her usual hard time."

"Why would you think *that?*"

"Well, let's just say, I'm about to fulfil her greatest wish."

"You can't possibly mean...."

Darcy turned his gaze to focus on an obscure point outside the carriage window. He could hardly believe it himself; therefore, he could understand his cousin's confusion. Had he not argued against such a union for years? He turned his eyes back to look directly at his cousin.

"Yes, I have decided to ask Anne to be my wife."

"Well man, don't just sit there; tell me everything!"

"There isn't much to tell. I've given it a great deal of thought and it seems to be the only logical solution. You know how much I've been worried about Georgie's fragile state since Ramsgate. She has lost all confidence since the ordeal she suffered at the hands of Wickham. She no longer trusts herself to make good decisions after being so deceived in his character. I believe that if I marry Anne and bring her to Pemberley, Georgie will improve in her company. Plus you must agree this will make our Aunt Catherine exceedingly happy."

"What of your own happiness, Darcy?"

"After all of these years, I've come to the conclusion that there is no one out there that would meet all the requirements I would desire in a wife. I see no other choice in the matter. You know an heir for Pemberley is demanded of me. Besides, I admit a desire for a child. If I do not love Anne the way I ought, the way I have imagined a man should love a woman, at least she is my equal in stature and consequence and is someone whom I can respect. And since she brings to the marriage a fortune large enough to rival my own, I do not need to concern myself with her motives."

Richard raised an eyebrow. "Do you think Anne will agree to all of this, Darcy? I know our aunt has harped on it for years, but I have never heard Anne's opinion on the subject. Also, there is the question of her health."

"I admit I am anxious to see if there is any improvement since our last visit. If Anne *does* agree to become my wife, I want it to be with her full understanding that she must eventually produce an heir. I will wait for a chance to speak to her alone before Aunt Catherine has a chance to impose her will. I am hoping there is enough mutual affection between us that Anne will not find this arrangement objectionable."

Richard chuckled to himself at the thought of Aunt Catherine's reaction to Darcy's proposal to Anne. He doubted Anne would be allowed to refuse, even if she wanted to. This was going to be a very interesting visit to Rosings indeed.

Darcy and Richard had been very close all their lives despite the fact that Richard was a few years older. Since he was the second son of an earl, he would not inherit. That distinction went to his older brother, who would inherit both title and property. Needing an occupation, Richard had chosen the military as his vocation and was fairly happy with his lot in life. He did not begrudge Darcy his wealth and position in life, for they each had to play the cards they were dealt.

Knowing the burden of responsibility that had fallen to Darcy after his father's death, Richard often felt sorry for him. He always had been a serious young man and, after inheriting Pemberley, he had seemed to withdraw even further into his own restrictive world of duty and propriety.

Upon his father's death, he also had become his younger sister's guardian, a responsibility Richard and he shared. Richard knew the scandalous circumstances surrounding Georgiana's near elopement with Wickham that summer at Ramsgate. Darcy thought of Richard as a friend and confidant, for heaven knew he needed someone with whom he could unburden himself and someone he could rely upon to be discreet.

Because of this closeness, Darcy had no reservations about telling Richard of his decision regarding Anne. He knew he could be completely honest with him in revealing his reasons to marry, knowing he would always have his cousin's full support and unfailing loyalty.

As they approached Rosings, Darcy inhaled a deep breath of air and slowly released it.

"Is that my nephews?" cried Lady Catherine de Bourgh as Darcy and Richard entered the large parlour. Both gentlemen approached their aunt and bowed in greeting before her. She was seated on her usual "royal throne," presiding over all who attended. As Darcy looked around the room, he saw Anne sitting quietly next to her companion, Mrs. Jenkinson. She did not look at him but stared at the floor before her. Aunt Catherine introduced the man and woman seated next to Mrs. Jenkinson, a Mr. And Mrs. Collins; the gentleman obviously a clergyman from his form of attire.

Upon his introduction and his benefactress's compliments, Mr. Collins immediately began his effusions. "Oh! My dear Mr. Darcy, it is indeed an honour to finally make your acquaintance. Your esteemed aunt, my benevolent patroness, has spoken of you often; it is my greatest pleasure, indeed it is my privilege, to have this opportunity to acquaint myself with you and your noble and esteemed cousin, the son of the Earl of Matlock." While he took a moment to draw breath, Darcy and Richard used the opportunity to bow curtly and remove themselves from his immediate presence. They both acknowledged Mrs. Collins and then proceeded to address Anne.

Darcy bowed before Anne and took her hand. For the first time, her eyes left the floor and met his own. "It is so nice to see you again, Anne," said Darcy. "You are looking well this evening."

She blushed slightly at his words.

Richard then approached Anne and gave her his finest bow. "Indeed, Anne, Darcy is correct. I am delighted to see that your health improves."

Unaccustomed to such attention and praise, Anne was at a loss for words, a condition that did not afflict her mother.

"Do sit down, Darcy! There is a place next to Anne. I hope you intend to stay longer than your usual fortnight," said his aunt.

In Derbyshire he might be the Master of Pemberley and worthy of the deference of his acquaintances, but at Rosings his authority was not recognized. It had taken a certain amount of finesse on Darcy's part over the years to outmanoeuvre Lady Catherine and her marital machinations. But now that he had made his decision to propose to Anne, there seemed little need to oppose his aunt's wishes any further.

"Our plans are not yet fixed," said Darcy as he took his seat next to Anne. Richard tried to hide his amusement as he watched his cousin. If Lady Catherine knew of Darcy's intent this visit, she would have done cartwheels around the parlour. Picturing in his mind such a sight, Richard turned away to hide his grin.

Not paying much attention to the company around him, Darcy listened with little interest to Mr. Collins as he explained his very good fortune in having recently inherited an estate in Hertfordshire. Gathering what he could from his conversation, the estate had been entailed away from the female line and had fallen to the clergyman. To his delight, Mr. Collins told of his immediate possession of the property. As a sign of good faith, and because he did not wish to lose Lady Catherine's good opinion, he had agreed to come back to Rosings until such time as the new clergyman would arrive at the parsonage at Hunsford. Something about the clergyman's story sounded vaguely familiar to Darcy, but he couldn't bring the exact situation to mind. As he had no desire to engage Mr. Collins in further conversation, he did not pursue the subject.

As the entire party was staying for dinner, Darcy knew he would not have a chance to speak with Anne alone tonight. He would have to wait until tomorrow.

Darcy was grateful to find Anne alone at breakfast and requested her company for a walk around the gardens.

"Of course, Cousin, I would be happy to," replied Anne shyly. "I shall meet you in the foyer in a few minutes."

When she approached Darcy who was awaiting her, he offered his arm. Upon taking it, she looked up at him, trying to imagine what he was about. As many times as he had visited Rosings, he had rarely, if ever, sought her out for private conversation. On the contrary, because of her mother's constant inference to a marriage between them, he usually avoided being alone in her company at all.

Her mother's single-mindedness in regard to a union between herself and Darcy was a constant annoyance to Anne. She might have had a more pleasant relationship with her cousin if not for her mother's interference. How could her mother not see that her constant badgering only made things awkward between them? Surely, Darcy would have been more attentive all these years, had he not felt like every word and gesture he made towards her was being observed and scrutinized.

The two walked some distance before a word was spoken between them. Darcy was trying to gather his thoughts before approaching the delicate subject he wished to discuss.

"Anne ... I ... I have a reason for asking you to accompany me this morning. I wish to discuss a subject that is of great importance to us both."

Anne looked up at him and nodded for him to proceed.

"As you are well aware, it is your mother's greatest wish that we marry."

At this statement Anne blushed profusely but said nothing.

"I have, of late, been giving the subject of marriage a great deal of thought, and I have decided that it is time that I chose a wife. I have always had affection and great respect for you, Anne. I truly believe a union between us could be agreeable to us both. I do not make this decision lightly, as whomever I choose will be the Mistress of Pemberley and the mother of my children. I have often heard your mother's opinion of our union, but I have no idea of your feelings on this matter."

Again, Anne said nothing, her mind a mass of confusion upon hearing Darcy's words. *Is he proposing to me? Is he asking me to declare my feelings?*

Surmising that Anne was of a mind not to speak, he continued again. "I wanted to discuss what our expectations would be if we were to marry. I know this does not conform to propriety, but our situation is such that I would not wish to make you an offer of marriage if we could not come to a mutual understanding. Once an offer is tended, we both know your mother would not allow you to *refuse*, even if that were your wish. So, before I declare myself, I need to know that such a declaration would be welcomed and that you would agree to …that is …that you are aware of… that you accept the *duties* that would naturally accompany being the Mistress of Pemberley."

As he exhaled a sigh of relief, he felt uncertain still that his meaning had been properly professed. To make sure he added, "I am sure you understand that our union must result in an heir to Pemberley." He did not look at her as he spoke this declaration, showing great concentration on the path they were following.

After what seemed like an eternity, Anne finally responded. "As you have spoken so honestly of your feelings, I will try to do likewise, Fitzwilliam. Even though my mother has often spoken of a marriage between us, I have always believed that it would never occur. I knew you did not possess feelings of love or passion for me, feelings I assumed you would require before entering the marriage state. I have always held you in high regard, and I do have affection for you. To protect my own heart, I have never allowed myself to feel anything beyond that."

She could not look into his eyes as she spoke these words, afraid she had already revealed too much of her feelings. She took a deep breath and continued, "I am not so naïve as to believe that you could ever truly love me, but a marriage of mutual respect and affection would not be objectionable to me. I believe that I could do honour to the title of Mistress of Pemberley, and I am willing to take on *all* the responsibilities that go along with that title."

With this last statement, she *did* look directly into Darcy's eyes so he could make no mistake of its meaning. None was perceived.

Darcy had never heard his cousin speak so earnestly before, and, at that moment, he admired her immensely. He was also relieved that he would not have to pretend feelings he did not possess. They both knew she spoke the truth. He did not desire her as a husband should desire a wife, but many couples had gone on to sustain enduring marriages where no such amorous feelings existed.

Darcy turned to look at Anne directly. Her soft auburn curls framed her delicate face. Her eyes, which had always reminded him of the colour of emeralds, looked up at him in anticipation. He took her hand in his and looked into those trusting eyes. "Would you then do me the great honour of becoming my wife?"

"Yes, Fitzwilliam, I will."

Darcy lifted her hand to his lips and kissed it softly. They stood and looked at each other for a moment before Darcy said, "I guess I'd better go speak to my aunt."

Anne smiled. "I hardly think there's much chance she will not give her blessing, Fitzwilliam."

"Yes, I dare say, I think we are safe on that matter."

Since the entailment of Longbourn, Mrs. Bennet and her three youngest daughters were somewhat uncomfortably settled in a small cottage on the outskirts of Meryton. The only saving grace was its easy walking distance from her sister, Mrs. Philips. With the Militia encamped in town, Kitty and Lydia were quite pleased to be so close to their aunt. Mrs. Philips loved company; when her nieces visited, she would also invite Mr. Denny and Mr. Wickham, along with some of the other officers, for an evening of supper and cards and sometimes dancing.

Lydia, the liveliest of the Bennet girls, now had free reign over her mother, who had always favoured her youngest daughter. When Colonel Foster's wife invited Lydia, as her particular friend, to accompany them to Brighton for the summer, Mrs. Bennet practically swooned at the thought of her Lydia being in such esteemed company.

Jane had written her mother to express her opinion against Lydia going to Brighton, reminding her of Lydia's careless and imprudent manner. But Mrs. Bennet had argued that Lydia was a young woman who should have the opportunity to socialize and that she would be well chaperoned by Colonel Foster and his wife. And hadn't Lydia suffered enough, wearing black for six months after her father's death? Now that her long period of mourning was well over, what better way to re-enter society than a trip to Brighton?

Even though they could ill afford it, Mrs. Bennet acquiesced to Lydia's request, or rather demand, that she be allowed to purchase new clothes for the trip. After all, there would be balls to attend, and she wanted to make a great impression on the officers. Kitty could not contain her grief at learning of her sister's invitation to Brighton and almost convinced her mother that they should *all* go to Brighton for the summer.

"If Lizzy had accepted Mr. Collins's proposal, we *would* all be going to Brighton," exclaimed Mrs. Bennet. "When I think of that selfish, thoughtless girl! We could all be back at Longbourn right now instead of that artful Charlotte Lucas taking my place as Mistress.

"Oh well, if the Collinses can enjoy themselves settled in someone else's estate, so be it. I know *I* could never be happy living on an estate that was entailed away from its rightful owners! Lydia will go to Brighton with the Fosters for the summer and meet the officers. At least one of my daughters will not throw away a chance to marry well."

CHAPTER THREE

The carriage's wheel bounced in and out of a rather large hole, shaking it quite thoroughly, waking Elizabeth with a startle. She looked out the window in an effort to determine her whereabouts, but only an unfamiliar landscape greeted her. They were no longer in the city, but rather in a more bucolic setting. Removing her bonnet, she placed it on the seat beside her. When she had lived at Longbourn, a day like this would have pleased her very much. She would have gone on a ramble and explored the woods beyond her home. Such simple joys were now in her past.

The carriage turned onto a gravel road and slowed its pace. They must be getting close she thought. She picked up her bonnet but did not put it on. It was just too hot. The carriage stopped in front of a manor house, small, though somewhat larger than Longbourn. A footman immediately opened the carriage door and helped her out.

Elizabeth looked up at the house, her heart beating loudly in her chest. There certainly was no turning back now. She at least had to go through with the interview. What that would be like, she could not even begin to imagine. It was of little matter; she would find out soon enough.

A young woman led Elizabeth down the hallway and motioned towards the door. Elizabeth stepped into the room, which seemed rather dim, considering it was early afternoon. All the curtains were drawn tightly. In the middle of the room, a small table held only a single candle, next to which sat a single chair.

She could vaguely make out the older woman who sat at the far end of the room, behind a large desk. The desk, too, held only one solitary candle.

Elizabeth hesitantly walked toward the middle of the room; her eyes having difficulty adjusting to the lack of light.

"Please, take a seat, dear," the woman offered.

"Thank you," replied Elizabeth as she eyed the uncomfortable looking wooden chair. Elizabeth was extremely nervous, though the woman had a kind face and spoke in a gentle voice.

"Would you tell me a little about yourself?" asked the woman.

"I was informed I would not need to reveal any personal information."

"I'm afraid such an intimate situation requires *some* personal details, though your identity is not one of them," stated the woman. "Are you fully aware of the position for which you are being interviewed?"

"Mr. Gallagher briefly explained what would be expected of me."

"You look full young to be contemplating such an endeavour," observed the woman.

"I am almost two and twenty; old enough to make my own decisions."

The older woman silently eyed her for a few moments.

"Have you any health impediments?" she asked.

"No, aside from the normal childhood ailments, I have never been ill."

"What of your parents and siblings, do they also enjoy good health?"

"My father died about a year ago, but the rest of my family is alive and well."

"What of mental impediments? Do any members of your family suffer from such a malady?"

If it wasn't for her state of unease, Elizabeth might have found that particular inquiry almost humorous, for it was certainly subject to conjecture. Her mother suffered from *many* nervous conditions.

"Not to my knowledge," was the best she could offer.

Elizabeth heard whispering and, for the first time, realized that there was someone else in the room. She looked slightly to the left of the woman and saw a silk screen that was completely devoid of light. Someone was sitting behind the screen, and, although she could not see them, they obviously could see her.

After the whispering stopped, the woman asked her to stand. Elizabeth rose from the chair and stared directly into the woman's eyes. She then turned her gaze slightly to the left towards the source of the whispering voice. Imagining that she was staring directly at whoever was behind the screen, she raised her chin in an act of defiance.

Elizabeth was then asked to turn around and then finally to sit again. She complied with all that was asked. She was so nervous that she was starting to get lightheaded. She was also starting to get angry.

Again the woman conferred with the mystery person behind the screen. "Is there not some other more conventional way you might obtain the money you require?"

"No, there is not," replied Elizabeth.

"No relatives from whom you might borrow? Or perhaps some young gentleman who might offer for you and resolve your financial situation?"

Elizabeth's mind immediately went to Mr. Collins. She knew her mother still had not forgiven her for rejecting his offer of marriage.

When he had proposed that day, Elizabeth had been adamant in her refusal. She was grateful that Jane had left for London on the previous day with her Aunt and Uncle Gardiner. She knew if Mr. Collins had met Jane first, she most likely would have been his first choice, as Jane was five times as pretty as the rest of the Bennet sisters. She knew, too, that Jane would have acquiesced in order to save her family.

"If borrowing the money I required was a possibility, I would not be here. And despite my situation, I have vowed never to marry if I cannot do so for love."

Again, the whispering began. However, this time Elizabeth could discern that it was a male voice coming from behind the screen. The anger she had been suppressing began to rise in her chest.

"Does the *gentleman* suffer an impediment, a defect of speech perhaps, that prohibits him from speaking to me himself?" asked Elizabeth, trying to keep her voice as even as possible.

Taken somewhat by surprise at the young woman's impertinence, the older woman said, "I'm sorry, but you cannot know the identity of the gentleman. This situation is of a very personal and confidential nature. If a mutual agreement is reached, a future meeting time and place will be arranged. Of course, he must have your word that you will not disclose any of the details of this arrangement to anyone."

"I am not asking that he make himself known to me, only that I be allowed the opportunity to hear his voice."

"To what purpose, my dear?"

Before Elizabeth could reply, the gentleman spoke. His voice was deep, yet softer than she had expected. "I have no objection to speaking with you directly, if that is your wish; though I cannot perceive what hearing my voice would reveal to you."

"I believe the sound of a person's voice and their manner of speaking can be quite telling, sir."

Thursday's Child

The room was silent for a moment. Then the gentleman asked, "Can you tell me for what reason you require this money?"

"Just as you, sir, do not wish to have certain personal information disclosed to others, I, too, wish to keep the particulars of my situation private. I will only say that it is a personal family matter that must be acted upon quickly if it is to be resolved in a satisfactory manner."

The gentleman again whispered something to the older woman who nodded her head. The gentleman then asked, "Is this something you have done before?"

"No, never, sir!" came Lizzy's immediate reply.

The silence this time went on longer than the last. He stared at her from behind the screen. She sat uncomfortably in the straight back wooden chair. After several moments, the silence was broken as the gentleman finally spoke. "Do we have an agreement then?"

Elizabeth looked down at her hands in her lap and replied in an almost inaudible voice.

"Yes."

~*~

Elizabeth was told to wait in the adjoining room. After a quarter of an hour, the older woman joined her. She explained to Elizabeth the particulars of the arrangement that would take place in less than a fortnight. A carriage would again be sent for her, and she would be travelling to a small village in Scotland, where all accommodations would be made for her. Elizabeth was surprised by the destination but was told that it was of the utmost importance that they travel to a location where no one would know either the gentleman or herself.

She then offered Elizabeth some food and refreshments. Elizabeth was hardly up to eating as she doubted she would be able to hold anything down. She did agree to a cup of tea, however, and sipped it slowly.

The woman stared at Elizabeth for a long moment, and then gently put her hand on Elizabeth's arm. "It must be indeed a heavy burden you carry, my dear. To do such an unselfish act for your family is most admirable." They looked into each other's eyes. Elizabeth's unshed tears were her only reply.

Elizabeth was soon again riding in the carriage back to London. At least the sun had now begun to lower in the sky, and the heat was dissipating. She then realized that she had left her bonnet on the small table in the room she had just occupied. It was of little consequence.

Her mind was reeling with all that had just occurred. Her hands were slightly shaking, and her heart was racing. Had she really agreed to do this?

She remembered the older woman's last words. It was almost as if the woman could read her mind. Elizabeth knew why she was doing this. She was doing it to save her family from scandal. She had let them down before, but now she could make it up to them. Even if her mother never forgave her, she would do this for her sisters. They deserved to have a chance at happiness.

True, the esteem in which the family was held had been somewhat diminished upon her father's death due to the entailment, but they were still a respectable family. Her sisters' prospects for marriage may not have been grand to begin with but, still, they could be expected to make well-regarded matches. This scandal that threatened would make it certain that no decent gentleman would associate himself with any of them.

Of course, the irony of her situation was apparent. In order to save her family from a prodigious scandal, she was about to involve herself in an even more salacious situation should the particulars ever become known.

For herself, Elizabeth did not care what calamity might befall her. Indeed, her refusal of Mr. Collins confirmed her conviction that she would rather remain single forever than to marry without love. After this episode, she knew she would be unfit for any gentleman to marry. Even if the truth was never discovered, Elizabeth would be obligated to inform any suitor of her past. No, it was not for her own future happiness that she was entering into such an agreement. It was for her sisters. If she could secure their happiness, she would be content.

For this reason, Elizabeth quite agreed that the precautions being taken to ensure concealment of this arrangement were well warranted. The gentleman would never know her name, and she would never know his. All future communication would be conducted through the gentleman's attorney, Mr. Gallagher, who would be the only person to know Elizabeth's identity.

However, she was more than curious about the gentleman. She wondered what circumstances might warrant his seeking such a situation. She wondered if he was married, the very thought increasing her unease. Perhaps the less she thought of the situation, the better. If she were to think about the situation at all, she preferred to think of herself as doing an unselfish act for another. Yes, if one looked upon it in a prudential light, she was doing a very noble thing.

Most difficult for Elizabeth was recognizing she would have to conceal the truth from Jane. She had never lied to Jane before. Knowing Jane's goodness, Elizabeth was in a small way relieved that she would not have to divulge the details of her arrangement. Not that she felt Jane would judge her harshly, but because she did not wish to burden Jane with this knowledge. The less Jane knew of this whole affair, the better.

CHAPTER FOUR

Darcy stood outside Anne's bed chamber with a worried look. He had sent for the doctor as soon as she had collapsed. They had been walking in the gardens, enjoying the beautiful June morning when it happened. He had watched her face drain of all colour, and then she had fainted. Barely catching her before her body reached the ground, he had gathered her in his arms and hurriedly climbed the stairs. But it wasn't until he had placed her on the bed that he noticed the blood.

As his housekeeper, Mrs. Reynolds, waited downstairs for the doctor's arrival, Darcy went to Anne's side and took her hand. She looked so pale. She was unresponsive to his voice, and her eyes remained closed.

When the doctor arrived, he was shown immediately to Anne's room. "Where is Dr. Chisholm?" Darcy asked as he eyed the unfamiliar gentleman and took a protective stance in front of Anne's unconscious body.

"I am Dr. Adams, Mr. Darcy. I have been Anne's doctor since she was a child; surely you have heard your Aunt Catherine speak of me."

"Yes... yes, of course. What has brought you to Derbyshire, Dr. Adams?"

Thursday's Child

"It was just by luck that I happened to be in Lambton conferring with Dr. Chisholm on another patient when your note arrived," replied the doctor as he attempted to approach Anne's bedside.

Darcy seemed reluctant at first to relinquish his position but then nodded his acceptance and stepped aside.

Noting Darcy's tentativeness, the doctor tried to alleviate his worry. "I understand your concern, but I assure you Dr. Chisholm was in complete agreement that I should be the one to heed your summons. If it will help put your mind at ease, Mr. Darcy, you are welcome to stay while I examine your wife."

As Darcy momentarily thought over the doctor's offer, he realized that though they had been married for almost two months, he could not recall ever having seen Anne completely unclothed. Resignedly he told the doctor he would wait outside until his examination was completed.

After waiting in the hall for nearly a half hour, Darcy went down to the library and poured himself a drink. As he paced the length of the library, the doctor was finally announced.

"Mr. Darcy, I have examined your wife. She remains unconscious, and her breathing is shallow." He hesitated slightly before continuing. "I must unhappily inform you that she has suffered a miscarriage. Were you aware of her condition?"

By the look on Darcy's face, it was evident to Dr. Adams that he was not. "We have only been married since the end of April; it has barely been two months," said Darcy, "and we did not think it likely that Anne would be so soon with child."

"The miscarriage has left her extremely weak. I am well acquainted with Anne's history of ill health, and I'm afraid this episode has only added to her frail condition. The next few days will tell us what we can expect of her recovery. I have left detailed instructions with Mrs. Reynolds as to her care."

Before his departure from Pemberley, Dr. Adams informed Darcy he would remain in Lambton for several more days and to inform him immediately if Anne's condition changed. Darcy and Georgiana kept vigil over Anne for the next two days and witnessed little improvement. However, on the third morning, while Georgiana was sitting beside her bed, Anne opened her eyes.

"Anne!" exclaimed Georgiana, unable to contain her surprise and relief. "We have been so worried about you. Fitzwilliam left your side only moments ago. I shall go and retrieve him."

Anne looked into her sister's eyes.

As Georgiana searched Anne's, she could see the concern in them. "Do not be alarmed, Anne. All will be well."

Anne managed to give her sister a reassuring smile as she watched her leave.

Within moments Darcy was by her side. "I have sent for Dr. Adams, Anne. Pray, how are you feeling?" Anne's eyes fixed upon a pitcher of water, and Darcy immediately poured her a cup. He helped her to an upright position and gently guided the cup to her lips.

"I'm feeling somewhat weak," she managed to say. "Have I been asleep very long?"

"No, Anne, not very long," said Darcy. He did not wish to frighten her. They would have time later to talk about what had occurred. Right now he just wanted to make sure she was well. She closed her eyes again, and Darcy eased her back down upon the pillow.

By the time Dr. Adams arrived, Darcy was pacing the hallway. He met him at the top of the stairs and relayed everything that had occurred during the last three days. Dr. Adams immediately went in to examine Anne.

He again joined Darcy in the library to relate his findings. "I believe that Anne shall recover," said Dr. Adams. "However, I feel it is my duty to warn you that if she suffers another similar episode, the outcome may not be as agreeable. Even now, I cannot assure you that her recovery will be complete."

"Have you told her of the miscarriage?" inquired Darcy.

"Yes. You would not wish to keep it from her, would you?"

"No, of course, I would not. My only concern is for her health. I was afraid such news at this time would only impede her recovery."

"I understand, Mr. Darcy," said Dr. Adams. "I am sure you will see to her wellbeing."

Dr. Adams departed with the promise to return to check on Anne's progress before his return to London. Darcy immediately went to Anne as the doctor's carriage pulled away. She was sitting up in bed and, as he entered the room, he observed the tears in her eyes. He went to her side and secured her hand in his.

"I am so sorry, Fitzwilliam. You put your faith in me, and I have failed you," she sobbed. "I cannot bear it…"

Darcy sat on the bed beside her and embraced her tightly to his chest. He wanted to comfort her, to tell her it would be all right. Most of all he wanted to reassure her that one day she would again be with child, but he could not.

"No, Anne, you are not to blame. Do not distress yourself. You must rest and regain your strength." He kissed her on the forehead and helped her get settled under the covers. She closed her eyes, but sleep would not come easily.

~*~

Darcy made his way down to the library. He poured himself a brandy and sat before the unlit fireplace. He felt as if his life was spinning out of control. His intentions couldn't have been simpler. He would marry Anne. She would produce an heir. They would live a quiet life and watch their child grow. Was that not what every gentleman wanted? He had been willing to forsake love and passion in order to attain an heir. Was that now to be denied him too?

By the age of nine and twenty, Darcy was hardly unfamiliar with the intimate company of women. Over a decade ago his cousin Richard had taken his passage into manhood to task, introducing him to a world where, for a price, women would gladly attend his every libidinous need.

Since his initiation to such pleasures, he had enjoyed, if not many, more than a few such intimate liaisons. He would admit that at first these illicit associations had produced some feelings of guilt—or was it shame?—on his part. But as the years had progressed, he recognized that such liaisons were his best defence against succumbing to the many wiles of the daughters of the ton. Hence, his guilt eventually abated.

As physically gratifying as those sexual experiences had been, they had always left him feeling empty. There had to be more to it than the physical connection. His two months of marriage had at least taught Darcy that much.

If he was sure of one thing, it was that he was not going to jeopardize Anne's life again. There would be no further attempts to produce an heir.

He thought back to the fleeting days before his marriage.

He had noticed a slight change in Anne's health prior to their marriage. At first, he had attributed it to all the anxiety of preparing for the wedding and then the excitement of the actual day itself. Aunt Catherine had insisted upon an almost immediate wedding, perhaps afraid he would change his mind.

Also, it did not escape his notice that Anne was extremely nervous and distressed on their wedding night. He had thought that once she was settled at Pemberley, she would relax and her condition would improve. That had not been the case.

When the doctor had disclosed that Anne had been with child, his thoughts immediately went to his mother. Could history be repeating itself? Was he doomed to the same fate as his father? He could not let that happen. He would abstain from exercising his marital rights in order to protect Anne.

On thinking of the few occasions that he *had* taken Anne into his connubial embrace, he had to admit, it was not romantic or passionate. It had been done with the one thought of procreation. This would not do. He lowered his head into his hands. He was a man torn. He would never do anything to bring harm to Anne, yet he desperately wanted an heir—for Pemberley, for his family, but most importantly, for himself.

CHAPTER FIVE

Elizabeth was quite fatigued by the long journey. This was the third day of travelling and, she desperately hoped, the last. They had gotten underway again very early in the morning and, though she had slept part of the way, it was far from restful.

She knew she was travelling to a small town in Scotland named St. Andrews. But that was about all she knew of her destination. By the length of the trip, she was convinced she would not meet anyone of her acquaintance. She was certainly a long way from Hertfordshire. The carriage finally stopped at their final destination.

The Fairmont Inn was a quaint looking place. It was not lavish, but Elizabeth thought it quite pleasing. As she walked in, she noted it had a small dining room that overlooked a picturesque view and a sandy beach.

She apprehensively approached the man behind the desk and gave the name she was instructed to use. She was handed a key and shown to her room by a young girl who informed her that, even though it was still late August, the nights could get quite cool with the wind blowing off the coast and that a fire would be lit for her each evening after dinner. It was not a very large room but tastefully furnished and boasting a small adjoining dressing chamber.

After she had attended her toilette, she went down to the dining room. She sat at a small table and ordered a modest meal. She didn't eat very much but spent a great deal of time moving the food around her plate. She was trying desperately to appear calm. There were several other people in the dining room, and Elizabeth felt like every one of them knew why she was there.

She wondered if the gentleman was seated somewhere in the dining room observing her. He did have that advantage over her: he had seen her; she had not seen him. She prolonged dinner as long as she could, even indulging in a second glass of wine, which she normally did not do. When she felt she could delay no longer, she rose and climbed the stairs to her room. She turned the key and opened the door.

A small gasp escaped her lips as the sight of a gentleman seated before her took her quite by surprise. The key fell from her hand to the floor.

"I am sorry to have startled you," he said as he immediately rose from his chair.

Elizabeth recognized his voice at once as the voice from behind the screen. She had tried to picture the face that went with that voice many times over the last fortnight, her only reference being that of a gossiping woman declaring that he must be most abhorrent.

The woman had been quite mistaken.

He walked towards her and bent down to pick up the fallen key.

"For propriety sake I thought it best to await your arrival in here than to be seen in your company downstairs."

Elizabeth nodded as he handed her the key, a small shock accompanying his touch.

There was an awkward silence. She looked around the room and noticed that there were no candles lit, but the fireplace was aflame as had been promised. It was the only light in the room, and it gave off a warm, golden glow.

"Was your journey without incident?" he inquired as he took a step back to increase the distance between them.

"Yes, though much longer than I had anticipated," replied Elizabeth, grateful that her voice had not failed her.

"And your accommodations, do you find them suitable?"

"They are most comfortable, sir."

Again there was an awkward silence. Elizabeth looked up at him as if to ask for some direction. She could discern that he was as uncomfortable as she.

He cleared his throat. "I must take no chances of us being seen together. My reputation and the honour of others are at stake. We must be as discreet as possible."

Elizabeth sat down, suspecting that her trembling legs were losing their capacity to support her weight. The gentleman produced a bottle of brandy and poured himself a glass, then took a rather large swallow. He took a seat across from her but did not attempt to meet her eyes.

"We will not acknowledge each other beyond the confines of this room. I will meet with you here for three evenings."

"Is . . . *this* to be one of the evenings?" asked Elizabeth.

"Yes," he said. "If you need some time to prepare, I could return later."

"That will not be necessary, sir," said Elizabeth as she endeavoured to sound as business-like as he. "I see no need to delay. I am prepared to begin now."

He stared at her for a long moment. The look in his eyes as he gazed upon her did not lessen her anxiety. He then rose and poured more brandy into his glass. She gave a thought to requesting some for herself, as her nerves could certainly use some calming. Instead, she straightened her shoulders and stood. She then walked purposefully towards the dressing chamber. She returned a few minutes later, wearing only her chemise.

As he looked upon her, he could not help but notice that the light from the fire was revealing her naked form through the sheerness of her gown. He could feel his body's reaction to the sight of her. Even though their mutual unease was apparent, along with *his* uneasiness, he was surprised to discover a certain amount of excited anticipation.

She looked down at herself and smoothed her hands over her chemise. "I . . . I would prefer to keep...." She took a deep unsteady breath. "Is this acceptable?" she asked as she met his gaze.

Afraid his voice would betray him, he simply nodded.

Elizabeth slipped into the bed and pulled the covers up to her neck. She did not look at him as he silently undressed, but turned her head to stare at the fire. She then felt his weight upon the mattress as he moved in beside her.

He slowly took the covers from beneath her chin to expose her neckline. He looked for some reaction from her and, seeing that she voiced no objections, continued drawing the covers down until they were completely free of her body. Elizabeth's heart was beating so loudly, she was sure he could hear it.

She looked into his eyes for fear of looking at any other part of his anatomy. He was lying on his side next to her. He reached down to the hem of her gown and slowly brought it upwards, never taking his eyes from hers.

He wanted desperately to say *something* that might help relieve the awkwardness of such a situation but could think of nothing. He was there to accomplish a task, and his body was telling him to proceed. He moved his knee between her thighs.

Petrified as she was, Elizabeth was also fascinated as each movement he made progressed them towards their prearranged conclusion. She watched with an almost voyeuristic fascination as he positioned his body over hers. When he leaned over her, she unconsciously reached up to brush a lock of his dark brown hair from his forehead.

From the moment he had discerned her supple body through her translucent gown, he had felt his arousal build. He guided himself to the opening of her core and slowly entered her. Elizabeth's body stiffened. He started tentatively, leaning into her a little further each time as he gathered momentum. His pace increasing, his thrusts became more forceful. To his surprise, he was met with some resistance, and, in that split second, he realized that she was an innocent. However, that realization came just as he felt the barrier between them break, and he was immediately buried deep inside her.

Elizabeth inhaled sharply as the pain invaded her body, her hands clutching the bed cloth on either side of her. He looked down at her, afraid to move, and witnessed a single tear roll down her cheek as she looked away.

He was now completely surrounded by her tightness, and, although he knew he should be concerned for the pain he had just inflicted upon her, his body could not help but respond to the moment. Their eyes met as he again began to move inside her, pleasure taking higher precedence over any guilt he may have been feeling. His rhythm again building, his self-imposed abstinence combined with the enticing uniqueness of their situation soon brought about his uncontrollable release, as he did his best to suppress the deep guttural moan that accompanied it.

It took several moments for his breathing to return to normal. He rolled away from her and lay on his back, his arm covering his eyes. They did not speak. They did not look at each other. The only sound in the room was the crackling of the fire. After another minute of silence, he rose from the bed, dressed, and left her room.

~*~

Darcy quickly and quietly made his way down the corridor to his own chamber. He fumbled for the key and, after several attempts, finally got the door open. He immediately poured himself a brandy. He paced the room for several minutes. He looked down at his glass and, noting it was again empty, refilled it. So many different emotions were fighting each other to take over his mind. Once again, his intentions couldn't have been simpler. Once again, he discovered that nothing was ever simple.

Darcy had obtained the services of an elderly attorney by the name of Mr. Gallagher. He thought it best not to use his regular attorney for such matters, certain he would advise against such a scheme. With Mrs. Reynolds's reluctant assistance, he had discreetly arranged for five ladies to be escorted to a rented estate. He had devised it so that he would be present in the room to observe each lady, but would keep his presence unknown.

The first two days produced ladies of somewhat questionable character. The lady on the first day was rather vulgar and appeared to be well past her child bearing years. The lady on the second day appeared to be *already* with child.

On the third day he saw *her*. At first glance, he had thought her rather pretty. When Mrs. Reynolds had asked her to stand, she turned her head slightly and stared directly into his eyes as if she could see him. As he had stared back into those fine eyes, he conceded an attraction. When she had almost defiantly requested that the gentleman speak to her himself, he knew there would be no need for further interviews. She was the one.

Upon her departure that day, he had discovered the bonnet she left behind. He immediately had picked it up. He had recognized the sweet aroma of lavender, the same sweet aroma that he had inhaled as he lay over her only minutes ago.

Over the past two weeks, he had tried to imagine what misfortune had led her to make such a desperate decision. If he were honest with himself, he would have to admit he had imagined her in *many* ways since he first saw her. She had invaded his dreams regularly. He had reasoned he could not control his dreams, and what harm did they bring to anyone but himself? Certainly duty and propriety could at least allow him that small concession.

Though he allowed himself to indulge in such dreams, he knew it best to banish all thoughts of her from his mind. He need not worry about his heart. In his nine and twenty years, no woman had ever gained entrance there, that likelihood being even less so for a woman who would enter into such an agreement as theirs.

As in any business endeavour, it would be ill advised to display any emotion. To ensure that end, upon his departure to Scotland, he had made his list of mental notes: *he would remain as detached as possible; he would not engage his emotions; he would conduct himself in a business-like manner; he would walk away in three days unaffected by anything that occurred.* After all, he was paying her most handsomely for her services.

But as self-incriminations began to surface, he acknowledged that he had some guilt with regard to her maidenly status. He had taken her virginity, a circumstance he had not foreseen.

During their interview, when he had asked if she had ever done anything like *this* before, he had meant had she ever entered into such an agreement before; obviously she had meant something of far greater import.

He had assumed that any woman who would agree to the terms of an arrangement such as theirs was no longer a maiden. *Why would an innocent young lady, regardless of her lower social standing, consent to such an agreement?*

He poured himself another brandy and sat before the dying fire. As he reflected upon all the events that had led up to this evening, he concluded that he should not feel guilty at all. After all, he had not forced her to do anything. It had been *her* decision to enter into their agreement. However, this train of thought did little to ease his conscience.

As he finished off the bottle of brandy, he truly hoped he would pass out from the alcohol, for he feared that it would be his only chance for any rest tonight.

CHAPTER SIX

Elizabeth awoke the next morning to a steady rain. She welcomed the grey and gloomy day as it matched her mood perfectly. The brightest thought that entered her mind all morning was that, with any luck, the worst of it was over. She could not imagine anything more humiliating than what she had gone through the night before. But, despite the previous night's experience, she was determined to maintain as much of her dignity as possible.

Not wishing to be in company, she had requested that her breakfast be brought up to her room. She sat before the now cold fireplace and poured herself another cup of tea. Her mood was melancholy.

She held no resentment towards the gentleman. Had she not willingly consented to the terms of the agreement? After all, she told herself, it could have been much worse. When she had entered her room the previous evening and saw the gentleman seated before her, she was not repulsed by his countenance.

Over the last fortnight, when her thoughts had anticipated the abhorrence of their first intimate encounter, she had prepared herself to keep her eyes firmly shut as not to look upon the disagreeable visage that must surely be his. However, the exact opposite had occurred. She had found herself unable to look away from him.

But it was more than his physical beauty that had kept her eyes transfixed with his. She somehow had felt a connection with the gentleman. Perhaps it was a normal phenomenon that occurred while indulging in such intimacies. Being a neophyte to such activity, she could not say.

She was grateful that he was a man of his word. He had promised to provide part of the money in settlement of their arrangement prior to their designated meeting, acquiescing to her entreaty to Mr. Gallagher.

The unpleasantness of that entire episode would not be easily forgotten.

In July when Elizabeth had visited her sister Jane in London as they had planned, she had not expected the turn of events that quickly followed her arrival.

~*~

With their Aunt and Uncle Gardiner travelling in America, Jane had made arrangements with the Morgans that she would stay with Lizzy at their uncle's townhouse on weekends and return to Grosvenor Street during the week. She wanted to spend as much time as possible with her sister.

During the week, Elizabeth would walk the several blocks from Gracechurch Street to the park where Jane took the children to play. The flowers were now in full bloom and the trees' foliage afforded shade over the park benches. The sisters sat and caught up on all that was happening in their lives. Elizabeth was truly enjoying her visit.

During the second week of her visit, Jane received an express letter from their sister Kitty. Since it was a rare occasion for Kitty to write, she was doubly curious as to why she would send an express. Elizabeth watched Jane's face as she read the letter and saw the myriad of emotions displayed upon it.

"Jane, tell me!" said Elizabeth. "What does our sister write that distresses you so?" Jane could not speak. Tears immediately filled her eyes as she handed the letter to Elizabeth.

Elizabeth took the letter and read:

July 27, 1812

Dear Jane,

I am writing with the most dreadful news. Our mother has received a communication from Colonel Foster in Brighton. He has informed us that Lydia has run off with one of his officers. To be more precise, she has run off with Mr. Wickham. He has no further information other than he believes they have gone to London.

He has sent two of his best officers in hopes of locating them and has promised to keep us informed of any news.

Our mother has taken to her bed and refuses to see anyone other than our Aunt Philips. I will write you again as soon as we have received any further information.

Love, your sister

Kitty

Elizabeth slowly put down the letter. She looked over to Jane who was now crying openly. "Who is Mr. Wickham, Jane? Have you made his acquaintance?"

"No, Lizzy, I have not," she answered through her sobs. "But I understand that he was a frequent guest of our Aunt Philips when the Militia was in Meryton. If the rumours that our aunt has relayed to me are true, he has left many debts to the shopkeepers in town, and his scandalous behaviour has ruined more than one young lady's reputation."

What was to be done? The only person who could help them was their Uncle Gardiner. Even if they knew where to write him, it would take him weeks to get back to London. By then, all would be lost.

Elizabeth decided that the best course would be for her to go to Meryton. She would be aware of any new communication from Colonel Foster much sooner if she were there.

As she left for Meryton the following morning, she promised Jane she would keep her informed. "Do not distress yourself, Jane. Maybe things are not as grave as they seem. We should not lose hope." The sisters hugged, each one thinking they would remain strong for the other's sake.

Upon her arrival at her mother's cottage, her sister Kitty came running to her and hugged her tightly. "Lizzy! I can't believe you are here! I am so happy to see you."

Elizabeth returned her sister's hug. She hadn't seen her since the week of their father's death. She had grown into a lovely young woman, and she appeared much improved in sense and behaviour in the short time away from her sister Lydia's influence.

When they were settled into the house, Elizabeth said, "Now tell me all you know, Kitty." Her sister relayed all the details she had learned thus far. Mrs. Foster had sent along a letter that Lydia had left for her the night she ran off with Wickham. The letter had indicated that Lydia believed Mr. Wickham intended to marry her, as she said she would return from Gretna Green as Mrs. George Wickham. Elizabeth knew that was not likely. Lydia had no money or connections. Certainly nothing that could tempt Mr. Wickham into matrimony.

Knowing she would have to face her mother sooner or later, Elizabeth approached her bed chamber and slowly turned the knob. She peeked into the room and found her mother lying on her settee, her hands wringing her handkerchief.

"Hello, Mama," said Elizabeth softly.

Mrs. Bennet looked over towards the door and gave her least favourite daughter a glare. "Lizzy! We are all ruined, and it is your fault! If you had married Mr. Collins, we could all have gone to Brighton, and your sister would now be safe."

Thursday's Child

Elizabeth approached her mother. "Really, Mama, I hardly think you can blame me for Lydia's imprudent behaviour."

"Oh, yes, yes! Had I but been there, I would have made sure she behaved herself in front of the officers. I also blame Colonel Foster for not keeping a watchful eye on her. My poor Lydia!"

"Have you been able to reach our Uncle Gardiner?" asked Elizabeth.

"I have sent a post to his last address, but I fear he is travelling again. I will not be able to contact him until he next writes to me. Oh, my poor nerves! How could he leave us at a time like this? He should not have made such extensive plans! Oh, what is to become of us? We are all ruined!"

"Mama," sighed Elizabeth. She knew there was no point in continuing. Her mother was never one to listen to reason. "I will have some supper sent to you in a little while, Mama."

Conversation at dinner was stilted, even with Mary quoting what she thought to be relevant passages from her book of Fordyce's Sermons. Kitty and Elizabeth tried to carry on pleasant conversation, but they just didn't have it in them. They were too worried to pretend. Elizabeth knew all they could do was wait.

That night Elizabeth found no sleep. Even though she knew her mother's propensity for hyperbole, she could not dismiss the fact that there was truth in her words. Her refusal of Mr. Collins had left her family susceptible to the harsh realities of life. Might this situation have been avoided had she married Mr. Collins? Would they all have accompanied Lydia to Brighton? Of course, there was no way to judge such things, but she could not deny the guilt she felt.

The following morning two officers appeared at the cottage door. "Allow me to introduce myself, Miss Bennet. I am Colonel Fitzwilliam, and this is Captain Grayson. We have been sent by Colonel Foster, and I wish to assure you of our full cooperation in the search for your sister."

"I am surprised that this situation would require someone of your rank, sir."

"Well, normally it would not Miss Bennet," said the colonel. "May I speak freely?"

"Yes, of course."

"When I discovered that Mr. Wickham was involved in this situation, I informed Colonel Foster that I would like to lend my assistance to your family. I have had previous dealings with Mr. Wickham in a similar matter, and I thought I might be of some use. We are on our way to London where I hope to locate former associates of Mr. Wickham's who might know of his present whereabouts."

"That is very good of you, Colonel Fitzwilliam. We certainly could use your help, and we are most grateful for it."

"I cannot promise that we will be successful, but I will let you know of any progress in locating your sister."

The gentlemen bowed as they left her company. However, Colonel Fitzwilliam turned back one last time to admire the young lady who possessed the finest eyes he had seen in a long time.

~*~

Three days later Elizabeth received a communication from Colonel Fitzwilliam. The colonel had located a Mrs. Younge on his first day in London. Mrs. Younge had been associated with Mr. Wickham in the past and would most likely know how to contact him. Since she knew the colonel by sight, Captain Grayson had approached the woman advising her that he represented the Bennet family and was acting on their behalf.

The following day Mrs. Younge informed Captain Grayson that Mr. Wickham refused to meet with him but was willing to relay his unyielding demands. There would be no negotiating.

Mrs. Younge revealed exactly what it would take to induce Mr. Wickham to marry Lydia, namely that all of his debts in town be paid, and that he receive an additional sum of ten thousand pounds. Unless the family agreed to his terms, he would not marry Lydia nor divulge her whereabouts.

Colonel Fitzwilliam and Captain Grayson returned to the cottage the following day. "I'm sorry we were not successful in obtaining your sister's location," stated the colonel. "I wanted to be able to assure you of her wellbeing. We can only hope that she has been unharmed."

"Believe me, Colonel; I am grateful for everything you have been able to accomplish. I would not have known where even to begin looking for Mr. Wickham."

"Are you in possession of the money he is demanding?" he asked, his tone almost apologetic.

"No," said Elizabeth, "but if it means saving my family from ruin, I will find a way to raise it. I will go to London and discuss the situation with my sister. I will contact you as soon as we have found a way to acquire the money."

The colonel bowed before her and departed. Had it not been for the unfortunate circumstances of their acquaintance, he might have acted upon his undeniable attraction towards the young lady, but certainly the grievous nature of their association made any such conduct inappropriate. It was probably for the best; for as a second son he knew he must marry a woman of means. Still, he could not deny her appeal.

~*~

Elizabeth met Jane at their usual bench in the park. As she relayed to her sister what had transpired over the last few days, Jane could not help express her great concern.

"Oh Lizzy, how are we ever to come up with such a sum of money?"

Elizabeth shook her head. "I don't know, Jane. Perhaps, I could borrow it from Mrs. Worthington."

Elizabeth highly doubted that Mrs. Worthington possessed such a large sum of money, and, even if she did, Elizabeth was certain her son and only heir would not approve of her making such a loan with no guarantee of its repayment. She did not relate these thoughts to Jane, as she wanted to give her some hope to cling to.

Unable to come up with a feasible resolution, the sisters sat in silence. After some time had passed, Jane stood. "I promised Mrs. Morgan I would stop by her salon and make an appointment for her for Saturday." Elizabeth offered to accompany her, stating she needed a diversion from her thoughts. They gathered the children and made their way towards the centre of town.

As they entered the salon, Elizabeth lifted Caleb into her arms while Jane guided Jaime and Sarah toward the counter. The shop was very busy accommodating London's most upper class of clientele. As Jane tried to gain the attention of the lady behind the desk, Elizabeth sat with Caleb in the waiting area.

Several ladies were seated about the room and looked over at Elizabeth as she entered. She immediately became self-conscious of her appearance. It was obvious that Elizabeth was not a member of their social circle. Her attire, though neat and clean, was simple in nature and contrasted with the fashions worn by those around her. Elizabeth could see the look of disdain on the ladies' faces.

She sat down avoiding all eye contact and focused on Caleb. The two ladies closest to her were engaged in a conversation that was conducted in a stage whisper. Elizabeth was sure this was done for her benefit to produce a reaction of shock.

"Have you ever heard of such a thing?" said one young lady to the other. "I have it on good authority that it is absolutely true!"

"No!" said the other, "How deliciously scandalous!"

"Yes, I heard that whoever he is, he is willing to pay a very large sum of money. Can you imagine paying someone to have your child?"

"If that's the case, I'm sure he must be most disagreeable. Who else would have to do such a thing?"

"Oh, I quite agree, my dear. I'm sure he is most abhorrent."

"How did you ever learn of such circumstances?"

"Well, promise you won't breathe a word of this to anyone, but one of my servants has a cousin who works for Mr. Gallagher, the attorney handling all the arrangements."

Elizabeth saw that Jane had concluded her errand and was walking in her direction. She stood, holding Caleb in her arms. As she turned to leave, she looked back at the ladies who remained still deeply immersed in their gossip.

When they exited the salon, Elizabeth begged to be excused. "I just remembered an important matter that requires my attention, Jane." She handed Caleb over to Jane and kissed her sister on the cheek. "I will see you on Saturday at Gracechurch Street. I'm sorry, but I really must hurry."

"Where is Lizzy going, Jane?" asked Jaime.

Jane stood there quite perplexed as she watched her sister hasten away. "I truly cannot imagine."

CHAPTER SEVEN

Elizabeth nervously awaited Colonel Fitzwilliam's arrival. She had insisted that he allow her to accompany him, and she was grateful that he understood her anxiety in wanting to be assured of Lydia's safety as soon as possible.

She was also extremely thankful that the money from her "business arrangement" had been sent to Mr. Gallagher's office by special courier on the previous morning, as promised by the gentleman.

When she informed the colonel she was in possession of the money demanded by Mr. Wickham, he arranged to meet her at Cheapside. Jane was not even a little suspicious when Elizabeth informed her that Mrs. Worthington had agreed to lend her the money.

When the colonel finally arrived, he apologized for his tardiness. "It was my hope that my cousin would accompany us to meet with Mr. Wickham. I know he would be very interested in the outcome of this situation, as he also has had dealings with Mr. Wickham in the past."

"Did he not wish to make the trip?" inquired Elizabeth.

"When I arrived at his townhouse, I was informed that he had some urgent matters to attend to with an attorney here in town, and then he would be departing to Scotland on business. His housekeeper was not sure when he might return, but expected him to be away for a fortnight or possibly more."

Elizabeth was startled for a moment at the mention of Scotland but quickly dismissed it from her mind.

As their carriage approached the more dissolute part of the city, the colonel reached into his pocket and pulled out the paper Mrs. Younge had given to Captain Grayson. "I'm afraid this is not the best of neighbourhoods. I am certainly glad that circumstances did not prevail upon you to go alone, Miss Bennet.

"Once we have established that your sister is unharmed, it would be best if I were to speak with Mr. Wickham in private. I think I might be more persuasive in convincing him that an immediate wedding would be prudent."

Colonel Fitzwilliam unconsciously touched the sheath of his sword at his side. He could not help but feel protective towards the young lady in his company. She appeared so vulnerable and trusting. Alone, she certainly would have been no match for Wickham.

When the carriage stopped at the address, Elizabeth looked around in disgust. There seemed to be a foul odour in the air and a feeling of depression hovered. As soon as she was handed down from the carriage, several children, dressed in little better than rags, clamoured about her, begging for change.

The colonel immediately endeavoured to chase them away, but Elizabeth begged his patience whilst she reached into her reticule and produced several coins and handed them to the children. She could not help but feel sorry for their wretchedness.

"I'm afraid that will only attract others" he said. "We'd better hurry inside." He offered her his arm, and they crossed the street to the apartments they were seeking. As they climbed the stairs, the colonel instructed Elizabeth to stay behind him. He approached the door to the particular apartment they sought.

He knocked soundly, and, after a few moments, Wickham swung the door open. Upon seeing Colonel Fitzwilliam standing in front of him, he immediately tried to slam it shut. However, the colonel was too quick for him and stopped the door from closing with his boot. Jerking the door forward, he pushed his way past Wickham and entered the room.

Lounging upon the bed was a rather scantily clad Lydia.

Elizabeth was close at Colonel Fitzwilliam's heels. "Lydia!" she exclaimed. "Have you no decency? Put on something to cover yourself!"

Lydia sat up and gave her sister a look of indifference. "What are you *doing* here?"

Unable to hide her shock, Elizabeth immediately grabbed Lydia's dressing gown and demanded that she put it on.

As Wickham made a lunge toward Colonel Fitzwilliam, Elizabeth heard the sound of a sword leaving its scabbard. As she turned, she saw Wickham, quite pale, with a blade pressed under his chin.

"Why don't we go somewhere private and have a little conversation?" suggested the good colonel. Wickham was barely able to nod his head. The colonel withdrew his sword, and the two men exited the room and proceeded downstairs.

As soon as they left, Elizabeth was standing over her sister. "How could you act so imprudently? Have you no idea what scandal this will cause our family should the particulars become known?"

"Oh la, who cares of such things? Wickie and I will be married, and then all will be well."

Elizabeth was on the verge of informing Lydia the price demanded for such a marriage to come about but thought better of it. She knew if Lydia was indeed to marry Mr. Wickham, it would be best if she didn't discover, practically upon her wedding day, the scoundrel that he was. *She will have the rest of her life to learn that*, thought Elizabeth.

Downstairs the two men were seated at a table in the pub. Wickham had a smirk on his face that the colonel was just itching to wipe off. Had it been up to him, Wickham would never have survived the Ramsgate incident. He was not going to let Wickham get away with this sort of thing again. He would either marry Lydia, or he would find himself at the end of the colonel's sword.

"Where is my money?" demanded Wickham.

"Do you think me fool enough to hand over the money before you are married? The family has agreed to pay your demands only on the condition that you immediately proceed with the wedding. And," continued the colonel, "I am here to see that you do. You will not receive a farthing until *after* the ceremony."

Wickham's smirk was sufficiently wiped off as far as the colonel was concerned. He knew Wickham would be facing debtor's prison if he didn't come up with some money soon. He had no choice but to go through with this marriage.

Never one to show any sign of weakness, Wickham commented, "I see you are making a good impression as the hero for Lydia's sister. She is exceedingly pretty. Too bad I did not meet her first. I would certainly have liked to have had my way with *that* one. Her ample figure could keep me well occupied for weeks!"

"You win the prize, hands down, as the most despicable man of my acquaintance, Wickham. That girl upstairs is far too young and naïve to know what she is getting herself into. I pity the day she learns of the misery she will have to endure as your wife. No one deserves such a fate."

"Perhaps we could come to some other resolution," suggested Wickham.

"What do you mean?" the colonel practically growled.

Leaning across the table, Wickham lowered his voice. "Lydia is already ruined. One more gentleman's attentions could hardly make a difference. She can be *quite* entertaining. You could have her and half the money too. All you would have to do is let me escape."

Wickham quickly felt the sting of a fist upon his jaw. The colonel swore under his breath as he felt the pain radiate throughout his hand. However, he had to admit he felt much better having let off a little steam. Wickham was fortunate they were in full view of other patrons; for given the opportunity, the colonel would have gladly beaten him senseless. A few customers looked over, but upon seeing the venom of the colonel's countenance, quickly determined it was best to mind their own business.

It was decided that the wedding would take place in London in three days' time. It would take some doing, but it would be accomplished nevertheless. The colonel could not spare any more time babysitting Wickham as he had to return to his regiment, and Elizabeth had a previous engagement in Scotland.

A special license would be required, and Colonel Fitzwilliam escorted Mr. Wickham to make the necessary arrangements. Elizabeth had the carriage drop her off at Cheapside. The next morning she walked the several blocks to the park and met Jane at their usual bench. She told Jane of the prior day's occurrences, leaving out anything that she thought might offend Jane's sensibilities. The two sisters would attend Lydia's wedding. They agreed it would be best for everyone involved not to inform their mother until after the wedding had taken place.

Three days later, the wedding proceeded as planned. A very uncomfortable looking Mr. Wickham took a very young and misguided Lydia Bennet as his lawfully wedded wife.

Both Jane and Elizabeth thanked Colonel Fitzwilliam for all his help. "Indeed," said Elizabeth, "our whole family will be forever indebted to you."

He bowed deeply to both sisters and graciously accepted their thanks, then headed out to rejoin his regiment.

When it came time for Lizzy to depart from London, the two sisters hugged and promised to write each other often. Jane expressed her deep regret that she would lose her dear sister's company, and Lizzy wanted so desperately to tell her that perhaps she would visit again during the holidays, but even as she considered the words, she knew that would not be possible given the events that would soon occur in Scotland.

All of this deception was most upsetting, but she knew there was nothing to be done for it. She must go to Scotland and fulfil her part of the agreement. Elizabeth knew it might well be a year before she would see Jane again.

CHAPTER EIGHT

Elizabeth had stayed in her room for the entire day. When it was time for the evening meal, she descended the stairs once again and proceeded towards the dining room. There were very few people about. Since it was a Monday, most of the weekend guests had departed the night before.

She was seated at the same small table, her appetite no better than it had been on the previous evening. Again she tried to prolong her dinner as long as possible. She sipped her tea very slowly and ordered a dessert, though she didn't touch it.

One by one, the other tables around her became vacant. Raising her eyes from her cup, she realized that there was now only one other patron in the dining room: *him*.

As soon as their eyes met, she quickly turned away, feeling the blush his stare had created. When she rose from her seat, his eyes followed her every move as she climbed the stairs once again to her room. She knew he would not be long behind her as she went to the dressing chamber to ready herself for his arrival.

Again in her chemise, she was grateful that the fire had been lit, for there was a slight chill in the air and a steady mist was still falling outside. She sat in front of the fire and waited. An hour later she was still waiting.

Thursday's Child

Maybe he isn't coming, she thought. *He certainly saw me climb the stairs. Perhaps he no longer finds me suitable for his purpose. Has he changed his mind about the entire scheme?*

Before Elizabeth's mind could conjure up further explanations for his absence, she heard the fumbling of a key in the door. She rose from her chair, and he was immediately standing before her. He looked upon her, starting with her bare feet and continuing up to her chestnut hair and finally lowering his gaze again to linger on her eyes.

"I did not think you were coming," said Elizabeth softly.

He took an unsteady step closer to her, and she could detect the smell of whiskey. For some reason Elizabeth was not alarmed. She knew she had no reason to fear him. He reached out and gently touched her cheek. He then turned his concentration to her hair as his hands caressed the curls that were so neatly arranged.

He removed a hairpin and watched as a dark chestnut ringlet slowly unwound, falling to her shoulder. He continued this employment several more times, and Elizabeth found herself barely able to breathe, frozen in place by the unexpected feeling of intimacy.

With a tortured look, he turned away. "Please, forgive my lateness, Madam. Are . . . are you ready to . . . *proceed*?"

Elizabeth nodded. She walked slowly in the direction of the bed. As she turned back towards him, she observed him struggling with the knot of his cravat. The picture he presented could either induce mirth or tears. He certainly looked quite ridiculous, standing there unsteadily, trying unsuccessfully to undo his cravat. Yet, there was such sadness in his countenance that she could not help but feel sorry for him.

She returned to stand before him once again. She lifted her hands and, although she had no experience with untying a gentleman's cravat, began trying to loosen the garment from around his neck. As she did so, he looked deep into her eyes. Again his stare had the ability to undo her. She averted her gaze and concentrated on her task, her hands slightly shaking.

He gently rested his hands on her shoulders as she untied the last of the knots and removed the neck cloth. He drew her closer. As their eyes locked, Darcy felt a sudden jolt of panic pierce his heart, and he quickly released her.

Trying to compose himself, he walked towards the small table that held the bottle of brandy. As he lifted the bottle to pour, Elizabeth asked, "Do you think that is wise, sir?"

He looked over to where she stood. He could not deny her effect upon him. "No, you are right. Forgive me," he said as he returned the bottle to its original position. He knew he should not have anything more to drink; he had already over indulged. However, as much as he had imbibed that evening, his senses had not been dulled. His body was already reacting to her nearness.

Elizabeth climbed into the bed, bringing the covers to her chin while she watched him unbutton and remove his shirt. It was not an unpleasant sight. As he started to unfasten the buttons of his breeches, she quickly turned away to stare at the fire. When he had freed himself of the garment, he climbed onto the bed beside her. He moved closer to her and inhaled the lavender scent of her hair.

Darcy had to remind himself that this was not a romantic interlude; this was a business transaction, nothing more. However, that fact did not deter him from speculating on what it would be like to kiss her lips. How strange, he thought, he could take such liberties with her body, but to kiss her would be deemed inappropriate for their purpose.

When he reached over to remove the covers from her, his arm brushed across her breasts, unconsciously tantalizing her nipples. A shiver went through Elizabeth's body. As she looked into his eyes, he reached for the hem of her gown and raised it slowly to her waist. Upon feeling the soft fabric of her gown glide over her thighs, she automatically opened her legs slightly as if in anticipation.

However, he did not move over her as he had the previous night. Instead, he lightly stroked her thighs, causing a ripple of pleasure to radiate through Elizabeth's entire body. Elizabeth was mortified that this man, a man she hardly knew, was causing her body to react in such a manner.

He saw the look of distress on her face and immediately realized the inappropriateness of his action and ceased his ministrations. He knelt between her thighs, his arousal becoming painful from the want of her. As he entered her, the tightness of her engulfed him, and his pain became his pleasure.

As he increased his pace and drove deeper into the recesses of her body, Elizabeth unwillingly let a moan escape her lips. Her hands pressed against his chest as she touched his naked body for the first time. The feel of her hands, so warm and enticing, spread a trail of fire in their wake, causing Darcy to lose all control. He came in a quick succession of quakes and collapsed over her.

~*~

Elizabeth could not sleep. After the gentleman had departed, she immediately was up and pacing the room. She could not account for what was happening to her. Until yesterday all knowledge of any intimacies had been erudite in origin. As a young girl, she had discovered in her father's library some very exotic literature, but even that had not prepared her for the feelings she had just experienced. Was not a lady supposed to be indifferent to such activity and only tolerate it for the sake of procreation?

It seemed quite unfair that unmarried young women were kept in the dark about such things. Was her reaction to this evening's encounter depraved? One thing was for certain: she was anything but indifferent.

Every movement, every touch had brought a reaction. The feel of his breath on her neck as he lay over her, the tingle throughout her body as he brushed against her breasts, and the feel of his hands caressing her thighs had caused her such excruciating pleasure; it had taken every ounce of control she possessed to remain motionless. As he had entered her, she wanted to cry out, but she stifled her voice, emitting only an uncontrollable moan. When she had reached up and touched his bare chest, she felt pure desire for the first time in her life.

She must get control of both her body and mind. She only had to get through one more evening.

Elizabeth sat down before the fire. She did not wish to be in the bed that the gentleman had just vacated. She could still smell his musky redolence upon the bed clothes. She closed her eyes; he was there before her. This would not do. However, she did not try to erase him from her mind.

She awoke a few hours later still in front of the fireplace. She could see the dawn approaching. The rain had passed, and the sun was beginning to rise. After spending the entire previous day idle in her room, Elizabeth was anxious to be outdoors. She decided to dress early and take a walk along the beach. Carrying one of her books under her arm, she made her way down the stairs and onto the boardwalk. It was so early that there wasn't another soul to be seen.

She rather enjoyed being the only person about. She couldn't imagine why she was in such a good mood, considering her situation and the confusion she had felt just a few hours before.

But she had a wonderful sense of freedom as she now walked along the shoreline, enjoying the sun, the sand, the breeze, and the beautiful waters of St. Andrews Bay. As the waves rushed the shore, Elizabeth made a game of chasing them back to the bay and retreating as they rushed the shore again. She was so engrossed in this activity that she hadn't noticed the gentleman standing a short distance away. He was looking at her intently.

Darcy also had endured a rough night with not much sleep. With each of their encounters, he was becoming more conflicted and confused. Last night he was convinced he had discerned some reaction on her part during their intimacy.

While he watched her playfulness upon the shore, he could not help but wonder at her. She was indeed an enigma. Despite her unfortunate situation, she was here before him, enjoying the gloriousness of the day as if she hadn't a care in the world.

They shared a brief look. He certainly could not pretend he had not seen her. He approached where she was standing.

"Are you not jeopardizing your reputation by being seen in my company?" she asked.

Darcy looked around the beach. "I believe no one else has yet awakened from their beds," he replied.

They began walking along the shore. "I see you are *also* an early riser," he observed.

"Yes, I would often awaken early and take long walks around the woods near my home. I am very fond of walking."

"Are you also very fond of reading?" he inquired, noting the book she carried.

"I admit I do have a love of books. My father instilled that in me from a very early age. He had a wonderful library, and I loved to visit him there. When I was young, I would sit on his lap, and he would read to me. Then as I grew older and learned to read myself, we would sit there for hours, each engrossed in our own pursuits."

"Do you still visit your father's library?" he asked.

"No," said Elizabeth, "I'm afraid that after my father's death, our home was entailed away to a distant male cousin. I only managed to take a few of my favourite volumes upon our departure.

"I see that you are allowed to ask personal questions of me, sir," Elizabeth said in an almost teasing voice. "Is that not against the rules?"

"Ah, I see your point, Madam. I guess I must allow you to ask a personal question of me then."

Elizabeth gave this opportunity her full attention. With only one question at her disposal, she didn't want to waste it on something trivial. She looked up at him and asked quite seriously, "Do you believe yourself to be a good man?"

Somewhat surprised by the question she had chosen to ask, he thought for a long moment. "That, I'm afraid, is not such an easy question to answer. I believe I have good intentions. My entire life I have always tried to do the right thing. But, sometimes life presents situations that make it hard to remain true to that ideal. I would like to believe that *I am* a good man. However, I will admit that the past weeks have caused me to ponder that very question myself."

Elizabeth noting the troubled look upon his countenance, wished to return the conversation to a more congenial subject. "Might I ask a small favour of you, sir?" Elizabeth asked as they continued their walk.

"If it is within my power, I shall try to accommodate you, Madam."

"I know we are not to know each other's identity, and I am of the same opinion, but to keep calling you 'sir' seems a little absurd. Do you not agree? Is there not some name I might call you?"

Darcy thought for a moment. He had always been Fitzwilliam or Darcy to everyone he knew, his mother the only exception. She had sensed that he was less than happy that he had been saddled with such a name as "Fitzwilliam," and when they were alone together, she would call him "William." No one had called him that since his mother's death.

"Yes, I believe I can accommodate you, Madam," said Darcy. "William. You may call me William."

As he said the name, he displayed a smile that made Elizabeth catch her breath. It produced the most irresistible dimples she had ever seen. She had already judged him quite handsome without ever observing a smile upon his countenance. With that added enhancement, he was devastatingly so.

"And may I call you something other than 'Madam'?"

Elizabeth thought of the names her friends and family called her. There was, of course, Elizabeth, and then there was Lizzy, and some acquaintances were known to call her Eliza, which she did not favour. *How about Liz?* she thought. It sounded very sophisticated. But no, she didn't want him to call her that. She wanted to hear him call her Lizzy. Surely that would not compromise her identity.

"Yes, you may call me Lizzy."

He studied her face, watching her lips as they turned up to form a bewitching smile. For a brief moment he again wondered what it would feel like to kiss those lips. He quickly chastised himself for such a foolish notion.

"It is a pleasure to make your acquaintance, Lizzy," said Darcy as he bowed before her.

"Thank you, William," Elizabeth responded with a curtsey.

They continued their walk for some time, discussing composers they preferred, books they had read and debating the merits of certain poets. When Elizabeth expressed her partiality to Byron, Darcy raised an eyebrow and smiled at her. "Is there any young woman in all of England who does not favour Lord Byron?" he asked in amusement.

As their conversation continued, they unconsciously stopped walking. He looked deep into her eyes. They were dark and hypnotic, revealing the intelligence and warmth of the woman who possessed them. He reached out and touched her hair, brushing a wayward curl away from her face.

As a group of people approached, he immediately withdrew his hand. Elizabeth followed the direction of his stare and knew he must depart. He bowed slightly as he left her company. As he walked away, he could not help but smile at the irony of the book she carried. It was one of his favourites also . . . Milton's *Paradise Lost*.

CHAPTER NINE

The weather turned out to be so beautiful that Elizabeth decided to spend the entire day exploring St. Andrews. She discovered many enchanting gardens, castles, and cathedrals and visited several shops.

She made several purchases as she passed through the main street of the small town. In one particular shop, she selected three new ribbons and a lovely tortoise shell comb for her hair. In another, she purchased the palest pink silk dressing gown—one of extraordinarily fine quality and of the sheerest fabric. And finally, as she was making her way back to the Inn, she spotted a painting for sale in the window of a small art gallery, depicting the boardwalk and beach she had just walked upon that morning. There was even a little plaque in the middle of the lower frame identifying the beach and name of the town. It captured the entire scene so perfectly; she knew she had to buy it. She had no idea why was she was feeling so frivolous.

It was almost six o'clock by the time Elizabeth finally made her way back to the Inn. She decided to take a long leisurely bath and to have a light dinner served in her room. She did not feel like going through the motions again in the dining room.

With her toilette completed, she looked at her purchases. She eyed the tortoise shell comb and ran her fingers over the smooth surface. Yes, she would wear it in her hair tonight.

Moments later, Elizabeth was seated before the pier glass, draped in the beautiful pink dressing gown she had just purchased. As she adjusted the comb in her hair, she suddenly stopped as she stared wide-eyed at her reflection.

"What are you doing, Lizzy?" she asked aloud to her mirror image. "What are you *doing*?"

She slowly stood. As she studied the length of her reflection, she imagined she looked as a bride might on her wedding night.

She was far from a bride. How foolish she must look, dressed this way as if waiting for her husband to come to her.

She rushed to the dressing chamber and flung off the lovely silk gown, her frenzied motions contradictory to the gown's gentle fluttering to the floor. She quickly put on her chemise and, wiping the tears from her cheeks, returned to sit before the pier glass.

What is wrong with me? she thought. *I must pull myself together.*

Elizabeth did not want to examine her feelings. But she had to face the fact that she was feeling *something*. She knew if she could just get through this final evening without betraying herself, she would be all right.

Starting with their early morning walk, her day had been almost perfect. She truly had enjoyed being in his company. She thought she would have felt embarrassed, considering their previous nights' endeavours, but she did not. It seemed the most natural thing in the world as they walked together and engaged in pleasant conversation.

That feeling of wellbeing had followed her the entire day, a feeling she hadn't experienced in such a very long time, since before her father's death. She did not want to give up that feeling. Not yet. She had one more evening before she must return to her staid existence as a lady's companion. She and the gentleman would go their separate ways come the morning.

~*~

Darcy was taking an unusually long time to dress this evening. He was constantly distracted by the thought of her. Their unexpected encounter that morning was being replayed over again in his mind. He had never met anyone who had completely captured his imagination as she had. Despite his social awkwardness, they had very naturally slipped into easy conversation. He felt a closeness to her that he could not explain.

He presumed his fascination with her was based upon their carnal experience of the past two evenings and would fade along with his ardour once he returned to Pemberley and his well-planned life. After all, it was not as if he had never known the pleasures of intimacy with a woman before. Indeed, he had certainly had previous encounters with women whose experience in the art would make them far more superior partners.

This would be their final evening together. His anticipation was accompanied by a certain amount of apprehension. He should not be this eager to see her again. He would force himself to remember the reason why they were both there. Again he repeated to himself his list of mental notes: *he would remain as detached as possible; he would not engage his emotions; he would conduct himself in a business-like manner; he would walk away unaffected by anything that had occurred.* He inspected his reflection in the pier glass and headed down towards the dining room.

As he entered, he tried to casually look about the room. Not seeing her, he assumed she would be down shortly. He ordered his dinner and waited. By the time he had finished, she still had not appeared. *Where was she?* He was becoming impatient.

He rose from his table and headed toward the stairs, taking them two at a time. As he stood before her door, he did not use his key but pounded his fist upon it. She responded immediately and, saying nothing, backed away, allowing him entrance. As he silently entered the room, she arched an eyebrow.

He noticed her hair was fixed differently, arranged in an upsweep, held by a single tortoise shell comb. Her eyes were dark and penetrating as they stared deeply into his. The scent of lavender was fragrant upon her smooth skin.

She was beautiful.

He studied her face, trying to read her thoughts. His eyes settled on her lips and, again, he was struck with the urge to kiss them. *If I kissed her, would she resist?* He could not help but wonder why this act upon her person had become so paramount. After all, they had been far more intimate than a kiss. And yet . . .

As if against his will, he stepped closer to her and moved his arm around her waist. She lifted her head and met his stare; that stare that made her heart beat faster. He gently kissed her brow, holding her tightly to his chest. He then moved his lips lower, brushing them against her cheek. He could feel her tremble in his embrace, or was it he who trembled?

As he kissed the hollow of her neck, she let out a soft moan. He pulled back to again look into her eyes. Slowly he lowered his head and placed his lips upon hers.

Her lack of experience at this endeavour did not go unnoticed. From her response, he could discern it was most likely the first kiss in which she had ever engaged. As he placed his mouth over hers, he realized she had lost her virtue before she had ever been properly kissed, and that knowledge made him want to hold her dearer.

He moved his mouth, opening it slightly over hers, his tongue lightly beckoning her to allow him entrance. Her lips were warm and inviting as Darcy guided her, teaching her, until at last they kissed a kiss of lovers.

Elizabeth was bewildered at how easily she had allowed him to enfold her. How eager her lips were to meet his. She had imagined his kiss, how it would make her feel. Her imagination paled to the reality of what she was now feeling. A sweet sensation flowed throughout her body. Her hands unconsciously reached up and caressed his shoulders as she returned his kiss with a desperation she could not explain.

As their tongues comingled, a moan of pleasure escaped Darcy's lips as he continued to devour her mouth, each kiss leading to another. And then another. He had never suspected that mere kisses could bring him to such a state of arousal.

Darcy's arms were now the only form of support for Elizabeth's limp body. Her legs had given out kisses ago. He picked her up and carried her to the bed, his lips still upon hers.

He withdrew from their kiss and gently placed her on her feet. Elizabeth had to grasp the bedpost to keep steady. He then reached up and touched the tortoise shell comb that held her hair. In one sweep of his hand, the comb was removed, and her hair tumbled down around her shoulders.

They still had not exchanged a single word; there seemed no need. As much as she wanted to hear the deep resonance of his voice, Elizabeth did not want to disturb the silent pact that now existed between them, allowing this divergence from their agreement.

She moved closer to him again, her hands upon his cravat. It was astonishing how easily it came undone, once she knew how. She began unbuttoning his shirt. As she did, he ran his fingers through her chestnut curls. But his lips were soon again upon hers. He just could not resist kissing her.

As his lips sought hers at every measure, he moved his hands down her body, his arms encircling her as he stroked the small of her back. He lowered his hands still further and embraced the curve of her hips and cupped her lower posterior as he pressed her to his arousal. His hands then moved up along her sides and touched her breasts through her gown. She let out a low moan as he traced over her nipples.

Darcy tried to slow their pace; he wanted this to go on forever. He tried to appear calm, despite his laboured breathing, as he stepped back and wrenched his tailcoat and vest from his body. His shirt came next as he lifted it over his head.

He looked into her eyes before he reached for the buttons of his breeches. Their eyes held for a brief moment, and he then returned his attentions to his task. Elizabeth did not turn away to look at the fire. She watched him as if in a dream, unable to move, as he removed the last of his clothing. The sight of a naked male body was completely foreign to her, yet she instinctively knew that his body was perfection. She could think of no other word to describe him than *beautiful*. He was trim, yet muscular; masculine, and yet graceful in his movements.

Now standing naked before her, Darcy reached for the hem of her chemise with both hands. As he slowly brought it upwards, their eyes never disengaged. When the garment was at her waist, she raised her arms, allowing him its removal.

He lifted her and placed her on the pillows of the bed. He began kissing her again as his hands slowly explored her body. He was now a man on a mission.

He wanted desperately to erase their two previous encounters from her memory. He needed to show her that *this* was how it was supposed to be; *this* is what occurred between a man and a woman when they made love.

He cupped her breasts, running his thumbs over their tips; the coolness of her skin a direct contrast to the heat of his hands. His mouth followed the path of his hands as he traced over every curve of her body. Elizabeth felt as if she were drowning. She had never known such pleasure existed.

Even in his wildest fantasies of her, Darcy had not imagined such passion; his own as much a surprise as hers. He had never reacted so strongly to any other woman's touch. He wanted to give her as much pleasure as she was giving him.

His hands travelled down to her stomach, his light touches causing her to shiver. He was now stroking her thighs, tempting them to surrender their sentry. He moved over her and slipped his fingers into her, finding her most sensitive spot. She gasped as the sensations he caused overtook her entire body.

He knelt between her thighs and pulled her hips toward him guiding himself slowly into her, silently praying he would not lose control too soon. As he began a rocking motion, she lifted her hips to meet him, each crescendo of their perfectly timed rhythm bringing them closer to their ultimate goal.

She once again felt the arousal of his touch, causing her body to tighten around him. As this sensation of pleasure spread through her, Elizabeth allowed herself to give in to its exquisiteness, her body surrendering to the climax of their passion.

"Oh god, Lizzy," he cried as his release followed hers with his final thrust.

After several moments their sated bodies calmed and stilled except for the steady rhythm of their breathing. Darcy allowed himself one final kiss from her sweet lips.

~*~

Darcy moved over to the side of the bed and rested his head on the pillow next to hers. He pulled the bed clothes up to cover them. He stayed like that for some time, trying to decide what he should do. Should he leave as he had the two previous nights? They only had a few hours left before they would be parted forever.

Maybe she would want him to go. Thinking her asleep, he sat up and swung his legs over the side of the bed. He turned his head to look back at her and could just make out her silhouette in the shadows of the dying fire.

He let out a breath as he stood. When Elizabeth felt his weight lift from the mattress, she turned to look at him.

Their eyes found each other in the barely discernible light of the remaining embers.

"I should go," he said.

Pat Santarsiero

She looked away.

He did not want to leave her like this. How could he leave her after what they had just shared? He could not deny he wanted to stay, his list of mental notes now completely abandoned.

He hesitated. For a full minute he stood there, guilt and longing fighting a battle within him.

Elizabeth then felt his weight once again upon the mattress. He slipped in behind her, drawing her back to his chest in one sweeping movement of his arm.

"If it is all right, I will stay with you a while longer, Lizzy."

Her only response was to snuggle closer to his warmth.

Elizabeth drifted off to sleep with the sound of his deep voice calling her Lizzy still resonating in her ear.

A few hours later, the sunlight filtered through the curtains of Elizabeth's room. She looked over at the empty pillow beside her, and a dull ache filled her heart. He had departed before the light. She would never see him again.

CHAPTER TEN

Caroline Bingley was quite pleased with herself. She had managed to persuade her brother to abandon Netherfield, at least long enough for her to enjoy part of the Season in London. She had most definitely had enough of the country to last a lifetime.

"Charles, you know you prefer London to the country. Why don't you just admit it?" she asked as she sat at the breakfast table of their townhouse.

"That's not entirely true, Caroline," he said. "I admit I have missed some of the social activity of London, but I was also enjoying being master of an estate. I agreed to stay in London until Michaelmas, and now it is almost November. I think I have been quite tolerant of your transparent ploys to keep me here, but now I must insist that we return to Netherfield."

"Really, Charles, I just don't understand how you can enjoy being around such primitive people. Why, in the last two months, we have been in the company of a countess and two dukes! How can you compare that with the likes of Hertfordshire society?"

"I hardly consider attending the same play as the Countess Isabella as being in her company," said Bingley. "And the two dukes," he continued, "rode by us in their equipage and nearly ran us over!"

Ignoring her brother's last comments, Caroline continued, "I think we should have a dinner party before you exile us back to

Hertfordshire. Maybe we could invite Mr. and Mrs. Darcy. I'm sure they would attend if *you* invited them, Charles."

"I *would* like to see Darcy again," admitted Bingley. "It has been more than six months since I last saw him at his wedding. We could invite Georgiana also and maybe Colonel Fitzwilliam too." Bingley was beginning to brighten at the prospect of seeing his good friends once again.

Caroline was also anxious to see Mr. Darcy again. She could not believe he had married that plain and sickly girl. Certainly it was a marriage of convenience. Perhaps he needed to be reminded what it was like to be in the company of an elegant lady of society, such as herself.

~*~

Darcy had thrown himself into his work since his return from Scotland, trying to keep his mind and body as active as possible. He was determined not to think upon her. If only he had not allowed himself to become preoccupied with kissing her. That preoccupation had led to his discovering the sweetness of her mouth. Once he had tasted her lips, he knew he wanted more than just another night of sexual achievement.

Before his departure, he had given Dr. Adams his consent to discuss with Anne the consequences to her health that would most likely occur should she again find herself with child. Actually Darcy was somewhat relieved that he would not have to be the one to broach such a delicate subject.

Anne never discussed her conversation with Dr. Adams, but, from that day forward, an unspoken agreement existed between the two of them. They each retired nightly to their respective bedchambers. Aside from that, Darcy was attentive to Anne in every other way.

As he opened the mail that morning, he came across Bingley's invitation. He would like to see his good friend again, but he feared Anne would not be up to travelling to London. In the two months since he had returned from Scotland, her health had not improved.

She had expressed a desire to visit Rosings when she was feeling better, and he did not wish to deny her this small consideration. Her pleasures were few of late. Travelling to both London and Rosings might prove to be too much for her frail condition.

Every thought of Lizzy provoked fresh guilt over what had occurred in St. Andrews. Of course, he had expected to feel *some* guilt when he first devised his plan to produce an heir. After all, he did not approve of gentlemen who indulged in sexual activity outside of the marriage bed. But he had believed his plight was quite different from those gentlemen. He had not been seeking sexual congress for the act itself, but for its end result.

On their first evening together, he had applied himself as perfunctory as possible. As he watched her walk from her dressing chamber towards him wearing only her chemise, he had quickly reviewed his list of mental notes to ensure no deviation from his plan. However, as he had lain over her, he could not escape the intensity of her stare. She had looked inside him, and he felt a connection far beyond the mere coupling of their bodies.

On their second evening together, he had been determined to keep all personal aspects of their union under strict regulation. He would remain immune to whatever arts and allurements she possessed. He had hoped the whiskey he indulged in that evening would dull his senses and render her charms ineffective; however, the alcohol only seemed to intensify his desires. When he had looked into her eyes as she untied his cravat, he felt something he had never felt before. Whatever that feeling was, it had shaken him to his very core.

On their final evening together, he had been lost as soon as he tasted her lips. He could no more control his desire for her than he could control the tide. He had wanted to possess her body and soul. To his amazement, she had returned his ardour with equal passion.

He knew the time he had spent with her had affected him greatly; however, he also knew he could not allow it to change his life. He had gotten carried away by their intimacy, but, now that he was home again, he hoped the spell would soon be broken.

She had come into his life in a most unconventional way. She was certainly beneath his society. If he had met her before he had married, he would have never allowed himself to become associated with someone so far below his own station in life. It seemed he was fated to regret her no matter how or when their paths may have crossed. There was no point dwelling on such matters. He had made his choices in life. His priorities had been duty and obligation. So be it.

But fate had given him a glimpse of what his life might have been under different circumstances. He knew whatever time he had been granted to spend in her company, he would always cherish. For the sake of his marriage, his family and his reputation, he would remember her only as the woman who once fulfilled his fantasies. He must now get on with the reality of his life.

He would not know the outcome of their union for at least another month or more. She had been instructed to contact Mr. Gallagher as soon as she was sure, one way or the other, preferably upon experiencing the quickening of the babe.

Darcy had arranged it so that once it was confirmed she was with child, she would have a comfortable place to live during her confinement. He was now glad that his attorney had made all of those arrangements beforehand. He did not trust himself to know where she might soon be living.

As he was headed toward his study to reply to Bingley's invitation, he heard a horse approaching. To his surprise, his cousin Richard was announced.

"Darcy, you're a hard man to track down," said his cousin.

"So I hear. Mrs. Evanston said you came looking for me a few months ago but that you did not say what it was about."

"Let's go into the study and have a drink," suggested Richard, "and I will relate the entire story."

"Is it not rather early in the day?" quipped Darcy.

"Believe me, Darcy, when you hear the story I have to tell, you will not think it too early."

Darcy shrugged and obediently entered the study and poured out two glasses of brandy.

"Well," started Richard, "you're not going to believe the events that have taken place. I didn't want to reveal the details to your housekeeper as they involved Wickham."

At the mention of the name, Darcy's eyes immediately grew cold. "What has that blackguard done now?" he asked.

"Well, it seems he was up to his old tricks. He ran away with a fifteen year old girl from Hertfordshire under the pretence of an elopement. Unfortunately they were not found before she was compromised."

The look of bitter disgust was apparent on Darcy's face. He would be forever grateful that he had discovered Georgiana before such an occurrence had taken place.

"And what has become of her?" asked Darcy.

"Wickham demanded the family pay all his debts and ten thousand pounds to proceed with a wedding. Since her father is deceased, her elder sister accompanied me to meet Wickham. I, fortunately, was able to locate Mrs. Younge to make contact with him. I had thought you might be interested in joining us, so I went to your townhouse to see if you were available."

"And what was the outcome?"

"After some persuasion, Wickham agreed to marry the girl. I made sure he abided by his agreement and that the money was not exchanged until after the ceremony. I believe he has gone into the regulars now and has been relocated to Newcastle."

"I'm sorry I wasn't there to accompany you."

"What business took you to Scotland?" asked his cousin.

Darcy startled slightly at his question as he was not prepared to answer anything regarding his trip. He took a gulp of his drink, now grateful that the liquid was already in his hand.

He had always been honest with Richard. Should he disclose to him this confidence? After thinking upon it for a moment, he considered that until he knew the outcome of his assignation, there would be no need to tell him anything. After all, Lizzy might not be with child.

"I met with a gentleman who has designed a new irrigation system," stated Darcy, quite pleased he had come up with such a reasonable explanation so quickly. "I may be interested in applying such a system here at Pemberley." This was not an outright lie, as he had met with a gentleman regarding that very thing only last month.

There was a light knock at the door, and Anne and Georgiana entered the study. "Richard!" cried Georgiana, as she rushed to his side.

He hugged her and gave Anne a kiss on the cheek. "It's so good to see you both again."

"Oh, Richard, I am very glad you are here. I think my brother could use some cheering up," said Georgiana. "He seems much distracted since his return from Scotland."

Darcy blushed slightly, trying to hide his discomfort at such an observance. "Indeed, Darcy. And what distracts you so?" queried Richard.

"I assure you, I am not," he said, using the haughty tone he reserved for such occasions. In an effort to change the subject, he relayed, "I have received an invitation from Mr. Bingley for a dinner party in London. The invitation includes all of us. I have not yet decided as to my reply."

"Oh Fitzwilliam!" exclaimed Georgiana. "I would love to go. It would be so wonderful to see Mr. Bingley again. And Anne and I could do some shopping whilst in London."

"How do you feel about travelling to London, Anne?" asked her husband. "If you are not feeling up to the trip, we will, of course, decline the invitation."

Not wishing to disappoint her husband or sister, she said, "I believe I am well enough to make the trip, Fitzwilliam."

Darcy sat down next to his wife and took her hand. "Are you sure, Anne? It is of little importance. Your comfort is my main concern."

"I am very sure, Fitzwilliam. I think we all could use some diversion. And besides, it will give me a chance to see how you two behave out in polite society," she said teasingly.

Darcy and Richard both looked at her. "We will do our best not to embarrass you too much," replied Darcy with a smile, happy to see his wife in such good spirits.

"Perhaps, we could travel to Rosings upon leaving London," she suggested.

"Whatever you wish, Anne," he said.

Turning towards his cousin he asked, "What about you, Richard? Do you think you can make it? It's in ten days' time."

"I shall make every effort."

"Then it's settled," said Darcy. "I shall reply to Bingley and accept for us all. I'll write to Mrs. Evanston immediately and have her open up the townhouse for our arrival."

CHAPTER ELEVEN

"How was your visit with John and his family?" asked Elizabeth.

"I had a wonderful time. My grandchildren are growing so big, I hardly recognized them!" said Mrs. Worthington. "I hadn't realized how much I missed seeing them. John has again asked me to move in with him and Henrietta, but I still can't make up my mind. It would mean selling my home. I have so many fond memories here, but it does seem silly for me to live in this big house all by myself. I'll give it some more thought. Nothing has to be settled right away.

"I'm glad you returned before me, Elizabeth. I hate coming home to a stuffy house. I see you had it aired out properly. You always think of everything. Now sit down and have some tea with me and tell me about your visit with your sister."

Elizabeth made her way over to the divan and sat down next to Mrs. Worthington. She poured a cup of tea for each of them. "Well, it was anything but dull," said Elizabeth. "I got to see all of my family actually. As it so happened, I had occasion to travel to Meryton and visited with my mother and younger sisters also."

Elizabeth really didn't want to expand on the circumstances of seeing all her family, since most of it revolved around her sister Lydia's scandalous affair and hasty wedding.

"It was wonderful to see Jane again. She seems so happy in her position as governess. The children adore her."

Thursday's Child

"Since she is so good with children, I'm sure she would one day like to have some of her own," said Mrs. Worthington, "as I imagine you would also, Elizabeth. Have you not given that prospect some thought? Such pretty girls! Why some gentleman hasn't come courting is astonishing! What is wrong with the gentlemen of today? Why, in my day . . . oh well, I'm sure you don't want to hear about the way things were in my day."

Elizabeth tried to make light of Mrs. Worthington's words as she displayed a forced smile. The mention of bearing children had temporarily frozen her cup midway to her mouth. "I'm sure Jane will someday meet the right gentleman," said Elizabeth, hoping Mrs. Worthington hadn't detected her uneasiness. "Certainly someone with her goodness and beauty will find happiness."

"And what of you, Elizabeth?" asked Mrs. Worthington.

"I am quite content as I am," she answered. "I have my friends and family, and my books. Your groom is teaching me to ride, and I, of course, have your very enjoyable company," said Elizabeth. "I believe my life is quite full."

Mrs. Worthington eyed her dubiously. "Well, my dear, if you say so."

~*~

Over the next few weeks, Elizabeth settled back into her normal routine. She ran errands for Mrs. Worthington and helped her tend her lovely gardens. She read, then discussed, all the latest books, and on her idle afternoons, she would write letters to Jane.

She continued her equestrian lessons with Danny, the young groom, and he seemed quite pleased with her progress. He had tried to teach her to ride side saddle but, with no experience to draw upon, reverted to teaching her to sit astride. Elizabeth hardly minded as she could not imagine how anyone could ride a horse with any speed while sitting in such an awkward way, and one thing she loved about riding was the speed. Though she still enjoyed her rambles, nothing made her feel quite as alive as galloping through a field with the wind blowing across her face, enjoying all the freedom and excitement that it provided.

When she asked Mrs. Worthington when and where they were to travel next, the elder woman expressed a desire to stay put for a time. She was growing tired of so much travelling, she said. "After a while, one place looks just like another."

~*~

Elizabeth awoke to a beautiful early October morning. She had decided to walk the gardens around Mrs. Worthington's property. After her brisk walk she returned to the house, ready for breakfast. She poured herself a cup of tea and sat down before her usual fare of toast and jam while Mrs. Worthington was enjoying her customary kippers and eggs.

As their aroma reached Elizabeth's nose, she immediately jumped up. Without excusing herself, she made her way upstairs and went directly to the chamber pot. This routine continued for the next several days.

Knowing herself not to be ill, Elizabeth was slowly coming to terms with her condition. She was aware that many women who were with child experienced such nausea when in contact with strong odours. However, she did not want to acknowledge that possibility just yet.

As long as she could still convince herself that she was yet unsure of her condition, she would not have to leave Mrs. Worthington, and she could pretend that Scotland had only been a figment of her imagination. Until she felt the quickening of the babe, she would continue her usual routine. *Well, maybe I should forego the riding lessons*, she thought.

Suspecting she was with child, *his child,* she could not stop thinking about him. Up until then she had sufficiently kept her mind busy as to keep out thoughts of him, at least during the day. Nights were another story.

She had tried not to think upon their last night together. She had responded to him so naturally and surrendered to him so completely. She had often tried to imagine what might have occurred had they been subjected to subsequent evenings in such intimate proximity. The only word she could think to describe herself while in his embrace was *wanton*. Surely they were not well enough acquainted that she would think herself in love; if not love, then what?

She tried to determine if she would feel the same way for *anyone* under such circumstances. How could one not have feelings for someone they held in intimate embrace? Pondering that thought, she tried to imagine Mr. Collins in such a situation. Would *he* have inspired such responses? Would she now be spending her nights longing again for *his* touch? Elizabeth immediately shuddered at the thought.

No, it was William's touch, and William's touch alone, that had inspired her. He had awakened feelings in her she did not know existed. He had changed her forever. She wondered if he ever thought upon their time together or had he already forgotten her. And why should he not forget her? After all, it was never meant to be anything other than a business arrangement.

She had gone into their arrangement with no expectations other than those established by Mr. Gallagher. Indeed, when the agreement had been explained to her, she hadn't any knowledge of the gentleman whatsoever, aside from hearing his voice that day during her interview.

What if he had been abhorrent in looks and in manner? Had that been the case, would she care now that she would never see him again? Probably not. But she also knew that if that *had* been the case, their last night together—or for that matter, their first and second nights together—would have gone quite differently. She would not have been so strongly affected by their intimacy.

Mr. Gallagher had explained to her quite explicitly exactly what was to take place, the agreement being very precise. The terms stated that she and the gentleman were to engage in sexual congress, for the sole purpose of reproduction; there were to be no less than three attempts to accomplish the desired result, and any sexual act that would not achieve the desired result was prohibited. Mr. Gallagher had explained that this last provision was added for her benefit and protection, but to be honest, Elizabeth had not had the slightest idea what it meant and was too embarrassed to ask.

Once it was established that she was with child, the agreement further stated all of the arrangements would be made for her confinement, including the provision for living quarters to be provided during her confinement and for one month following the birth of the child. If she were to deliver the child in May, she could continue to reside in the living quarters provided until the end of June. Mr. Gallagher explained that his client wanted to give her ample time to recover from the birth and also give her time to relocate herself.

One servant would be provided to attend her during her confinement, and a midwife would be provided for the birth of the child. Further terms stated that neither party was to seek out the other nor would any communication between the parties be permitted. All communication would be conducted through Mr. Gallagher. Upon the birth of the child and the handing over of such child to Mr. Gallagher, the terms of the agreement would be fulfilled.

Looking over her copy of the contract, Elizabeth realized how cold it sounded to her now. Of course, now that Lydia's reputation was saved and her family was no longer threatened with a scandal, her point of view was quite different.

Sometimes at night as she lay in bed, she could not believe she had actually agreed to such a situation. Even now as she stared at the agreement in her hand, it did not seem real. Was she just beginning to realize the impact this entire affair would have on her? Had she really been so naïve?

Thursday's Child

Within the next few weeks, the nausea passed. She began to feel like her old self again and had even convinced herself that perhaps she had only suffered a touch of the flu to cause her such symptoms.

That diagnosis was quickly dismissed, however, when on the following week, she most decidedly felt someone kick her. The kick came from within. She knew she would have to contact Mr. Gallagher very soon.

CHAPTER TWELVE

Darcy's carriage pulled up in front of his townhouse in Grosvenor Square. He helped Anne and Georgiana down and called to the footman to help with their trunks. They had arrived two days prior to the dinner party and hoped to spend some leisurely time visiting with Bingley. Darcy quickly penned a note, sending his card around to inform him of their arrival. By that afternoon, Bingley was at his door. Unfortunately, he was not alone.

Upon their announcement, Caroline and Charles Bingley entered the music room. Darcy immediately rose from his seat to greet his guests. "Bingley! What a pleasure to see you again."

Before he could address Caroline, she was at his side and gave him a rather lingering kiss on his cheek. "Mr. Darcy, how we have missed your society! I am so glad you have accepted our invitation."

"It is a pleasure to be in your company as well," said Darcy with far less enthusiasm.

Georgiana rose from the pianoforte, where she had been playing, and went to her brother's side. "I'm so happy to see you both. I am so looking forward to your dinner party."

Bingley graciously took her hand and bowed. "You're looking very well, Georgiana. I must say you have grown into a most lovely young lady." Georgiana blushed shyly at his compliments.

"Oh, my dear Georgiana," said Caroline, "Charles could not be more correct—you have indeed grown. You must be at least two inches taller than last we met."

Georgiana hesitantly smiled in response, not quite sure if this was a compliment or not.

Darcy led the entire party over to Anne, who rose from the divan to greet her guests.

"How lovely to see you again, Mrs. Darcy," said Bingley. "Do you remember my sister Caroline? You met briefly at your wedding."

"Yes, of course," said Anne. "It is nice to make your acquaintance again."

Looking the woman over from head to toe, Caroline's insincerity was hardly disguised. "The pleasure is all mine, Mrs. Darcy."

With introductions and greetings finally out of the way, the party sat and tea was ordered. "Well, Darcy, what have you been up to?" asked Bingley. Realizing his friend was still practically on his honeymoon, Bingley's colour deepened at his own words.

However, connubial relations were the furthest thing from Darcy's mind, and he didn't notice his friend's embarrassment. "Anne and I are getting used to married life. We have been enjoying the peace and quiet of Pemberley, and Anne is learning about some of her duties as Mistress. Mrs. Reynolds has been most helpful in acquainting Anne with her many new responsibilities." With that he looked over to his wife, who smiled at him.

"I'm sure it is a most daunting task," said Caroline. "Running a household as large and prestigious as Pemberley must be very exhausting for someone as . . . *delicate* as you, Mrs. Darcy."

Darcy quickly tried to intercede on his wife's behalf. "Did you enjoy the London season?" he asked.

Both Caroline and Bingley answered together. "Exceedingly so," was Caroline's reply.

"Not really," was Bingley's.

"It is such a pleasant day; shall we take to the outdoors for a stroll?" offered Anne as she gave Darcy a look of gratitude.

"That is an excellent idea!" said Georgiana eagerly.

Darcy leaned over to Anne and whispered in her ear, "Are you sure you are up to a walk so soon after our arrival?" She gave him a smile and nodded.

As the entire party was making ready to leave, Colonel Fitzwilliam entered the foyer. "Oh, Richard, you made it!" cried Georgiana. Bingley and Darcy expressed their pleasure at the colonel's timely arrival to accompany them, and they all proceeded out to enjoy an afternoon in the park.

Maintaining a leisurely pace, they remarked on the beauty of the day and shared pleasant conversation. Upon approaching a park bench, both the colonel and Bingley eyed the blonde beauty seated, and each to the surprise of the other said simultaneously, "Miss Bennet?"

Jane Bennet looked up from her letter and eyed the three couples before her. She immediately recognized Colonel Fitzwilliam, having seen him only three months prior at her sister Lydia's wedding. As she looked at the other familiar face, she blushed, realizing it was the man who had so often occupied her thoughts. She immediately rose from the bench.

"Colonel Fitzwilliam! Mr. Bingley!" she exclaimed. "What a most unexpected surprise!"

"Indeed," said the colonel as he bowed to her.

Bingley's face immediately reflected his pleasure at seeing her even as he pondered on her association with Colonel Fitzwilliam and how it had come about. The next thing he noted was the small child playing at her feet.

He bowed and addressed her. "I'm so happy to make your acquaintance again, Miss Bennet. I was so sorry to hear of your father's passing. We only met on two occasions, but he seemed a most amiable gentleman."

"I thank you, sir."

There was a moment of silence before Bingley, remembering his manners, introduced Jane to the rest of their party. When he got to the colonel, he could not help but comment, "And you obviously already know Colonel Fitzwilliam."

The colonel said nothing, waiting to see how Miss Bennet wished to explain their acquaintance. "Yes, Colonel Fitzwilliam and I met a few months ago while attending my sister Lydia's wedding. The bridegroom was in military service and an acquaintance of the colonel." Her reply caused Bingley's demeanour to brighten considerably.

It also drew Darcy's attention. *Was this the young lady that Richard accompanied to London to meet Wickham?* He would have a private talk with Richard later.

Jane looked down at Caleb, who was tugging on her skirt to gain her attention. Reaching down, she scooped him up into her arms.

"What an adorable little boy," said Georgiana.

"Yes," said Jane. "He is adorable, but he can also be a handful. This is Caleb," she said to all, "one of the three children under my care." She gestured to the pond and indicated Jaime and Sarah also. "I have been their governess for over a year now."

Again, Bingley conveyed a look of relief at this news. He had not taken his eyes from Jane even once, and she could not help but notice.

Caroline, realizing that this was hardly someone who could further her position in society, dismissed her immediately. "Well, we really should be going."

"Yes, of course" said Jane. "It was very nice to meet all of you. I hope that we shall meet again." The gentlemen bowed at their departure, and the couples continued their walk.

Jane sat back down on the park bench. She felt out of breath. She could not believe the serendipity of such a meeting. Would he seek her out again now that he knew where he might find her?

As the couples continued their stroll, Bingley remarked, "Perhaps we should invite Miss Bennet to our dinner party, Caroline."

"You must be joking, Charles. Are we now inviting domestic help to our social affairs?"

"Really, Caroline, must you always be such a snob? Miss Bennet comes from a very respectable family. It is only due to the entailment of her family estate that she finds herself in need of such a position."

"Tell me, Bingley," asked Darcy, "do you know to whom the estate was entailed?"

"Yes, as a matter of fact, I do know. He, of course, is now a neighbour of mine. His name is Mr. Collins; he is a clergyman," stated Bingley.

"How unbelievable," said Anne. "We are acquainted with Mr. Collins! My mother was his patroness at the parsonage at Hunsford."

"Yes," said Darcy. "If I remember his conversation, I believe he said the estate was entailed to him since he was the only male heir."

"That's right, Darcy. There are five daughters. Mrs. Bennet lives with two of her younger daughters, Miss Katherine and Miss Mary, outside of Meryton. Miss Lydia, as you heard, was just recently married, and I'm not sure where Miss Elizabeth is living now. You remember I told you that I had met them once at Longbourn that week before we all attended the Meryton Assembly," said Bingley.

Colonel Fitzwilliam decided it was best to keep any information he had to himself at the moment. He certainly didn't want to mention in front of Georgiana that Miss Elizabeth had accompanied him to meet Wickham.

Darcy did not want to think upon these new revelations. He was sure his imagination was just running away with itself. But one thing he had to admit: it was certainly a small world, and it seemed to be getting smaller by the minute.

~*~

The next day Darcy was determined to speak to Richard privately. He summoned him after breakfast to meet him in his study. "I would like to ask you about Miss Bennet," said Darcy.

"I thought you might."

"Is that the young lady you accompanied to London to meet Wickham?"

"No," said Richard, "that is her sister. I went to London with Miss Elizabeth."

"Well, if Miss Elizabeth is half as agreeable as Miss Bennet, I do not think it was exactly a hardship," he said with a look of amusement on his face.

"No, it was not," agreed Richard. "She may not be as beautiful as her sister, but she is exceedingly pretty, and she has a smile that reaches all the way up to the most delightful eyes I've ever seen."

"How does she make her living?"

"From what I gathered, she has been a companion to an elderly widow since shortly after her father's death."

"I don't understand," said Darcy, "how Miss Bennet's employment as a governess and her sister's position as a lady's companion enabled them to afford to pay such a large amount of money to Wickham, not to mention the fulfilment of his debts in town?"

"That is indeed a very good question, Darcy," said Richard. "I know Miss Elizabeth made all the arrangements to obtain the money, but I never asked from whence it came. I just assumed she had managed to borrow it; from a relative, perhaps."

Darcy ran his hand through his hair. Why was he getting this uneasy feeling in the pit of his stomach?

~*~

When Bingley announced he was going out for the morning, he was relieved that Caroline had not offered to accompany him. He had his own agenda in mind.

"I'm sorry, Charles; I must stay here. I'm expecting Louisa and Mr. Hurst to arrive sometime this morning. Louisa and I are planning to go shopping with Anne and Georgiana."

Bingley tried to look disappointed.

Practically running from the townhouse to the park, he was hoping to find Miss Bennet somewhere within. He walked the same route as they had the day before, and, upon nearing the same park bench, he saw her. She looked up and eyed him immediately.

He approached her and bowed. "Good morning, Miss Bennet. I was hoping I might meet you again."

She blushed.

"Would you mind if I joined you?" he asked.

"Not at all, sir."

He sat beside her on the bench, a wide grin upon his face. "May I inquire as to your health?"

"I am well, sir," she replied.

"And what about your family, Miss Bennet, are they well?"

"They are all *very* well, sir."

There was an awkward silence. Even though he could think of nothing else to say to her, he could not help the smile that continued to reside upon his face. It must have been contagious, because soon Jane was displaying a similar smile.

As they sat there, grinning at each other, Bingley had an inspiration. He would defy his sister and invite her to his dinner party. After all, it was *his* dinner party.

"Miss Bennet, I am giving a dinner party tomorrow evening, and I was wondering if you might like to attend? I know it is rather late notice, but if it is at all possible, I would be most happy to have the pleasure of your company."

"I would be delighted to attend, Mr. Bingley."

"Excellent! I shall send a carriage for you, shall we say at seven? Just give me the address, and I will see to all the arrangements."

Jane stood and helped Caleb to a standing position. Bingley immediately followed her lead and took hold of one of Caleb's hands. As the little boy teetered between them, they looked into each other's eyes.

"Would you care to join us in a walk around the park?" inquired Jane.

"I would enjoy that very much."

Jane called to Jaime and Sarah. Sarah came running quickly, but Jaime approached slowly, eyeing the gentleman who stood next to Jane.

"Sarah, may I present Mr. Bingley," said Jane.

"It is my pleasure to meet you, Miss Sarah," said Bingley, bowing before her. The little girl's already rosy cheeks blushed a deep red at his words, and she giggled gleefully.

"And this is her brother Jaime."

"Indeed, a pleasure, sir," said Bingley. "I have been invited to accompany all of you on a walk around the park. I hope you do not mind."

Jamie instinctively took hold of Jane's hand and gave Bingley a wary look. Obviously, he did mind. Jane smiled down at Jaime, comprehending his gesture.

"Perhaps you would like to hold Mr. Bingley's hand during our walk, Sarah. That way you and I shall both have the protection of a gentleman to accompany us," said Jane.

Again Sarah blushed but quite willingly put her hand in Mr. Bingley's. Bingley and Jane each held one of Caleb's hands and smiled adoringly at each other as they all proceeded on their walk, both quite content just to be in each other's company.

~*~

Mrs. Reynolds was instructing the staff of their duties for the day. With the Master, Mistress and Georgiana all from home, she decided it would be a perfect opportunity to do a thorough cleaning of their bed chambers. She instructed the servants to open all the windows and remove all the bedding.

She gathered up the bed clothes from Georgiana's room first, and as she was next stripping the mattress in Anne's room, she noted several handkerchiefs stuffed beneath it. As she pulled them out to surrender them to the laundry, she noted the dried blood within each one. She quickly took them, hiding them in her apron pocket, not wanting the servants aware of her findings.

Although somewhat startled by this discovery, she was not surprised by Anne's deception. Anne had confided in her several times over the past months of her guilt regarding the situation of her marriage to Mr. Darcy, guilt derived from her feelings of inadequacy. She felt she had failed him. To make matters worse, despite these failings, he continued to be attentive and supportive of her as his wife. Mrs. Reynolds had tried to convince Anne that she should not give in to such self-deprecation, but she could not be convinced. The more accommodating Darcy was to her needs, the guiltier she felt.

If Darcy knew the extent of her illness, he would be even more solicitous, causing Anne even more remorse. It was a complicated matter to say the least. She would have to decide what course of action to take. If she removed the handkerchiefs from beneath the mattress, Anne would know she had been found out. She would need time to think over the situation.

Mrs. Reynolds had been in service of the Darcy household for five and twenty years. She knew almost all there was to know about the family. She had been caring for Mr. Darcy since he was four years old.

She was extremely proud of the fine young man he had become. She was also painfully aware of the current circumstances of his life. She knew his regard for Anne's health had forced them to abandon the hope of producing an heir together. She also knew of his plan to produce one elsewhere. Although she did not entirely approve of her master's plan, she could not deny him her assistance in helping him see it through. Her loyalty and devotion to the family was unquestionable.

She continued her supervision of the housecleaning chores throughout the morning. When the mail arrived after lunch, she shuffled through her master's correspondence and came across a letter addressed to her from Mr. Gallagher.

November 8, 1812

Dear Mrs. Reynolds,

I have received word from the young lady. She has informed me that it is her belief that she is now with child. She has experienced the quickening to confirm this. She relayed no other details and is requesting to receive further instructions. She has asked me to again assure her that I am the only person to know her identity, and I have written her with my assurance and to advise her of the arrangements being made for her confinement.

If there is anything you would like me to convey to the young lady, please write me.

Yours truly,

Arthur Gallagher, Esq.

Mrs. Reynolds refolded the letter and placed it into her pocket. She could not gauge her own reaction to this news. She knew how much Mr. Darcy wanted this child, but she also knew he had not come up with a feasible plan to claim the child as his own.

As much as she had disapproved of this entire scheme to produce an heir, she had to admit she found no offense with the young lady herself. She had been open and as honest as could be expected regarding her circumstances. She was bright and intelligent and had a certain warmth about her. Indeed, Mrs. Reynolds had agreed wholeheartedly with her master's choice. However, now that she knew for certain of the young lady's condition, she wondered how this warm, bright, and intelligent woman would be able to give up her child?

Mrs. Reynolds sat there for a long time. Her apron pocket held many secrets. Should she tell Mr. Darcy of Anne's failing health? Surely, he was already aware of it. She was sure it had not escaped his notice that Anne appeared weaker and that her cough could be heard long into the night. No, it was not her place to divulge such information. That was between a wife and her husband.

Of the other secret in her pocket, she knew what she must do. She would write to Mr. Darcy in London and inform him of Mr. Gallagher's letter and reveal its contents. By her accounting, if all went right, the baby would be born sometime in May.

CHAPTER THIRTEEN

The night held much promise for Jane Bennet, who arrived in anticipation of spending the evening in Mr. Bingley's company. As she entered the townhouse, she was met by Miss Bingley, who looked upon her with dismay. "Why, Miss Bennet, I did not expect to see you again so soon. My brother evidently neglected to mention that he had invited you."

"I hope my attendance does not displease you," said Jane feeling somewhat embarrassed.

"No, of course not. I could not be more pleased that you were able to leave your employment on such short notice," said Caroline as she did little to disguise the smirk on her face.

Noting Jane's look of distress, Bingley immediately made his way towards her. "Miss Bennet, how lovely you look this evening. Please come in. There are some people I would like you to meet."

Grateful for his presence, Jane took his arm, and they entered the parlour. As Jane looked around her, she recognized everyone she had met at the park. She again greeted Colonel Fitzwilliam, Miss Darcy, and Mr. and Mrs. Darcy. As she looked back at Miss Bingley, she could see her in conversation with two other ladies, who took turns looking over in her direction. It was obvious that she was the topic of their conversation.

She was introduced to Mr. Carlson and Mr. Wethersby, both of whom expressed their delight in meeting her as they eyed her appreciatively. Their enthusiastic approval alerted Mrs. Carlson and Mrs. Wethersby that their presence was required, and they immediately took their places beside their husbands. After a brief introduction, they steered their spouses away to another part of the room.

Anne could not help but notice Jane's unease. "Miss Bennet, we are so glad you were able to attend. Mr. Bingley especially, I believe."

She started to chuckle as she said this, but her chuckle soon turned into a series of coughs. Darcy was immediately at her side. As soon as she was again in control, Anne dismissed his concern, reassuring him she was now quite well.

Upon seeing Jane in Mr. Darcy's company, Caroline immediately made her way towards the parlour. "Isn't it delightful that Miss Bennet was able to get this evening off to attend our little dinner party?" she asked.

Jane's red face belied the calmness she was trying to maintain. Bingley, Darcy and Anne all turned to Caroline with disapproving looks upon their faces.

Of course, that did not deter Caroline from continuing; in fact, she was quite pleased to see she now had their full attention. "It has always been my experience that allowing the servants a night off keeps them content and helps maintain a more pleasant household. I dare say I often give our servants *two* evenings a week off to do as they please."

Bingley and Darcy both shifted uneasily from one foot to another. Wanting to ease the tension, Anne again addressed Jane. "Miss Bennet, I understand you have several sisters. That must have been a wonderful experience growing up. I am an only child, so I must admit I envy you such a situation."

"Yes, the five of us are so very different that at times it was difficult, but our diversity also made life quite interesting," said Jane, grateful to move on to another subject.

"Tell me, Miss Bennet," asked Darcy, "do you get to see your sisters often?"

"Not as often as I would like, Mr. Darcy, especially Li . . . Elizabeth. Being the two eldest, she and I have always been closer than the rest of our sisters. We only see each other occasionally when Elizabeth is not travelling with her companion, Mrs. Worthington, and when she has a chance to take a holiday. I'm afraid that has only happened once in the past year."

"So both you *and* your sister Miss Elizabeth are employed as domestics? Your family must have a calling for such employment," purred Caroline.

With that, dinner was announced, and they all entered the large dining room.

Darcy was hoping to engage Miss Bennet in further conversation during dinner but was not seated near her. He looked down at the end of the table and saw her conversing quietly with Bingley. He also saw the look on Caroline's face as she witnessed the same thing.

Caroline tried to ignore the obviously smitten couple and turned to Darcy, placing her hand on his arm. "Tell me, Mr. Darcy, do you plan to stay on for a while in London?"

His first reaction to her hand was to flinch and quickly remove his arm from her reach, but he managed to count to three before he nonchalantly reached for his wine glass, thus allowing her hand to fall to the table.

"No, we leave the day after tomorrow. Anne and I are planning to visit Rosings upon our departure."

"Oh, Mrs. Darcy, surely you would like to spend some more time in London, would you not?" asked Caroline.

"As much as I would like to enjoy the many diversions of London, it has been some time since I have visited my mother. I believe she desires my company," said Anne.

"But certainly you could spare another day or two to visit with us," urged Caroline, hoping not to lose Mr. Darcy's company again so soon.

"As agreeable as that prospect may be, Miss Bingley, I believe we must leave for Rosings as originally planned," said Anne, starting to get somewhat flustered at Caroline's insistent manner.

"Oh, I do wish you would reconsider, Mrs. Darcy. I'm sure Mr. Darcy would like more time to visit with his good friends. It has been so long since he has been in our company."

Anne looked over to her husband. *Does he desire to stay in London with his friends? Am I preventing him from enjoying himself?* Anne started to speak again, but her agitated state once again provoked another bout of coughing. Darcy became alarmed as he watched her try to catch her breath.

After several minutes, she was finally able to bring her cough under control, and she started to breathe more easily. Darcy poured a glass of water and instructed her to take small sips as he placed a protective arm across her shoulders. Once he was assured that Anne was able to maintain a steady breathing pattern free from further hindrance, Darcy rose from his chair, and with a glare in Caroline's direction stated, "I believe we must leave immediately."

"Fitzwilliam, I'm sure that I shall be fine now," stated Anne, not wishing to be the cause of her husband's departure from his friends.

"Yes, Mr. Darcy," interjected Caroline. "She now seems quite recovered."

Darcy had endured all he could take of Caroline Bingley for one evening. With an iron cold look in his eyes, he turned and directly addressed her. "Miss Bingley, I do not believe you are qualified to make such a determination regarding my wife's health. We are leaving . . . *now*."

~*~

Thursday's Child

Colonel Fitzwilliam assured Darcy that he would see Georgiana safely back home. He also promised to meet him at Rosings in two days' time. On the carriage ride back to their townhouse, both Anne and Darcy were still in an agitated state—Darcy, because of Caroline's insensitive behaviour, and Anne because she was feeling responsible for having caused their early departure.

"I'm so sorry I ruined your evening, Fitzwilliam," said Anne, unable to look at her husband. He took her hand.

"Anne, please don't say that. You did not ruin my evening. If anyone ruined this evening, it was Caroline Bingley."

"But I'm the reason you had to leave your friends," she said, almost sobbing.

"Do you really think I care about that?" he asked astonished. "Anne, you must believe me; I care only for your wellbeing."

After they had ridden in silence for several minutes, Anne turned to look at her husband. "Fitzwilliam, I think we should leave for Rosings tomorrow."

"Of course, Anne, I quite agree," said Darcy. "I will make all the arrangements." He put his arm around her shoulders and pulled her close to him, resting his cheek on her forehead. They remained like that for the rest of the way home. He wanted to comfort her. He did not need to be told that her health was deteriorating. He would do whatever he had to do, to make her happy.

~*~

They arrived at Rosings the next evening. Anne was quite done in by the journey and went to refresh herself upstairs. Darcy headed immediately for the study to get a drink. He would need to speak to his aunt. Anne's doctor should be summoned as soon as possible.

As he sat down by the fire, Lady Catherine entered. "I see you have arrived safely. Where is Anne?" she asked.

"She's upstairs at the moment but will be down directly. She has been experiencing some alarming coughing bouts of late, and I think it would be best to have Dr. Adams come and examine her while we are here," stated Darcy.

"I'm sure it's just a trifling cold," his aunt concluded.

"Indeed not; I would not be so concerned had I suspected it were merely a cold."

"Very well, if you think the doctor is necessary, I will send for him tomorrow," said his aunt. "However, I'm sure that Anne is in good health and will be able to continue to fulfil her role as your wife."

"Of what do you speak?" asked Darcy, quite taken back by his aunt's statement.

"I speak of your heir, of course. An heir for Pemberley must be attained from your union with Anne. I am just assuring you that Anne will be able to fulfil her obligations in that regard. Anne will do what is required of her."

"I'm glad to hear you know more about your daughter's health than her own doctor," replied an agitated Darcy.

At that moment, Anne entered the study. "Hello, Mother," she said timidly as she walked to the matriarch's side and gave her a kiss on the cheek. "It's nice to be back at Rosings . . . and of course, to see you again."

It was amazing to Darcy how his wife's demeanour changed so completely when in her mother's company.

"What is this I hear about you're being unable to perform your wifely duties?" asked her mother. With a look of horror on her face, Anne looked over to Darcy. Her eyes filled with tears as she fled the room.

Darcy glared at his aunt. "I did not say any such thing!" he growled at her as he immediately left the room to find his wife.

Anne was upstairs in her old room, her frail body flung upon the bed. He was immediately beside her and pulled her into his embrace. "How could you have told my mother?" she said through her sobs.

Thursday's Child

"I assure you, Anne, I did not say a word to your mother about . . . about our situation. I only suggested that we might have Dr. Adams examine you to see about your cough while we are here. I promise you, Anne, I did not betray anything to your mother."

"Oh, Fitzwilliam, why does it have to be like this?" Her tears were falling freely down her cheeks as she told him what was in her heart. "I would risk everything to be the wife that you desire. I want so dearly to be healthy enough to bear your child."

"I know, dear Anne, I know. But think upon it no more. I would not be able to endure the guilt should something happen to you."

"But what of your heir, Fitzwilliam? Will there be no heir to Pemberley?" she asked.

He did not answer her. He held her tightly until her sobs subsided. He lay next to her until she was asleep.

~*~

Having received word at his London residence on the previous evening, Dr. Adams arrived at Rosings the next afternoon. After spending a good hour with Anne, he made his way to the study to speak to Mr. Darcy.

"Please come in," said Darcy, anxious to hear the results of the doctor's examination.

Dr. Adams entered and gestured toward the side board, indicating his desire for a drink. Darcy nodded his head, and the doctor proceeded to pour himself a brandy.

"I'm afraid my examination is not too encouraging, Mr. Darcy. There has been a great deal of damage to Anne's lungs. I would like to make further tests, but it is my belief that she is in the early stages of consumption."

Darcy startled at the word. "Are you sure?" he asked. "I know she has been coughing a great deal of late, but consumption!"

"Of course, I would understand if you would like to have Dr. Chisholm examine her to get a second opinion," said Dr. Adams.

Darcy did not reply. He could hardly comprehend the words he was hearing. Realizing the doctor was waiting for him to respond, he said, "Yes, I will send for him once we return to Pemberley." He then hesitantly asked, "If it is confirmed to be consumption, Dr. Adams, how long . . . what kind of prognosis can we expect?"

"That's hard to say, Mr. Darcy. As I said, I believe Mrs. Darcy is still in the very early stages. Should she develop a fever, or should her cough produce blood, that would indicate a worsening of the disease. Anne has assured me that neither has occurred.

Darcy was almost in shock. He sat down and tried to think calmly.

"I know this is a difficult situation to face, Mr. Darcy. I also know that you have done everything you could to ensure Mrs. Darcy's continued health."

The two men eyed each other at the doctor's last words. Dr. Adams was well aware that Darcy had relinquished his marital rights for the sake of Anne's wellbeing.

"The only advice I can offer is to try to make her life as pleasant as possible. That is the only thing anyone can do. You are a good man, Mr. Darcy. You should have no guilt or regrets. I believe Mrs. Darcy's fate was sealed long before your marriage took place."

"Does Anne know of her condition?" asked Darcy.

"Well, I haven't told her in so many words, but I would venture to guess that she is aware of the seriousness of her illness. I will leave that up to you, Mr. Darcy. It would be very hard for her to go on without hope."

Darcy nodded absentmindedly at the doctor's words. "I should advise you that you may be susceptible to catching the disease yourself, Mr. Darcy, as it can be contagious. Even when Mrs. Darcy shows no symptoms of the disease, she can still be infectious. But since we have already established that you and Mrs. Darcy do not share . . . are not . . .

"Yes, Dr. Adams, I understand perfectly," interrupted Darcy.

Darcy thanked Dr. Adams for everything. He promised he would keep him informed of Anne's condition. As the doctor's carriage pulled away, Darcy was already on his second brandy.

He recalled Lizzy that morning of their walk on the beach asking the question, "Do you believe yourself to be a good man?" The doctor had just declared him so. But then again, the doctor did not know the entire story.

~*~

He had yet to tell his aunt of the doctor's prognosis. As she called for tea, he entered the parlour and greeted her. Anne had not yet come down from her room, and Darcy decided to take the opportunity to speak with his aunt.

"I have had a long discussion with Dr. Adams regarding Anne's health."

"And what has the doctor to say? I'm sure he agrees with me that she is in excellent health, except for perhaps a cold."

Darcy eyed her curiously. "I'm afraid that is not the doctor's opinion, Aunt. He believes that she is in the early stages of consumption."

"Don't be ridiculous, Darcy! The doctor is mistaken. Anne is in perfect health," she insisted.

"I know this is a most difficult fact that we must face, but I believe the doctor is correct in his opinion. Anne's condition has been deteriorating for the last few months."

He could not imagine having to learn that your only child might have a very short time to live. In that respect, he could understand his aunt's reluctance to accept what she was hearing as the truth. However, he could not understand her lack of concern. Did she really believe that if she disagreed with the doctor's prognosis, she could somehow change it? Could she really just ignore Anne's failing health?

"I, of course, will have Anne examined by my personal physician for a second opinion," said Darcy, desiring to show his aunt that he had not given up all hope.

"If it pleases you to do so, then do as you must, Darcy." She signalled with a wave of her hand that this topic of conversation was ended. Darcy shook his head but remained silent.

Anne joined them in the parlour a short time later. She looked pale. Darcy immediately rose and helped her to the seat next to his. He poured her a cup of tea.

"Has the doctor left?" she inquired.

"Yes," said Darcy. "He left some time ago. You must have fallen asleep."

"Did he speak with you before he left?" she further inquired.

"Yes, Anne," said Darcy, not knowing how much he wished to reveal.

"And?" She widened her eyes as she looked into his in question.

Lady Catherine opened her mouth to speak, but Darcy cut her off immediately. "He believes that you are in much need of rest and some time to regain your strength," Darcy prevaricated. Dr. Adams was right. It would be most difficult for Anne to live without hope. "After our visit here, we shall return to Pemberley where I will see that you get all the rest you require."

"Darcy is right, my dear. All you need is a little rest, and you will be fine. All this fuss over a trifling cold," said her mother.

Anne looked into her husband's eyes. She knew he was not telling her the truth. She knew he was lying because he truly cared for her. And that fact was enough to sustain her.

"Thank you, Fitzwilliam."

"Thank you for what, Anne?" he asked as he took her hand.

"Just . . . thank you," she said as she leaned over and kissed his cheek.

~*~

After dinner, Darcy escorted Anne to her room. He made sure she was comfortably situated and then returned downstairs. After an hour had passed, he heard his cousin announced. Richard entered the study where Darcy was seated, alone by the fire. He immediately observed his dejected state.

"I take it things have not gone too well here at Rosings," ventured Richard as he made his way towards the bottle of brandy.

Darcy looked up at Richard and nodded his agreement. "I'm afraid I have some rather alarming news regarding Anne's health."

Darcy proceeded to tell Richard of his conversation with Dr. Adams and also his conversation with their Aunt Catherine. As unpleasant as the news was, Richard was hardly shocked. They had known for years that Anne's health was frail, at best. Of course, that did not make the prognosis any easier to bear.

"What will you do?" asked Richard.

"I plan to take Anne back to Pemberley and make her as comfortable as I can. We will stay here for a short time, but I want Anne to see how beautiful Pemberley is at Christmas."

When Richard looked over at his cousin, he saw the sadness reflected in his eyes.

There was a long silence between the cousins. Neither felt the need to talk, for they were both lost in their own thoughts. Darcy was having a hard time reconciling himself to all that had happened. If what the doctor had suggested was true, then Anne's health already had been in jeopardy when they married. He needed to believe that their marriage had not caused her any harm.

He would devote himself to her for as long as she had left. That was the least he could do. As soon as Anne felt strong enough, he would retrieve Georgiana from London, and the three of them would go back to Pemberley. He rose from his seat and looked over to Richard.

"Care for another?" he asked as he raised his glass in the air. Richard nodded. Darcy poured each of them another drink and sat back down. There seemed to be nothing left to say.

He unconsciously touched his waistcoat pocket and felt Mrs. Reynolds's letter.

CHAPTER FOURTEEN

Despite the way the evening had started out, it was ending on a much brighter note. After the departure of Mr. and Mrs. Darcy, Bingley privately expressed his anger to Caroline and told her they would speak about her behaviour at greater length on the morrow.

When it was time for Jane to leave, Bingley offered to accompany her home. He handed her into the carriage and took the seat next to her. Jane was a bit nervous. Despite the fact that she was four and twenty, she had never been completely alone with a gentleman before.

Well, there had been *one* gentleman when she was but fifteen who had written her love poems that would have made the angels sing. However, his affections for her had never progressed beyond the occasional sonnet. He also had made it quite clear that his devotion to his dear widowed mother would always be his first priority.

As the carriage began its short journey, Bingley moved closer to Jane and took her hand. She smiled at him. He smiled back.

His voice was tentative as he addressed her. "Miss Bennet, I know we have not known each other very long, but I was hoping you might consider entering into a courtship."

A slight blush coloured her lovely face as she shyly looked up into his eyes. "I would be honoured to have you court me, Mr. Bingley."

She looked down at his lips, hoping he would take the hint. Even though she knew it would be most improper, at four and twenty she believed she had waited long enough to experience the thrill of a first kiss. Love poems might feed the soul, but Jane was anxious to feed her imagination.

Bingley lifted her hand to his lips and kissed it. It stirred the butterflies in her stomach as he did, but still she wanted more. *Please do not recite a poem*, she thought.

As the carriage stopped before the Morgans' townhouse, Bingley opened the door and stepped down. He took Jane's hand and guided her steps to the ground. "If it is agreeable to you, I would like to call on you tomorrow evening, shall we say about seven?"

"Yes," said Jane, "I would like that very much, Mr. Bingley."

He was again about to bring her hand to his lips. Jane, now realizing she was to be denied once more even the smallest of kisses, withdrew her hand and reached her arms around his neck, planting a kiss most decidedly, and quite accurately, upon his lips. His first reaction was one of surprise, but he very quickly recovered and kissed her back most ardently.

~*~

"Caroline, I wish to speak with you about your behaviour last night," said Bingley. "I cannot believe you were so rude to our guests. I wouldn't blame Darcy if he never wished to be in company with us again. And your treatment of Miss Bennet was unforgivable."

"Charles, really, you're overreacting," countered Caroline. "Mr. Darcy knows of my affection for him. And for Mrs. Darcy, too," she added as an afterthought. "I was only trying to be a good hostess. I was expressing my desire to have their company for a few days more. That is all. And as far as Miss Bennet is concerned, I still cannot believe you invited her without telling me. I think, under the circumstances, I was quite justified in my behaviour."

"Caroline, I'm warning you. You will desist with this fantasy you have of you and Darcy, and you will behave in a civil manner towards Miss Bennet."

"Or what?" she asked.

"Or you will find out what it's like to live within the confines of your stipend," he replied.

"You know I cannot do that," she said, a horrified look transforming her face.

"Well, the choice is yours, Caroline. And I should tell you that you will have ample opportunities to make it up to Miss Bennet, as I expect to be seeing a great deal of her from now on."

"I thought you were in a hurry to return to Netherfield?"

"Well, Caroline, you should be happy. You're getting your wish to stay in London a little longer." With that he turned and left his sister's company.

Louisa Hurst entered the breakfast room and sat down next to her sister. "Well, our brother seems to be in a most horrible mood this morning. Is he still upset with you about last night?"

"Oh, I'm sure he'll get over it soon enough. I'm just trying to stop him from making a fool of himself over that *servant*. We'll all be the laughing stock of London if he continues to see her.

"And I'm sure Mr. Darcy would quite agree with me. After all, the only reason he married Anne was because of her wealth and social status. Mr. Darcy is a man who understands the importance of such things. I'm sure I'll have an ally in him. I will make sure to discuss this with him when he returns to London."

"How do you know he will return to London?"

"Well, Georgiana is to accompany them, so he must come to London for her before they proceed to Pemberley. Maybe we should call on her in the meantime. This way it will not look suspicious when we visit her when he returns. We will be good friends by then."

"Caroline, you really are so devious!" said Louisa.

~*~

Elizabeth took the letter from Mrs. Worthington's hand and eyed the handwriting. Noting it was not from Jane, her hand immediately began to tremble. She excused herself from Mrs. Worthington's company and went out to the gardens. The letter, as she suspected, was Mr. Gallagher's reply. He instructed her as to when and where a carriage was to meet her.

Elizabeth knew she would now have to speak with Mrs. Worthington. She needed to inform her of her imminent departure, and she also needed to ask a favour of her. She waited until it was time for their afternoon tea. As she poured out a cup for each of them, Elizabeth took a deep breath. Mrs. Worthington noticed her unease.

"I hope your letter did not bring you bad news, Elizabeth."

"Not exactly," she replied. "However, the news it bears will have an immediate effect on my circumstances."

"How so?"

"I'm afraid that I must leave here, Mrs. Worthington. A personal matter has arisen that I must attend to." Mrs. Worthington eyed her curiously but said nothing. "I do not wish to appear mysterious, but I cannot disclose any of the details," continued Elizabeth.

"Elizabeth, if you are in any trouble, please tell me. I may be able to be of some assistance."

"I assure you, I shall be fine. It is something that I must face alone," said Elizabeth. "I do, however, need to ask a rather large favour of you."

"What is it Elizabeth? You know I will try to help you if I can."

"Since this matter is highly personal, I'm afraid I cannot even divulge the details to Jane. She cannot know that I have left your employ. Therefore, I would ask that you forward Jane's letters to me. I shall give you the address where I will be residing for the next several months. Would you be willing to do such a thing for me?" asked Elizabeth.

"If that is what you wish. When must you leave?" asked Mrs. Worthington.

"In four days' time."

"Elizabeth, I know I am just an old woman. I'm sure you think me very thick and naïve. But, I was once a young woman such as yourself. I am not unacquainted with the fancies of young men and women. And, I am not completely unaware of the changes in you since your return from holiday. I do not wish to interfere in your life, but I want you to know that if you ever need me for anything, I would be most willing and happy to assist you in any way I can."

They looked into each other's eyes; Elizabeth's already brimming with tears. "I thank you" was all she could manage to say.

~*~

Despite the vastness of Rosings, Darcy was beginning to feel claustrophobic. It seemed he could find no refuge from the company of his aunt. His only escape, a temporary one, came in the mornings when he would choose a mare from the stables and ride.

It was almost December, and the mornings were getting colder. He wanted to be heading back to Pemberley soon. The last thing he wanted was for the weather to prohibit their departure. Anne was not getting any better. She had refused to see any more doctors or to have any further tests. He could have insisted, but he did not. He could not blame her. What was the point? Why did he need to have further confirmation of her fate? Whether Dr. Adams was right or wrong in his diagnosis, they would know soon enough.

Even with all that had been happening with Anne, Darcy still could not stop thinking about *her*. Ever since he had read Mrs. Reynolds's letter, she had been in his thoughts constantly. She was with child, *his* child. Despite the fact that they were never to meet again, they would always have this bond. Nothing could ever break it.

He wondered where she was. He wished he could see her again. Just once more. The last few months had taken their toll. He longed for the sanctuary of her embrace. He wanted to feel that closeness again. He both blessed and cursed her.

Before her, he had felt nothing. He was a man driven solely by his sense of duty and responsibility. But now, now that he had experienced what it was to feel such a connection to someone, to have his passions awakened, how could he go back to the nothingness he had before? Yet, he knew he must. Would it not have been better never to have known such feelings?

He had tried not to think of all the coincidences that had been surfacing lately; the entailment of Longbourn, for one. Mr. Collins had inherited Longbourn due to an entailment. Lizzy had lost her estate to a distant male cousin, due to an entailment. Was this just a coincidence?

And what of Wickham and the ten thousand pounds? Lizzy had said that her predicament was of a personal family matter that had to be acted upon quickly. Could that have been Wickham? Was the money she needed to pay him? If that were the case, then Richard had been in her company. It also meant that she was Miss Bennet's sister, which meant that Bingley had been in her company also.

Darcy shook his head, thinking he must be suffering from paranoia. He was convinced his mind was playing tricks on him. Not *everything* is connected to *her*, he thought. Still he could not help but be curious.

They would be leaving for London next week. He would spend only a few days there; just enough time to see Bingley again and to give Anne sufficient rest before they departed for Pemberley with Georgiana. He told himself once safely back home, he would rid Lizzy from his mind once and for all.

CHAPTER FIFTEEN

Darcy and Anne arrived at his townhouse much later than he had planned. He had wanted to get an earlier start, but his aunt had delayed their departure. She had insisted that they stay the evening in order to share the company of Mr. and Mrs. Collins, who had been invited to dine. Even though Darcy had no desire to be in the obsequious clergyman's company, he thought it might be a good opportunity to learn more about the clergyman's recent inheritance.

As they entered the parlour, Mr. Collins bowed so low before Lady Catherine that his wife had to help him back to an upright position. His added delight at seeing Mr. Darcy was apparent. He was somewhat stunned by the appearance of Mrs. Darcy as she was pale and much thinner than the last time he had seen her. He, however, did not let that deter him from finding some compliment to offer.

"How delightful to see you again, Mrs. Darcy. And may I say the colour of your gown is most complimentary to your slippers."

Anne tried to join in pleasant conversation, but her fatigue grew with each passing moment. She begged to be excused, and Darcy escorted her to her room and made sure she was comfortable.

"I shall have some supper sent up. I promise not to be too long, Anne. As soon as dinner is over, we will depart for London. Get some rest if you can."

As they sat at the dinner table, Darcy was anxious to ask the clergyman some questions regarding the entailment. "Tell me, Mr. Collins, how do you like living at Longbourn?"

So enthralled was he at the fact that Mr. Darcy had actually taken an interest in him, he was only too happy to proceed to tell Mr. Darcy anything he would like to know on the topic.

"Well, Mr. Darcy, I can honestly say that I am quite enjoying being the master of my own estate. Oh my dear sir, not to compare my position with yours, of course, but I must admit living the life of a country gentleman is quite appealing."

"It must have been very hard on the Bennet family to lose their home to an entailment," offered Darcy.

"Oh, are you acquainted with the family, sir?"

"I have only recently met Miss Jane Bennet. I have not had the pleasure of meeting her mother or any of her sisters." *At least to my knowledge,* thought Darcy. "Are you acquainted with the rest of the family?"

"As it happens, Mr. Darcy, Miss Jane Bennet is the only sister I have *not* met. She had already departed for London by the time I reached Longbourn. But I am acquainted with Mrs. Bennet and her other four daughters."

"I see," said Darcy, not wishing to appear too interested. However, he could not help himself as he asked, "Are you *much* acquainted with the other four daughters?"

Mr. Collins looked down to the end of the table and saw that his wife was deep in conversation with Lady Catherine. He turned his body slightly in Darcy's direction, as if to avoid his wife's notice and spoke in a low voice.

"Well, to be honest, Mr. Darcy, when I arrived at Longbourn to claim my inheritance, it was my intention to choose a wife from one of Mrs. Bennet's daughters. I thought it only my duty to try to make things right. As I mentioned, Miss Jane Bennet had already departed for London, but, when I saw Miss Elizabeth, I thought I had found my future wife. Indeed her wit and her vivacity were qualities to highly recommend her as my life's companion."

Darcy sat in complete silence, listening to every word he had to say. He dared not ask any more questions for fear of arousing the clergyman's curiosity. But, then again, there was no need to ask any further questions, as Mr. Collins was only too delighted to continue. Noticing how absorbed Mr. Darcy was in his story, he threw caution to the wind and revealed every detail.

"I had decided to ask for her hand the very afternoon of my arrival. I am not a man who is swayed by appearances, Mr. Darcy, but upon seeing Miss Elizabeth, I will admit I was enthralled by her dark eyes, her beautiful chestnut hair and," again looking down at the end of the table to make sure his wife was not listening to their conversation, "her most pleasing figure."

Darcy tried not to react to his description of Miss Elizabeth. He merely nodded for him to continue.

"I know it is very hard to believe, considering my position, but she refused me! I explained to her I was offering to save her family, but to no avail. I pointed out the unlikelihood of her ever being offered another proposal of marriage, and still she refused! Can you imagine such an imprudent young woman? Upon witnessing such reckless behaviour, I was somewhat relieved; for I'm sure we would not have been of the same mind."

Darcy could not help but ask his next question. " Did she give you a reason for her refusal?"

"Such foolishness to be sure," replied the clergyman. "She vowed never to marry if she could not do so for love. Can you imagine such folly?"

Darcy sat there stunned for a moment. Was that not the same response Lizzy had given during their interview?

His aunt's voice brought him back to his surroundings. "Of what are you speaking, Darcy? I must have my share in the conversation!"

The two gentlemen proceeded to join the ladies' conversation, and the rest of the evening passed unremarkably.

~*~

Georgiana was delighted to see her brother and Anne seated at the breakfast table the next morning. Her delight was somewhat diminished upon noting the pallor of Anne's skin. She tried not to look alarmed as she greeted them both.

"I am so glad you have returned from Rosings. I have missed you both so much," she said.

"Have you had nothing to pleasantly divert you since our departure?" asked Anne.

"Well, I have been visited on several occasions by Miss Bingley," said Georgiana. "However, the diversion was not necessarily a pleasant one."

Feeling embarrassed by her uncharitable admission, she added, "I do not mean to sound ungrateful for her companionship, but sometimes I feel I am just a poor substitute for you and my brother, that it is not me that she truly wishes to visit."

"I'm sure that is not the case," said Anne. "Why would she have visited then, knowing we were away?"

"I guess that's true," said Georgiana, still not completely convinced.

"I promised Miss Bingley we would all call on her and Mr. Bingley as soon as you returned."

Darcy looked over at Anne. He could tell she was not fully recuperated from their journey from Rosings. "Perhaps Georgiana and I should go alone," suggested Darcy. "That will give you another full day to rest, Anne. I do not want to exhaust your strength. We still have a long journey ahead of us to Pemberley."

"Perhaps you are right, Fitzwilliam," said Anne. "Please make my apologies to Mr. Bingley and Miss Bingley. I am sure I shall see them again soon."

After breakfast, Darcy and Georgiana headed out towards Bingley's townhouse. Darcy was anxious to speak to Bingley on a private matter. He would only have a few days in London, and he had much to accomplish.

Caroline and Mrs. Hurst greeted Georgiana and Darcy most graciously. Upon noting that Anne had not accompanied them, Caroline was immediately at Darcy's side and escorted him personally into the parlour. "How good of you to call so soon upon your arrival in London," she said. "I'm sure Georgiana has told you how close we've become during your absence."

Darcy looked over to Georgiana who smiled at Caroline as she spoke. Despite his best efforts, he could not help but roll his eyes, causing Georgiana to stifle a giggle. "Yes, I just mentioned that very fact this morning," said Georgiana with a grin.

Bingley made his way towards the parlour and greeted his guests. Darcy straightaway suggested they leave the ladies for a short while. "I have some business I need to discuss with you," said Darcy.

"But, of course, Darcy. I would be most happy to be of any help I can."

They entered Bingley's study where they made themselves comfortable before the fireplace. "What is it you wish to discuss with me?" asked Bingley.

Darcy hesitated. He didn't really know how to broach the subject, so he just blurted out "Have you been seeing much of Miss Bennet?"

Bingley, somewhat surprised by this question answered defensively, "Don't tell me you, too, are going to start in on me!"

"Whatever do you mean?" replied Darcy.

"Well, it's just that since I started courting Miss Bennet, Caroline won't give me a moment's peace. She insists that I stop seeing her. And she has assured me that you would wholeheartedly agree with her."

"I have never even discussed Miss Bennet with her, so I don't see how she could know my feelings on the matter," said Darcy.

"So, you are not here to try and talk me out of seeing Miss Bennet?"

"I assure you, I am not."

"Well, that's a relief." Bingley smiled at his friend. "I cannot tell you how happy I am to hear you say it. Well, what did you wish to discuss then?"

"Actually, the matter I wish to discuss is not wholly unconnected to Miss Bennet. I know this will sound like a strange request, and I must insist that you not ask me the reasons why I seek this information."

Bingley's face was one big question mark. "Whatever are you talking about?"

"I need you to find out if Miss Elizabeth Bennet is still employed as a lady's companion," said Darcy.

"Whatever for?" exclaimed Bingley.

Darcy let out an exasperated sigh. "I just explained that I cannot give you the reasons why, Bingley. I just need to know if she is still living with her employer as a lady's companion."

"However am I to find that out without raising suspicions?" asked a very confused Bingley.

"Can you not work it into a conversation with Miss Bennet?"

"I suppose I can," admitted Bingley. "As a matter of fact, Miss Bennet is dining here tonight. Perhaps you and Georgiana would care to stay? I'm sure Caroline would be more than happy to accommodate you both."

"I think I can manage that. I would like to send word to Anne to let her know that we will not be home until later this evening."

~*~

It was unusually warm for a December day. Anne was not in the least disappointed that she had not accompanied Fitzwilliam to Mr. Bingley's. As much as she liked Mr. Bingley, she could not tolerate an entire afternoon watching Miss Bingley fawn over her husband and listening to her make unkind remarks at her own expense. She decided to spend the afternoon in the small parlour off the breakfast room. The room was completely infused with light, and Mrs. Evanston had placed several floral arrangements throughout the room, giving it a most wonderful outdoorsy effect.

Anne had slept but little the previous night due to her cough. The nights seemed worse than the days. She knew that as Fitzwilliam never brought up the subject of her health, the situation must be grave. He avoided the subject entirely, and she was grateful that he did. She did not want to deceive Fitzwilliam, but in her own mind she had good reason not to mention any other symptoms to him or Dr. Adams. There was no point in making her husband worry more than he already was. There was certainly nothing that he could do to relieve her distress. She knew her fate was in the hands of God.

~*~

Jane Bennet arrived at seven o'clock. She was greeted by an anxious Mr. Bingley and an even more anxious Mr. Darcy. After greetings were exchanged, they all sat down in the parlour before dinner was called.

Darcy tried to situate himself as near to Bingley and Miss Bennet as he could without raising curiosity. After some conversation had passed between the two, he saw that Bingley still had not approached the subject he wished to discuss. He finally decided to take matters into his own hands.

"Miss Bennet, I recently had the opportunity to dine with your cousin, Mr. Collins. During our discourse he happened upon the subject of your family. He informed me that you were the only family member he has not met."

"That is true, Mr. Darcy. I had already left for London with my Aunt and Uncle Gardiner when Mr. Collins arrived at Longbourn."

"He mentioned that your mother and younger sisters were situated on the outskirts of Meryton."

"Yes. As you know my youngest sister, Lydia, is now married and living in New Castle, but my mother and two younger sisters live in a cottage just outside of Meryton."

"He did not know where your sister Miss Elizabeth was now residing," Darcy said rather cautiously. "I heard you mention at the dinner party that she is employed by a Mrs. Worthington. Is she still in that lady's employ?"

He steeled himself for her answer. He knew from Mrs. Reynolds's latest letter that Lizzy was now living in the accommodations arranged by his attorney. She would stay there until the end of her confinement. He held his breath as he waited for Miss Bennet's reply.

"Well, yes, Mr. Darcy," Jane replied, somewhat surprised by his interest in her family. "As a matter of fact, I just received a reply to my last letter this morning, and Elizabeth said that she and Mrs. Worthington would not be travelling much in the near future. She said she was most happy to be staying in one place for a while and that I should continue to write her at Mrs. Worthington's home."

Darcy thought the look of relief on his face must have been quite apparent to everyone in the room. "I am glad to hear it. I trust she is well?"

"Yes. She sounded quite well. I thank you for your interest, sir."

Bingley had sat and listened to this entire exchange in complete bewilderment. In all the years that he had known his friend, this was indeed the most loquacious Darcy he had ever witnessed.

What in the world was he about? Why was he so interested in Miss Elizabeth's whereabouts? He knew it would be futile to ask.

As dinner was announced, Caroline immediately went to Darcy's side and, with her arm entwined around his, led him towards the dining room. Darcy was so relieved that Miss Elizabeth Bennet was not the "Lizzy" of his acquaintance that he actually indulged Caroline with conversation throughout the entire dinner.

It was quite late by the time they departed Bingley's. During the carriage ride home, Georgiana soon fell asleep, leaving Darcy alone with his thoughts. He concluded that if Jane Bennet was writing to her sister at Mrs. Worthington's and she had received a reply to her last letter just this morning, then it must follow that Elizabeth Bennet was still a lady's companion where she had been employed for the last year and a half. She was not the Lizzy he had met in St. Andrews.

Now that this was no longer plaguing his mind, he began to relax. He couldn't even imagine the awkwardness such a situation could have presented. Imagine, Bingley courting the sister of . . . of . . . *can I even think the thought?* . . . the mother of my bastard child! No. That is not how it shall be. I will find a way to bring this child into my home and raise it as my own. I must find a way to conquer this.

With thoughts of his child running through his mind, he immediately thought of what his child might look like. With Lizzy's dark eyes and hair, he knew the child would be beautiful. How could it not be? He thought of *her*; about seeing her again. Would it really be so imprudent to see her once more? Just to be in her company one more time before she was lost to him forever. Would she be willing to see him again? Did she miss him at all?

CHAPTER SIXTEEN

The sun shone brightly down on Grosvenor Square as Darcy assisted Anne and Georgiana into the carriage. It was Georgie's plan for her and Anne to get some Christmas shopping accomplished before their return to Pemberley. Darcy had offered to accompany them stating that he had business in town which needed his attention. As he dropped them off at the prominent shops along the main thoroughfare, he arranged to meet them at the book sellers across the street in two hours. Once he left their company, he headed north three blocks to the office of Mr. Gallagher.

Two hours later, as planned, Darcy walked into the book sellers. Noting his wife and sister had not yet arrived, he started perusing the shelves. Perhaps he would purchase some books for Georgie for Christmas. He approached the clerk and, after asking for the latest novels and biographies suitable for a seventeen year old girl, made several selections. He asked the clerk to wrap them quickly in case his sister should arrive in the meantime.

He again wandered the rows of books, sighting many of his beloved possessions. He then came upon *Paradise Lost*, and his heart sank in his chest. He pulled the book from the shelf and leafed through several pages, reacquainting himself with the verses. The eternal fight of good and evil, he thought. A fight he knew he was losing, just as surely as Adam and Eve had lost their paradise. Impulsively he pulled several volumes of poetry from the shelves and quickly brought them to the clerk, once again requesting that they be immediately wrapped.

The bell above the door tinkled, announcing that Anne and Georgiana had entered the shop. They both carried several packages, and Darcy rushed directly to help them. "Anne, whatever possessed you to carry such a heavy load?" She was unable to answer. He could see she was winded and was having trouble breathing. She began to cough and gasped for air. He immediately picked her up and carried her to their carriage. The clerk helped Georgiana gather the rest of their packages and packed them into the boot of the carriage.

With a distressed look upon her face, Georgiana asked, "What is the matter with her, Fitzwilliam?"

"She is just out of breath," he replied, not wishing to alarm his sister.

He knew he would have to reveal the truth to Georgie soon, but for now he preferred to preserve the possibility that Anne's health could still improve with time. If Georgiana knew the truth of Anne's condition, he was sure she would not be able to conceal her grief in Anne's presence.

Anne's coughing subsided after several minutes. Darcy pulled her close, and she rested her head on his chest, her breathing still laboured.

Once back at their townhouse, Darcy saw to Anne's comfort and care. His heart was heavy with concern. Each episode seemed to come more quickly and last longer than the previous one. He would give her at least a day or two of complete rest before they journeyed home. He was convinced that the healing effects of his beloved Pemberley would help restore her health. He would see that she received the best of care.

~*~

Caroline Bingley entered the foyer of the Darcy townhouse. Even though Mrs. Evanston had informed her that, unfortunately, the family was not receiving visitors today, she had insisted on being announced.

"I'm sure they will make an exception in my case," she stated with conviction. "I'll wait in the music room," she said as she brushed her way past the housekeeper. Several minutes later a very agitated Darcy entered the music room and approached his unwelcomed guest.

"Thank you so much for seeing me, Mr. Darcy," said Caroline as she rose to greet him. "I told your housekeeper that there must be some mistake. I knew you would not refuse to see *me.*" Caroline sat back down upon the divan, waiting for Darcy to sit next to her. He remained standing.

"I'm afraid both Georgiana and Anne are indisposed this morning," said Darcy barely able to contain his annoyance.

"Oh, I *am* sorry to hear that. Nothing serious I hope?" she asked trying to sound sincere.

"No, just tired after a long day of shopping yesterday," he said. "I'm sure they will both be well recovered and ready to travel to Pemberley by tomorrow."

"So soon? I thought after our pleasant evening together you might delay your departure a little longer," she said as she again stood and placed her hand on his arm.

"Our 'pleasant' evening together?" asked Darcy with a genuine look of confusion on his face.

"Why, yes," she said, "the other night at dinner?"

Darcy removed her hand from his arm and stepped back. As he was about to speak, she continued, "Oh, I know we must be discreet, Mr. Darcy. It must be very difficult for you, with Anne being so often indisposed. I'm sure you frequently find yourself in need of companionship. That you've turned to me is indeed most flattering, but I must advise you, sir, I will not be involved in a scandal." As she said this, she moved her hand along the lapel of

Darcy's tailcoat somewhat diminishing the sincerity of her declaration.

As he again removed her hand from his person, Darcy was confident his look of abhorrence conveyed his feelings. *Surely she must be delusional.* "Miss Bingley, I assure you that I have no intentions of involving you in a scandal. I have no intentions towards you whatsoever. I'm sorry if anything I've said or done has led you to believe otherwise."

"I understand, Mr. Darcy," Caroline whispered as her eyes darted about the room. "We must be very careful not to raise any suspicions. How fortunate that Georgiana and I have become such good friends. I can always use visiting her as an excuse for us to be together."

With an exasperated look on his face Darcy asked, "Why are you here, Miss Bingley?"

"I have come to talk to you about my brother and Miss Bennet. I am counting on you to talk some sense into him. Certainly you must agree that it is imperative that he stop seeing that . . . that *servant!*"

"Your brother is a grown man. I'm sure he is capable of making such decisions on his own."

"But certainly you would never think of courting a woman in domestic service yourself, Mr. Darcy. I know you far too well to believe that you would."

Most undoubtedly he agreed with Caroline's assertions; however, the hesitation that preceded his response caused both of their brows to crease slightly. "I . . . I believe that my circumstances greatly differ from those of your brother. My family has always instilled certain expectations in me, and there are certain rules of propriety that must be followed," said Darcy. "You cannot compare my place in society with that of your brother."

"Well, Mr. Darcy, I see you feel yourself quite above the rest of us. Would you not wish to counsel Charles with the same good sense and respect for propriety that you yourself received?"

Darcy pondered this for a long moment. What was the world coming to when the likes of Caroline Bingley actually made sense? Bingley forming an alliance with Miss Bennet would not advance his position in society. Granting that perhaps Caroline had made a valid point he stated, "I promise to do no more than point out the disadvantages of such a match. He must make up his own mind on the subject."

"That is all I ask of you, sir. You know how much Charles values your advice.

"I will leave you now, Mr. Darcy. I will look forward to our next meeting. I am sure you will find some reason to visit us in London again very soon." Looking around the room, she whispered, "You can count on my discretion in all matters, sir."

~*~

Darcy, knowing he hadn't much time to speak with Bingley regarding Miss Bennet before departing for Pemberley, decided the best course would be to send a note requesting his company for lunch at his club. He did not want to be in Miss Bingley's company again and resolved to avoid Bingley's townhouse at all cost.

Darcy was already seated at his usual table when Bingley arrived. Bingley greeted his friend warmly, happy as always to be in his company. "I can understand why you wished to meet me here," said Bingley. "Caroline has been out of control lately. I never know what she will say or do next to embarrass me. I truly apologize for her behaviour."

"There is no need for you to apologize. I admit she can try one's patience at times, but that certainly is no reflection on you, Bingley."

"So, tomorrow you leave for Pemberley?"

"Yes, but there was one thing I would like to further discuss with you before I leave," said Darcy.

"Oh? What might that be?"

"I was wondering how things are going with Miss Bennet?" inquired Darcy.

"Why, very well, Darcy. I don't see her as often as I would wish, due to her duties as governess, but we have had several pleasant evenings together. Is she not a perfect angel?" replied Bingley grinning quite openly.

"I believe those were the very words you used to describe that young lady you met last year at the Banister's party, was it not? You know the one you courted for several weeks before she mentioned that her betrothed was away on business?"

"No, it was not!" insisted Bingley. "I believe I said that *she* was a heavenly creature."

"Oh, I hadn't realized the distinction."

"What are you getting at, Darcy?" demanded Bingley.

"I'm merely trying to point out that you have a tendency to fall for every beautiful girl you meet, regardless of their feelings for you or their situation," explained Darcy.

"I thought you said you had no intention of talking me out of seeing Miss Bennet?"

"And I meant it. If you are sure of Miss Bennet's feelings for you and if you have no problem with the fact that she is employed as a governess, then I would not try to talk you out of it. I'm sure her family will be quite pleased with the prospect of you for a son-in-law. That would help their situation most decidedly.

"I'm only suggesting that you take a step back and look at the situation from every aspect before you make any decisions about your future. As your good friend, I only want what's best for you, Bingley."

Bingley found he could not respond unkindly to Darcy's sincere request. "Well, I only promise to give your words some thought. After all, I know you would not advise me unwisely."

Now that Darcy was convinced that "Lizzy" was not Miss Bennet's sister, he held no real objection to Bingley courting her, aside from her lack of fortune and connections. However, considering Bingley's history with women, he felt some justification in his words of caution, and he had kept his word to Caroline in expressing his concern. He could now return to Pemberley with a clear conscience.

"That is all I ask, Bingley. Shall we order lunch then?" asked Darcy, glad to have that topic of conversation behind them.

CHAPTER SEVENTEEN

Darcy eyed the secluded cottage with trepidation. He allowed his horse, Marengo, to slowly amble upon a large ridge which afforded a perfect view of the grounds. As he sat there gazing down on the small but pretty cottage, his heart beat loudly in his chest, just knowing she was there causing both panic and longing. He was not totally convinced that this was a good idea. He had changed his mind several times along the way.

Even now, he still was undecided as to his next course of action. Would he travel down the path that led to the gate, or was just knowing where she was the reassurance he needed?

He could make up some excuse as to why he had come. Did he need an excuse? Was it not enough just to be concerned for her wellbeing and that of his unborn child? Certainly he had that right.

With much hesitation, he dismounted and led Marengo down the path to the gate and tied his reins to a nearby tree branch. As he made his way towards the door, he tried to think what to say to her.

He would be polite, of course. He would inquire as to health. He would make sure she had everything she needed. And above all, he would conduct himself as a gentleman.

He adjusted the lapels of his greatcoat and knocked on the door. A plump young woman with a pleasant smile answered his knock and asked him his business. He remembered now that Mr. Gallagher had mentioned that a local girl had been retained to help out. She stared at him in wait for his reply. "I have business with the mistress of the house," he informed her.

She curtsied and told him to wait in the small sitting room. Darcy entered the cottage and looked around him. It was indeed tiny, but he felt it somehow fit its mistress perfectly.

As soon as she entered the room, he could feel her presence. He turned to look at her; as he did, a look of surprise shown upon her face. She was more beautiful than he had remembered. His first impulse was to rush to her and take her in his arms.

Elizabeth was at first stunned into silence. Her second reaction was one of embarrassment as her mind immediately recalled her actions upon their last encounter. Her complete abandonment of propriety on that occasion had been fuelled by the knowledge that she would never see him again. Certainly she never would have acted so wantonly had she ever expected to again be in his company.

"William! What are you doing here?" she asked, the look of surprise changing to confusion and morphing just as quickly to fear.

"I was assured that Mr. Gallagher would be the only person to know of my whereabouts."

"Please forgive my intrusion," said Darcy. "I know this is quite unexpected, and I must assure you that your identity has not been compromised. I had business with Mr. Gallagher recently in London, and I'm afraid I used trickery to learn of your present location."

"Trickery, sir?" asked Elizabeth as she arched an eyebrow at him.

He remembered that look. He also remembered what had followed that look. God, not being able to touch her was torture.

Looking into her eyes as she waited for his reply, he continued. "I requested to see the leasing bill for the cottage and noted the name of the leasing agency. I then visited the estate agent. He was only too happy to oblige me with the address when I offered to pay the entire lease in advance."

"You seem to have gone to a great deal of trouble to find me. May I inquire why, sir?" asked Elizabeth.

"I had to see you again," said Darcy, knowing it would be senseless to lie. "You have been much in my thoughts. I know we were never to meet again, but I could not help myself. I wanted to see you once more."

Knowing that her identity was safe comforted her somewhat, but she did not understand his meaning by coming there.

"What did you hope to accomplish by seeing me again?" asked Elizabeth.

That was indeed an excellent question. One for which he had no answer. Truly he was hoping her presence would pale in comparison to his memory of her. He was hoping her eyes were not as dark and seductive as in his dreams of her. He was hoping her essence was not as intoxicating as when last he held her. He was a fool to have entertained such hopes.

"I wanted to assure myself that you were well and that you were comfortably situated." With some hesitation he added, "I was hoping that you wanted to see me again also, Lizzy." He moved closer to where she stood.

"Forgive my manners, sir. Please sit down," said Elizabeth uncomfortably. "Hannah," she called, "please bring some tea." The young woman made a brief appearance at the doorway to acknowledge that she had heard the request and was gone again in an instant.

Elizabeth sat down on the divan and offered William the chair across from her. She eyed him suspiciously.

"I believe that your part of our agreement has been fulfilled, sir. I am with child as was our intention, and I have received the compensation we agreed upon. I can see no reason why we should need to meet again."

Hannah returned with the tea and placed the tray on the table between them.

"You need not bother, Hannah, I will pour," said Elizabeth. "I will call if I need you."

"Very good, Miss," said Hannah as she left the two alone in the small room.

Handing him his tea, her nervousness was obvious. She bit down on her lip to try to steady her nerves as well as her hand as he took the offered cup.

"I must admit I am surprised to see you here," said Elizabeth. "The agreement stated quite clearly that once I was with child, we should not meet again. I believe Mr. Gallagher said that point was one of the conditions on which you were most vehement."

"I know that my coming here is highly improper, and I have done so at the risk of injuring those who are most dear to me," said Darcy. "I offer no excuse other than my own selfish desire to be in your company one last time. Unless . . ."

"Unless what, sir?"

Darcy stood and began to pace the carpet, running his hands through his hair. As he turned to look at her, he searched her eyes for some sign of understanding. He returned to sit beside her on the divan, leaning his body towards her as he inhaled her lavender scent, bringing back memories that were painfully exquisite; memories he had tried to forget.

"Have you not thought upon our time together?" he asked. "Have you not wished that we might again share the closeness we once had? Surely you cannot deny your feelings."

He could not help himself. He needed to be in the comfort of her arms once more. He quickly rose to his feet, pulling her up into his embrace as he did. With a swift motion he lowered his head and secured his lips upon hers. He sighed as their lips met, and his arms automatically went around her, enfolding her in his embrace. Remembrances of their last encounter filled his memory. He knew he had already crossed the line of decorum, but his passion, not his head, was now controlling his actions.

Elizabeth was unsteady on her feet as she grabbed the lapels of his coat to maintain her balance. As she started to speak in protest, he took advantage of her now open mouth to deepen their kiss.

One of his hands slid up her back and foraged through her hair, holding her head in place to keep her lips securely intact with his own. His other hand now had free reign over the delicate curves of her body.

For one stolen moment Elizabeth allowed herself the guilty pleasure of his intoxicating kiss as she reacquainted herself with the sweet familiar taste of his mouth and revelled in the warmth of his embrace before she struggled to release herself from his hold upon her.

"Sir, this is not to be borne! Are you suggesting that we continue in the same manner as we did in St. Andrews? Are . . . are you asking me to be your . . . your mistress?"

The tension in the room was palpable. They stood there, looking at the each other, afraid to breathe.

"Yes."

He took in a large breath of air, as if shocked by his own response. Undoubtedly he had dreamed about such a thing; he had allowed himself to fantasize about it often, but certainly he had never expected to suggest that they actually engage is such a relationship. He already regretted his answer.

He felt his heart pound in his chest. As much as he wanted her, he would never ask her to take on such a role. He had never given any thought *ever* to taking a mistress. What was it about this woman that made him disregard his every good intention and behave as he should not? Would he sound foolish now to withdraw his offer? It did not matter, foolish or not he must tell her it was a mistake.

"Lizzy, I must . . .

But before he could get the words out, she spoke.

"Sir, what you suggest is quite out of the question. Were you the last man in the world, I would never agree to be your mistress. I must insist that you leave at once."

He breathed a sigh of relief that she had refused him. What would he have truly done had she willingly agreed? However, despite his relief, he could not help but react to her offensive words and total dismissal of him. His pride overtook his common sense; he had to know *why* she had refused him.

"And is this all the reply I am to expect?" asked Darcy. "I might ask why with so little regard to your situation, you have rejected me? Is the prospect so abhorrent to you?"

Elizabeth could feel her indignation rising and with a calmness she did not truly feel, she gathered her courage and addressed him.

"And I might ask why with so evident a desire to offend and insult me you have come here under the guise of concern for me and your unborn child, while your true intention was to engage me as your mistress?"

She now looked directly into his eyes, her emotions spurring her on. "Sir, when you speak of injuring those most dear to you, I assume you speak of your family." Elizabeth closed her eyes for a brief moment and took a breath before she continued.

"I, too, do not wish to see innocent people injured. I was foolish enough to believe that while I was resolving my family's financial burden by entering into our agreement, that I was also doing something good and noble for someone else."

Darcy was about to speak, but she put up her hand and said, "Please, sir, let me have my say.

"My first reaction to your suggestion was anger. But, upon reflection, 1 can understand why you would think that a woman who would sell herself and her child would easily agree to be your mistress." In a voice just above a whisper she said, "I am not proud of myself.

"I have no false expectations as to my future. But whatever my future holds, I am convinced that it will not include such an arrogant and selfish man as yourself. I may no longer be considered a lady, but you, sir, have behaved most ungentlemanly. If you seek a mistress, I suggest you look elsewhere. I desire no such attachment."

"You have said quite enough, Madam. I will not impose myself upon you further. I need only your assurance that you intend to fulfil the remaining terms of our agreement."

"I have given my word, sir, and will abide by our agreement." With that she walked towards the door. "And I must have *your* word that you will also abide by the terms of our agreement and not seek me out again."

"You can be assured; I shall not bother you again. I'm sorry to have taken up so much of your time. Please accept my best wishes for your health and happiness." He afforded her the slightest of bows and was gone.

Elizabeth's legs barely carried her back to the divan. As tears threatened, she felt the quick movements of the child within her and sighed.

"Well, I see you and I are of the same opinion of your father, little one. He makes me want to kick someone, too."

CHAPTER EIGHTEEN

Christmas at Pemberley was as festive a sight as was to be seen. Darcy had made sure that no expense was spared to ready the grand house for the occasion. Decorations adorned all the common rooms, and the most splendid of the many handsome fir trees on his property was selected to be displayed in front of the window in the music room. Darcy had chosen this room as it was the one in which Anne and Georgiana spent most of their day.

Five days before Christmas, Richard arrived with his parents, Lord and Lady Matlock, and his elder brother, the Viscount of Matlock, with his wife and their two children. Lady Catherine arrived the following afternoon, demonstrating her usual flair for the dramatic; lamenting on her long journey, the cold weather, the horrid condition of the roads, and, strangely enough, the lack of cushions in her carriage. Darcy wondered if it was possible that Lady Catherine and Caroline Bingley were somehow related. They both seemed to have the same innate ability to offend his sensibilities.

On Christmas Eve, as was tradition, a large feast was provided for all the tenants on his land. Many of them had gone carolling, and their voices could be heard through the cold night air. Darcy was trying to make this the best Christmas Anne had ever had. After a large and well turned out dinner, they withdrew to the music room for some Christmas carols.

Georgiana's confidence was indeed growing in the company of Anne. Normally she would never have thought of performing in front of such a large number of people but, with Anne's encouragement, agreed to play the pianoforte and even offered to sing, as long as Anne would accompany her.

Anne, knowing that she would not be able to get through an entire song without coughing, declined her sister's offer, suggesting instead that Christmas carols should be sung by everyone. And indeed, everyone joined in.

As the night wore on, Darcy could not help but notice Anne's fatigue. As he made his way over to her, she smiled up at him. "Oh Fitzwilliam, this is indeed the happiest Christmas I have ever experienced!" He sat down beside her and took her hand.

"I'm happy to hear you say it. I believe that was my intention," he said, giving her his most devastating smile. She couldn't help but laugh at his self-satisfied grin as he squeezed her hand. "Do you think you should retire for the evening? We still have another busy day ahead of us."

"Perhaps you are right. I do not want to overdo it. Will you take me up, Fitzwilliam?"

"It would be my pleasure" he replied as he smiled at her.

When they announced that Anne would be retiring for the evening, the rest of the company agreed that perhaps they all should do the same. They would all be departing tomorrow following the Christmas brunch, except for Richard who had two more days before he was expected back at his regiment. Even Georgiana would be departing to Matlock to spend a few weeks with her aunt and uncle.

As the group disassembled, Darcy took Anne's hand and led her up the staircase to their respective chambers. Stopping at her door, he kissed her on the cheek and wished her a good night. When he was about to depart, she clutched his hand again and brought it to her lips. She kissed it lightly. "Fitzwilliam, you have indeed made this the best of Christmases. Would it be ungenerous of me to ask one more thing of you?"

"You know you can ask anything of me, Anne. If it is mine to give, you shall have it," he answered.

Hesitating somewhat, she finally asked, "Would you spend the night with me?" A blush coloured her pale face as she spoke. "I know that we cannot be intimate, but I would be most content just to lie in your embrace."

He looked into her eyes and saw the love she had for him. How he wished he could return that love. He knew he did not feel the same love for her that she felt for him, but he recognized that love comes in many forms, and, in his own way, he did love her very much.

He pulled her into the warmth of his embrace, and she melted into his arms. Then he easily lifted up her slight body and opened the door to her bed chamber, closing it behind them.

~*~

Elizabeth Bennet had still not fully recovered from the effects of her visitor. She wanted to hate him for his arrogance in thinking she would agree to be his mistress. But she could not. Whatever the circumstances of his life were, she would not judge him. How could she judge him without judging herself?

It had been most shocking to see him standing there in the sitting room of the tiny cottage, his looming presence causing it to appear even smaller. She was sure she had turned crimson as their eyes first met.

With some embarrassment she would acknowledge the fact that she had fantasized about him often over the last four months. However, his short visit had done much to dispel all her fantasies. His arrogance and conceit had been revealed to their fullest.

He was obviously a man who was used to getting whatever he desired, and apparently he desired her. That fact was more pleasing to her than she cared to admit. However, on that she would not dwell. He had made it quite clear what he thought of her and what he wanted from her. Why that had upset her so, she could not say. After all, what did she care for his good opinion?

Their positions were clear. His visit had revealed far more than she wanted to know; he belonged to another. The only place for her in his life was mistress. Had he been free, she was convinced he still would never have considered her his equal. Perhaps once, long ago, when her father was still alive and she was a gentleman's daughter, he might have found her worthy.

With renewed determination after having witnessed the gentleman's true character, she vowed to think of him no more.

It was Christmas Eve, and she was quite alone. Even Hannah had departed at Elizabeth's insistence that she spend Christmas with her family. Elizabeth assured her she would be fine by herself for a day or two. Hannah had reluctantly left, stating that she would return the next day as soon as Christmas dinner was over.

Elizabeth sat by the fire and read Jane's letter again. She wondered at the absence of any mention of Mr. Bingley. Her last two letters had been filled with details of their time spent together, but not once was his name to be found in this one. Jane told of her plans for the holiday. All their family would be spending the day at their Aunt and Uncle Gardiner's townhouse. The Gardiners had just recently returned from America and were anxious to share their experiences with everyone.

When Elizabeth had realized that they would never be able to get in touch with their uncle in time to save Lydia's reputation, they did not make further attempts to contact him. Since Wickham had agreed to marry Lydia, the truth was never made known to her family. As far as all her family knew, George Wickham had been a loving and willing bridegroom. Only she and Jane knew the truth.

Her family was under the impression that she was spending Christmas with Mrs. Worthington and her family. So there she was, all alone on Christmas Eve. She and Hannah had put up some decorations earlier in the day, and the little cottage looked quite festive adorned with holly berry boughs and pine cones. As she was about to see what Hannah had left her for dinner, she heard someone knock.

Pat Santarsiero

With some hesitation she approached the door. Opening it just enough to see who stood behind it, she was surprised by the sight of an unknown young man carrying a rather large package. He looked to be harmless, as it was all he could do to hold the heavy burden in his arms. She opened the door to him.

"Scuse me, Miss," said the young man. "I 'ave a delivery fer this address. Are yew bein' the mistress of the 'ouse?"

"Yes," said Elizabeth cautiously.

"Then this 'ere package is fer yew," said the young man with a grin.

Elizabeth moved aside, allowing him in to set the package on the floor of the small sitting room. When Elizabeth went to her reticule to give the young man a coin for his trouble, he put up his hand. "No, Miss. I was told not to take nothin' from ya. Already been paid fer me services."

"Who paid you, young man?" asked Elizabeth.

"The gentleman di'nt give 'is name, Miss," said the boy as he tipped his cap to Elizabeth and left.

She opened the package directly upon the boy's departure, her curiosity piqued. She was indeed surprised as she pulled out one of the many books the package contained, a volume of poetry by Byron. Was it just a coincidence that a braid of gold and blue threads marked the page that contained the following poem?

When We Two Parted

When we two parted
In silence and tears,
Half broken-hearted,
To sever for years,
Pale grew thy cheek and cold,
Colder thy kiss;
Truly that hour foretold
Sorrow to this!

Thursday's Child

The dew of the morning
Sunk chill on my brow;
It felt like the warning
Of what I feel now.
Thy vows are all broken,
And light is thy fame:
I hear thy name spoken
And share thy shame.

In secret we met
In silence I grieve,
That thy heart could forget
Thy spirit deceive
If I should meet thee
After long years,
How will I greet thee?
With silence and tears.

~*~

Darcy arose later than his customary time the next morning. For a moment he forgot where he was, so unaccustomed was he to awakening in Anne's bed chamber. She was not in bed, but he could hear her attending her bath. She had not slept well, her cough keeping them both awake through most of the night. She had expressed her concern at disturbing his rest, but he soothed her worries until finally she relaxed in his arms. It was only during the early morning hours that her cough had finally subsided and she found some relief in sleep.

She entered the room and, upon seeing him awake, greeted him with a warm smile. "Good morning, Fitzwilliam."

"Good morning, Anne. How are you feeling?" he asked, concern showing on his face.

"Do not look so distressed, Fitzwilliam. I assure you I am well," she offered. She felt so happy, and her heart was filled with such love for him that she did not wish to spoil the mood with talk of her health.

"If you don't mind waiting, I will hurry and complete my ablutions so we can go down to Christmas brunch together," suggested Darcy.

"I would like that very much."

An hour later, both Darcy and Anne, dressed in their holiday best, opened the door to Anne's bed chamber and walked right into Lady Catherine as she was passing Anne's room. Having witnessed their intimate exchange at that very spot on the previous evening, Lady Catherine was quite delighted to see that her daughter was spending nights in Darcy's company. She bid them good morning with such a lascivious smile that it made Darcy cringe.

Christmas brunch was all one would expect from the master of such a grand estate. The buffet was complete with a carved turkey and all its trimmings, venison and three different kinds of potatoes, followed by every pastry and dessert imaginable. By two in the afternoon, most of the party was ready to leave. Lady Catherine had offered to stay an extra day or two, but thankfully remembered that Mr. and Mrs. Collins would be calling on her at Rosings in a few days, giving her just enough allowance to make the journey home and prepare for her company.

With all the party gone, except for Richard, Anne expressed her desire to rest upstairs. Darcy escorted her to her room and returned to the library and his cousin. It had been such a long time since the two had been able to spend any amount of time together. Darcy had missed Richard's companionship. After spending some time discussing the military and Richard's recent assignments, their conversation eventually turned to Anne's health.

"Has there been much change in her health of late?" inquired Richard.

"I'm afraid the only change has been for the worse. Her cough has been the cause of much distress, and she seems to tire quite easily. She can barely catch her breath after she has ascended the stairs to her room," said Darcy.

Thursday's Child

"She did not seem to be that bad the last few days. I did not witness much coughing; maybe once or twice."

"She has gotten very proficient at deception. She usually finds some reason to excuse herself when she feels a coughing bout coming on. I know she does so for my benefit," said Darcy with a genuine look of sadness.

Darcy walked over to the sideboard and poured himself a brandy. "Would you care for one?" he asked his cousin.

Richard nodded.

They sat down before the fire with drink in hand. Darcy looked over to his cousin and started to speak, but changed his mind. Upon doing the same for a second time, his cousin inquired, "Do you have something on your mind, Darcy?"

"Yes, I do, Richard. However, the subject is such that I am somewhat reluctant. I know that you and I have always been able to discuss any situation without fear of judgment, but this time I may be asking too much of you."

Intrigued by Darcy's words, Richard encouraged him to proceed. "I don't even know how to begin," he stated as he stood and began his customary pacing.

Darcy took a deep breath followed quickly by a large swallow of his drink. He was not sure just how much he wished to reveal. That he had been so affected by Lizzy and that he had been tempted to take her for his mistress were not facts he wished to make known. Since it was of little consequence now, he saw no need to mention either. No, he would only disclose the most pertinent information.

And so he began. "I have done something that has set in motion an inescapable chain of events."

CHAPTER NINETEEN

Caroline Bingley was once again feeling the triumph of victory as she took her place at the head of the table. Convincing her brother that it would be most advantageous to spend Christmas at Netherfield had been so easy, thanks in part to Darcy's little heart to heart, that it was almost undeserving of her diligent machinations.

Even though she herself would much have preferred Christmas in London, she knew a little sacrifice on her part now would help guarantee her future. She looked around the table at her guests. *I suppose this is the best that Hertfordshire has to offer,* she thought meanly to herself.

Charles sat at the opposite end of the table, Mr. and Mrs. Hurst to his left, Mr. and Mrs. Collins to his right. On Caroline's left were Mr. and Mrs. Lucas and to her right were the Lucases' youngest daughter, Maria, and a very distinguished looking gentleman by the name of Dr. Adams. They had met recently while attending a small dinner party given by Sir William. She did not think much of him upon his introduction, but when she had overhead Sir William talking with his eldest daughter, Mrs. Collins, it was the mention of Mrs. Darcy that drew her attention. Apparently, Dr. Adams had attended the sickly Mrs. Darcy at Rosings. Since Dr. Adams was a recent widower, Caroline had generously offered, and he had graciously accepted, an invitation for Christmas dinner at Netherfield.

Without trying to appear too obvious, Caroline was using her limited charms to try to obtain any information she could regarding Mrs. Darcy's health.

"How were Mr. and Mrs. Darcy when last in their company?" she asked casually.

Dr. Adams, always the consummate professional, answered with a non-committing, "Very well."

"I had heard that Mrs. Darcy has been quite ill recently. Indeed, she had a most persistent cough when I last had occasion to dine with them," Caroline pressed on.

"Yes . . . well. . . I believe she was in need of much rest, and I advised her accordingly. I have no doubt Mr. Darcy is attending to her needs admirably," he replied uneasily.

Seeing that this was not going to be as easy as she thought, Caroline decided to postpone this topic of conversation for a more private setting. As she looked upon the gentleman, she assessed his appearance and deemed him quite presentable, though much older than herself. Perhaps if she were to become better acquainted with the good doctor, he might be more amenable to discussing his patient. What did she have to lose? She might as well occupy her time in a useful manner, as it might be a long while before she was again in Mr. Darcy's company.

At the other end of the table, Charles Bingley was anything but cheerful. His usual happy demeanour was nowhere to be seen. He could not stop thinking about Miss Bennet. He had imagined her reaction to his letter many times in the last week, and each time it brought him pain.

How could he have been so insensitive? If it had been only Caroline's displeasure with his attentions toward Miss Bennet, he would not have acquiesced to her will. However, the fact that his best friend, the man whose opinion he valued above all others, had also expressed his concern regarding his choice of Miss Bennet, caused him to feel obligated to follow his counsel.

Darcy had not exactly objected to Miss Bennet, he only wanted to advise him to act in a more prudent manner. Bingley could understand Darcy's concern. There had been countless young ladies who had practiced their charms on the rich Mr. Darcy for no other reason than his wealth and position. But surely Miss Bennet was not like that. He could not be mistaken with regard to her feelings for him. But he could not disregard his friend's advice.

He looked down at the end of the table and saw the satisfied grin on Caroline's face. *How could I have taken romantic advice from a woman who owns no heart?* he thought as his eyes met hers.

~*~

Jane Bennet gave a deep sigh as she entered her small room at the Morgans' townhouse. Christmas at Gracechurch Street had been very pleasant. She had missed her Aunt and Uncle Gardiner and was happy that they were back from America. Her mother had been her usual self and relentlessly questioned her regarding Mr. Bingley. But it was good to be in her family's company again and to see her younger sisters. Even Lydia had shown up with her husband, who was on leave from New Castle.

How she missed Elizabeth and longed to speak to her. She had not written to her yet of Mr. Bingley's departure to Netherfield, for she did not want to elicit her pity. She would wait until the holidays were over before she burdened her sister with that news.

She had been quite surprised to find the letter from Mr. Bingley tucked inside a short note from Caroline which arrived a week ago. While Caroline's note was obviously inconsequential and used only as a ruse to deliver Mr. Bingley's letter, she could not help but react to the insensitive sentiment of Caroline's words as she read:

December 17, 1812

My Dearest Jane,

I hope this note finds you and your family well. Charles and I wish you a happy Christmas, and while we do not expect to be again in your company very soon, we wish you joy in the coming year.

Your friend,

Caroline Bingley

The attached letter from Mr. Bingley was almost as formal, informing her of his decision to return to Netherfield, stating he had neglected his duties to his estate far too long, and he must now turn his attention to his business affairs. He had given no indication of when he might return to London.

Was their courtship over? Had she displeased him in some way? She now regretted her forwardness that night of his dinner party. At the time, he had not seemed to be offended by her actions. On the contrary, he had appeared rather delighted. Upon subsequent evenings, it was he who had initiated their intimacy, to which she had gladly been a willing participant. Their kisses had become more and more passionate with each new encounter. Upon their last evening together, she had to admit, things had gone a bit further than they had intended.

She felt a blush rise within her as she recalled the memory of his hand at first lightly brushing the skin of her décolletage and, as their passion escalated, his hand finding its way inside the neckline of her gown to encompass the bare skin of her breast. She thought she would faint at his touch, but she did not pull away. And now he had gone back to Netherfield. Could there be any other explanation? He had found her wanton, and it disgusted him. After crying herself to sleep for many nights, she decided it was time to pull herself together.

She was hoping that Lizzy would be able to visit her again soon. According to her last letter, the earliest she would be able to travel to London would be sometime in June or July. That seemed so far away. How was she ever going to survive until then?

~*~

Anne made her way back up the long staircase; her cough slowing her progress. As she approached her door, she paused to allow herself a chance to catch her breath. She stood with her hand on the knob for several minutes and finally, as her gasps for air subsided, she entered her chamber. She leaned back against the door, tears stinging her eyes. She walked slowly to her bed and sat on the edge, staring straight ahead, not moving a muscle, her mind a whirling mass of thoughts.

Having awakened from her rest, she had made her way downstairs to find Fitzwilliam and Richard. As she approached the library she had heard her husband's voice and was about to enter the room. Upon hearing his words, she had immediately stopped in her tracks. She could tell by the sound of his voice that the subject was of a serious nature. Thinking he was discussing her health with Richard, she had stood outside the door to hear their conversation.

"I have done something that has set in motion an inescapable chain of events." There seemed to be no reply forthcoming from Richard. As she moved her body slightly as to see inside the room, she again heard her husband's voice.

"Do you recall my trip to Scotland?" asked Darcy.

Richard nodded.

"My true purpose for travelling there was not for the reason we discussed. I travelled there with quite a different purpose in mind."

Here he paused, not sure how to word his next statement. He paced the room to give himself time to form his thoughts. He stopped in front of the fireplace, looking into the flames. Finally he said, "I had arranged to meet a young woman there." He did not have to look at Richard to gauge his reaction.

Anne was holding her breath. She could hear her heart pounding in her chest. This could not be true! There must be some reasonable explanation. But even as she thought this, her eyes were filling with tears.

"I entered into an agreement with this woman. For a specified amount of money, she would bear my child and heir." Darcy kept his eyes on the fire, watching the flames, afraid to face his cousin.

After several moments of complete silence, Richard spoke, his voice barely above a whisper. "I will not judge you, Fitzwilliam. That is for a much higher authority than I. You and you alone will have to bear whatever the consequences may be."

With that, Darcy turned to look at his cousin. He could see the compassion in his eyes, and he knew they would be all right.

"Is the woman now with child?" asked Richard.

"Yes," said Darcy. "The child shall be born in May. I engaged the services of an attorney, who has made all the arrangements as to the provisions of the agreement and has provided for her needs during her confinement. He is to be notified upon the birth of the child."

"How do you intend to claim the child as your heir?" asked Richard. Darcy again began a slow pacing of the room. "I'm afraid my plan did not extend that far. I could say that the child was abandoned and left here at Pemberley. I just don't know Richard, but I must find a way to bring this child into my home and raise it as my own."

"What of the woman? Can you trust her? Will she keep your secret?" asked Richard.

"Yes, of that I am certain," replied Darcy. "Every precaution has been made to conceal our identities from each other. Our association extends no further than the terms of our agreement." He turned toward the fire again, and, if one were listening closely, one could almost hear the sadness in his voice as he said, "We are never to meet again."

Pat Santarsiero

Anne could feel her breathing becoming more laboured. She knew it would only be a matter of seconds before she would start coughing. As quickly as she could, she made her way towards the staircase.

~*~

Elizabeth put down the book of poetry she had been reading. She stood and walked to the window, looking out at the night. She pressed her forehead against the coolness of the windowpane. She could feel the movement of the child within her. Her child, a child she would never know. So many nights she had cursed this hell she had created for herself. Had she really thought she would be unaffected by this?

How could I have known I would love this child even before it was born? How will I ever give it up? She knew she need not worry as to the child's welfare. William could obviously afford to see to his child's care and education. He was, after all, a man of means. The child would be well provided for. She only prayed that the child would also be loved.

CHAPTER TWENTY

The next few weeks saw Anne and Darcy settle into a comfortable routine. Now that she was receiving the best of care, her health was at least stable. She was no better, yet no worse.

The severe weather of the northern county of Derbyshire quickly enveloped the large estate in a blanket of snow. Although most of the county's residents did not venture out into such intolerable weather, Darcy did still manage to ride Marengo at least once or twice a week on days when the weather's severity lessened.

Most usually his destination was unplanned, but more likely than not, he would find himself riding the half hour it took to reach the ridge that overlooked the small cottage that housed Lizzy.

He told himself his only purpose in travelling there was to ensure that she and his unborn child were safe. On one occasion he had actually seen Lizzy as she walked a path near the cottage, but that was at least a month ago, before the snow had fallen. He had not seen her since. Occasionally he would see Hannah as she went about her duties. Sometimes she would be gathering wood for the fire, or throwing out a basin of water.

He had been tempted on several occasions to visit her again. He wanted to let her know he regretted his words that day. He wanted to tell her he had not meant to insult her and to ask her forgiveness, but he had promised he would not bother her again, and he was sure she would refuse to see him anyway. He also had to admit to his admiration of her for having refused him. He knew that not many women in such a situation would have done likewise.

He wondered what her life might be like after this. Would she seek a position as nursemaid or companion? Even those options would be closed to her should the particulars of their agreement become known. She could still perhaps marry. But he knew her well enough to know she would never enter into a marriage without revealing her past. Would she lead a life of degradation? He could not bear to think of Lizzy with other men, uncivilized men who would treat her poorly. *After all, she is soon to be the mother of my child, a child who will someday inherit all of Pemberley.*

The thought of taking a mistress had always been abhorrent to him; there must be some other way to keep her safe.

As he watched the cottage, he observed the post's arrival and saw Hannah as she ran from the cottage to offer up a letter. Darcy was now familiar with the routine of life that stirred about the small cottage. On Tuesdays and Fridays supplies were delivered by an elderly man and his young helper. The young boy would carry the parcels inside the cottage, while the elderly man stood outside and talked with Hannah. The postman arrived with less consistency, but usually two or three times a week.

On the previous Thursday, a new precedent had begun as he watched a carriage arrive and a woman descend, carrying a black satchel. She stayed for about an hour. Darcy knew this to be the midwife hired by his attorney. He knew this for no other reason than that he had followed the carriage upon its departure. Was it not his right to know all the comings and goings of a cottage where he had paid the lease in full?

He would have preferred that his own personal physician, Dr. Chisholm, be the one to attend Lizzy. However, Mr. Gallagher had convinced him that obtaining a local midwife would be more prudent and attract less attention. He assured him that he had thoroughly checked out the woman's experience and reputation. He also assured him that the woman would be discreet. She would visit once a month until the end of April to make sure everything was progressing normally. Darcy had insisted that starting the first of May, as the birthing day approached, she would visit each afternoon. Even though she had not asked, he agreed to pay the woman twice her usual fee for such diligent attention.

Satisfied that all was as it should be, he slowly turned Marengo back towards Pemberley.

~*~

"Fitzwilliam," said Anne, "I have received a reply to my recent letter to my mother this morning. I must inform you that it is very likely she will visit us soon, although I will attempt to forestall her for as long as I may."

Darcy continued his entry into the parlour where Anne was about to partake in her afternoon tea. He made it a point each day to join her in this ritual, as it seemed to please her very much. He smiled as he approached her and took the cup from her hand as she offered it up to him.

"What is it that you have written that would cause her to travel to Pemberley again so soon and in such unsuitable weather?" asked Darcy as he seated himself next to his wife.

"I have informed her that I am with child," stated Anne quite calmly.

Darcy dropped the cup from his hand, spilling the tea on his breeches. He quickly stood as the hot liquid scorched his thigh. Surely he had not heard her correctly. "Forgive my clumsiness," he said as he picked up the cup and returned it to its saucer. He brushed off his breeches with his napkin and again took a seat.

"I'm afraid I must have misunderstood you, Anne. What was it you said?"

"I said, Fitzwilliam, that I have written to my mother informing her that I am with child," said Anne again, slowly and succinctly.

Darcy said nothing but looked curiously at his wife. He watched as she refilled his empty cup, her hand steady. He waited to see if she continued, but she silently offered the tea to him, apparently waiting for his response.

Not quite knowing how to reply to such a statement, he took her hand and said softly, "Anne, I know how much you wanted this to be so, but surely you do not truly believe that you are with child?"

Looking at him now just as strangely as he was looking at her, she said, "I did not say that I *was* with child, Fitzwilliam, I said that I informed *my mother* I was with child."

This explanation did little to alleviate Darcy's confusion.

She took the cup and saucer from his hand and placed it on the table before them. She then took both his hands into hers. Darcy looked into her eyes, searching for the explanation that was beyond his immediate comprehension.

"I have a small confession to make," she said as she still held his hands in hers. "On Christmas night, while you and Richard were in the library, I came downstairs to find you. As I approached the door, the serious nature of your voice convinced me you were discussing my health, so I waited outside the door to listen to your conversation."

At the recollection of that conversation, Darcy immediately stood and turned away from her. *She knows! She knows what occurred in Scotland. She knows of the child!*

"Anne . . . I. . . I . . . what is it you heard?" he asked, still not looking at her. He would wait to hear her full explanation.

"You know what I heard, Fitzwilliam. Is it your desire to hear me repeat it?" she asked.

Her calm demeanour still convincing him she did not know of his transgressions, he turned back to where she sat and grabbing her shoulders pulled her up to stand in front of him. "Tell me what you heard!" he demanded.

Pulling herself from his grasp, she took a step back. With only a trace of anger in her voice, she complied with his demand. "I heard of your true purpose in travelling to Scotland. I heard of the child, *your child,* that shall be born in May."

Darcy stood there and looked into her eyes for a long moment. Neither spoke nor even drew breath. Finally he reached out and pulled her again, this time into his embrace. He had no words that might comfort her. What good would words do now? He could not defend himself against the charges laid at his door. He had betrayed her and their marriage. As much as he wished to deny it, he could not.

As he embraced her frail body, Anne put her arms around his waist and rested her head against his chest. She remained silent, enfolded in his arms, for several minutes. She did not cry. When Darcy finally released his hold and looked upon her, she said, "Come sit down with me. We have much to discuss, Fitzwilliam."

Pat Santarsiero

CHAPTER TWENTY-ONE

Miss Anne de Bourgh had grown up a lonely only child. She had little memory of her father, Sir Lewis de Bourgh, even though she was nine years old when he died. He had rarely spent time in her company and seemed to travel a great deal.

Anne had mostly been raised by governesses, having had several over her early years; none of them staying long enough to form any kind of attachment. At first she had thought that she was the cause of each one's departure, but upon overhearing a conversation one afternoon between the upstairs maid and Miss Nethercott, her fourth, or was it her fifth, governess, she learned the true reason why so many governesses had come and gone.

Apparently, Sir Lewis had no difficulty in showing his affections to ladies outside of his immediate family. Either a governess was appalled by his attentions and would leave of her own accord, or a governess was *not* appalled by his attentions and Lady Catherine would dismiss her from service as soon as she suspected any inappropriate behaviour. Lady Catherine had tried hiring only older and less attractive governesses for a while, but that had not seemed to deter Sir Lewis.

The only affection Anne could bring to memory was that of her earliest years. Their cook, a Mrs. Harrigan, had several daughters. The eldest, Meg, a pretty and lively young girl with copper hair and green eyes, had taken kindly to her, displaying an open warmth and fondness that Anne sought whenever Lady Catherine bestowed her disapproval upon her, which was often. Meg would lift her upon her lap and with soothing words would make her forget her distress and would soon have her smiling again.

Some of her fondest memories were of the afternoons they would walk to the herb garden just beyond the small creek behind Rosings. Meg would hold her hand as they stepped from stone to stone across the shallow water to reach the basil, or perhaps the parsley, that was required for the evening meal. Once their task had been completed, especially on fine summer days, they would stretch themselves out, side by side, lying on the sun-warmed grass and inhaling the exquisite mixture of scents the garden emitted. There they would look up at the white puffs of clouds and, using their imaginations, would discern their likeness to anything from a teapot to a fire-breathing dragon.

At night she would sometimes sneak into Anne's room with some delightful baked treat or just simply to wish her sweet dreams. However, not long after her father's death, Meg disappeared from the kitchen and from Anne's life.

Anne's relationship with the great Lady herself had been at best tolerable. A less affectionate mother could probably not have been found in all of England. Right from the start, the fact that Anne was a fragile child had seemed to annoy her mother. The only time she had spoken to Anne was to correct, instruct or criticize her. That Anne turned out to hold herself in low esteem was hardly surprising.

Anne had tried to become the child her mother wanted, but nothing she did seemed to please her. By the time she was in her youth, she had long stopped trying to attain her mother's approval. Anne knew that her biggest disappointment to her mother was her inability to entice the great Fitzwilliam Darcy. Her mother had preached to her daily regarding her hopes for a union between the two of them.

As much as she had preached, Anne knew her mother never truly believed such an alliance would ever come about; her sickly, unsophisticated, unrefined and untalented daughter attracting one of the richest, handsomest and most powerful gentleman in the county? Never! But still she had preached.

By the time she was five and twenty, Anne had been resigned to the fact that she would live the rest of her life under her mother's thumb. She had no prospects for marriage, and her mother would never permit her to do anything outside of Rosings that might allow her to feel useful. No, she would forever be a disappointment to her mother and would most likely die a lonely old maid.

Her lack of vigour had never been of great concern to Anne. It would have been far worse to be in such a stifling environment and be healthy. At least her ill health had given her an excuse for her idleness.

But all of that had changed in one glorious morning stroll in the gardens of Rosings. Fitzwilliam Darcy had proposed. You could have knocked her over with a feather. As nonchalant as she had tried to appear, she was shocked beyond belief. She had so wanted to see the look on her mother's face when Fitzwilliam asked for permission to marry her. Oh, to have been a fly on the wall!

Even though Anne had known it wasn't exactly a love match, at least on Darcy's part, she also had known that her life would benefit by this union in so many ways.

Firstly, and most importantly, she would no longer be under her mother's rule. She would be free of her mother and free of Rosings. She would speak, dress, associate with, learn, laugh and love in any manner she so desired.

Secondly, she would be mistress of her own home. She would be respected as the wife of a gentleman. She would no longer be idle. Her life would have purpose.

And thirdly, but equally as important, she would be able to give her love to someone, to care for another person and show her affection. Even though she had known he married her only out of duty to family, she would make her husband happy in any way she could. She would show her gratefulness every day for the honour he had bestowed upon her.

All of this, she was sure, had not even occurred to Fitzwilliam Darcy. He had no idea how he had saved her, how much better her life was because of him.

The disappointment of her miscarriage still grieved her. She had wanted so dearly to have his child. Had he asked, she would have gladly acquiesced to share her bed with him again.

But now she knew that was not her fate. She would never be well enough to produce his heir, a fact that her husband obviously knew as well. Of course, he did not know the extent of her illness, or perhaps he did but did not speak of it.

If her plan was to work, she would need an ally. She knew she had one in Mrs. Reynolds. On their first night back at Pemberley on their return from Rosings, Anne had stuffed another bloody handkerchief under her mattress and noted that the previous ones were not where she had hid them.

She immediately had risen from the bed and searched under the mattress. As she lifted it, she had found her four previously hidden handkerchiefs, perfectly laundered and folded.

They had not spoken of the incident, but each time they were in each other's company, Anne was sure she detected a look of understanding in Mrs. Reynolds's eyes.

Anne knew how badly Fitzwilliam longed for an heir. That he had jeopardized his reputation as a gentleman and risked a scandal to produce one, was proof indeed. Although she was not happy with his deception, she understood his motive.

Now that his plan was set in motion, she wanted to see that it would come to fruition. The child would only be accepted as his rightful heir if they could convince their families that the child was a result of their union.

If she could not produce an heir for him herself, she would see that he would be able to raise the child he had fathered. Her only fear was that God would not grant her the time she needed to complete her plan.

Her first task had been to write her mother informing her of her supposed condition. She had sat down at her desk and written:

January 18, 1813

Dear Mother,

I am writing you with the happiest of news. It has now been confirmed that I am with child. Fitzwilliam and I can hardly contain our joy at such a prospect. The child is due in May. I have been under the care of Fitzwilliam's personal physician. It was at his suggestion that we not reveal my condition at Christmas since my health has always been so fragile. But now he feels I am far enough along that we may share this good news with our families.

Please do not bother yourself with a visit during this harsh weather. Be assured that I am well and am receiving the best of care.

With love,

Anne

Anne knew that writing this one letter would be the equivalent of writing to half of England. Her mother would tell anyone who would listen that her daughter was soon to produce the heir to Pemberley.

Her next task was to implore Mrs. Reynolds to assist in her charade. Certainly she would need someone to intervene when her mother came to visit. Not that she believed her mother would inspect her person. Even during her worst childhood illnesses, her mother had never attended her. Surely, this would be no different. As long as there was a servant about to handle such necessities, her mother would refrain from any solicitous behaviour. However, she would still need Mrs. Reynolds to help perpetrate the illusion of her alleged confinement.

She was grateful that her condition had not worsened since their arrival at Pemberley. Fitzwilliam was so convinced that her health could not possibly decline in such a beautiful environment that Anne truly believed he had willed her ill health into remission. Whatever the cause, she was happy to have the time she required. However, she worried yet. May was still a long way off.

Pat Santarsiero

CHAPTER TWENTY-TWO

Darcy opened the letter and, upon observing the several blotted ink spots on the page, knew its writer immediately. Bingley was never one to demonstrate patience whilst writing a letter. He usually scrawled his thoughts with speed rather than precision. It was obvious that he had been in an agitated state during *this* correspondence. He informed Darcy that he and Caroline had returned to London where they would be spending the Season. He expressed his wish that Darcy might meet him there.

As an added inducement, Bingley had emphasized that he wished to meet with him alone, assuring him that Caroline would not be in attendance. Darcy could tell by the tone of his letter that the matter was of great concern and importance to his friend.

The weather was just beginning to lessen from its severity. March had brought some milder temperatures to the area, and the snow was slowly dissipating throughout the county. Darcy had no objection to travelling to London but thought perhaps he would make the trip on horseback rather than by carriage. Since it was still early in "the Season" he had no need for his carriage, and he could make the journey much faster on Marengo. He did not want to be away from Anne and Georgie for too long, nor did he wish to relinquish his faithful guardianship of the small cottage.

The past two months had brought a new and unusual understanding between Anne and himself, one that had taken him quite by surprise. He had thought that upon discovering his most ungentlemanly transgressions, she would have demanded release from their marriage. That she had not even suggested such a course of action relieved him greatly. There would be no scandal, no damage to his reputation or that of his family.

But far beyond that was the fact that she not only accepted the situation, but she also had devised a plan and was determined to see it carried out to an agreeable conclusion. She was truly a remarkable woman. He could honestly say, upon observing her during the last two months, that despite her health impediments, he had never seen her happier. The thought of having a child to care for was obviously giving her much pleasure.

Darcy was also extremely glad that Georgiana would not know of his indiscretions. They had informed her that Anne was with child, and fortunately she was not one to ask too many questions regarding her condition. The fashions of the time also helped conceal the fact that Anne was not increasing. It was Darcy's plan to have Georgie away to Matlock as the time drew near to the birthing day.

He sat down at his desk and responded to Bingley's letter, informing him of his arrival date in London. He had decided not to take Bingley into his confidence regarding the truth about Anne and the child. He felt too many people already knew. He had written to Bingley the previous month to inform him that he and Anne would be expecting a child in May but had not revealed any particulars. All that was needed was one slip of a tongue, and lives would be ruined, and all of this careful planning would be for naught.

As he finished his letter, Anne entered the library. She smiled a hello and stood before him.

"Mr. Bingley has requested my presence in London next week. His letter sounds urgent. I have written that I will meet with him as he has requested. I will also call upon my attorney while I am there and take care of a few business matters. I have decided that if I go on horseback, I can make it there, conclude my business and return all within a se'ennight or so."

"You shall hardly miss my company anyway," said Darcy in a teasing voice.

"Why would you say such a thing, Fitzwilliam?" Anne asked in surprise.

"Well you have been so busy with your plans for the nursery, that I sometimes think you forget I am here."

"Forgive me. I do admit it has taken over much of my time these days. But Fitzwilliam, it makes me so happy to be engaged in such a delightful activity."

Darcy gave his wife a hug. "And it delights me to see you so happily engaged." To Anne's added joy, he whispered, "I shall bring you back a surprise from London."

~*~

"You seem quite astonished by my news," remarked a curious Caroline. "As her physician, I thought you would have been aware of her condition." She touched his arm, letting her fingers run provocatively over his sleeve.

"I admit I am somewhat astonished at learning that she is with child," said Dr. Adams.

Although it was not prudent for her to be entertaining a gentleman caller whilst her brother was out for the evening, Caroline thought it the perfect opportunity to try to inveigle some information regarding Mrs. Darcy's health.

She had brought up the subject on several previous occasions, but had been unsuccessful in learning anything of consequence. Having noted Dr. Adams's preference for her company, she decided that this might be her only chance to engage him in conversation without her brother's censure.

As they sat on the divan in the parlour, Caroline shifted slightly closer so that their shoulders were touching.

"Why should this surprise you? They are, after all, man and wife," she stated.

Feeling somewhat uncomfortable with the topic of conversation, Dr. Adams tried to divert her thoughts elsewhere, knowing he had already expressed his opinion far too imprudently. He inquired as to her previous evening at the theatre.

Without reference to either the play or the performances she answered, "Oh it is obviously much too early in the Season for anyone of consequence to have attended. I admit I found it rather dull."

"I am sorry to hear you say so. Perhaps it was not an exceptional production. I am sure there will be much more satisfying experiences as the Season progresses."

Attempting again to bring the conversation back to the Darcys, Caroline replied, "Oh, I am sure once Mr. and Mrs. Darcy arrive in town, they will undoubtedly invite Charles and me to share their private box. I am sure you are aware how close my brother and I are to Mr. and Mrs. Darcy. Why Charles and Mr. Darcy are almost like brothers! And I certainly consider Mrs. Darcy one of my closest acquaintances.

"That is why I am so concerned for her condition. I would think her rather delicate body would not be able to tolerate the burden of such a situation." She placed her hand on his arm to emphasize the sincerity of her words.

Although he did not want to reveal any confidential information regarding Mrs. Darcy's health, he also did not want to disappoint Miss Bingley. She seemed to have a genuine concern and only wished to be reassured of Mrs. Darcy's wellbeing.

"Since I have not attended Mrs. Darcy in some time, I cannot opine on her current state of health. Mr. Darcy has obviously sought the services of his private physician in the care of his wife. However, my last examination did warrant me to advise Mr. Darcy that perhaps it would be prudent to avoid those . . . activities . . . that might . . . um . . . result in Mrs. Darcy being again with child."

"Again?" asked a shocked Caroline.

"Did I say again?" responded a red faced Dr. Adams. "If I did, it was a slip of the tongue, I assure you."

There was a long minute of silence as Dr. Adams composed himself. Caroline, observing his obvious discomfiture, decided not to press him further on that point. However, she also did not want to leave the subject entirely yet.

"And did you believe that he had heeded your advice, sir?" asked an innocent looking Caroline as her hand left his arm and travelled lightly over his lapel.

"At the time, I believed he had. But then again, her health may have shown some signs of improvement since my last examination." There was another long moment's pause. "I really do not think we should discuss this topic any further, Miss Bingley."

Caroline moved her body closer, her face was inches from his lips. "I hope you know that I ask these things only out of concern. It would be devastating for me to lose such a good friend as Mrs. Darcy," she whispered.

Dr. Adams turned his head towards her, and as he did Caroline brushed her lips against his. Her hand still upon his lapel, she began to move it slowly across his chest. Dr. Adams, at first stunned by her boldness, responded to her kiss. After all, it had been almost two years since his wife had passed, and he had not felt the touch of a woman's lips on his in all that time. To be honest, he had never expected to experience such a thing ever again.

When they broke from the kiss, Caroline looked pleadingly into his eyes. "Tell me, sir, is Mrs. Darcy in any . . . danger?"

A disoriented Dr. Adams, having had most of the blood leave his brain to travel due south, answered, "I am sorry to say that I will be very much surprised if both she and the child survive."

As he again leaned towards her lips, Caroline abruptly rose from the divan. "Dr. Adams! This is most improper, sir! I think you would be best advised to monitor your behaviour!"

~*~

At seven and a half months along, Elizabeth's walk had a distinctive gait. Mrs. Pearson, the midwife attending her, had assured her that her confinement was progressing at a normal and anticipated pace. The constant movement from inside her womb was not at all the annoyance one might expect, but a reassuring sign that her child was developing as it should.

Grateful that the weather was steadily improving, Elizabeth had once again begun taking her daily exercise, each day following a different path in the woods that surrounded the small cottage. In the evenings she would retrieve one of her now many books of poetry and read aloud to her unborn child.

The postman had delivered Jane's latest letter that morning, forwarded most kindly by Mrs. Worthington. She had not opened it as yet, planning on savouring its contents after dinner.

She was torn between wishing this were all over with and wanting it never to end. Once she gave birth, she must give up her child. At least for now, she had the pleasure of knowing her child was safe within her. Right now, no one could take her child away.

On the other hand, she had to admit she was getting restless in the small cottage. She had not seen nor spoken to anyone other than Hannah and Mrs. Pearson, except the delivery boy on Christmas Eve, since William's most unexpected and disconcerting visit. Her vow to think of him no more was not as successful as she had hoped. He was often in her dreams, and her resistance to him there was just as non-existent as it had been on their last night in Scotland.

Her opinion of him had not improved, but he was a man to which she could not be indifferent. Every thought of him brought a reaction of one kind or another. He seemed to evoke every emotion from her.

Knowing that this man was to raise her child, she wanted desperately to think well of him. That they had parted on such disagreeable terms was distressing. He had hurt and insulted her most exceedingly. He may have expressed a desire for her, but no, he did not think well of her either.

Elizabeth knew she should start making plans for her future. She would be allowed to stay in the cottage for one month after the birth of her child. She had never asked Mrs. Worthington if she would again take her into her employ, not wanting to put the kindly woman in an awkward position. She would write her soon to inform her that she would be available for employment in August. It would be up to Mrs. Worthington whether she would offer such employment or not.

Elizabeth was hoping to visit Jane in July. She missed her sister dearly. She wished she could confide all that she was feeling to her. She needed her calm serenity and voice of reason to help her through this difficult situation. She had no one else to turn to. But she could not bear to expose Jane to the hardship she was about to face.

Hannah had become her life line. Though they never spoke of the particulars of Elizabeth's situation, she was sure that Hannah had some notion of the circumstances. Certainly she had been witness to William's visit, and, although she had discreetly removed herself to her room that day, the tiny cottage did not accommodate private conversation. Hannah had proven herself to be a loyal and devoted companion. She would dearly miss her company.

CHAPTER TWENTY-THREE

Darcy arrived in London late in the evening. He had not informed Mrs. Evanston of his pending arrival, and she was quite surprised as he entered the townhouse. She immediately ordered the servants to prepare a hot bath and to arrange for a light supper. Darcy had requested that the tray be brought to the sitting room off his bed chamber. A fire was being lit as he headed towards his bath.

With the mud of the road washed from his body, he sat before his light repast and poured out a glass of his favourite brandy. His bath had relaxed him, and he sat by the fire, enjoying all the comfort and warmth that his wealth and position afforded.

As he sat there staring into the flames, he conceded that he had little to complain about in his life. His wife's health, though not improved, was at least steady, and she was most happily anticipating the child to come. His sister's confidence was growing daily, and she seemed to be well recovered from the ill effects of her traumatic experience at Ramsgate. He had good friends and family whose company he enjoyed. His estate was flourishing, and this year's crops were promising increased prosperity for Pemberley and for his tenants. He knew he had much to be thankful for.

With the acknowledgement of all of these things, he should be peaceful and content; yet, he was not.

He wondered why his life still felt so incomplete. He truly believed that the birth of his child would help fill the void that was missing in his life. In less than two months, he would become a father. The joy that thought ignited in his heart was immeasurable.

He thought back to his visit to the cottage. The very thought of it tortured him. Did she hate him now?

Suddenly a disturbing thought entered his mind which made him jolt, causing his brandy to splash over the rim of his glass. If he was feeling such pleasure at the prospect of becoming a father and Anne was also deriving such great delight at the anticipation of caring for this child . . . what was Lizzy feeling? What must she be going through? He shook his head in wonderment at his own insensitivity. Was Lizzy's opinion of him correct? Was he the arrogant and selfish man she had described?

God help him, *he was.*

~*~

Charles Bingley entered Darcy's townhouse. The look of determination of his face was unmistakable. "Darcy, it is good to see you again." His words came out automatically and without thought as he brushed past his friend to enter the study.

"It is indeed a pleasure to see you again too, Bingley," said Darcy with more sincerity.

Noting that Bingley seemed rather tense, it was obvious he had something he wished to get out in the open. "Won't you join me in a brandy?" Darcy asked.

Bingley paced the room, seemingly unaware of the unanswered question still resonating in the air. By the look on his face, he was obviously gathering his thoughts in anticipation of their conversation.

"Bingley, whatever is the matter with you? Come sit down and join me in a brandy," said Darcy, slightly amused at his friend's distracted state.

Bingley did as he was bid and sat down in one of the comfortable overstuffed chairs in front of the fireplace. As Darcy handed him his drink, he took a seat in the matching chair across from Bingley's.

"There, that's better," said Darcy. "Now, what seems to be the cause of your distress?"

After a slight pause, Bingley took a deep breath. "I have thought long and hard about what I am about to tell you, Darcy. And although I truly value our friendship, I am afraid that what I have to say will greatly jeopardize our future relationship." Bingley did not look at his friend during this discourse. He knew he would not be able to continue if he did.

Darcy sat very still as he listened to his friend's words. He had never heard Bingley speak with such resolve before. Whatever the subject matter was, he knew it must be of a very serious nature and that his response would be of the utmost importance.

"I have tried to be a grateful friend and have always appreciated how well you have counselled me on both business and personal matters. I am also well aware that your friendship and good opinion has reinforced my position in society." With that, Bingley rose and started to pace the room.

Darcy looked up with great concern as his eyes followed his friend's path across his study. Indeed, it seemed their roles were now reversed. Was it not usually Darcy who was the one pacing the room?

Again, Bingley continued, still unable to make eye contact with his friend. "I have never questioned your counsel in the past, for I have always believed that you had my best interests at heart. But now I must challenge the motives of your advice regarding my attentions towards Miss Bennet."

"Miss Bennet?"

"Yes, Miss Bennet! Miss Bennet!! Surely you do not believe that I have forgotten her? I have not had a moment's peace since I wrote that horrid letter to her. What must she think of me?"

Darcy was at first at a loss for words. He had to admit to himself he was somewhat relieved. He was imagining something far worse than this. But, to think that Bingley had put himself through such torture over Miss Bennet because of something he had said to him was astonishing. Did Bingley truly think he would lose his friendship if he continued to see her?

Darcy stood and walked to the mantle, at first staring into the fire. After a few moments, he turned to face his friend.

"Bingley, I am saddened and truly sorry that I have caused you such distress. I had no idea that my words to you that day would be taken in such a way. It was never my intention to discourage your relationship with Miss Bennet. If not for Caroline's insistence that I speak with you, I would not have intervened at all. I only promised her that I would point out the disadvantages of such a match, just as I would advise any gentleman whom I consider a friend.

"You are master of your own destiny, Bingley. It is your opinion and your opinion alone that should rule your actions. I felt that if you were truly in love with Miss Bennet, my words of caution would have little influence over you. I truly apologize for my interference."

"But what about your abhorrence to her being a governess? Are you saying that you do not find this to be unpardonable? Surely *you* would never have considered courting someone in domestic service."

For some reason, when Caroline had expressed that opinion, it did not seem to have the same impact as Bingley saying it now. Darcy shook his head and smiled a mirthless smile.

"I will tell you something, Bingley, although I doubt very much you will believe me. I have learned much about life this past year. Some of the things that I thought were most important have turned out not to be so. I have learned that regardless of one's station in life, where matters of the heart are concerned, we are all on equal ground. Do not be so quick to judge me."

Bingley looked at his friend as if for the first time. Was he just as vulnerable and susceptible to life's uncertainties as everyone else? Apparently, he was. For some reason that made his friendship even more valuable than before. For the first time since their acquaintance, Bingley felt that they were equals; that their friendship would take on a whole new meaning from this day forward. And for that he was grateful.

"I have been a fool. To blame you for my own lack of conviction is indefensible. Can I then assume I have your approval?" asked Bingley.

"Do you need my approval?" retorted Darcy.

"No, but I should like to think I have it anyway."

"Then, you have it!" said Darcy with a smile as the two gentlemen shook hands.

Pat Santarsiero

CHAPTER TWENTY-FOUR

It was April, and Anne had used every excuse she could think of to avoid a visit from her mother. Now she knew she could no longer keep her away. With Easter approaching, Lady Catherine had insisted she would journey to Pemberley to spend the holiday with her dear daughter and nephew.

Anne's cough, which had been somewhat subdued, had begun again to worsen. Darcy blamed himself for not curtailing her activities in the preparation of the nursery. She was obsessed with its being completed before May and had spent many hours going over every detail. When she was seen moving the bassinette to a different location in the room for the third time in one afternoon, Darcy finally had to ban her from the room altogether.

The crowning glory of the nursery was the rocking chair Darcy had sent her. He had seen it shipped before he left London, and its arrival had coincided with his, so that both Darcy and the rocking chair reached Anne the same afternoon. It was exquisite. The beautifully handcrafted wood was carved with small delicate butterflies, and she could just imagine herself rocking the baby to sleep each night whilst sitting in it.

Darcy was more nervous than he cared to admit upon receiving the news of his aunt's visit. He did not know how proficient Anne was at play acting, but he doubted his own abilities with much certainty. How Anne had persuaded Mrs. Reynolds to go along with her scheme, he had no idea, but the elderly housekeeper seemed more than willing to be an accomplice in their charade.

As he paced the foyer, he anxiously awaited Richard's arrival. He needed to make sure that his cousin was well acquainted with the circumstances and that he would behave himself in front of their aunt.

It was decided that they would have Anne nestled on the larger divan in the parlour amidst many bed clothes for most of Aunt Catherine's visit. With so much bedding, it would be hard to discern where Anne ended and the bed clothes began. Hopefully this camouflage would help complete the illusion of Anne's increased size.

When she finally arrived, Lady Catherine entered the parlour with a vigour that belied her years. "Oh, my dear daughter, how good it is to see you!" She then approached Anne and bent down to kiss her cheek. This action caused Anne to startle, and an amused smile spread across her face. *I have finally been able to please my mother,* she thought.

Mrs. Reynolds, for her part, executed a flawless performance. She exhibited just enough concern for Anne to convince Lady Catherine that her daughter's condition was cause for a certain amount of apprehension as with any confinement, but that there was no need for any undue anxiety.

Darcy's nervousness at the deception was misinterpreted by Lady Catherine as worry over Anne's ability to successfully bear the child she carried. On one particular evening after dinner, Lady Catherine felt it her duty to proclaim that Anne would have no difficulty giving birth and, of course, assured Darcy that she would bear him a son.

Georgiana spent most of Lady Catherine's visit with a perplexed look on her face. She could not account for her brother and cousin's strange behaviour; Fitzwilliam looked to be a nervous wreck, and Richard acted like the cat that swallowed the canary. What were they about?

One evening Darcy almost panicked as Lady Catherine approached a sleeping Anne and patted her stomach. To his surprise, his aunt did not react with alarm to this endeavour. To his relief, he later learned that Mrs. Reynolds had placed a small pillow under Anne's dressing gown for just such a likelihood.

Richard was having an exceptionally good time enjoying himself at Darcy's expense. He spent most of the visit with an amused look on his face and on a few occasions had even burst into laughter at Darcy's obvious unease.

As for Anne herself, to her surprise, she was quite enjoying being the centre of attention. Her mother had never displayed such condescension towards her before, and the pleasure was acute indeed. She had also discovered a little ploy to help her with her coughing bouts.

At Easter dinner, Anne, though never one to indulge in alcohol, had partaken in a glass of wine to celebrate the day. She noticed that after she had imbibed the wine, she did not cough for several hours.

On this particular evening, she had already partaken in *three* glasses of wine in order to subdue her cough. This was done without anyone's notice, except for the servant who dutifully refilled her glass each time she emptied it. After dinner had been completed, Georgiana had been called upon to play the pianoforte. She happily took her place in front of the instrument.

As she began to play, to everyone's surprise, Anne suddenly broke into song. Her voice, at first faint, grew in strength and was not particularly melodious.

Richard, who was highly amused by this, immediately joined his cousin in her vocal efforts, and both were now singing off key and at the top of their lungs. Georgiana at first faltered with her playing, but quickly recovered and accompanied their singing as best she could.

Observing their joyful countenances, she could not resist joining in, and soon all three were singing gaily. As they sang, they all looked at each other and displayed the happiest of smiles.

Lady Catherine sat quite horrified with her mouth agape, wondering what had gotten into her quiet, well-bred daughter. Expecting to see the same look of dismay on her nephew's face, she turned towards Darcy only to find him grinning from ear to ear. It was the first time since Aunt Catherine's arrival that he had actually relaxed and enjoyed himself.

~*~

Jane Bennet took a seat on the park bench she had adopted as her own. Caleb, now three, was no longer content to sit idly beside Jane and so joined his brother and sister as they played by the pond. It was one of those perfect early May mornings.

She had spent the previous evening in the company of her Aunt and Uncle Gardiner and had read them Lizzy's latest letter. All three were in much anticipation at seeing her again, but Elizabeth's letter indicated that she was still unsure of her plans. She said she hoped she would be able to visit sometime during the summer, but as yet her plans were not fixed.

As Jane sat there contemplating such a happy event, a figure was approaching in her direction. She caught a glimpse of the gentleman from the corner of her eye, and as she turned her attention to look upon him, she immediately startled at the recognition.

As he approached the park bench, he slowed his pace, giving himself time to gauge her reaction. When he saw her surprised look change to one of dismay, he felt his determination waver, but knowing it was too late to turn back, he continued his course until he was standing before her.

"Jane . . . eh, Miss Bennet, might you favour me with your company this fine morning?" he asked with a great deal more confidence than he felt.

She looked up into his eyes. The shock of seeing him so suddenly, combined with the stress she had endured over the past several months, overwhelmed her. She immediately burst into tears, hiding her face in her hands.

Bingley sat down, quite at a loss at how to comfort her or even if she would welcome his efforts. The desire to embrace her was almost irresistible; however, the situation of their public viewing prohibited any such indulgence.

He felt the full force of his guilt at causing her such pain. "Please, Miss Bennet, I beg you, please do not cry." He slowly pulled her hands from her face and looked lovingly into her eyes. He then gently wiped her tears away.

"Can you ever find it in your heart to forgive my callous behaviour?" he asked.

Despite her tears, Jane managed a weak smile.

"I have been a fool. I know I deserve no such consideration from you, and you have every right to reject me, but I beg you to please give me another chance."

Jane sat in bewilderment. Able neither to speak nor even to form a coherent thought, she continued to stare at him in silence. Bingley, misinterpreting her silence, hung his head and looked down, his only thought being, *I've lost her!*

As he was about to rise to leave, he felt the gentle touch of her hand on his cheek. As he lifted his eyes to meet hers, he saw the love she felt for him, the love he had heartlessly disregarded. He put his hand over hers and brought it to his lips, kissing her palm softly. They both stood and, defying propriety, embraced. Without need for words, they came to a complete understanding. They would be together for the rest of their lives.

CHAPTER TWENTY-FIVE

The lateness of the month was beginning to take its toll on the many awaiting the arrival of the future Master of Pemberley. Georgiana was probably the least concerned, as she was enjoying her visit with her Aunt and Uncle Matlock. She was looking forward to becoming an aunt, and such was her nature that she could not imagine anything untoward happening that might diminish that happy prospect.

Caroline Bingley had been anxiously awaiting any news related to the event, especially after hearing Dr. Adams's surprising disclosure. She felt confident that if either Anne or the child should not survive as the doctor had suggested, she would still have a chance to win Mr. Darcy.

If only the child survived, Mr. Darcy would, of course, need a wife to raise the child. If only Anne survived, he would have to acknowledge his mistake in choosing such a sickly girl to bear his future heir. Caroline was certain she would find a way to benefit from either outcome.

The only drawback at having used her charms to persuade Dr. Adams to divulge Mrs. Darcy's condition was that he was now convinced of her affection for him. Not wanting to completely discourage his advances, certain there was still more to the story than he had revealed, she had allowed him the liberty of her kisses. Although it was not wholly unpleasant to be the object of such attentions, she would have to sever the relationship soon so that she might be free to pursue Mr. Darcy once again.

~*~

Anne's nervousness could not have been more genuine had she actually been with child herself. Each day she waited patiently for some news. Her anxiety and anticipation were having their effects upon her health. She confined her daily activities between her bed chamber and the nursery, which was now completed to perfection. Many afternoons found her rocking in the beautiful chair Darcy had bought for her. She longed for the day that she would hold his child in her arms.

~*~

Elizabeth's demeanour was abnormally calm. She was determined not to dwell on the inevitable fate that awaited her and her child. She knew she must abide by the terms of the agreement.

In moments of pure fantasy, she envisioned herself fleeing from the small cottage, her child in her arms, to seek refuge with Mrs. Worthington. Or perhaps she and her child could secure passage aboard a ship destined for America. Even after the fulfilment of all of Wickham's demands and the money she had sent her mother, she still had some funds available to her. But she knew such thoughts were all just idle musings. She awoke each morning with the hope that today would be the day that ended this torture.

~*~

Darcy had been sitting there for almost a half hour looking down at the cottage. He had not witnessed any activity since his arrival and was deep in thought. For the last several days, he had made the journey religiously in hopes of discerning some news regarding the birth of his child. Monday, Tuesday and Wednesday had passed, one day into the next, without incident.

If daily routine was followed, Lizzy would soon be walking the nearby woods behind the cottage. This practice had resumed two months prior, upon the arrival of more pleasant temperatures.

Just as he thought upon it, she appeared in the doorway of the cottage. He watched as she tied the ribbons of her bonnet and noted that her hair was not pinned but fell around her shoulders. She stretched her arms over her head and gave an approving look at the day around her.

Most recently she had taken to walk the same route each day, as it was the shortest and accommodated her now somewhat limited capabilities. As she made her way behind the cottage and towards the wooded area, he lost sight of her. She would usually reappear about fifteen minutes later. This was always the longest fifteen minutes of his day.

He decided to make use of today's time by thinking of names for his child. If it was a boy, he was partial to George after his father, or perhaps Geoffrey after his grandfather. If it was a girl, he thought Anne would be appropriate as it was his wife's and his mother's name.

His mind then wandered, and he let himself entertain the thought of naming the child after its mother. He wondered if Lizzy was short for Elizabeth. He had imagined it was. Would Elizabeth Anne be inappropriate? He made a mental note to look up his family history to see if there was indeed an *Elizabeth* somewhere amongst his past relations to which he could point, should he be questioned about such a choice.

He pulled out his fob and noted that it had been more than twenty minutes since Lizzy had entered the woods. Given her condition, he decided to give her a few more minutes before he became alarmed. After all, she was moving much slower of late.

At first he thought the sound he heard was emanating from the branches below as their leaves swayed in the wind. However, as the sound continued, he realized that the trees were not the source of such sounds. He suddenly saw Hannah run from the cottage towards the woods. Quickly he kicked Marengo into action and galloped down the ridge, past the cottage, to where he had last seen Lizzy.

As he manoeuvred Marengo into the woods, he called to her. Upon hearing her again, he followed the sound of her voice. He was soon upon her and immediately jumped from Marengo to her side. She was on her knees, both hands protectively over her stomach. She was obviously in much pain.

"Lizzy!" he cried. "What has happened? Are you hurt?" He lowered himself and knelt beside her. "Tell me what has happened!"

As she looked into his eyes, the surprise on her face was immediately replaced by one of relief that he had so quickly come to her aide. She tried to calm herself as her accelerated breathing made it very difficult to speak. "I do not know exactly. I was walking . . ." again she took a moment to catch her breath, "I was walking back towards the cottage, when I suddenly felt a sharp pain . . . here." She indicated the lower portion of her very protruding belly and immediately turned a crimson red. "I . . . I tried to continue . . . but another pain . . . brought me to my knees."

"Do you think you can stand?" he asked.

"I do not know. I shall try." As she spoke another pain gripped her, and she grabbed his hand, squeezing it tightly.

At that moment, Hannah reached them. "Quickly!" he said. "We must try to get her into the cottage. As Hannah went to Lizzy's other side, Darcy instructed her to help him lift Lizzy to a standing position. Slowly, they gently raised her from her knees. As Lizzy was about to place her weight on her feet, another pain seized her, and she immediately crumbled. Darcy caught her and lifted her up before she reached the ground.

Without another thought, he positioned her carefully in his arms. "Hold on to me," he instructed. She did as he asked and put one arm around his neck, resting her head against his shoulder as another pain swept over her body.

As quickly and carefully as he could manage, he carried her back to the cottage. Hannah ran slightly ahead and led Darcy towards

Lizzy's bed chamber. He gently placed her atop the covers. As he went to leave her side, she grabbed his hand and once again squeezed it tightly.

He quickly turned towards Hannah and asked more sharply than he had intended, "When is the midwife expected?"

"She usually arrives around three o'clock, sir," answered a much shaken Hannah.

With his free hand he pulled out his watch; it was just eleven o'clock.

"I will go and bring her," said Darcy.

"No!" cried Elizabeth as she strengthened her hold on his hand. "Please, do not leave me!"

He reached for the chair beside the bed and moved it closer to sit beside her. Softly he spoke to her. "Lizzy, you cannot stay like this for another four hours. I will go and bring the midwife back as quickly as I can. Hannah will be here with you. You will not be alone."

He brought her hand to his lips and kissed it tenderly, then stoked her fingers reassuringly. "I promise you, Lizzy, I will make haste. You must try to relax and calm yourself. Promise me you will try."

"I am sorry; you are right, of course," she breathed. "Yes . . . I shall try to do as you ask." Their eyes locked for a long moment.

"I will leave you now," he said as he slowly withdrew his hand from hers.

"William," she called as he turned to her one last time. "Thank you."

Pat Santarsiero

CHAPTER TWENTY-SIX

Mrs. Pearson quickly entered the cottage, immediately calling to Hannah to boil water and bring some towels. As she approached the bed, she took Lizzy's hand. "Are you in much pain, dear?"

"It . . . it comes and goes," she answered. At that moment another contraction bore down on her, and she cried out.

Darcy had immediately followed Mrs. Pearson into the cottage and rushed to the doorway of the bed chamber upon hearing Lizzy's cries.

As Mrs. Pearson turned to see him there, she demanded that he stop. "Sir, you must not be here! This is woman's work. You must wait outside!" When he made no attempt to move, she became more adamant. "Sir, unless you are this woman's husband, I must insist that you leave immediately!" With that, she instructed Hannah to close the door behind him.

He dutifully left the room and heard the closing of the door. As much as he knew he should not be there in the cottage, he could not bring himself to leave. His son or daughter was being born in the next room, and he would not rest until he knew that his child had been safely delivered.

His departure from her room did little to lessen the sounds emanating from Lizzy's bed chamber. He could hear the reassuring and encouraging voice of Mrs. Pearson instructing Lizzy to breathe and not to bear down yet. As her cries increased in length and volume, he was now somewhat grateful to be on his side of the door. After many hours of pacing, he finally heard the sound that he had been praying for—the sound of a child's hearty cry.

Inside the bed chamber, an exhausted Elizabeth looked up to see Mrs. Pearson holding a tiny bundle. She automatically reached out to the child, and Mrs. Pearson carefully placed it in her arms. As she moved the soft fabric away from the tiny infant's face, her heart melted.

"Boy or girl?" she quietly asked.

"It is a healthy little girl," said Mrs. Pearson. "And she appears to be the exact likeness of you, her eyes especially."

Indeed, there was no doubt about it. The tiny little girl was already graced with swirls of dark chestnut curls and the same dark eyes as her mother.

Tears filled Elizabeth's eyes as she gazed upon her daughter. She wondered how much time she had before the child would be taken from her; how long before her heart would break. Afraid to ask, she clung to the little girl and softly wept.

As the full effects of her strenuous afternoon converged upon her, Elizabeth succumbed to sleep. Hannah had been waiting in anticipation for just that occurrence and lifted the child from atop its mother.

Just before she was about to place the baby girl in the cradle, she had a second thought and started towards the door.

"Where are you taking the child?" asked Mrs. Pearson. Without answering her, she continued into the other room where she had no doubt the gentleman still remained.

Their eyes met briefly in understanding, and she gently placed the child into his hands. "It is a girl, sir," she stated.

Darcy looked down at his daughter. As he gazed upon her dark eyes and dark curly hair, the love he immediately felt for her overwhelmed him. He then turned towards Hannah. "How is Lizzy?" his voice hoarse and barely above a whisper.

"She is sleeping now, but I am told she will be well. She came through the birth with no problems, sir." Hesitantly she added, "Mrs. Pearson is to notify Mr. Gallagher of the birth immediately upon her return. Mistress will have only a day or two at the most to spend with the child."

She collected the tiny baby from his arms and returned to the bed chamber.

~*~

As Darcy made his way back to Pemberley, his mind was much engaged. The thrill of holding his child in his arms had not yet left him. He was intoxicated with happiness and pride. He did not care that he was not granted a son. He had neither title to pass down nor entailment to cause him concern. The birth of this child, this beautiful little girl, was his finest hour.

He had wanted to break down the door to Lizzy's bed chamber and get on his knees to her, to thank her for this wonderful gift she had given him.

How could he just walk away from her now? His mind recaptured the look in Lizzy's eyes as she had grasped his hand and implored him not to leave her. Knowing that their association would now be terminated was unbearable. He no longer had any excuse to seek her out.

His emotions dictated that he must profess to her his feelings of gratitude and admiration for all she had endured. Yes, he would write her and thank her for providing him with the greatest gift of his life.

~*~

There was much excitement and activity as the news of the birth spread throughout Pemberley. Mr. Gallagher had arranged it so that the child would be brought to the estate in the middle of the night. As soon as Mr. Darcy had informed Mrs. Reynolds of the birth, she had immediately sent for the wet nurse she had hired the month before.

With the child now safely nestled in Anne's arms, her joy was boundless. She gently traced her fingers over the little girl's cheek as she slowly rocked her. The child looked so much like her husband, she thought, with his many dark features. Yet there was something different about the eyes. Fitzwilliam had deep brown eyes, but these eyes were almost black as coal. The child was undeniably beautiful. She would love this child as her own.

As Darcy entered the nursery, he smiled at the picture of his wife and daughter in the rocking chair. Anne looked up and greeted him as he kissed her cheek and his daughter's brow.

"We have yet to discuss a name, Fitzwilliam," said Anne.

"Tis true. Have you given it any thought?" he answered.

"I admit, I have not thought of girls' names at all, so convinced was I that it should be a boy. After all, did not my mother assure you of it?" she asked with a slight smile upon her face. "Have *you* any preferences?"

He remained silent for a moment. "I assumed if it was a girl we would name her after you and my mother," he said. "Perhaps we could use "Elizabeth" as a middle name. I . . . I believe it was the name of my mother's aunt. How does Anne Elizabeth sound to you?" he asked, not quite audacious enough to suggest Elizabeth Anne.

"I rather fancy it, Fitzwilliam, but I think it best we not call her Anne. That might prove to be too confusing. We could call her by her middle name perhaps.

Startled for a second, he almost flinched. "I have no objections if you do not. Are you sure that is your desire?"

"Yes, I think that would suit her. We could call her Ellie or perhaps Beth," replied Anne. "There are several names that are short for Elizabeth."

"Good, then it is settled. Miss Anne Elizabeth Darcy, welcome to Pemberley," he said with a gallant bow before his yawning, unimpressed daughter.

As the child began to fidget, the wet nurse was called for. Anne handed her daughter over to be fed, and Darcy helped his wife up from the chair and offered her his arm.

"Shall we have breakfast sent up to the sitting room? he inquired.

"Yes, that will be fine, except I need a moment to refresh, Fitzwilliam. I will join you there shortly."

As she made her way towards her chambers, her cough could no longer be suppressed. She knew the remission that had subdued the ill effects of her condition was abating. Fitzwilliam was sure that the return of her once again persistent cough was attributed to her recent exertions in preparing the nursery and that it would soon desist. She hoped, rather than believed, it to be true.

God had granted her the time she needed to complete her plan, but she selfishly wanted more. She prayed for more time to be a mother to their child, time for them to be a family.

~*~

Hannah awakened to find the cottage empty. As she ran outside to find her mistress, her search was quickly and with much relief truncated as she discovered Elizabeth slowly pacing the path in front of the cottage.

"Miss, you ought not be on your feet so soon!" cried Hannah. "Mrs. Pearson said you should not venture outside the cottage for several days."

Her words seemed to have little effect upon her mistress, as she gave no indication that she had heard them. Hannah went to her side and gently led her back towards the cottage door. "Please,

Miss, come inside and lie down. You need rest to give your body a chance to restore itself."

Although she complied, she barely comprehended Hannah's words. Her mind was numb. It was best right now that it remain so.

It was the thirtieth day of May, three days following the birth of her daughter. Even though she had relinquished her child to Mr. Gallagher in the early hours of the preceding morning, Elizabeth could still smell the newborn's scent on the small bed clothes she had been wrapped in. She could still feel the warmth of the tiny body cuddled closely to hers and the small mouth on her breast as Mrs. Pearson had instructed her to the suckling of her child. To know she would never experience these things again was unbearable. She only wanted to feel nothing.

As she looked around the cottage, her only thought was to flee. She could stay there for another month if she wished, but she had no desire to remain where memories of her child flooded her mind. At that moment she had no idea *what* she wanted to do. She did not want to stay there, but it was too soon for her to face Jane or her Aunt and Uncle Gardiner. She would not be able to conceal her grief from them.

She went to her dresser and pulled out the letter she had read several times already, the letter that William had handed to Hannah yesterday.

May 29, 1812

Dear Lizzy,

Be not alarmed on receiving this letter, for my only purpose is to express those feelings which I must unburden to you.

Though propriety may disallow it, I must speak of what is in my heart. I am filled with such gratitude that I know my mere words cannot do justice to convey my feelings. Nothing else in my life will ever compare to the joy I now know as I look upon my daughter's beautiful face. To know that my joy must also be your sorrow brings me pain.

I know at what cost to your happiness you have sacrificed for the good of your family. Your selflessness and goodness have shamed me.

Above all, I wish to tell you of my deepest regret for my words and actions that day I visited you at the cottage. To have made such an improper suggestion was quite unforgiveable, and yet, I beg your forgiveness for it would be hard to know that you are alive in the world and thinking ill of me.

I will always think upon you with great affection and tender regard, for you have truly changed my life in ways you cannot possibly know. You will always be in my thoughts and prayers.

May God bless you and keep you safe.

Yours most gratefully,

William

The tears she shed made the last line impossible to read, but it mattered not, for she now knew the letter by heart.

She thought of Mrs. Worthington. She had offered her help several months ago. Perhaps she could seek refuge there until she was strong enough to face her family. She would write to her this very afternoon.

CHAPTER TWENTY-SEVEN

"Caroline, I have received wonderful news. Mr. and Mrs. Darcy are the proud parents of a baby girl!" exclaimed an enthusiastic Bingley.

"Are you sure?" asked a surprised Caroline. "Both the child and Mrs. Darcy survived?"

"Yes, of course, I'm sure. I just received a letter from Darcy himself, telling me of the event. He has asked us to attend the christening ceremony next month."

"Who are to be godparents?" asked Caroline hopefully.

"Well, he did not say, but I am assuming it is to be his sister and Colonel Fitzwilliam. They stood up for them at their wedding. Is it not customary that they be godparents to their first born?"

"And Mrs. Darcy has suffered no ill effects from the birth? You are sure?" inquired a much agitated Caroline.

"I know of none. Darcy did not elaborate in his letter, but I assume all is well. What makes you ask such a thing?" inquired her brother.

"No particular reason, Charles. I am just aware of how fragile Mrs. Darcy's health has always been."

Though he would like to believe that Caroline truly had concern for Mrs. Darcy's wellbeing, he could not help but doubt the sincerity of her words.

"Well, you shall see for yourself when we visit next month," said Bingley.

"Yes, I am most looking forward to it, Brother. Oh, by the way, Charles, I think I will invite Dr. Adams to dine with us this evening. Will you be at home?"

"I'm afraid I have already made other plans, Caroline. But, please do not change your plans on my account. Louisa and Mr. Hurst can help you entertain him," replied Bingley.

Caroline already knew that her sister and brother were going out for the evening but made no mention of it. There was definitely something not quite right about this whole situation, and Caroline was determined to get to the bottom of it. Dr. Adams had been quite adamant in his opinion that Anne would not be strong enough to bear a child. He had even intimated that she had previously failed at such an attempt. If she could procure any information regarding the birth from Dr. Adams, perhaps she could use it to her advantage.

"Yes, I think that would work out well, Charles," she said as she smiled her sweetest smile.

~*~

"I was most . . . delighted . . . to hear of Mrs. Darcy's safe delivery," said Caroline as she led Dr. Adams from dinner into the parlour. "I hear that she encountered no difficulties giving birth."

"I, too, was quite surprised on learning such news," replied Dr. Adams as he took a seat on the couch. "But as Lady Catherine informed me herself of the birth I had no cause to doubt it."

As she settled in next to the doctor she allowed for little room between them.

"*Did* you have cause to doubt it, sir?" she asked as reached for his hand.

"I admit I did find it a rather perplexing verity," suggested Dr. Adams.

As she held his hand in hers, she slowly brought it to her breast as she whispered, "Dr. Adams, you indeed make it sound quite mysterious."

Encouraged by such an act, Dr. Adams allowed his arm to encircle her. "I would say indeed it is almost miraculous," he replied. "But a happy outcome for everyone, I assure you, Miss Bingley."

The truth was that if Lady Catherine had not personally informed him of the birth, he *would not* have believed it. Indeed, he had his own theories as to the actual circumstances that had produced an heir to Pemberley. Since he had advised Mr. Darcy regarding the danger to himself should he resume intimacies with his wife due to the consumption and he had also cautioned him of the danger to Anne should she again find herself with child, he found it almost incomprehensible that he would so thoroughly disregard his warnings. No, he was convinced Mr. Darcy had taken his advisements most seriously.

Caroline put her head on his shoulder and sighed, "Oh, you don't know how happy I am to hear such news, Dr. Adams."

"Your devotion to your friend is admirable, Miss Bingley. I am sure she is grateful for such a friend as you."

"You flatter me, Dr. Adams," said Caroline as she now looked deep into his eyes.

He moved closer and slowly moved his mouth towards hers. Just before their lips were about to meet, she asked, "So, it is your opinion that Mrs. Darcy is now in the best of health?"

Dr. Adams found his usual strict adherence to his Hippocratic Oath somewhat obscured by the amount of wine he had partaken at dinner and the fact that his libido was causing havoc with his better judgment. "Well, I wouldn't exactly say that," he replied as he again made his way towards her lips. As they kissed, Dr. Adams was at first tentative, but, as he gauged her reaction, he allowed that she was receptive to his attentions.

Caroline, certain the doctor had knowledge which would help her plight, was prepared to take whatever measures were necessary in order to attain the information she needed. However, the only way she could tolerate Dr. Adams's lips upon hers was to pretend that those lips belonged to Mr. Darcy. With that thought in mind, she found she was able to bear Dr. Adams's advances quite tolerably. As they broke from their kiss, she pulled away and asked, "What do you mean by that, sir?"

Not wishing to spend the rest of the evening discussing Mrs. Darcy's health when there were other things he would much rather be doing, he quickly intimated, "I believe Mrs. Darcy successfully bearing a child in her precarious health has raised many questions in my mind, but perhaps it is best not to speculate on such things."

"Of course, I understand, Dr. Adams. But are you suggesting you do not believe that all is at it seems?"

Reluctant to let this opportunity of intimacy pass, he had no choice but to appease her. He hastily replied, "Miss Bingley, I promise I will tell you all I know later," while impatiently pulling her into a deep embrace.

"Do I have your word, sir?" asked Caroline as she resisted his arms.

"You have my word, Madam."

As she heard his declaration, she willingly succumbed to his embrace, knowing that by evening's end she would learn everything there was to know. She was almost giddy with anticipation as she tried to imagine what truths she would soon uncover.

Refocusing her mind to the task at hand, Caroline acquiesced to the demanding lips that sought hers, and with thoughts of Mr. Darcy running through her head, she surrendered to the doctor's attentions. As his hands began to explore, Caroline was in heaven as she again imagined that it was Mr. Darcy's hands that now swept enticingly over her body.

Thursday's Child

So engrossed was she in her world of fantasy that she did not notice the point at which hands no longer caressed her nor lips sought her own. As she pulled back to look at Dr. Adams, his eyes were wide with fright. He grabbed his chest as his body slumped forward and fell atop of hers.

With a scream that would shatter glass, she wrenched her body from beneath his and quickly stood. As she slowly moved back towards him, she could discern no breathing. "Dr. Adams?" she called softly. There was no response. Her voice now giving rise to panic, she spoke more sharply. "Please, Dr. Adams! You cannot die! You must tell me! Dr. Adams! Dr. Adams!"

Such was the scene that Charles Bingley observed as he entered his parlour that evening.

~*~

Darcy had spent the morning with his steward, inspecting the crops on his land. The vegetation was growing hearty, and it promised to be a profitable season for his tenants. He had spent an overly abundant amount of time recently attending to such business, and his steward had repeatedly assured him that his presence was not necessary and that he would not need his assistance again until the harvest. But, Darcy had insisted on accompanying him.

When he returned to the house, he immediately went to the nursery to look upon his daughter. The wet nurse, Mrs. Hawkins, was sitting quietly in the corner reading a book. She nodded her head as he entered. Ellie was sleeping peacefully with her thumb strategically placed in her mouth. He brushed his hand across her soft chestnut curls and kissed her tenderly on her ear.

He made his way down to the music room, following the sounds emanating from the pianoforte. Anne was seated at the instrument and looked up, making an effort to smile as he approached her. "You are back early today, Fitzwilliam," she stated as she stopped her playing.

She quickly hid her handkerchief within the folds of her gown. Had he arrived fifteen minutes earlier he would have witnessed a very distressful coughing bout. Hoping that her countenance had returned to a composed state, she asked about his morning.

He approached her and kissed her forehead and, with some concern, asked how she was feeling. "I am quite well, Fitzwilliam. Why do you ask?"

"Your forehead felt a little warm just now," he replied. "Do you think perhaps we should send for Dr. Chisholm?"

"No. Really, Fitzwilliam, I do not require a doctor. Perhaps it is just that it is so hot today. Truly I am well."

The news of Dr. Adams's death had been extremely upsetting for Anne. He had been her doctor her entire life, and she was not comfortable allowing anyone else to attend her. Also, she did not want to have to answer any questions from Dr. Chisholm regarding the birth of their child. Dr. Chisholm and Dr. Adams had each believed the other had attended her during her "confinement." What if he could somehow detect that she had not given birth? It was best that he stay away. No, she did not want any doctor to examine her. She had more to lose than gain by his attendance.

Dr. Adams had recommended some elixirs to help her resistance when he had first attended Anne at Pemberley. Mrs. Reynolds had made sure that she continued to faithfully drink the concoction each morning, being quite convinced that it had been the miracle cure that had sustained her these many months.

Anne, however, knew differently. She knew her life was going according to whatever plan had been devised for her by someone with much a more pre-eminent title than "doctor."

~*~

Darcy paced the length of his library. It was Friday morning, and once again he was determined to occupy his day in some useful manner, but even *he* could not impose himself on his steward for the fifth day in a row. He knew he was using his presence overseeing the fields as a deterrent to riding where he really wanted to go.

He wanted to say goodbye to her. He wanted one last look at the woman who had changed his life and the way he looked at the world. He wanted to hear her voice call him "William" one more time.

It was mid-June. In two weeks she would be gone. If he did not go to her soon, it would be too late.

As he headed toward the stables, he shook his head at his own obstinacy. He had his groom saddle up Marengo, and both he and the horse knew exactly where they were headed.

When he approached the cottage, he looked down from his perch upon the ridge and saw Hannah conversing with the older man who delivered the supplies. He felt reassured as he witnessed this scene that no changes to the daily routine of the cottage had yet occurred.

A moment later the young helper exited the cottage dragging a large trunk and carrying several parcels. After placing all that he carried into the wagon, the young man helped Hannah onto the seat and within moments all three of them were gone.

Perplexed as to why Hannah would leave Lizzy alone, he approached the cottage. He hoped she would see him. He hoped his letter had softened her opinion of him. He hoped she no longer hated him.

He knocked at the door and waited . . . there was no answer. He again knocked, a bit louder this time, thinking perhaps she slept; still . . . no answer. He called to her . . . silence. He then tried the latch, and it turned easily in his hand as he opened the door. He called to her again, but only the echo of her name filled the room.

As he entered the cottage, he looked around the small sitting room they had occupied that first day he had visited. He remembered pacing this same carpet just three short weeks ago as he awaited the birth of his child, and he now stood in the same spot where

Hannah had first placed his daughter in his arms. The room was now empty.

As realization dawned, frantically he entered Lizzy's bed chamber to find it also empty and devoid of all personal affects. Gone were the ribbons and hair brush that had been just recently sitting atop the dresser. Gone was the bottle of lavender scented water that she had used in her hair.

As he turned to look upon the barren room, he saw the painting that had escaped his notice that day. As he studied it, he noted the small plaque confirming the familiar scene of the beach he and Lizzy had walked upon together. Had she bought this as a reminder of their time together? Why had she left it behind?

He removed the small painting from the wall and looked upon it with sadness. He knew in his heart why she had not taken it with her. She was leaving all that had occurred between them behind her. She wanted no reminders of their attachment.

However, he also knew that she would not be successful in this endeavour, just as he would not. No matter where they each travelled or how much distance and time lay between them, they would be forever connected through the child they had created.

Darcy left the cottage and carefully tied the painting to his saddle. He looked at the cottage one last time as he turned his horse back towards Pemberley. He knew it was for the best, but that did not stop the flood of sadness and regret that filled his heart.

Monday's child is fair of face,
Tuesday's child is full of grace,
Wednesday's child is full of woe,
Thursday's child has far to go.

TO THINE OWN SELF BE TRUE

CHAPTER TWENTY-EIGHT

"Lizzy!" cried her sister Jane. "What a happy surprise! Why did you not write us of your plans?" The two sisters hugged for several minutes as Lizzy could barely find the strength to pull herself away from Jane's comforting arms. Her tears would not be denied.

"Lizzy, are you unwell?"

"No, no. I am well, Jane. I am just so happy to see you. I have missed you so much," said an overcome Lizzy as she hugged her dear sister once more.

Mrs. Gardiner rushed to the two sisters and gave Lizzy an equally long and comforting embrace. "Oh, my dear niece, what joy to finally see you! When you did not come this summer, we had almost given up hope of ever seeing you again! You have been gone so long, Lizzy. But why did you not write to tell us you would be with us for Christmas?"

"I. . . I did not want to give you false hope in case I was unable to come."

"Well, come inside and have some tea," said her aunt. "You must be exhausted from your long journey."

"Lizzy, are you sure you are well; you look so pale," said Jane with much concern in her voice.

"Jane, I assure you I am fine." Wanting desperately to change the focus of attention away from herself, Elizabeth congratulated Jane on her engagement.

"I only met Mr. Bingley briefly, but I could tell that day that he was already in a fair way to being in love with you."

Jane smiled back at her sister and immediately offered her left hand, displaying the engagement ring that graced her third finger.

"It is beautiful, Jane. Mr. Bingley has exquisite taste in rings as well as in fiancées." Happy tears filled both sisters' eyes.

"Have you informed Mrs. Worthington that you will require some time off to attend my wedding in April?"

"No, it makes little difference as it does not signify. I was unable to take my leave earlier due to Mrs. Worthington selling her home. She needed my assistance in packing up her possessions. She has gone now to live with her son John and his family in Oxford. So you see, she will no longer require my services as a companion. I am afraid I am quite at my leisure at the moment."

"But Lizzy, that is wonderful news!" cried Jane. "Not that I am glad you are no longer employed, but, well, I did mention to Charles that should your situation with Mrs. Worthington change, I would love to have you come live with us at Netherfield."

"Oh, I don't know, Jane. The last thing newlyweds need is an unwanted sister hanging about."

"You are not unwanted, Lizzy. And besides, Netherfield is quite large, and Mr. Bingley has informed me the walls are quite thick." Jane smiled a wicked little smile at her sister as they both blushed with laughter.

"Your wedding is several months away. I would still need to find something to occupy me until then. You know I am not one who finds pleasure in idleness. I have written to a . . . a recent acquaintance of mine regarding a job here in London. It is only to be for a few months, but it sounded quite interesting."

"What is it?"

"At the Melbourne House where my friend is employed, they are installing a small library for the use of their guests, and they are looking for someone knowledgeable to help stock it. Since my friend was aware of my love of books, she suggested I apply for the position. I have an interview in two days. The position is only for the short duration until the library is organized and fully stocked, but one of the provisions would be a small room in which to stay during my service there. If the library proves to be successful, they may need my services again in the future to keep it current."

"Oh, Lizzy, that sounds perfect for you. It is all too bad you had to give up all your beautiful books at Longbourn. I know Papa wanted you to have them," said Jane with sadness in her voice.

"I know, Jane, but perhaps I shall start my own library. Oh, that reminds me; I had some recently acquired books sent here. They should arrive in a day or two, Aunt. I hope you won't mind storing them for me until I am settled somewhere."

"Of course not, Lizzy. I shall be happy to keep them for you as long as you like," said Mrs. Gardiner.

When Lizzy muffled a yawn, her aunt insisted that she rest upstairs until dinner. "We will have plenty of time to discuss everything tonight."

Too tired not to obey, she hugged her aunt and sister one more time and climbed the stairs.

In her room Elizabeth released a sigh of relief that she had gotten through this first reunion with Jane and her aunt without revealing too much emotion. Over the last six months, she had become very adept at hiding her true feelings. She was sure that with a little more practice, she could learn to adopt an air of indifference, but that was the best she could hope for under such circumstances. Happiness was not an option.

She was glad to be spending the holiday with her family, even though she was uncertain that she was mentally equipped to handle the emotions that day would bring . . . wondering about her child's first Christmas.

She gave a thought to last Christmas, alone in the small cottage. It seemed so long ago.

She was certainly not the same woman she was a year ago. Life had taught her some hard and cruel lessons, and she had learned well from them.

She thought of all the tears she had shed, not only for the loss of her daughter, but for William too. William . . . the man she had given herself to so freely. She did not regret the loss of her virtue, for that was part of the agreement; no she had given much more than that. She had given of herself, a piece of her heart.

How dare he make love to her and engage her emotions! He had not that right. She would always mourn the loss of her daughter, but she vowed she would shed no more tears for William.

~*~

Darcy entered the nursery and watched his daughter as she slept soundly in her cradle. With each passing day, she grew more beautiful.

For the first few months of Ellie's life, he and Anne had happily spent every moment of their time devoted to their precious child. He had never felt such contentment in all of his life. He knew that Anne felt that same joy as he witnessed her delight in caring for their daughter.

However, the last two weeks had brought about a severe worsening of Anne's condition. He knew that her health had reached some irreversible juncture. Each night her cough grew worse, and each day she found it harder to attend to even the simplest of tasks.

Against her wishes, he had sent for Dr. Chisholm, who confirmed his suspicion that Anne's condition was indeed advancing and that there would be no further remissions.

Darcy had already silently begun to fear for his daughter's safety. He knew little of consumption, but the one fact he did know, was that it was contagious. Anne was also becoming extremely weak, adding the fear of her dropping the little girl to his worries.

The time had come that he must deny Anne the pleasure of their child's company. Knowing that caring for Ellie was the only source of her limited happiness, he was not looking forward to that duty, but he would not jeopardize his daughter's life.

As he told her the heart-breaking news, he could not hide the tears that welled in his eyes.

"Fitzwilliam, you must not be sad for me. Should I have lived another fifty years, I could have achieved no greater fulfilment than what you and Ellie have given me these past few precious months. It has meant everything to me."

The lump in Darcy's throat made it impossible to speak. There was nothing he could say or do, except silently grieve for what was soon to pass.

CHAPTER TWENTY-NINE

January brought grey days and icy temperatures to the now nearly deserted streets of London. Elizabeth was well settled into Melbourne House and was grateful for the hours she spent contentedly engaged in her new position. During those hours her mind was busy and free from melancholy.

She was in close proximity to Jane, who was now immersed in the many details of preparing for a wedding. Their mother had made several trips to London to assist Jane with such preparations and to attend to her trousseau. On the two occasions they had been in each other's company, Elizabeth had made several attempts at civil conversation, but it was obvious Mrs. Bennet still held fast to her feelings of resentment.

Elizabeth had learned about the availability of her present position through Hannah, as the two women had agreed to correspond upon Lizzy's departure from the cottage. It was both pleasing and unsettling to see her again, as the sight of her brought back so many memories.

Hannah's position as chamber maid at Melbourne House presented many opportunities for their paths to often cross. Though Hannah had felt herself far below Elizabeth's station, she never felt uncomfortable in her company. To know such intimate details of someone's life was to her a privilege, and she felt a deep honour-bound loyalty to that lady.

It was only in Hannah's company that Lizzy let down her guard. She told her of her sleepless nights and worse, of the nights that she did finally succumb to sleep only to be haunted by dreams of her child. She spoke of her anguish and regret. Hannah would mostly listen without comment. She knew Lizzy was not looking to her for answers. Her only need was to express these feelings to someone, someone who would not judge her.

Upon noting Lizzy's pale colour and highly agitated state, Hannah suggested that she seek a doctor who might prescribe something to help her. At first reluctant to go, she finally acquiesced and visited the local apothecary who prescribed some sleeping powders. She used them but rarely, as they made her feel more dazed than sleepy.

The library was coming along but would require at least another two months of preparation before its completion and before Lizzy's services would no longer be required. One evening as Elizabeth was locking up for the night, she heard a familiar voice call her name.

"Miss Bennet!"

"Colonel Fitzwilliam!"

Smiling at the sight of her, he bowed. "I cannot tell you how happy I am to see you again."

"And I, you."

"I trust you have been well?"

"Yes, sir. I have been quite well," said Elizabeth. "Have you been in London very long?"

"My regiment has been stationed here for the past month."

Upon observing the two engaged in pleasant conversation, one might have perceived both to be in good spirits, but each one recognized in the other an underlying unhappiness for neither's smile had reached their eyes.

Elizabeth then noticed the black arm band positioned over the colonel's sleeve. She raised her eyes in question.

"Ah, yes. I am afraid my family has suffered a most sorrowful and untimely loss."

"I am most sorry to hear that, Colonel."

"I hope you do not find this forward of me, Miss Bennet, but I was about to partake in some dinner and was wondering if you might care to join me? We could continue our conversation in a more comfortable setting."

"Yes, that would be most agreeable. I would welcome the opportunity to renew our acquaintance, sir."

As they sat in the dining room of Melbourne House, the colonel was more than pleased by her company. She was just as pretty as he had remembered her, but she seemed to possess a maturity that she did not have before. Perhaps maturity was not the word he was looking for; wisdom might be a better choice. After some pleasantries, he brought the conversation back to that of his family's loss.

"It was my cousin Anne who was so cruelly taken a few months ago. She had been in poor health most of her life, but the circumstances of her death were most upsetting. She was married to my cousin Darcy, and they had just recently had a child."

"That is most grievous," said Elizabeth softly.

"Indeed it is. My cousin has been inconsolable since her death. He has barely spoken to anyone in all that time, and his sister has written to me expressing her concern for his wellbeing. If it were not for my duties in town, I would have travelled to Pemberley directly. But I cannot leave my regiment's training for several months."

"I did not realize Mr. Darcy was your cousin," said Elizabeth.

"Are you acquainted with him?"

"No, not at all, sir, but I believe I shall have the pleasure of meeting him soon at Netherfield, as my sister Jane is to be married to his best friend, Mr. Bingley. I am told that he is to be Mr. Bingley's best man, and, as I am to be Jane's maid of honour, I suspect we will be quite often in each other's company."

"Yes, of course. I had heard of Mr. Bingley's impending marriage through my cousin. Please convey my congratulations to Mr. Bingley and your sister. They did seem very well suited. I have been invited to visit Netherfield as well. I would consider myself fortunate indeed if our visits should coincide."

Since the colonel was to be stationed in London for the next several weeks, they agreed to meet again for dinner, and Elizabeth was grateful for the friendship he offered.

~*~

Darcy stared at the letter in his hand trying to focus his eyes. It was from Bingley, once again imploring him to reconsider his decision not to attend his and Jane's wedding. *Why won't he just leave me alone! Does he not understand I do not wish to be in company? He will just have to find another best man!*

Darcy walked unsteadily towards the bottle of brandy and poured another glassful. His thoughts were jumbled, and he knew it was not all due to the effects of the alcohol. He was grieving, that he knew to be sure. But the true source of his grief still lay unacknowledged for it shamed him.

There was a light knock on the door. "Enter," he commanded.

Georgiana, carrying Ellie in her arms, stepped through the doorway of the study. "We have come to say goodnight, Fitzwilliam," she said, now accustomed to seeing her brother in such a state. "Please, Fitzwilliam, we cannot go on like this. Your daughter has lost her mother. She needs her father now more than ever. Do not abandon her."

Darcy took his daughter into his arms and looked into the eyes that haunted his dreams, the eyes she had inherited from her mother.

He could not look upon his daughter without being reminded of Lizzy. He kissed her gently on the forehead and handed her back to his sister.

"I need more time, Georgie. I am not fit to be in anyone's company at present," he said as he turned away from them both.

As she gathered all the confidence she could find from deep inside her, she placed a hand on his arm. "No! That will not do, Fitzwilliam! For months you have given me the same wretched answer. This has to stop now!"

He turned, giving her his best haughty look, but she would not back down. "I am writing to Mr. Bingley tonight. We are expected at Netherfield in a fortnight. You will attend his wedding and serve as his best man. I will not stand by and watch you alienate all of us who love you."

Much softer she said, "I know how much you grieve the loss of dear Anne. But you must turn your thoughts to the living now. Your daughter needs you. I need you, Fitzwilliam. You must carry on as you know Anne would have wished."

He turned and looked at Georgiana holding his daughter in her arms. Knowing the tears she shed were because of him, grieved him even more. Sadly he said, "I shall try, Georgie, I shall try."

"You must do more than try. You know Aunt Catherine has already threatened to take Ellie away to live with her at Rosings. She is just waiting for some excuse that will allow her to do it. Do not give her a reason, Fitzwilliam. Ellie must remain with you. Anne would have wanted it so."

~*~

As he lay in bed that night, his guilt was overwhelming. Of course, everyone assumed his grief was for Anne and for Anne alone. However, only he knew that was not entirely true. Only he knew that the depth of his grief was for the loss of another woman entirely.

While he had been immersed in caring for Anne, he had been left no time to dwell on thoughts of Lizzy. But now, she was all he seemed capable of thinking about. However, to admit such a thing would mean betrayal to Anne's memory. It was easier for him to drown his guilt in brandy than to admit the true source of his grief.

He was no stranger to heartache, and for the third time in his life he would try to put aside his grief as he had done with his mother's passing and then his father's. He would do what his family and everyone else expected of him. He would go to Netherfield and play the dutiful father, the good brother, and the loyal friend.

Pat Santarsiero

CHAPTER THIRTY

As the carriage pulled up in front of Netherfield, Bingley rushed to greet his guests. He had been waiting with much anticipation throughout the long afternoon, and now, as evening descended, he could not hide his eagerness. Before the carriage had come to a complete stop, his hand had already secured the handle of the coach's door. He reached for Jane's hand as she stepped from the carriage and immediately enfolded her in his arms as a blush covered her countenance.

Lizzy smiled, patiently waiting for the two lovers to conclude their greeting before Bingley finally pulled himself away from his angel to help Lizzy down as well.

"Miss Elizabeth, what a pleasure to see you again. I was delighted when Jane informed me that you would be accompanying her to Netherfield."

"The pleasure is all mine, Mr. Bingley. I was happy to learn that Jane will be married from Meryton rather than London. That we shall be able to spend two weeks here before your wedding is most welcomed. Your hospitality is much appreciated, sir."

"Not at all; for there is nothing that I love better than having a house full of family and friends. Let us get you both inside, and I will introduce you to my other guests," said Bingley.

Upon their entrance into the parlour, Caroline Bingley immediately rose to greet the newest arrivals. She knew that in a short span of time she would have to relinquish her hostess duties to Jane, who would soon be Mistress of the house. However, that thought was not as upsetting to her as one might suspect, for she had the highest hopes of becoming Mistress of a much grander estate. It was her intention to finally secure the affections of Mr. Fitzwilliam Darcy, and what better opportunity than during this period preceding her brother's wedding. They would certainly be much in each other's company over the next two weeks.

"Jane, how lovely to see you again," said Caroline. "And this must be your sister."

As she eyed Elizabeth, she noted that she displayed the same unfashionable country attire as her sister and immediately dismissed her as any threat. With Mr. Darcy arriving soon, she did not want any distractions that might take his attention from her. She saw little that might tempt him in Miss Elizabeth Bennet.

Mr. Bingley made the introduction. "Yes, this is Miss Elizabeth Bennet. Miss Elizabeth, my sister, Miss Caroline Bingley."

At that moment, Georgiana, having just seen to settling Ellie in for the night, entered the parlour and was introduced to Elizabeth as well.

After greetings were exchanged, Elizabeth, Jane, and Georgiana all expressed their desire to be called by their given names. "I am so happy to make your acquaintance, Georgiana," said Elizabeth. "Did not your brother accompany you? I understand he is to be Mr. Bingley's best man."

"Yes, I expect him shortly. He had some estate business to finish before he left, but he assured me he would arrive sometime later this evening." She had a slight look of concern on her face, as she wished to believe her own words.

Darcy had Georgiana travel with Ellie and Mrs. Hawkins plus two rather large and burly armed guards as well as all of the paraphernalia necessary to care for a ten-month-old child, while he promised he would follow in two days' time, travelling upon Marengo.

After tea was served, Caroline excused herself to see about the arrangements being made for dinner. Charles and Jane quickly took the opportunity for some time alone and announced their intention of taking a walk in the gardens. To their credit, they *did* ask if anyone would care to join them, but Elizabeth and Georgiana gave each other a knowing look and graciously declined.

The two young women, now alone in the parlour, slipped easily into conversation. "I understand you are to be Jane's maid of honour, Elizabeth," said Georgiana.

"Yes. Besides being sisters, we have always been each other's best friend."

Georgiana was quiet for a moment. "Yes . . . I can certainly understand that. I was fortunate to have a sister for a short time," said Georgiana as tears suddenly appeared in her eyes.

Taking her hand, Elizabeth said, "Oh, how thoughtless of me, Georgiana. Your cousin, Colonel Fitzwilliam, told me of your family's loss. Forgive me."

"No, please do not distress yourself. There is no need for my forgiveness. I seem to cry rather easily these days."

Elizabeth put her arms around the young woman and, for a moment, both were lost in their own thoughts.

Upon seeing tears in Elizabeth's eyes also, Georgiana gave her a questioning look.

"I guess I am suffering from the same malady. I seem to cry rather easily these days myself."

Hoping to introduce a more pleasant line of conversation, Elizabeth asked, "You have a niece, do you not?"

"Oh, yes!" A smile quickly illuminated the young girl's face. "Ellie is the most beautiful child I have ever seen! She had quite a full day today and is fast asleep now, but you will have the opportunity to meet her tomorrow."

"Oh, she is here also? How delightful! I look forward to meeting her *and* your brother."

~*~

Dinner had come and gone with no sign of Darcy. Georgiana had begun to worry, as an obvious furrow made its appearance across her brow. Trying hard not to alert the other guests of her concern, she graciously consented to play several concertos on the pianoforte.

As was her customary reaction to anything Georgiana did, Caroline fawned over her performance. "How proud your brother must be to have such an accomplished sister."

As she was the only one who was directly facing the young girl, Elizabeth could not help but notice Georgiana's eyes roll upward towards the ceiling at Caroline's statement, and she suppressed a smile at the young girl's reaction.

Elizabeth was persuaded to play two songs, and Caroline did likewise. When Charles let out a rather noisy yawn, they all agreed that it was indeed time to retire for the night, noting it was well past midnight.

Caroline tried unsuccessfully to convince her guests that it was not *that* late, hoping there was still a chance of Mr. Darcy's arrival.

As Caroline and Georgiana retreated to their rooms, Mr. Bingley offered an escorting arm to each sister. Before climbing the stairs, he pointed out the library as they passed, suggesting that perhaps they would like to select a book before retiring. Elizabeth and Jane both assured him they were much too tired to read, and Elizabeth wished him and Jane a good night, as she suspected the engaged couple would wish a few moments alone.

Once again, grateful for the chance to let her guard down, Elizabeth sat on the chair before a roaring fire, watching the interplay of red and yellow amongst the flames. The long day of travelling and the burden of keeping up social pretences had taken their toll on her.

She did admit that she was pleased to meet Georgiana but felt somewhat uncomfortable in Caroline Bingley's company. It wasn't anything she could pinpoint, but there was a distinct coolness in her address. Perhaps once she got to know her better, she would be more at ease in her company.

After readying herself for bed, she noted there was a small decanter of brandy on the dresser. Observing the masculine décor of the room, she surmised that it was usually reserved for gentlemen rather than lady guests, knowing brandy would not be intentionally provided in a lady's chamber.

As an hour passed with still no sleep in sight, Elizabeth rose from the bed. She glanced at the dresser and eyed the decanter. *Maybe a small glass of brandy will help me sleep*, she thought.

She poured out a glass and sipped it slowly at first. Noting how easily it had passed her throat, she finished the rest of the glass quickly. Hoping it would have some immediate effect upon her, she made her way back to the bed and waited.

As she continued to toss and turn, she decided that perhaps another glass was warranted. She again rose from the bed and poured out another glass; this one slightly fuller than the last. Again the reddish gold liquid slid easily down her throat. Satisfied that her mission was now accomplished, she once again padded back to her bed.

As she was just entering the twilight of sleep, she heard a child's cry. Sitting up immediately in her bed, she looked around the darkness of the room for her child's cradle. As consciousness brought her back to reality, she realized the cry was that of Mr. Darcy's daughter. And again she wept for the child she had given up.

She was again wide awake and now pacing the room. *Is there no sleep to be found tonight?* She went to her travelling case and, after a brief search, pulled out the sleeping powders her doctor had prescribed. After she mixed the powders with some water, she quickly gulped it down. Though harder to swallow than the brandy, she was at least confident that this would bring about the result she so desperately sought.

Trying to escape thoughts of her daughter, Elizabeth only increased her melancholy by letting her mind wander to William. How could she not think upon the man who was father to her child; the man who now enjoyed her daughter's smiles and laughter and took comfort in his ability to assuage her daughter's tears; the man who now had the pleasure of seeing her daughter daily while she was left with nothing?

A resigned Elizabeth finally gave up her useless attempt at sleep and reached for her dressing gown, slipping it over her night rail. With candlestick in hand, she made her way down to the library. Perhaps a dull book would finally grant what had eluded her thus far this night.

Pat Santarsiero

CHAPTER THIRTY-ONE

The moonlight guided Darcy as he rode Marengo through the woods and fields towards Netherfield. It had been his intention to arrive much earlier in the evening; however, his last stop to rest had resulted in his partaking of several whiskeys which he was convinced he required to face the social situation awaiting him.

He made his way towards the Netherfield stables, startling the young boy who was attending the horses. He gave up Marengo's reins, relinquishing the stallion to the lad's care for the night.

He walked towards the darkened house, relieved his late arrival had saved him from at least one night of feigned interest and contrived conversations.

As Bingley was new to the business of estates, he had no old family retainer, such as Mrs. Reynolds, to place at Netherfield as housekeeper. He had hired a younger and less experienced woman by the name of Mrs. Walker, who informed Mr. Darcy that indeed the entire house had gone to their chambers hours before.

"Mr. Bingley said you might be arriving late, sir. Your usual room is ready for you."

He mumbled a thank you to the housekeeper but did not go up to his room. Instead he went to Bingley's study and poured himself a drink. Why had he ever promised Georgiana he would come? He would have been perfectly content to remain at Pemberley forever.

He had no need for social engagements. He never wished to be in society again!

As he drank the brandy, he felt the tension begin to leave his body. *Just a few more drinks and my mind will be free of her*, he thought. That was what he waited for each night . . . the alcohol induced click in his head which turned off his memory of her and allowed him some peace. Some nights it took more alcohol than others.

He removed his tailcoat, vest and cravat. He picked up the bottle and walked, glass in one hand, bottle in the other, towards the library. His mind had not yet disengaged, and he knew there would be no point in attempting sleep until it had, for she would be there in his thoughts, in his dreams, in his fantasies. She was *always* there, taunting him.

He entered the library and sat in an overstuffed chair before the dying fire. With her much on his mind, he was not surprised that he imagined the scent of lavender in the air. His mind often played such cruel tricks on him.

She was gone from his life forever. The guilt he felt, knowing the grief he now endured was attributed to that fact and no other, made him refill his glass yet again.

He had grown to love Anne in many ways, but he had not desired her as he did Lizzy. She had not made him feel as if he might die if he could not look upon her face or hear her voice . . . or touch her. This ache in his heart as he thought of her now only reinforced that fact.

He wondered where she was, who was she with? Was she safe? How had she managed to go on with her life after all that had happened between them? How had he?

He knew he must rid himself of her memory and get on with his life. Georgie was right; they could not go on like this. Ellie was now the most important thing in his life.

He finished the last of the bottle and stood. He hoped the alcohol, coupled with the exhaustion of his journey on horseback, would grant him a peaceful night's sleep. Unsteadily he began to pace the room. As he turned past a row of books, he saw the flicker of a candle. Swaying slightly he looked toward the couch by the window. She was there. Once again, his dreams of her would not be denied.

As much as they tortured him, he could never resist these dreams. He approached her, daring to see where *this* dream would take him. He looked down upon her and softly called her name.

She stirred.

He moved in beside her sleeping form. The candle had all but gone out, but the moonlight streaming through the long windows illuminated her beautiful face. He leaned toward her and gently placed a kiss upon her lips.

She opened her eyes.

As Elizabeth looked upon William's face, she did not seem at all surprised. *Ah, the brandy and sleeping powders must have finally accomplished their task,* she thought, *for I am certainly dreaming.*

"Lizzy, I have found you," he whispered.

She stared at him as if bewildered. "We are dreaming, are we not?"

"Yes, my sweet Lizzy, we must be dreaming, for these dreams are all that I have left of you. I curse them because they torture me, yet I thank God for them, for I could not live without them. Only in these dreams can I hold you in my arms and kiss your sweet lips."

Again he kissed her—a deep, warm and passionate kiss, and she responded as she had done in so many of his countless other dreams of her. He inhaled the lavender scent that brought back the memories of what they once had shared.

Through her night rail, his hands traced over the familiar curves of her breasts, and his fingers easily found the heightened peaks his touch had aroused. He heard the moan of pleasure she released as their mouths continued their exploration.

He felt her hands move lightly over his chest as she mimicked his own movements. His body responded to her touch, and as his arousal grew, to his astonishment, her hand slowly moved towards it. When, at last, she caressed him there, he nearly sobbed.

The torture of this sweet dream was more than he could bear. It seemed too real, too intense, too painful to endure. He must wake up. He started to pull back from her, but she wrapped her arms around his waist to secure herself against him.

"Stay with me, William," she breathed out on a sigh.

As he felt her body conform to his, he held on to her tightly, now afraid if he let her go, the dream might end, and he would be without her once more.

He did not know which was worse: the pain of having her only in his dreams or the pain of not having her at all.

She nestled against him, and, with her lying in his arms, he at last felt the contentment he had so longed for; his mind at peace. Exhaustion now hitting him full force, he kissed her once more and just before sleep conquered his mind and body, he whispered, "You are the mistress of my dreams as well as my heart, Lizzy."

A short time later, a knock at the library door brought him to full consciousness. Bingley peered into the room and, in a low whisper, called Darcy's name. Startled, Darcy managed his way around the row of books.

"I knew I would find you here," stated Bingley with a smile. "My housekeeper said you had arrived, but you were not in your chambers."

Unsteady on his feet, Darcy stumbled towards him as Bingley eyed the empty bottle. "I can see you have had too much to drink, my friend. Well, at least you have excellent taste. That was one of my best bottles of brandy. Here, let me help you to your bedchamber."

Putting his arm around him for support, Bingley helped Darcy up the stairs and deposited him on his bed. *I can see Georgiana has not exaggerated his condition*, thought Bingley.

A few hours later, a much disoriented Lizzy awoke. *I must have fallen asleep while reading*, she thought. She quickly made her way back to her room and safely locked herself inside her door.

She cursed herself for her dream. She had dreamed of William again. She had banished him from her heart; now she just had to find a way to rid him from her dreams.

CHAPTER THIRTY-TWO

"Good morning, Mr. Darcy," said an eager Caroline. "Or should I say good afternoon?"

As Darcy approached the breakfast room, he stopped short at the sound of Caroline Bingley's voice. It was just his luck that she would be the first person he would encounter today. His head was throbbing, and he was in no mood for her cloying manner. He tried to keep a civil tone, remembering that she was his best friend's sister.

"Good morning, Miss Bingley," said Darcy. "I'm afraid I arrived rather late last night and was unable to get much sleep. I see that everyone else has already partaken of their breakfast."

"Oh, quite. Charles left hours ago, meeting a neighbour's shooting party. He informed me of your very late arrival. I thought I would await your appearance downstairs this morning, so you would not have to breakfast alone." Here Caroline gave Darcy the most genuine smile in her repertoire.

"Where is everyone else?" he inquired.

"Georgiana is with Miss Bennet taking a walk around the grounds. Mr. and Mrs. Hurst are yet in London and will not arrive for another week. They plan to join us a few days before the ball. I guess Miss Eliza was unable to sleep last night either, as she has not made an appearance thus far this morning."

"Miss Eliza?" he inquired as he unfolded the newspaper that had been left on the table.

"Oh, that's right. You have yet to meet Jane's sister Elizabeth. She is hardly worth your notice, Mr. Darcy, as it is obvious that Jane is the beauty in the family."

Ignoring her last words, he inquired, "And where is Ellie?"

"I believe she is just getting up from her nap. The wet nurse is attending her. Here, let me get you some more coffee, Mr. Darcy. I know exactly how you like it," she said brushing his hand as she reached for his cup.

Perusing the newspaper as he ate, Darcy felt no compulsion to make idle conversation and, as soon as he had finished his meal, quickly rose from the table. Taking his coffee with him, he bowed as he left Caroline's company.

Finally able to enjoy his coffee alone in the library, he stood looking out the long windows at the bright April day. He had a slight remembrance of recently standing in this very spot, only it was not the sunlight he recalled filtering through the window panes; it was the moonlight. For some reason that recollection soothed him, and strangely his spirits were lifted. Unable to produce any further images from his memory, he turned away.

As he left the library, he found Mrs. Hawkins with his daughter about to embark on a walk. Ellie eyed him and seemed to cling tighter to Mrs. Hawkins. As he observed his daughter's reaction to the sight of him, he admonished himself, acknowledging it had been far too long since he had spent time in her company.

As he looked upon her adorable face, he knew that Georgiana's words rang true. His daughter needed him now more than ever. Why did she have to look so much like her mother? How could he look upon her without thinking of Lizzy?

"I would be happy to take Ellie out for some fresh air, Mrs. Hawkins, if you have other things to attend," he stated.

"That is most kind of you, sir. I *would* like to take an early luncheon if that would meet with your approval. Ellie had me up quite early this morning."

"Yes, of course," said Darcy as he took the child from her arms.

"Oh, Mr. Darcy," exclaimed Caroline as she came upon them. "I was just planning on taking to the outdoors myself. How fortunate; now we can walk together."

Darcy resigned himself to the fact that there would be no escaping Caroline Bingley today and resolved that he would plan better in the upcoming days to avoid her company.

~*~

Elizabeth awoke, observing that it was well past her usual time as the sun was already exceedingly high.

She dressed quickly and made her way downstairs, hoping there was still a chance for some breakfast. Relieved to see that a servant still awaited her arrival in the breakfast room, she went about procuring her tea, toast, and jam, and enthusiastically broke her fast. Any ill effects from last night's endeavours seemed to have completely vanished. On the contrary, she felt exceedingly well and could not recall the last time she had slept so long or so peacefully.

With her breakfast completed, she retrieved her pelisse and bonnet from her room and headed outdoors in search of her sister. In the distance she could see Jane and Georgiana strolling amongst a grove of trees and waved her arm to gain their attention. As they espied her, they happily waited for her to reach them.

As the three continued on their walk, they felt much at ease in each other's company. Georgiana, though obviously shy, made easy conversation with the two sisters. Addressing Elizabeth, she said, "Mr. Bingley informed me of my brother's arrival. I have not yet seen him, as he was still asleep when Jane and I left for our walk."

"I am sure you are much relieved that he has arrived safely," said Elizabeth.

"Yes, I admit I was worried last evening at his delay. I am truly hoping this visit will help him recover, if only a little, from recent events. He has been so grief stricken; I do not know what to do to help him," said Georgiana sadly.

"Surely Ellie will be a comfort to him during this difficult time," said Elizabeth.

"Yes, Georgiana," said Jane. "I am sure he will pull himself together for her sake."

"I have been praying for that," she said. "But he seems to have withdrawn from her. He is rarely in her company. I know if I can just get through to him he will again be the doting father he once was. I know he loves Ellie very much."

Elizabeth took the young girl's hand and squeezed it lightly. "Give him some time, Georgiana. From everything I have heard of your brother, I am sure he will not let you and little Ellie down."

Georgiana gave Elizabeth a smile, and, as she turned her head, her smile grew into a wide grin. "Look!" she cried. "There they are!" Georgiana pointed in the direction of a distant garden where they could see a woman seated and a gentleman standing with a small child in his arms.

Elizabeth looked in their direction as she shielded her eyes from the sun's glare. As they walked towards the threesome, she recognized Caroline Bingley as the woman who was seated on the bench while the gentleman stood nearby. She watched as he raised the young child up over his head to the delightful squeals of the little girl who flailed her arms and legs.

As she, Jane, and Georgiana drew nearer, Elizabeth slowed her pace and tilted her head to one side. Again she brought her hand up as a shield from the glaring sun, trying to focus her eyes on the scene before her.

As she gazed upon the little girl, she was unable to catch her breath. Feeling her heart pounding in her chest, her eyes immediately went to those of the gentleman who stared back at her, his eyes as wide as hers. The last thing she remembered before her body hit the ground was Jane calling her name.

"Lizzy!"

Pat Santarsiero

CHAPTER THIRTY-THREE

"I assure you, Mr. Bingley, I do not require a doctor," said Elizabeth. Jane sat beside her on the bed and held her hand. "I . . . I must have gotten dizzy for a moment. Really, I am quite recovered now. I am sorry to have caused everyone so much trouble."

"Are you sure, Lizzy? I have been worried about you lately. It would not hurt to at least have Mr. Jones look at you," said a much concerned Jane.

"Please, Jane, you ought to believe me. I am fine. I will rest for the afternoon, and I'm sure I will feel like myself again by dinner."

"Please do not hesitate to ask for anything, Miss Elizabeth," said Bingley with his usual friendly demeanour. "I will be at your service if needed."

Elizabeth thanked Mr. Bingley again and asked if she might have a moment alone with Jane.

"But, of course. I will go see to my other guests and inform them of your progress." As he left the room, Lizzy motioned to Jane to shut the door.

"What is it, Lizzy?"

"Tell me everything that happened after I fainted, Jane," said Lizzy in a whisper.

"What do you mean? We, of course, all rushed to your aide."

"Tell me *exactly* what happened," she said.

Jane looked at her sister rather curiously. "Well, at first we were all a little stunned. Mr. Darcy was the first to react. He handed Ellie over to Georgiana and immediately came to your side and picked you up. He carried you all the way back to the house and placed you here on the bed. We all followed him, and, when I entered the room, he left. A few moments later, you opened your eyes, much to my relief."

"Oh, I wondered how I had gotten here," said Elizabeth. "Did Mr. Darcy say anything?"

"No, not really. Only that he hoped you would be feeling better soon."

Suddenly wishing to be alone with her thoughts, Elizabeth said, "I think I should try to rest for a little while."

"Yes, that would be best. I will come and check on you before dinner," said Jane as she kissed her sister's cheek before departing.

Despite her light-headedness, Elizabeth could not stay abed. Her mind would not permit it. She aimlessly roamed the room, seeking answers to the many questions each new moment provided.

Elizabeth shook her head. She had much to think upon. Her daughter was here! They were under the same roof and would remain so for the next two weeks. She would have a chance to acquaint herself with her child. Her tears were of joy.

To be presented with such a situation after she had spent the last ten months of her life reconciling herself to the fact that her daughter was lost to her forever was quite overwhelming. Indeed, she had spent most of the summer and autumn within the confines of Mrs. Worthington's home, protected from the rest of the world, learning to cope with her grief.

The elder woman's kindness to Elizabeth could never be repaid. She had not asked any questions of her and simply allowed her the time she needed to heal, offering her solace when she wanted it and solitude when she did not. While there, Elizabeth had resumed her riding lessons with a vengeance, finding the demanding activity calming to her mind and exhausting to her body, thus allowing her a modicum of sleep at night.

Now Elizabeth was almost afraid to have hope. She feared that this opportunity would be taken away from her just as quickly and unexpectedly as it had been presented. She wanted to run downstairs and demand to see her child; demand to hold her in her arms. As difficult as it would be, she must somehow rein in her emotions.

And then there was William . . . or should she say Mr. Darcy. Confident that he would not betray their prior attachment, she let herself relax a little. Her mind began to piece together all the known events of his life as she had become acquainted with them.

Recalling Colonel Fitzwilliam's words, she remembered him saying that Mr. Darcy was inconsolable since his wife's death. He had taken to excess drinking, from what she could perceive from Georgiana. *How he must have loved her.*

The colonel also revealed that Anne had been in ill health most of her life, which may have meant she was unable to bear a child; hence, Mr. Darcy's need for a surrogate.

Was he looking for another kind of surrogate when he asked me to be his mistress?

She would not dwell on that. He had apologized. Besides, whatever her feelings were for William now, she knew she must be civil to him if she wanted to remain in her daughter's company. And above all, she wanted that more than anything else.

Was the arrogance and conceit William had revealed that day an accurate reflection of his true character?

Of course, she had heard Jane speak of Mr. Darcy. She had also written of him many times in her letters. He had been a good friend to Mr. Bingley for many years and had advised him in his business endeavours. She also remembered Jane writing that he had become his sister's guardian after the death of their father many years ago and was now master of his late father's estate, Pemberley. All of these things spoke well of him.

Who was the real Mr. Darcy? She would have two weeks in which to try to find out the answer to that question.

No matter how awkward the situation, she was left with the one thought that outweighed all others; she had found her daughter! Knowing the heartache and suffering she had just endured over the last ten months, she knew she would do anything to keep her daughter close to her . . . anything.

Elizabeth could not predict the events that might unfold over the next two weeks. How were they to act while in each other's company? Would William allow her to acquaint herself with Ellie, or would he deny her that pleasure? And most curiously she wondered . . . *who named the child Ellie*?

As her body gave in to the fatigue of her overactive mind, she climbed back onto the bed and was asleep in minutes with dreams of holding her child in her arms.

~*~

While Elizabeth slept, the rest of Mr. Bingley's guests gathered in the parlour for afternoon tea.

"May I inquire as to your sister's health, Miss Bennet?"

"I thank you for your concern, Mr. Darcy. She has assured me she is quite well and plans to join us for dinner."

"I am happy to hear it," said Darcy as he bowed slightly before her and moved to the window. He might have taken a seat on the couch, but Caroline Bingley was seated there, anticipating his company.

"Yes, Jane, that is indeed good news. I'm sure Miss Eliza just needs to get some rest. I fear she did not sleep well last night," said Caroline. "One of the servants informed me that she spent most of the night in the library."

Bingley looked over to his friend by the window. Noting Darcy showed no particular reaction to this information, he dismissed it from his mind.

Darcy, however, did not.

When he had gazed upon her in the gardens, his shock was as great as hers. As he had held her in his arms and carried her back to the house, her lavender scent filled his senses, just as it had last night in his dream of her.

As he continued to stare out the window, he tried to recall the previous evening. He remembered the moonlight streaming through the long windows of the library and could picture Lizzy lying next to him as he held her in his embrace. Certainly it had been a dream. *We are dreaming, are we not?*

~*~

Elizabeth was seated before the pier glass, mindlessly staring at her reflection, deep in thought.

Why did you not answer my knock?" asked Jane as she approached her sister.

"What?"

"I knocked several times before I entered, but you did not answer."

"I guess I was thinking about this afternoon," replied Elizabeth.

"Well, you *do* look so much better, Lizzy. You were white as a ghost," said Jane.

"Yes, I guess a little rest was all I required."

"That is what Caroline Bingley said."

"What do you mean?" asked Elizabeth as she finished fastening the tortoise shell comb into her hair.

"Miss Bingley mentioned you had spent most of last night in the library reading."

"Yes . . . I guess I did," said Elizabeth, unsettled by the remembrance of her dream.

"Shall we go downstairs together? Charles has informed me that dinner shall be served within the hour," said Jane.

Elizabeth smiled at her sister and nodded. She gave her reflection a final glance and braced herself for the evening before her.

Pat Santarsiero

CHAPTER THIRTY-FOUR

The two sisters entered the parlour and were immediately greeted by Mr. Bingley. "It is a pleasure to see you so well recovered, Miss Elizabeth."

Georgiana immediately came to her side and echoed Mr. Bingley sentiments. "It would give me great pleasure, Elizabeth, to introduce you to my brother." The young girl took Elizabeth's arm, leading the way.

Elizabeth allowed her eyes to glance towards the window. He stood there with his back to the room, tall and erect, his hands clasped behind his back. She remembered those hands caressing her body, touching her, arousing her. In a moment he would turn towards her, and she must not react. She would not give him that pleasure; she would show him that her heart was now immune to him.

Darcy heard the sisters enter the parlour, and he listened as Georgiana offered her their introduction. Staring out the window, he waited. She was approaching, and in a moment they would be face to face. He tried to prepare himself. Would his feelings show? Would she know the moment she saw him, how much he had missed her, how many nights he had longed for her?

"Brother," Georgiana called, beckoning him to turn towards them, "May I introduce Miss Bennet's sister, Miss Elizabeth. Miss Elizabeth, may I present my brother, Mr. Darcy."

Their eyes met and held for a long moment as if each was trying to gauge the other's reaction. Darcy executed his most proper bow before finding his voice. "I . . . it is a pleasure to meet you, Miss Elizabeth. I am happy to see you have suffered no ill effects from this afternoon."

Elizabeth managed an unsteady curtsy. "I thank you . . . Mr. Darcy, for your kind words and also for your coming to my aide. I understand it was you who brought me back safely to the house."

"I was happy to be of assistance. I trust you are fully recovered?" he asked.

Hardly thinking herself fully recovered from the shock of seeing both her child and William, but noting the others in the room awaiting her reply, she offered, "I'm afraid a combination of brandy plus some sleeping powders last evening had an adverse effect upon me. I guess my fainting was one of the results. I do not anticipate any further consequences."

Again their eyes remained fixed for several moments. Then Darcy's eyes were drawn to the tortoise shell comb in her hair. Remembering the last time he had seen it, he quickly turned away, desperately looking for something else on which to focus his eyes. Luckily at that moment Mrs. Hawkins appeared in the doorway with Ellie in her arms.

Elizabeth turned and held her breath. She had to force herself to stay in place, not to rush to her daughter.

"Oh good," said Georgiana. "You will finally have a chance to meet Ellie!" Georgiana took the child from Mrs. Hawkins and walked back over to Elizabeth.

"Did I not tell you she was the most beautiful child," said Georgiana enthusiastically.

Yes, yes, yes! Has any mother not thought that of their child? she thought.

"Yes . . . indeed, she is," said Elizabeth, as she felt her body tremble. "May I . . . would it be all right . . . if I were to hold her?" Elizabeth asked as she turned her gaze from Georgiana to William.

As he stared into her beseeching eyes, he gave her a small smile.

"Of course, you may, Miss Bennet. You need not have asked," he replied. *Did she think I would deny her that pleasure?*

Elizabeth closed her eyes as she hugged her child to her breast, inhaling her scent. *Oh my sweet child.* Trying desperately to keep her composure, she fought back the tears that threatened. After several moments, Elizabeth pulled back to look into her daughter's eyes. The little girl giggled and brought her tiny fingers to the smile of Elizabeth's mouth. Elizabeth kissed her fingers and then pretended to bite them, to the little girl's delight.

Darcy watched closely at the reverence in which she held her daughter in her arms. He wondered if he was the only one in the room who observed the similarity of their eyes and the same chestnut colour of their hair. Surely everyone else must also see their likeness.

He tried to appear unaffected by her presence, but he could not draw his eyes from her. He watched as she held Ellie as if she had done so every day of the child's life, and Ellie responded to her just as naturally. His heart actually ached as he observed them together.

Darcy excused himself from their company and walked towards the table containing the bottle of brandy. He poured out a glass and, as he brought it to his lips, realized he did not want it. He did not want anything that might dull his senses. He wanted to remember this moment forever.

As he stood across the room, his eyes sought her again. He watched as she and Georgiana effortlessly made easy conversation. He could not help but wonder at their discourse and walked back in their direction. When he saw Miss Bingley approach, he changed his course and walked once again to the window behind them.

As she watched Mr. Darcy, Caroline was immediately alerted to something amiss and strode towards Elizabeth. Noting the precious scene before her, without ceremony she plucked the child from Elizabeth's arms stating, "We cannot take any chances that you may again faint while holding our dear little Ellie, Miss Eliza."

The little girl began to cry at such a manoeuvre, and Georgiana was rendered speechless. Darcy did not turn from the window, his clenched fist at his side the only discernible reaction to such rude behaviour.

Elizabeth assured Miss Bingley she was in no danger of again fainting, but her assurance had little effect, as Caroline summoned Mrs. Hawkins who took the child and left the parlour.

Georgiana, recovering from her embarrassment, looked apologetically at Elizabeth. "I will go see that she is settled in for the night."

Elizabeth nodded and gave her an understanding smile.

Knowing she was within easy earshot of Mr. Darcy, Caroline could not help but take advantage of such a situation, engaging Elizabeth in conversation.

"Ellie is such a dear, is she not, Miss Eliza? I have become much attached to her these past few days."

"Yes," said Elizabeth softly. "Indeed, she is perfection."

"To be deprived of one's mother at such an early age is such a misfortune. She is in great need of a mother's love," continued Caroline, stressing the words for Mr. Darcy to hear.

Elizabeth recalled Georgiana's words that afternoon. *He seems to have withdrawn from her. He is rarely in her company.* She had not given up her precious child just to have her disregarded by her father.

"Yes, on that we are in agreement, Miss Bingley. However, I believe in such cases as these, in the absence of a mother's love, a *father's* love and attention is essential and most beneficial to a child's happiness and wellbeing."

Not missing the slight upon Mr. Darcy, Caroline retorted, "I assure you, Mr. Darcy is as attentive as may be. He is a very busy man who has the management of a very large estate to attend. When he is unable to do so himself, only his most trusted servants attend her."

Caroline smiled smugly at Elizabeth, quite convinced Mr. Darcy would be well pleased by her defence of him.

At that moment Jane and Mr. Bingley joined them, and the conversation turned to other topics. Caroline soon left their circle and walked to the window, approaching Mr. Darcy.

"I believe I can guess *your* thoughts at this moment Mr. Darcy."

"I should imagine not," he replied.

"You are thinking it insupportable that you must remain in the company of one as opinionated and impertinent as Miss Eliza Bennet. Imagine *her* giving such advice, a woman who could not possibly know of the deep bond one has with one's child."

Unable to respond with any truth to such a statement, Darcy made no reply at all; he merely turned away from Caroline and continued his vigil at the window until dinner was called.

That night in his room, Darcy tried to reason out his thoughts. Their situation was precarious at best. He would not wish for their past association to be known; it would not serve anyone's purpose. Both of their reputations would be destroyed, not to mention the dishonour to Anne's memory and the wrath of his Aunt Catherine.

After the initial shock of seeing her again, his second reaction had been one of relief, relief that she was safe. He would do everything in his power to see that she remained that way.

He could not gauge her reaction to him. In company, she was as he would expect her to be, polite and pleasant. But what were her true feelings towards him?

Adding to his unease was the knowledge that Lizzy had learned of his recent dereliction in the care of his daughter . . . of *their* daughter . . . most assuredly adding to her already low opinion of him. He had much to prove to her. Would she give him the chance?

He could not say if she had even read his letter. When he had travelled that day to the cottage to deliver it, Hannah had informed him that her mistress had endured two long and sleepless nights and had just finally succumbed to sleep. She had not wished to disturb her, and he had quite agreed. However, that had left him with no choice but to hand the letter over to Hannah.

Had she thought enough of him to at least read his letter? Or had she destroyed it?

He hoped that their two weeks together at Netherfield would at least help improve her opinion of him. He told himself he would be content with that.

CHAPTER THIRTY-FIVE

Elizabeth had to restrain herself each morning as she arose with the sun and waited patiently for the time of her daughter's morning walk to commence. She would make sure that she was already set on the path that Mrs. Hawkins took each day at half past nine.

There she would just happen to meet them and, as always, the kindly and accommodating Mrs. Hawkins would agree to Elizabeth's suggestion that it looked as if Ellie was getting heavy and that perhaps she might assist her by carrying the little girl for a while.

Elizabeth relished these private moments with her daughter. She must find a way to stay with her.

~*~

"Ah, there you are, Mr. Darcy. We have been wondering where you had gone off to," said Caroline who was seated on the couch next to Georgiana and Jane Bennet. He entered the parlour at the appointed time for afternoon tea and greeted the three ladies.

He had managed to elude Miss Bingley's company for the last two days, finding some excuse or another to be away. Today he had been out riding Marengo, examining Netherfield's grounds so that he might better advise Bingley on its management. He had come up with several recommendations that might improve production by rotating the crops and fields used each season. It felt good to focus his mind on such useful endeavours. He had been idle far too long.

"I have been surveying the estate," he replied taking the cup of tea she offered and taking a seat in a nearby chair. Turning to Georgiana he asked, "Where is everyone else?"

"Miss Elizabeth had expressed a desire to see the stables, and Mr. Bingley accompanied her. Mrs. Hawkins just took Ellie up for her bath and said she would attempt to persuade her to nap."

They engaged in pleasant conversation, discussing nothing more controversial than the weather and the plans for Charles and Jane's upcoming wedding ball. After what Darcy deemed a reasonable length of time, he rose from his chair and addressed all three ladies. "Perhaps you will excuse me, as I would like to spend some time with Ellie before she takes her nap."

Georgiana could not have been more delighted. "Of course, Brother. We shall see you later."

Caroline hardly tried to hide her disappointment. Turning toward Georgiana she said, "It seems your brother is keeping himself much occupied these days. We must find an activity in which we can all engage. We can come up with something, I am sure."

"Yes, that sounds like a good idea," said Jane "I would be happy to help you devise a plan that might entice Charles away from his daily shooting party."

Georgiana heartily agreed, and the three of them set their minds to coming up with some entertaining diversion.

~*~

Darcy entered Ellie's room and watched as Mrs. Hawkins finished dressing her. "Has she been fed?" he asked.

"Yes, sir; bathed, fed and changed," she cheerfully replied. "She should be ready for her nap now."

"I will stay with her for a while, Mrs. Hawkins. You may go."

"Yes, sir. Thank you." She smiled at the two and left the room.

Darcy picked up his daughter and brought her face to his as he kissed her noisily on the cheek. The little girl stared at him, and, by the look on her face, Darcy could see she was poised to either laugh or cry. When had his daughter's reaction to him become so tentative?

As he heard a noise at the door, he turned. Elizabeth had entered the room and, upon seeing him there, stopped. "Oh, I am sorry, Mr. Darcy. I did not expect to find you here." She turned abruptly back towards the door.

"Wait," he called. "You do not . . . please, I would have you stay."

As Ellie looked over to Elizabeth, the little girl's face immediately brightened. She displayed her beautiful smile, showing the dimples that she had inherited from her father, and reached her arms out towards Elizabeth.

"It would seem she prefers your company to mine," said Darcy.

"I am sure that is not the case. It is just that I have been visiting her here before her nap for the last few days," said Elizabeth. "I hope that meets with your approval, sir."

Elizabeth looked at him steadfastly, raising her chin in the way she always did when either showing her contempt or feeling intimidated. At the moment she was both.

"Please believe me, Miss Bennet, I have no wish to deny you Ellie's company during your stay."

"Thank you, Mr. Darcy. I cannot express my joy to find her here. I never thought I would see . . . I'm sorry . . . forgive me," said Elizabeth as her emotions got the better of her. She quickly wiped her eyes and tried to regain her composure.

Darcy restrained himself as he observed her tears. His first instinct was to hold her, to comfort her, but he knew he should not.

She then looked around her, searching for something.

"May I be of some assistance?" he asked as he watched her eyes peruse the room.

"I was reading a book of fairy tales to Ellie yesterday, but I do not see it now."

He looked about the room and saw the book she spoke of, half hidden under some bed clothes. Retrieving the book, he handed it to her.

She sat in the chair and held her arms out to him. At first, not comprehending her gesture, he looked at her quizzically. Then realizing it was Ellie to whom she held out her arms, he placed the little girl in her lap.

"That chair looks most uncomfortable, Miss Bennet. At Pemberley there is a handsome rocking chair in Ellie's nursery for such endeavours." Softly, almost speaking to himself, he said, "Anne would sit in that chair for hours, just rocking Ellie in her arms."

Elizabeth looked up at him, and their eyes met. "I was sorry to learn of your loss, Mr. Darcy. Georgiana has told me how much you have grieved. You must have loved her very much."

"She was indeed an exceptional woman," replied Darcy sadly.

He looked into Elizabeth's eyes, wanting to tell her more, but not knowing what to say. Instead he endeavoured to change the subject, observing Ellie's restlessness. "I think you had better get on with your reading; Ellie seems to be impatient."

They shared a brief smile.

Elizabeth opened the book to the page where she had left off the day before. She nestled Ellie to her bosom and began reading. As she did, the little girl snuggled her body to Elizabeth's.

Darcy watched in silence as he listened to Elizabeth's voice, soft and caressing. He had not meant to stay, but could not seem to get his feet to depart the room. Before Elizabeth had finished reading the third page, Ellie was fast asleep on her lap.

Darcy walked over and picked his daughter up in his arms and placed her sleeping body gently in her cradle. He kissed her softly on her cheek and then walked back to Elizabeth. She rose from the chair and, putting her finger to her lips to indicate silence, led them out into the hallway.

"Ellie seems to respond well to the sound of your voice, Miss Bennet."

"Perhaps you forget, Mr. Darcy, I read to her for many months during my confinement. I believe Byron was her favourite," said Elizabeth as she smoothed the folds of her skirt, "for she never kicked while I read her Byron."

Darcy smiled at her reference to their conversation that day on the beach in Scotland; for it was Elizabeth who had argued the superior talents of Lord Byron, while Darcy's preference led more towards the battle-plagued verses of Thomas Campbell.

Upon mentioning the poet, Elizabeth was reminded of the package of books that had arrived at the cottage that Christmas Eve and wondered if he had been her benefactor. As she was about to relate the mystery to observe his reaction, Caroline Bingley approached them.

Observing the two of them alone in the hallway, Caroline could not conceal her annoyance. "Did you lose your way, Miss Eliza? Allow me to direct you to your room. I'm sure Mr. Darcy has more important things he needs to attend."

"Thank you, Miss Bingley, but that is quite unnecessary. I believe I can find my way myself."

As Elizabeth left their company, Darcy started his retreat also, but before he had taken two steps, Caroline stayed his progress with her hand on his arm.

"I would be very careful if I were you, Mr. Darcy. You would not wish to be found with Miss Eliza in a compromising situation. Indeed, there already seems to be some talk amongst the servants

Thursday's Child

regarding a night in the library." Caroline lifted her chin in her attempt at superiority. Darcy, however, was not to be intimidated.

As he moved his arm from her grasp, he addressed her. "One should never listen to the idle gossip of servants, Miss Bingley. They often embellish to elevate their own importance." He then afforded her the slightest of bows and headed down the stairs.

~*~

Darcy found Bingley in the billiards room and immediately grabbed a cue stick and joined him. "I think I should warn you, Darcy, I overheard Caroline planning some diversion that will include us all."

Darcy rolled his eyes. He knew his avoidance of her company would be thwarted sooner or later. However, he admitted to himself that an activity including the entire party would not be wholly unwelcomed.

"I understand Miss Elizabeth asked to see the stables," said Darcy as he lined up a shot. "Do you know if she rides?"

"Yes. She said she learnt while in Mrs. Worthington's employ. I selected a mare for her use during her visit. She also asked if I could supply her with a pair of breeches," said Bingley, displaying a wide grin.

Hearing this comment mid-shot, Darcy missed the cue ball completely, causing his cue stick to become airborne as it hurled towards Bingley like a spear.

As Bingley sidestepped impalement, Darcy asked, "Are you joking?"

"Not at all," said Bingley. "It seems the young groom who taught her to ride had no idea how to teach her side-saddle, so he taught her astride."

"I cannot believe Miss Elizabeth would defy convention in such a way. I can just hear your sister now, disparaging her for such improper behaviour." Darcy walked over to pick up the cue stick from the floor. Although he was shocked to hear that "Miss Elizabeth" would conduct herself so improperly, he was strangely aroused at the thought of "Lizzy" wearing breeches and riding a horse astride. *This I will have to see.*

"Miss Elizabeth was concerned for propriety also and informed me she only plans to ride early in the morning so that there will be less chance of her being observed," said his friend.

"She seems a most unusual and intriguing young lady. Do you not think so, Darcy?"

~*~

Once again he found himself making a late night visit to the library in the hope that she would again make an appearance, but she did not. Now convinced it had not been a dream, he wondered if she had any recollection of that evening.

Obviously Lizzy had believed their encounter to be a dream, a result of too much brandy combined with sleeping powders. *We are dreaming, are we not?* Was it her habit to dream of him?

When the startling realization had finally saturated his brain that his "Lizzy" was indeed Miss Elizabeth Bennet, he tried to remember all the coincidences that had led him to that suspicion in the first place.

There was the matter of the entailment. He recalled his conversation that evening at Rosings with Mr. Collins. She had refused his offer of marriage. She would not marry to secure the comfort of hearth and home where love was not in attendance.

He recalled the clergyman's words, the very same words she had used at their interview, "*She vowed never to marry if she could not do so for love.*" That prospect was now highly unlikely for no reason other than that Elizabeth would insist upon being completely honest with any gentleman who sought her hand in marriage.

But the realization that had made his heart pound in his chest and his pulse race was the reason she sought their agreement in the first place. Wickham!

She had selflessly sacrificed her virtue in order to save her family from a scandal at the hands of that blackguard. She had given up any chance she had to secure her own future for the sake of her sisters' happiness. And he could have prevented it all!

When Wickham had persuaded Georgiana to an elopement, she had been but fifteen years old, the same age as Elizabeth's sister. If he had not kept Wickham's character a secret from the world because of his pride, Wickham would not have been able to prey upon other unsuspecting young ladies. He would have been shunned by all decent society.

It was his fault that Lizzy sought their agreement! It was his pride that had been the catalyst that had diverted Lizzy from her previous course and redirected her fate. Would he ever be able to make it up to her?

Pat Santarsiero

CHAPTER THIRTY-SIX

To Caroline Bingley's delight, the weather cooperated most pleasantly, and her planned group outing was about to commence. As the temperature reached a dazzling sixty-five degrees, it was decided that a picnic was in order. The servants prepared, packed and carried the food, plates and silverware needed for the "simple" luncheon Caroline had planned. Bingley had picked the perfect spot and, by noon, the entire party was happily engaged in various outdoor activities.

Mr. Bingley and Jane were the first to suggest a walk around the pond situated a short distance away at the bottom of a sloping hill. Hoping for some time alone with Jane, Bingley held his breath, waiting to hear if there was anyone who cared to join them. To his relief, there was not.

Elizabeth sat with her back resting against a tree reading a book. At every sound of her daughter's laughter, she would look up to see what had amused her. More than once it had been William— *no, I must think of him now as Mr. Darcy*— who had enticed these lilting vocal responses. Finding it hard to concentrate, Elizabeth finally gave up her reading but still held the book in her hand, using it as a ruse for her observations. She was more than content just to watch Mr. Darcy's efforts to entertain Ellie and Ellie's delighted reactions to his efforts.

Even though it was a "simple" picnic, Caroline was dressed in her finest silk, the colour not unlike that of a pumpkin. She carried a parasol and daintily twirled it overhead as she stood not five feet from Mr. Darcy. As was her customary manner, she commented regularly on all that he did.

"Mr. Darcy, you are such an attentive father. How delightful to see you and Ellie so happily engaged!"

On rare occasions, a deep-voiced response was heard, but Elizabeth could not quite make out what his reply was to such effusions. Not far from them, Georgiana was instructing the servants where to unpack the lunch and lay out the blankets. This duty should have fallen to Caroline, but she seemed to be unaware of anything other than attending Mr. Darcy.

The sound of a horse's neighing commanded everyone's attention as they all looked up from their activities. "Richard!" cried Georgiana.

"There you all are!" he said.

After attending his horse, Colonel Fitzwilliam immediately strode to his cousin. "Darcy, how good to see you looking so fit! After Georgiana's last letter, I was almost afraid of the condition in which I might find you."

As he spoke Georgiana came to his side and kissed him on the cheek. "Is it not astonishing?" she asked. "I would not have believed that so little time amongst his friends would bring about such a change."

Uncomfortable with the conversation, Darcy turned their attention towards Ellie. "I believe I have come to see that Ellie is my first priority. I shall do my best to keep her happy and make her feel secure." As he spoke, he quickly looked over to Elizabeth. As she caught his eye, he gave her an almost imperceptible nod accompanied by the slightest of smiles.

As Colonel Fitzwilliam turned, he saw the recipient of that barely detectable gesture. "Miss Bennet! We finally meet again! I was hoping our visits might coincide."

Elizabeth rose from her resting place to join the colonel and Mr. Darcy. She and the colonel then proceeded to carry on a lengthy conversation in which Darcy discovered they had met for dinner on a few occasions in London. This displeased Darcy more than he cared to admit.

He imagined Elizabeth was grateful to his cousin for his part in locating Wickham and the wedding that quickly followed. Did she feel indebted to him for his role in saving her family?

"Tell me, Colonel," asked Elizabeth, "how did you find us so easily?"

Richard smiled at her. "I would like to think that fifteen years of military training has at least prepared me to locate a large party of picnickers."

"Then perhaps," responded Darcy dryly, "we should hope that Napoleon soon decides to go on a picnic."

Richard eyed him curiously and wondered if he had somehow unwittingly offended his cousin in some way to deserve such a remark.

Realizing he had not yet acknowledged his hostess, Richard turned to Caroline. "Miss Bingley, a pleasure to see you again. I thank you for your kind invitation. Where is Charles?"

"I am here," said Bingley as he and Jane approached the colonel. "I was just showing Miss Bennet the pond," Bingley explained while Jane blushed.

"Ah, yes," said the colonel smiling quite blatantly. "The pond holds many allurements."

After greeting Jane, the colonel again turned his attentions to Elizabeth and spent much of the next hour in her company, much to Darcy's vexation.

Soon lunch was served, and the group sat upon various blankets on the sunny hillside. As it happened, Darcy, Ellie, Elizabeth, and Caroline all occupied the same blanket—Darcy with a determination to situate himself near Elizabeth, and Caroline with an equal determination to situate herself near Darcy— while Charles, Jane, Georgiana and Colonel Fitzwilliam sat some distance away on another.

Eager to show Mr. Darcy her motherly instincts, Caroline was thwarted time and again as she tried to engage Ellie only to have her crawl back towards Elizabeth. After several attempts to forestall her, she finally scooped the squirming child up in her arms. Upon noting the wet condition of Ellie's bottom, she immediately held the little girl out at arm's length.

Looking about in desperation, she called to Mrs. Hawkins for assistance. Elizabeth was only too happy for the chance to remove her daughter from the woman's cloying grasp. Ever since that first night with Ellie, she had known everything about Miss Bingley she needed to know.

"I have finished my lunch, Miss Bingley. I shall be happy to take Ellie off your hands and locate Mrs. Hawkins."

Undecided whether or not to relinquish Mr. Darcy's precious daughter to this unsophisticated little country chit, Caroline quickly realized that doing so would allow her to be quite alone . . . with Mr. Darcy. . . on a sunny hillside . . . lounging on a blanket . . . just the two of them mere inches apart. She smiled ever so sweetly.

"I would do it myself, Miss Eliza, but, as you can see, my silk gown is much more susceptible to stains than your cotton muslin."

Ellie clung to Elizabeth's neck, content to be nestled against the softness of her body. "It is no trouble at all, I assure you, Miss Bingley."

Not wishing to be alone in Caroline's company, Darcy was about to stand when Caroline put her hand on his arm. "Mr. Darcy, how nice it is to finally be alone, is it not?"

No it was not, he thought, but said nothing.

Trying a different tack, she said, "I do believe that little Ellie gets prettier each day, Mr. Darcy; such a dear child."

"Yes, I see much of her mother in her looks," he replied, not realizing his indiscretion.

Surprised by such a comment, she retorted, "Hardly, Mr. Darcy. She is all *you* with her dark hair and eyes."

At this reply, he said nothing, concentrating fully on a blade of grass that he twirled between his thumb and forefinger.

"I did not wish to mention this in front of dear Jane, but I noticed that Miss Eliza seems to have some sort of fixation on the child. If I were you, Mr. Darcy, I would not leave Ellie alone in her company."

"That is absurd, Miss Bingley. I see no reason to be suspicious of Miss Elizabeth. She seems to have a genuine affection for the child," he said as he tried to hide his annoyance.

"Really, Mr. Darcy, you are much too trusting," objected Caroline as she again placed a hand on his arm. He immediately stood, not wishing to be pawed any further by the solicitous Miss Bingley. *Can this woman not take a hint?* "If you will excuse me, Miss Bingley, I have matters I need to discuss with my cousin."

As he left Caroline's company in search of Richard, he noted his cousin no longer sat on the other blanket. As his gaze travelled down the hill, he saw him once again in Elizabeth's company, heading towards the pond.

He was almost of a mind to follow them, but thought better of it. What was his cousin about? Was he taking advantage of her indebtedness to him? Surely he must know Elizabeth would not be a suitable candidate for marriage. Richard was a second son; he would need to make an alliance with a woman of some wealth, and his cousin was certainly aware that Elizabeth was not a woman of means.

She has little to recommend her, except, of course, for her fine eyes, or perhaps her light and pleasing figure, or maybe her wit and intelligence. Some might even find her determined independence and sense of adventure appealing, but beyond that, what could possibly be the attraction? And if his intentions were not honourable, if he was playing with her affections . . . Darcy clenched his fists at the thought.

~*~

"Tell me, Miss Bennet, are you enjoying your stay at Netherfield?"

"Yes, Colonel, I must admit, I am enjoying it far more than I ever would have imagined." Realizing that perhaps her reply was much more enthusiastic than called for, she added, "It is so good to be in Jane's company again."

"Yes, I daresay, your spirits are much improved since I saw you last in London."

As they approached the edge of the pond, they stopped. Richard turned, facing the hill they had just descended, while Elizabeth gazed upon the water. As he looked up, he could see Darcy staring at them from a distance.

"My cousin seems to have made a miraculous recovery. I wonder what has *caused* such a change. Even Georgiana, who never questions miracles, seems quite perplexed by his sudden improvement, but is grateful, nonetheless."

"I am sure it is just as Mr. Darcy stated, Colonel. He has realized that Ellie should be his first concern."

"I see you and Ellie have become well acquainted. She seems to have taken to you quite easily," he observed.

"Yes, she is a *wonderful* child, is she not?" enthused Elizabeth.

"Indeed, she is," replied the colonel as he glanced upward once more at Darcy's still-staring countenance. "She seems to have inherited many of Darcy's dark features, but her eyes appear even darker than the deepest brown reflected in his."

At this statement, Elizabeth coloured slightly, not meeting the colonel's gaze. "Did Mrs. Darcy possess such dark eyes?" inquired Elizabeth after regaining her composure.

"No, indeed, her eyes were as green as the clover," replied the colonel. "I had often wondered from what past relative she had inherited that unusual colour."

Elizabeth remained quiet for a long moment.

"What was she like?" Elizabeth surprised herself by asking. How could she not be curious about the woman who had cared for her daughter for the first several months of her life?

"Mrs. Darcy? She was a very sweet and kind-hearted woman," replied the colonel as he observed the woman before him.

"He must have loved her very much," she said, hardly believing she was again speaking of such intimate details of Mr. Darcy's life.

"I would say he was most devoted to her," he replied as Elizabeth's eyes met his.

An awkward silence prevailed, a circumstance that usually did not occur when they conversed, until the colonel finally spoke again. "I am looking forward to attending the ball."

"Oh yes," said Elizabeth "Besides many of their Netherfield neighbours, I understand some of Miss Bingley and Mr. Bingley's acquaintances from London are to attend. It should prove to be very entertaining."

"Will your family also attend?" asked the colonel.

Elizabeth's back stiffened slightly at the prospect of her mother and younger sisters attending the ball, but she was also looking forward to seeing her Aunt and Uncle Gardiner again. "Yes, all my family will attend, with perhaps the exception of Lydia and Mr. Wickham, as Jane received word that Lydia has begun her confinement."

The colonel was relieved to receive such news and was sure Darcy would be equally relieved. At the thought of Darcy, he looked again up the hill and found him in the same menacing pose.

"Perhaps we should rejoin the others," he said as he offered Elizabeth his arm.

She smiled at him as they proceeded up the hill. "How long do you intend to stay at Netherfield, Colonel?"

Though Darcy had now retreated from his post and no longer observed them, the colonel could not help but think, *One opinion may be that I have already stayed too long.*

Pat Santarsiero

CHAPTER THIRTY-SEVEN

"Elizabeth hurried down the stairs as quietly as she could, hoping the early hour of her departure would guarantee no encounters along the way. The breeches she had borrowed from Mr. Bingley were tighter than was her wont, but she would have to make do. As she passed the breakfast room, a servant stood at the ready to open the door for her to enter, but she gave him only a slight nod of her head as she passed him and headed outside.

As she reached the stables, the young groom who had been instructed by Mr. Bingley to attend her, approached. As he eyed her outfit, he smiled a wide grin, revealing every tooth in his head. He brought around the horse that had been selected for her use—a beautiful chestnut mare named Echoes, whose coat matched exactly the colour of Elizabeth's hair. He assisted her mount, and she thanked the young boy as she guided the horse away from Netherfield at a steady trot. When she reached the open fields, she kicked Echoes into a full gallop.

As the wind whipped over her face and through her hair, she felt the invigorating thrill that riding always gave her. It was a beautiful spring morning, and both she and Echoes were in high spirits.

As she passed below the ridge, Darcy looked down at her fleeting form as she skilfully governed the horse she rode. He observed her light hold on the reins and knew she would not be slowing her pace soon.

He had lain in wait for the last three mornings, hoping to catch a glimpse of her. His curiosity at seeing his Lizzy wearing breeches and riding astride had gotten the better of him. *She is not your Lizzy*, he reminded himself, but the knowledge that he had known her far more intimately than had any other man, gave him a small measure of solace and, as he had most recently discovered, an even larger amount of possessiveness.

She had not rejected his company over the last few days, but had not sought it out either. With the arrival of Mr. and Mrs. Hurst the previous afternoon, there was little chance of finding her alone. With so many guests now occupying Netherfield, she was always in company. When he did encounter her, their conversation was polite and always in full view of others. He hoped for a chance to talk to her alone. There were things that needed to be said.

Darcy led Marengo down the ridge and, once out in the open field, followed Lizzy's lead. She was far ahead of him but still within his sight. As he gained ground, he slowed his pace as he watched her urge her horse up a steep hill and then dismount.

Elizabeth walked to the edge of the plateau and stood there motionless for several minutes. Though she had walked to this spot many times when she had lived at Longbourn, she never had tired of the view. Indeed, it was the best prospect in the entire county. The sound of a horse behind her startled her.

"Mr. Darcy!"

"Miss Bennet." He could not conceal the slight smile that overtook his countenance as he eyed the breeches that showed off her figure to every advantage.

Elizabeth blushed with embarrassment at having been seen wearing the much too revealing garment. "Have you followed me, sir?" she asked.

Darcy dismounted and walked towards her. "Yes, but please do not be alarmed. I thought we could use some privacy . . . to discuss our current situation, Miss Bennet. I fear we have both avoided the subject far too long."

"It is a subject I am most happy to avoid, Mr. Darcy. I have tried with purpose to prevent my thinking upon it, sir." She turned slightly away from him, not wishing to expose her tears to him. "I never thought I would know such happiness again. To be able to see my daughter every day has been a true blessing. I do not want to think upon the time when I must leave her."

Darcy, too, was not happy at the prospect of her leaving. "Perhaps we could come to some amicable arrangement," he said, "something that might benefit us all. I have no set plan in mind, but I shall give it my fullest attention. I would welcome your thoughts on the subject as well."

"You . . . you would be willing . . . ?"

She stared at him for a long moment.

"Thank you, Mr. Darcy."

She could not describe the relief that she felt at hearing his words. He was going to allow her to continue to see her daughter in the future.

He wanted to move closer to her, but he let himself be content, knowing the smile she gave him was genuine and that his words had pleased her.

"I also wish to assure you that I intend to be the best of fathers to Ellie. Recent . . . events in my life had diverted my diligence in that pursuit, but I am committed to her happiness and wellbeing."

"I am pleased to hear that, Mr. Darcy. Her welfare had been much on my mind these past ten months."

"I assure you, it shall be so," he said as he granted her a short bow.

They stared for a moment into each other's eyes. He then turned to look around at the panoramic view. "Where exactly are we?"

"Why this is Oakham Mount, sir. Have you never heard of it? I used to walk it quite regularly when I lived at Longbourn."

He was glad that she did not seem in a hurry to part company with him, glad that she had finally smiled upon him.

"You ride extremely well, Miss Bennet. Despite whatever teaching skills your instructor was lacking, you have mastered the art quite proficiently."

"I thank you. Riding became my solace those first few months after Ellie was born." Thinking of her daughter's name, she could no longer contain her curiosity.

"May I ask who named her Ellie?"

It was now Darcy's turn to blush. "Well . . . her actual name is Anne Elizabeth, but Anne preferred to call her Ellie," he said, "and I . . . I had no objections."

She studied his face as he spoke. Then they turned their attentions to the vista, looking out over the mountains as they stood side by side in companionable silence.

As he kept his stare steady on the view before him, he said, "I had hoped you would mention my letter, Miss Bennet. Did you not receive it?"

"Yes, Mr. Darcy, I did."

She, too, did not turn her gaze. "When I first read it, I was too distraught to receive it with any civility. But upon subsequent readings, I learned to accept the sincerity of your words." She then withdrew her eyes from the far off view they had been observing and turned to look at him.

"Since we are to be much in each other's company, I would wish to put all unpleasantness behind us."

He turned to look directly into her eyes. "That is my wish also, Miss Bennet," said Darcy in earnest.

"For Ellie's sake I would wish that we can now meet as common and indifferent acquaintances, Mr. Darcy."

Common and indifferent acquaintances? "I would hope that we could do better than that, Miss Bennet. Could we not meet as friends, perhaps?"

"Yes, I believe that we could, Mr. Darcy."

They each presented the other with a smile.

"There is one more thing I wish to discuss, Miss Bennet, but because it might prove to be discomforting, I am afraid that it might diminish whatever harmony we have just achieved."

She looked at him curiously and replied with just a hint of amusement in her voice. "Considering our history, Mr. Darcy, it is hard to imagine any topic of conversation that might cause our discomfort. We are hardly strangers, sir."

He gave her an uneasy look as he debated whether to continue or not. Her now pleasant countenance and engaging, teasing manner made him reluctant to do anything that would upset their very fragile accord.

As she noticed his disquiet, she offered a suggestion. "If voicing this offense serves no real purpose, perhaps it would be best to leave it unsaid."

"Your charity is most generous. As much as I would like to remain in your good graces, I have learned that disguise of every sort is sooner or later revealed." He gave her a smile, but it immediately faded as he tried to temper his next words to her. He took a deep breath. "Do you recall the day you fainted?"

"I could scarcely forget it, Mr. Darcy."

"Besides the obvious reason known only to you and myself, you mentioned that it might have been the result of the sleeping powders and too much brandy imbibed the night before."

Elizabeth nodded, confirming his words.

"What exactly do you recall of that night?"

She stared at him and, observing his serious demeanour, set her mind to remembering that night's events. "I had not slept very well since . . . well . . . you know. For some reason there was a decanter of brandy in my room. In my desperate attempt to attain sleep, I drank two glasses and eventually started to drift off. I then heard a child's cry. Of course, I did not know at the time that it was my daughter. But I was again wide awake. I remembered the sleeping powders my doctor had prescribed and took them also. However, I still could not sleep and thought perhaps a dull book might help and went down to the library."

"What do you remember about the library?" Darcy asked as his gaze continued to meet hers.

"I remember getting a book down from one of the shelves and going over to the couch to read. I must have fallen asleep because the next thing I knew, I woke up several hours later."

"Did you dream while you slept, Miss Bennet?"

As soon as he asked the question, her hand went to her mouth, and she released a slight gasp.

"How could you be aware of my dream, sir?"

"I know of your dream because it was mine also."

As she suddenly realized the import of his statement, she turned a bright red.

"I'm afraid I arrived at Netherfield that night already under the influence of several whiskeys. Add to that a bottle of Bingley's best brandy, and, needless to say, I was quite inebriated. When I came upon you lying on the couch, I was convinced you were a dream."

They both stood there, staring at each other, recollecting the "dream" that was *not* a dream.

Expecting her contempt, he was surprised when she said, "I suppose I should have thought twice before I stated there was no topic of conversation that might cause our discomfort, Mr. Darcy."

Then offering a slight smile she said, "May I suggest that we add this to the unpleasantness we have just agreed to put behind us?"

He searched her eyes, as he confessed, "I will agree to put it behind us, Miss Bennet, but I must argue the unpleasantness."

Her colour only increased at his response, and she had to turn away.

Even though reluctant to leave her and the private domain of the mountaintop, he knew they should not be seen alone together in such an intimate setting. "I think it best I leave you to resume your morning's activities."

As he spoke, clouds overtook the sun and cast an ominous shadow over them. Elizabeth looked up and frowned. "Perhaps we should both head back before we get soaked."

He helped her mount Echoes and led the way down the hill. As they reached the fields, they did not gallop but cantered their horses, allowing him a few more minutes in her company.

As they approached the stables, the threatening rain began its descent. When the groom approached Elizabeth to help her dismount, Darcy denied him and assisted her himself, securing his hands on her waist and lowering her slowly to the ground. As her body slid down, brushing against his own, his breeches felt tighter than hers.

Indifferent definitely did not describe how he felt about her.

CHAPTER THIRTY-EIGHT

The heavy rains that had fallen the preceding evening did little to dampen the spirits of those inhabiting Netherfield on that overcast morning of the twenty-second day of April.

Georgiana eagerly headed for the breakfast room and, as she saw Elizabeth already partaking of her morning meal, joined her new friend.

"I'm afraid the weather has affected my plans," said Elizabeth. "I was hoping to ride, but last night's rain has made that prospect impossible. Have you any plans?"

"I was only intending to practice a new piece of music my brother brought me back from London," said Georgiana. "Perhaps we could go over it together after breakfast."

Elizabeth smiled and nodded in agreement while putting another spoonful of jam on her toast.

"I have not had a chance to acquaint myself with Mr. and Mrs. Hurst as yet," said Elizabeth. With a little hesitation she asked, "Is Mrs. Hurst much like her sister?"

Georgiana looked around the room and, seeing that they were quite alone, replied, "Well, she can be *very* much like Miss Bingley at times. But I have observed when she is not in Miss Bingley's company, she seems much friendlier. Sometimes I think Mrs. Hurst is afraid to disagree with her sister and that Miss Bingley has much influence over her."

"I certainly can understand such a situation," replied Elizabeth. "When we lived at Longbourn, my sister Kitty was influenced greatly by our sister Lydia. She often imitated her careless attitude rather than defy her. Thankfully, Kitty has much improved since then. You will be able to meet Kitty and Mary in a few hours. They should arrive sometime before lunch."

"Your sister Lydia is married to Mr. Wickham, is she not?" asked Georgiana.

"Why, yes; how did you know? Did Jane mention it to you?"

"No, my brother informed me. I . . . I was once acquainted with Mr. Wickham. He was our steward's son and lived with us for many years at Pemberley," replied Georgiana, reverting back to her shy demeanour.

"I once thought myself in love with him," she said looking down at her hands in her lap.

"I'm so sorry, Georgiana. I did not mean to remind you of unpleasant memories," Elizabeth said as she reached for the young girl's hand.

"No, you did nothing wrong, Elizabeth. I am well over that entire episode of my life. If your sister has found happiness with Mr. Wickham, then I am pleased for her."

"Believe me, Georgiana, whatever happiness Lydia has found with Mr. Wickham will, I am sure, be of short duration. As much as I love my sister, I must confess she was never a very sensible girl. I am sure *you* will find a gentleman of much higher character, someone who will appreciate all your wonderful qualities."

Georgiana hugged her friend, thankful for her kind words. As Elizabeth hugged her back, she glanced at the doorway and observed Mr. Darcy watching them. He gave her a look that conveyed his gratitude, and she acknowledged it with a small smile. After a moment he turned away and left the room, undetected by his sister.

The two women then turned their conversation to the evening's ball and to gowns, laces, and slippers. Even though she was not "out" yet, Darcy had conceded to allow Georgiana to attend the ball for Jane and Mr. Bingley on the condition that she would dance only with her cousin and himself. She had readily agreed and could hardly wait for evening to fall.

Mrs. Bennet, Kitty, and Mary arrived shortly before noon, and, to Elizabeth's great surprise, her mother's behaviour was, if not above reproach, at least much more subdued than Elizabeth could ever recall. It seemed that Kitty was not the only one to have benefited from the absence of Lydia from their daily lives.

Her mother was still a bit louder than necessary and, upon her observations of the estate, a bit too effusive with her comments, but on the whole her conduct was most amenable. In a somewhat stifled manner, Mrs. Bennet greeted her ill-favoured daughter, willing to concede some civility now that she knew Mr. Bingley had provided a home upon Netherfield property for her to comfortably live out her remaining years.

Elizabeth eyed Mr. Darcy as he was introduced to her relations and noted no particular reaction, other that his usual reticent, yet polite, demeanour.

After tea had been served, Mr. Bingley showed the newly arrived Bennets to their rooms. There was much to be done to prepare themselves for tonight's ball. Mrs. Hill, the only servant Mrs. Bennet could afford to keep after her departure from Longbourn, accompanied the ladies to attend their needs. She offered her services to Lizzy, as well, as she and Jane were always her favourites.

~*~

Jane knocked lightly on Elizabeth's door. "Lizzy, it's me." She entered her sister's room and took a seat on the bed.

"Mrs. Hill has outdone herself; you look beautiful, Lizzy," said Jane.

"And so do you, Jane," said Elizabeth as she rose from the dressing table to give her sister a hug.

"Jane, you're shaking! Don't tell me you are nervous?"

Elizabeth sat next to Jane on the bed and took her hand. "You will undoubtedly be the most beautiful woman in attendance this evening, and Mr. Bingley will have eyes for no one but you. Surely you do not regret your decision to marry?" asked Elizabeth.

"Oh no, not at all, Lizzy. It's just that I'm . . . well . . . to tell the truth, I was not too worried about the wedding night," said Jane as her complexion coloured, "until Mama came and told me what I am to expect. She did not make it sound very pleasant."

Elizabeth fought with all her might the urge to roll her eyes. If Jane's pained expression was any indication of what she had heard from their mother, she somehow felt obligated to relate what she could on the subject to alleviate Jane's concerns. How she would do that without revealing the source of her knowledge, she had no idea.

"Surely you and Mr. Bingley have shared some intimacy," said Elizabeth. "I have seen the way you look at each other."

The more than rosy hue of Jane's complexion did not diminish.

Lizzy thought of Mr. Darcy and their last night in Scotland. There had been nothing at all unpleasant about that night. She could easily recall his actions as he skilfully brought her emotionally and physically to a peak of desire.

"I know that many women are of the opinion that a wife's connubial duties can be a disagreeable requirement of marriage," said Elizabeth, unsure of how to continue. "I do not believe that will be case with you and Mr. Bingley. He loves you dearly, Jane, as you do him. Any discomfort will be brief, and the pleasure of sharing such intimacy will far outweigh any initial uneasiness. His love for you will assure he proceeds with care and tenderness."

"Oh, Lizzy, I know deep down in my heart that what you say must be true. You do make it sound so much more appealing than our mother has. But, how can you speak so confidently?" asked Jane.

Elizabeth's serious demeanour lingered for an instant, but noting Jane's look of confusion, she quickly tried to lighten the moment. "When you meet the man your heart has been waiting for, how can it be otherwise? I have imagined it many times . . . if I am lucky enough ever to find a love like yours and Mr. Bingley's, I am sure that is how it will be. Oh, Jane, I know you and Mr. Bingley will have a most perfect life together."

The two sisters hugged as Jane whispered, "Thank you, Lizzy. You have made me see the foolishness of my worry."

After they finally parted from their sisterly embrace, Elizabeth asked, "What of Miss Bingley? Will she be residing at Netherfield after you are married?"

"No, Charles informed me she will be staying with Mr. and Mrs. Hurst, at least for a while. She will be leaving with them right after the wedding. Have you made up your mind about staying here yet?"

"No, I'm not sure what I want to do. I appreciate your kind offer to live here, Jane, I really do. But I want to give it some more thought."

"Promise me you will stay here while Charles and I are on our honeymoon. Surely you can stay that long. Besides, you cannot leave until you have made a decision as to your future. You need some time, Lizzy, to think about what you want. You must stay at least a few days after Charles and I return; you must. I was so long without you, dear Lizzy. Please promise you will stay."

"All right, Jane. I promise, I promise! Should I warn Mr. Bingley *now* that you can be such a nag at times?!" teased Elizabeth.

"How are you and Mr. Darcy getting along?" asked Jane.

Feeling herself blush, she asked, "What do you mean?"

"I just happened to notice that he looks at you quite often," responded Jane.

"We get along fine, Jane, but I would not read too much into his looks. We are better suited as friends."

"So you have no feelings beyond friendship for Mr. Darcy?"

"My feelings are . . ."

Jane watched as her sister's face displayed her obvious struggle in determining the answer to that question. She wondered if perhaps her feelings for Mr. Darcy were more than she was willing to acknowledge.

"Jane, I am not interested in forming an attachment with any gentleman. But, if I were to judge Mr. Darcy solely upon my observation of him over the last two weeks, I would say I had an overall favourable opinion of him."

Elizabeth found herself surprised by her own admission, but she had to admit he had been nothing but kind to her since his arrival and, upon observing him with Ellie and his sister over the last two weeks, could find no fault with her declaration.

"Do you never wish to marry then, Lizzy?"

"I do not believe so." Elizabeth smiled at her sister. "But be not troubled, Jane, for I shall be the best of aunts and teach your ten children to embroider cushions and play their instruments very ill."

"You are very stubborn, Lizzy!"

"Of that I am sure. But I promise I will stay until you and Mr. Bingley return from your honeymoon. After all, it will only be for a few weeks."

"I guess that will have to suffice. Just remember, Lizzy, you will always be welcome here."

The two sisters hugged again. A moment later the door opened, and Mrs. Bennet entered the room, and the two sisters stood. "Come, Jane. You do not want to be late for your own ball! My, you do look most lovely. Oh Jane, I knew you could not be so beautiful for nothing!"

She then focused her eyes on Elizabeth. "You look very nice too, Lizzy. Of course, you will never be as beautiful as your sister."

"Thank you, Mama," said Elizabeth as she once again fought the temptation to roll her eyes.

As they made their way to the stairs, they found Mr. Bingley waiting to escort Jane. When he saw her, he smiled and eyed her lovely countenance appreciatively. The love in his eyes was quite apparent. He was indeed a lucky man!

To think he had almost thrown it all away. His own insecurities had almost cost him his happiness. He would always be grateful to Darcy for setting him straight. Thanks to his friend, he would never again allow another person's opinion to deter him from what he wanted.

As he thought upon that conversation, he smiled to himself. *One day I will tell Jane the entire story*, he thought. *But just to be on the safe side, it is best I wait until after we are man and wife.*

Pat Santarsiero

CHAPTER THIRTY-NINE

Jane and Mr. Bingley stood beaming at the entrance to the large room that had been transformed into the loveliest of ballrooms. As the prospective bride and groom greeted each attendee, their joy was obvious. Caroline stood next to the couple, as she officiated in what would be her final role as Mistress of the manor. In two days' time, her role would be relegated to that of "sister" as Jane would rightfully take her proper place as wife of Mr. Bingley.

The ball was well attended, with everyone in their finest apparel. Caroline wore a chartreuse taffeta that when seen reflected in light, turned a melon colour. The feather in her chapeau made her appear at least a foot taller than her already excessive height.

Elizabeth approached the happy couple and, as she did, many appreciative eyes followed her movements. She indeed looked lovelier than ever. Mrs. Hill had done an admirable job in fixing Lizzy's hair into a most attractive upsweep, allowing only a few loose curls to lightly brush against the back of her neck. The gown she wore was a delicate lavender chiffon that hugged Elizabeth's ample bosom and swept enticingly over the curves of her hips.

Elizabeth kissed her sister on the cheek and warmly greeted Mr. Bingley. As she next approached Caroline, Miss Bingley stated in surprise, "I see not *all* your dresses were bought in the country. Miss Eliza."

Colonel Fitzwilliam's gaze followed Elizabeth's progress as she entered the ballroom, and he watched as she greeted Mr. and Mrs.

Collins. Even though he would admit he felt an attraction towards the young lady, his suspicions regarding her connection to Darcy were mounting.

Kitty and Mary entered the ballroom, and Elizabeth went to greet them. She could not get over the change in her sister Kitty. She had somehow gone from a silly adolescent to a confident young lady overnight. It was amazing how the absence of Lydia's influence could have had such a positive effect on her. Colonel Fitzwilliam approached the three ladies, and Elizabeth made the introductions. He requested Kitty's third set, which she graciously accepted. Mary stood with a sheet of music in her hand, making her intention of exhibiting during the supper hour apparent.

As Elizabeth was next engaged in conversation with her Aunt and Uncle Gardner, she saw Mr. Darcy escorting Georgiana into the ballroom. When Georgiana spotted her, she led her brother in their direction.

As he approached, she noticed his cravat was tied in a most striking and intricate manner, and for a moment she was excessively diverted with the challenge untying such a knot would present. That thought brought an attractive flush to her already rosy complexion.

As soon as he saw her, his heart leapt in his chest. She had turned in their direction as he and Georgiana had entered the ballroom. Her face was luminous, and she appeared to be floating on a cloud of lavender chiffon. He drank her in from head to toe, admiring her every virtue. "Good evening, Miss Bennet," he said as he bowed.

"Good evening, Mr. Darcy, Georgiana. Allow me to introduce my aunt and uncle." After introductions were made, the sounds of the orchestra pervaded the ballroom as the musicians tuned their instruments to begin the first set.

Of course, Darcy would dance the first set with his sister, for to ask anyone other than Georgiana would attract too much attention. As he was about to lead her towards the dance floor, however, he turned and addressed Elizabeth.

"I would be honoured to dance the second set with you, Miss Bennet, and if it would not be too much of an imposition to place upon our newly formed friendship, perhaps the supper set as well?"

"Thank you, Mr. Darcy, I am not engaged for either set." He bowed slightly and, as he turned, caught a glimpse of his cousin approaching her. He watched as Richard took her hand and led her to the dance floor.

"May I say how lovely you look this evening, Miss Elizabeth?"

Looking up at him Elizabeth grinned. "Yes, you may indeed, Colonel."

Once again they engaged in easy conversation while in each other's close proximity during the dance.

Darcy tried to keep his attentions to the steps of the dance, but found himself often looking down to where Richard and Elizabeth were situated. He observed that they had much conversation. His eyes were then drawn to their hands as they were joined in requirement of the dance.

He felt his own hand twitch at the thought of touching Elizabeth, and the remembrance of their intimate caresses caused him to misstep. He quickly apologized to Georgiana and made a greater effort to focus his concentration.

When the set ended, the colonel led Elizabeth back to the edge of the dance floor. Darcy led Georgiana to the same vicinity, and, as the music started up again for the second set, the two gentlemen exchanged partners.

He took her gloved hand in his as he led her toward the centre of the dance floor. Before he released her, he let his thumb glide over her knuckles. Such a small gesture, but it caused a reaction in her, nonetheless.

As the dance parted them, he looked back towards her, paying no mind to the woman who now moved to his side. When the movements of the dance brought them once again back together, Darcy took advantage of her closeness. "Is it your plan to stay on at Netherfield after the wedding?"

"I promised Jane I would stay until they return from their honeymoon. She insisted that I remain a few days upon their homecoming. I have not yet decided what I will do after that."

"Might I ask a favour of you, Miss Bennet?" he asked as he guided her into the next turn of their dance.

"Yes, of course, Mr. Darcy."

"Georgiana and I must be away to London after the wedding. We will remain there for about a fortnight as we have a few social obligations we must attend. I would like to leave Mrs. Hawkins here with Ellie while we are gone. Would it be too much to ask of you to watch Ellie until our return?"

Elizabeth looked up at him and graced him with a smile. "I would be most happy to look after her, Mr. Darcy."

If a smile, he thought, could illuminate a room, it was most certainly Lizzy's. He watched as she whirled around him and moved on to her next partner in the dance. He knew his words had pleased her, and her reaction was all that he had hoped. Once again oblivious to his new partner, he followed Lizzy's every move with his eyes until she was once again before him.

The set came to an end far too soon and, reluctantly, he relinquished her company. Darcy moved to an inconspicuous location in the room and watched as she danced the next two sets. Though pleased that he was able to observe her undetected, he could not deny his jealousy as he watched the parade of men who requested her company.

Upon witnessing his cousin again about to approach her, he stepped from behind the shadows and was immediately detected by Caroline Bingley, who was in the company of a gentlemen whom he recognized immediately.

"Mr. Darcy! Where have you been hiding? Do you remember Lord Westcott and his daughter?" she anxiously asked, thrilled at the fact that she was able to secure such noble guests in attendance. *Wait until the London papers hear of my association with such aristocrats!* she thought. *I will undoubtedly be welcomed into the most prestigious circles of society once it is known.*

"Of course. How good to see you again, Lord Westcott. It has been some time, has it not?"

"At least two years," he responded. "I was just relating to Georgiana my astonishment at how she has grown since I last saw her. She reminds me much of your mother."

"Yes," agreed Darcy looking across the room at his sister with pride. "She has inherited many of our mother's features, although I believe she has already exceeded our mother's height."

"I must admit I am surprised to see you here. I hadn't realized you and Mr. Bingley were so well acquainted," said Darcy.

"I was surprised also upon receiving the invitation," replied Lord Westcott. "I have never been in his company aside from the few times I met him with you at the club. Had you not written your expressed desire that I attend on the invitation, I doubt that I would have. But now I'm glad I did. It's been such a pleasure to see you and Georgiana again." The Earl paused and tilted his head. "Darcy, you did send the invitation, did you not? It bore your name."

"Ah, yes, I did. I invited several of our acquaintances, my lord. It merely slipped my mind for the moment."

Knowing full well he had not written any such thing on an invitation, he looked over to Caroline, who was examining her nails. Not wishing to make a scene, he turned his attentions to Lord Westcott's daughter who patiently waited her turn at introduction.

Miss Westcott was several years younger than Darcy. The last time he had seen her, she could not have been more than ten. He imagined she was only a year or two older than Georgiana. She had grown into a most attractive young lady with hair the colour of honey. Her blue eyes stood out starkly against the alabaster of her flawless complexion, and she possessed a pleasing figure, though, if he were honest, much too thin for his taste.

As Caroline saw Darcy look upon the young woman with approval, she was beginning to doubt the wisdom of her deceitful ploy.

When Lord Westcott asked Miss Bingley to dance, Miss Westcott moved closer to Darcy, a becoming blush gracing her countenance.

"Will . . . will you be . . . residing in London this season, Mr. Darcy?" she finally managed to conjure up the words to inquire.

"I will travel there in a few days, but will remain only a fortnight. I have other business that calls me back to Pemberley."

Blushing again, she endeavoured to overcome her shyness to ask, "Dare I hope you might accept an invitation to dine with us during your stay in Town, Mr. Darcy?"

"If it coincides with my plans, I would be most happy to dine with you and your father, Miss Westcott."

As they stood there together, Darcy felt obliged to ask her to dance. Leading her to the floor, he observed Elizabeth dancing with Richard. Their eyes met.

Elizabeth immediately turned away as her complexion reddened. "Are you unwell, Miss Bennet?" asked the colonel.

"No, not at all, sir. I feel exceptionally fine this evening," she replied.

Elizabeth tried to maintain an air of indifference. Why should she care if Mr. Darcy danced with other women? So what if this one happened to be attractive, with honey blonde hair? Certainly he was free to do whatever he pleased. After all, she and Mr. Darcy were only friends. With determination she tried to ignore the presence of the attractive looking couple on the dance floor for the remainder of the set.

When the set ended, Caroline and Lord Westcott returned to Miss Westcott's and Darcy's company. As the music began again Caroline directed several hints toward Darcy. "This music is so inspiring, is it not, Mr. Darcy?" . . . followed by a subtle "It has been so long since I danced a reel."

Resigned to his fate, he asked her to dance the next set, which thankfully did *not* include a reel. During the dance, Darcy asked, "How is it, do you suppose, that a note bearing my name appeared on Lord Westcott's invitation?"

"I cannot imagine, Mr. Darcy," she answered as her eyes looked everywhere but at his.

Darcy decided since it had been a most pleasant surprise to see Lord Westcott again after so much time, that there was no reason for him to be angry with Caroline and let the matter drop.

At last, it was time for the supper set, and he again approached Elizabeth. She graciously accepted his hand, and once again he led her to the dance floor. This set was more intimate than the prior ones had been. The dancers were divided into groups of six, exchanging partners only within their group. As it happened, they were partnered with Bingley, Jane, and Mr. and Mrs. Gardiner, and the set was indeed a most pleasant experience. He spent the entire thirty minutes in her company, inhaling her delicate lavender scent and admiring her fine eyes. When the set ended, he had the added pleasure of offering his arm and escorting her into dinner.

As they stood in line to enter the dining area, Darcy could not help but comment, "You look quite lovely this evening, Miss Bennet. But I cannot recall a time when you have not, even when you were wearing breeches," he said as he smiled upon her.

Elizabeth tried not to blush at such a comment, remembering he had seen her wearing nothing at all.

"Thank you, Mr. Darcy. I admit this dress does make me feel quite elegant."

"I believe the dress has little to do with it," he responded.

He knew he was being far too attentive. But as usual, when in her company, he could not seem to restrain his responses to her, verbal or physical.

Pat Santarsiero

CHAPTER FORTY

As the ball was nearing its conclusion, Mr. Bingley engaged Elizabeth in what ended up being the liveliest set of the evening. Upon finishing the last of the set, Elizabeth excused herself and walked to the balcony to breathe in some much needed fresh air. While she stood overlooking the gardens, she heard a conversation in progress on the adjacent balcony.

"Whatever possesses him to show her such notice, I cannot imagine. Such a country nothing, just like her sister. I suppose he is just amusing himself. I have already heard rumours in the servant's quarters of a compromising night in the library."

The voice was unmistakably Caroline Bingley's. Elizabeth stood perfectly still, waiting for the conversation to continue.

"Do you not think he could form a serious attachment to her?" asked Louisa.

"Oh, do be serious, dear sister. Remember in London when I sought Mr. Darcy's help in separating Charles and Jane? I asked him if *he* would ever consider marrying someone with such low connections, and he assured me that his social standing and sense of duty would never permit an alliance with someone so beneath his society. And let us not forget the fact that he married Anne. Were they not preordained to marry since birth? Indeed his aunt, Lady Catherine, would brook no opposition on the matter, and he eventually succumbed to her wishes."

Having been in the woman's company for the past two weeks, Caroline's opinion of her was hardly surprising. How does a woman get to be like Caroline Bingley, she wondered?

"And as for that daughter of his, I am sure there is something amiss. I was so close to learning the truth from Dr. Adams."

"Yes," said Louisa. "How inconsiderate of him to die before he could tell you all he knew."

"Indeed, it was," replied Caroline, unaware of any sarcasm on Louisa's part.

"He was certainly of the opinion that Anne was hardly fit to bear a child. The girl is unmistakably Mr. Darcy's, but as to the identity of the mother, I cannot imagine. Whoever she is, I am sure she was always paid handsomely for her services."

Caroline and Louisa tittered behind their fans.

Elizabeth could not make out any further comments as the two women had now begun their departure from the balcony.

Elizabeth slowly turned and walked back towards the ballroom. When she found Jane and Mr. Bingley, she pleaded exhaustion and excused herself to her rooms. As she lay awake in bed that night, she thought about all she had heard on the balcony.

That Mr. Darcy had admitted *he* would never consider marrying someone so beneath his society should have had no effect upon her, since she had already purged her heart of him. Hadn't she? She could not account for why it bothered her so to hear it.

And had he tried to help separate Jane and Mr. Bingley?

Elizabeth took little offense to Caroline's insulting comments for they were of no consequence. Her only concern was being able to stay with her daughter for as long as possible. And if being in Mr. Darcy's good graces allowed her that pleasure, she would do everything she could to remain so.

She only prayed that Mr. Darcy would never entertain the notion of an attachment to Miss Bingley. The thought of Caroline Bingley as stepmother to her daughter made her cringe. It was unsettling just hearing the woman *mention* her daughter.

She was surprised, however, to learn of the circumstances of Mr. Darcy's marriage. Had he married Anne only out of familial duty? It had not been the love match she had surmised?

Mr. Darcy had been right about one thing. Disguise of every sort is sooner or later revealed. Their night of *dreaming* in the library was known by Caroline Bingley. But for some strange reason that did not bring her the angst she would have imagined.

~*~

"Can I interest you in a nightcap, Bingley?"

"As a matter of fact, Darcy, you can!" replied a fatigued but very happy Charles Bingley. "I think the ball was a great success."

At that moment Richard joined the two gentlemen in the study and agreed, "Indeed, it was."

Although the hour was late and all three had spent most of the evening on their feet, they did not wish to retire just yet, each one with his own reason to delay sleep. Charles Bingley's reason was obvious. He was still feeling the excitement of the evening and wanted a little time to unwind. A final drink with his two friends seemed just the thing. Richard's curiosity had gotten the better of him throughout the evening, and he now wanted to see if he could uncover any information from Darcy as to his quite blatant attentions towards a certain young lady.

Darcy, on the other hand, knew that his thoughts and emotions were so engaged that there would be no sleep for him tonight.

As the three gentlemen sat facing the fire, they lifted their glasses in a toast to Bingley and his forthcoming marriage.

"I envy you, Bingley," said a most reflective Darcy. "No one can doubt your happiness."

"I daresay, Darcy, you are the reason I now find myself in such blissful circumstances. But for your honesty with me that night I came to see you in London, I would never have had the courage to seek out Miss Bennet again."

Surprised to hear of his cousin's involvement in Bingley's love life, the colonel asked, "What did he say to you that had such an affect?"

"It was my own foolishness that led me to believe my sister Caroline's disparaging opinions of Miss Bennet. And she had me convinced that your cousin felt the same. Thankfully, I decided to confront Darcy and find out for myself what his objections were to Miss Bennet."

Knowing the strict code by which his cousin lived, he was sure Darcy had harboured *many* objections to his friend marrying someone with so little to recommend her.

"Well, Darcy, what *were* your objections to Miss Bennet?"

"I assure you, I had none," said Darcy as he now became defensive. "And I told Bingley as much that night at my townhouse. However, that was not the material point."

As Richard raised an eyebrow, he asked, "The material point being?"

Not quite understanding the chiding that was now volleying between the two men, Bingley felt the need to defend his friend and quickly answered in his behalf, "Why, that I should not allow my feelings to be swayed by the opinions of others, nor conform to the dictates of society when they do not serve my own best interest."

"That is all very good advice indeed, Darcy. However, you must admit it is somewhat perplexing since you have lived your entire life doing just that very thing," said Richard.

Several moments passed with not a sound but the crackling of the fire. Finally, Richard could stand the silence no longer and asked, "Can it be that you would wish to take some of your own advice?

Or do you still believe you must put your family's expectations before your own happiness?"

Again Darcy volunteered no reply.

"What do you mean?" asked Bingley. "Are you suggesting that Darcy has feelings for someone who might be regarded an unsuitable match?"

Darcy gave his cousin a look of warning. He was not sure exactly what Richard surmised, but if he had any inkling as to his past relationship with Elizabeth, he silently prayed he would keep it to himself.

"I think my cousin has found himself quite delighted with Miss Elizabeth."

"Really? Darcy, how extraordinary!" replied Bingley. "Why have you not mentioned it? Have you made your feelings known? Does she return your regard?"

Darcy let out an exasperated sigh. "Miss Bennet and I have formed a friendship, nothing more."

Richard raised a doubtful eyebrow, and Bingley was not the least bit convinced either.

Darcy put down his glass, still more than half full. Sometime over the last two weeks he had lost his taste for alcohol. He stood and was ready to leave, yet he felt he owed his cousin a response to his previous question.

"I shall always strive to meet the expectations of those whom I consider family."

CHAPTER FORTY-ONE

The day that Mr. Charles Bingley led his radiant bride towards their awaiting carriage to begin their future life together was indeed the most beautiful day one could have wished for. Tears streamed down Elizabeth's cheeks as she hugged her sister and new brother before their departure. She would miss Jane but was content knowing that she would live a most fulfilling life, married to a man who adored her and loving him in return.

Elizabeth acknowledged that perhaps some of the tears she shed were for herself, realizing she would most likely never experience that kind of happiness. But that was the price she had been willing to pay to secure the future of her most beloved sister. Hopefully, Kitty and Mary would also someday find themselves so agreeably settled.

Elizabeth stood next to her mother and sisters as they waved goodbye to Mr. and Mrs. Bingley. Her family would now be returning to Meryton to prepare for their move to their new home at Netherfield Park. Mrs. Bennet made it a point to mention that she was most unhappy that all the renovations she had requested would not be completed for at least another month.

As much as Elizabeth would have liked to comfort her mother at such a tragedy, she was a little relieved that her mother and sisters would not be occupying Netherfield Park over the next two weeks. She wanted Ellie all to herself, with no need for explanations.

Despite everything she had heard on the balcony, she was determined not to let anything spoil her time alone with Ellie.

Just then Colonel Fitzwilliam approached her. "I must be departing to Matlock. I hope we shall have the opportunity to meet again, Miss Bennet."

"I hope we shall, too, Colonel. I have enjoyed your company, sir."

Darcy watched as his cousin addressed Elizabeth and was relieved as he saw him bow and take his leave. He had been unable to find even the briefest moment alone with Elizabeth, and, except for the necessities of the day, they had hardly spoken. He was happy to grant her these two weeks alone with her daughter. He knew how she had restrained her activity with the child during her stay at Netherfield as not to arouse suspicions. He had offered her his friendship, and she had accepted. If friends were all they were destined to be, he would try to be content with that. He could never make up for the heartache she had endured because of him. Nothing could ever make up for that.

~*~

Georgiana and Darcy arrived at their London townhouse before noon. He would have preferred riding Marengo but did not want Georgie travelling alone in the carriage all the way to London. When given a choice, he always preferred riding Marengo than being cooped up in a carriage.

The day was turning out to be quite glorious. Spring was well under way. They had told few of their acquaintances of their plans as they anticipated attending only a handful of engagements that were deemed necessary to keep Georgiana in the social spectrum required of her as a soon to be "out" lady of society. Aside from those few occasions, Darcy was looking forward to a night at the theatre and perhaps a concert or two.

However, even the best laid plans can go awry, and unfortunately, as soon as they arrived, they were greeted on the street by Lady Waverly. Though not a particularly close acquaintance, Darcy had been in her company on a few occasions while attending dinner parties a few seasons back. Once she and her late husband, Lord Waverly, had been the toast of London, but soon after his untimely death, she had been plagued by scandalous rumours. Her social circle had since been limited to those of lesser consequence and similar situation.

"How very pleasant to see you again, Mr. Darcy," said Lady Waverly as she extended her hand. "I had not heard you were in town."

Darcy took her hand and bowed. "We have just now arrived. We do not plan to stay very long as we are expected back at Pemberley soon."

"Perhaps you will honour me with your presence this evening. I am having a small gathering. I believe you know some of the other guests who will be attending. They would be most happy to see you."

"I do not think that will be possible, Lady Waverly. Georgiana and I had planned an early dinner and to spend a quiet evening at home after our long journey. I would be happy to accept your invitation another time."

As he was about to retreat towards the townhouse entrance, Georgiana's voice interceded. "Fitzwilliam, you do not have to stay with me tonight. I'm sure you would have a much better time visiting with your friends. I will find a way to amuse myself, I am sure."

"How delightful; then it is settled. Shall we say eight o'clock, sir?" Lady Waverly asked.

Seeing no gracious way out of the invitation, Darcy nodded. "It shall be my pleasure to attend."

~*~

As he entered the townhouse, he noted the furnishings were well worn. Either from neglect or lack of funds, upkeep had been kept to a minimum. He was announced and several heads turned towards him. Lady Waverly approached and took his arm as she led him into a large parlour. Though he could still see traces of her past beauty, the years since her husband's death had not been kind. He felt some sympathy towards her as he remembered the woman she once was.

Upon entering the parlour, Darcy recognized a few people, though he could not place them. Certainly they were not among those of his usual social province. A drink was placed into his hand before an objection could be uttered, and he was immediately surrounded by a flock of ladies, though that particular appellation may have been too generous a term.

As he took the first sip of his drink, he realized that, except for a wedding toast to Bingley at the ball, he hadn't partaken of alcohol the entire two weeks he had been at Netherfield. The taste of the whiskey seemed bitter on his palate.

He was silently berating himself for acquiescing to Lady Waverly's invitation; then his eyes fell upon a woman across the room. He could not see her face, but the similarity of her dark chestnut hair to Lizzy's made him turn to look.

As the discourse around him continued, a refill for his empty glass was immediately summoned and placed in his hand. He was now in the company of a Mr. Chauncey and a matronly woman by the name of Lady Spencer whose choice of gown left little to the imagination. At first Darcy thought she required some assistance as she seemed to be leaning heavily upon her companion. However, he soon realized that the woman required no assistance other than a lesson in decorum.

He turned to find the dark haired woman walking in his direction. As she crossed the room, she stopped to talk with Lady Waverly, and then they both proceeded towards him.

"I have been requested to perform an introduction, Mr. Darcy," said Lady Waverly. "May I present Claire LaRoche? Mrs. LaRoche, Mr. Fitzwilliam Darcy."

He smiled to himself, for he assessed her far inferior in comparison to Lizzy, although she did hold a certain air of sophistication. She was older than he had first presumed, perhaps a few years older than himself, a fact she had tried to disguise by the application of powder and rouge. The bodice of her gown was lower than polite society would deem proper.

He learned she was a widow, recently from France, now visiting family in England. She expressed her pleasure in meeting him and offered her ungloved hand. Lady Waverly made a silent departure from their company, leaving Darcy alone with the woman.

They were seated next to each other at dinner. Darcy had already imbibed several glasses of whiskey and, during dinner, at least two different wines were served to complement each course. By dessert, the cognac had his head swimming.

As he escorted Mrs. LaRoche from the dining salon, she swayed slightly, and he had to quickly grasp her arm to keep her steady on her feet. "Perhaps you would be so kind as to accompany me out onto the terrace, sir. I believe I could use some fresh air."

He said nothing but nodded slightly to affirm his concurrence. He would have demurred, but he assessed that his own need for fresh air was equal to hers. As they proceeded through the terrace doors towards a small rooftop garden, Darcy voiced his thoughts.

"I believe there was more wine served than food. Even I find myself affected by so much alcohol."

After they had stood in silence for a few moments, Mrs. LaRoche finally spoke. "I have heard of your recent loss, Mr. Darcy. I imagine you have kept yourself secluded since your wife's death."

This was the last subject on which Darcy wished to converse. He would not discuss such a topic with someone so wholly unconnected to himself.

She turned towards him undaunted by his silence. "I also imagine you have been very lonely, sir. Perhaps that is something I could help remedy."

She did not seem as effected by the alcohol now as she had only moments before. As she drew nearer, she placed her hands atop his shoulders. "I can be very discreet, Mr. Darcy," she whispered.

He glanced down at her and, from his vantage point, could discern the fullness of her breasts. She leaned forward to ensure that he had the best view possible and moved her mouth just a hair's breadth away from his. She lingered there for a moment, tempting him, hoping he would be the one to breach the final gap between them, but he did not. She raised herself on tiptoes and placed a tentative light kiss on his lips. She waited for some response, but he seemed unmoved.

Darcy stood perfectly still as she again brought her lips to his. As he inhaled, he suddenly detected the fragrance of lavender, and his arms automatically reached for her. As the familiar aroma filled his senses, he closed his eyes, and his clouded mind pictured the woman of his desires . . . *Lizzy*. He pulled her tightly into his embrace as he deepened their kiss.

When he finally pulled back and looked into her eyes, disappointment consumed him. Hers were not the eyes he sought. Darcy struggled to clear his head and, when she moved closer attempting another kiss, he immediately grasped her wrists, stopping her advances.

"Come now, Mr. Darcy. What is it that prevents you from enjoying an innocent kiss?" she asked. "Or is it *someone*?"

Despite his inebriated state, he had experienced enough seasons to know when a woman was offering more than an innocent kiss.

"I'm afraid I have had too much to drink this evening, and its effects have impaired my better judgment. I must call for my carriage and make my departure at once."

"A pity, sir," she sighed. "Perhaps another time? If you find you have changed your mind, I will be staying at the Mayfair. I very much hope we shall meet again before you leave London, Mr. Darcy."

CHAPTER FORTY-TWO

The ostentatious carriage entered the gates of Netherfield. As it stopped before the main entrance, a liveried footman descended from his post at the rear of the carriage to open the coach's door for his employer. The amount of gold braiding upon his uniform rivalled that of a brigadier general.

Lady Catherine de Bourgh made her descent with all the pageantry of a queen and bustled her way past the servant who attended the door. She was draped in black, from her head to her toes, as befitting a woman in deep mourning of her only child.

"I have come to see my nephew," she announced to Mrs. Walker, the housekeeper.

"I am sorry, Ma'am, but *who* is your nephew?"

"Upon my word, madam, I am not a Ma'am, I am Lady Catherine de Bourgh, and my nephew is Mr. Fitzwilliam Darcy. I have been informed he is staying here at present with my granddaughter."

The housekeeper immediately curtsied, hoping she would be forgiven her ignorance. "I am sorry, your ladyship, but Mr. Darcy is away to London with his sister at the moment."

"And my granddaughter?"

"Oh, she is here, your ladyship," said the woman, glad that she would not disappoint Mr. Darcy's aunt a second time, "but out playing in one of the gardens at the moment."

"I see. I will wait for her in the study. Send her to me as soon as she returns."

"Yes, your ladyship."

~*~

Elizabeth awoke each morning impatient to see Ellie. She would dress quickly and immediately walk to Ellie's room. Mrs. Hawkins already knew the routine and would have Ellie fed and ready to go.

It was such a pleasure to have no hesitancy about attending her daughter. Aside from Mrs. Hawkins and the other servants, no one else was residing at Netherfield; no one to think it odd how she doted on the little girl. She had full reign over her daughter's care.

Elizabeth was blissfully unaware of any threat to her enjoyment as she basked in the pure bliss of her daughter's company, which today found the little girl quite engrossed with trying to catch a butterfly. As it landed on a flower, Ellie would point at it, urging her mother to hurry towards it, only to have it fly away again out of reach. This occupied much of the afternoon to Elizabeth's delight.

How she wished that this was the way it would always be. She knew her time alone with Ellie was growing short. Mr. Darcy would be back soon, and she would have to relinquish guardianship of her daughter.

While she was in no hurry for Mr. Darcy's return, she had to admit she was anxious to learn if he had devised a plan that would allow her to remain in Ellie's company. The subject had never been far from her mind. She hoped that he had been serious in his intentions on this matter. But she had to admit, whatever faults Mr. Darcy might have, he had always kept his word to her.

As they were making their way back to the house, she noticed a rather large and ornately decorated barouche in front of the entrance. She looked inside at the red velvet cushions and plush carpeting, wondering who could own such a thing. Certainly it was no one of her acquaintance.

The housekeeper greeted her nervously, opening the door before she had even approached it. As she stepped into the foyer, she observed Mrs. Hawkins pacing back and forth. A momentary look of relief passed over the woman's face as she saw Elizabeth, but the look of distress returned almost immediately.

"What is all the excitement?" asked Elizabeth, as she untied the ribbons of her bonnet. "It looks like we have visitors."

"Lady Catherine de Bourgh has been waiting for Ellie's return, Miss Bennet," said the housekeeper with a much worried look upon her face. "She is waiting for you in Mr. Bingley's study."

She had heard the name before, of course, from her cousin, Mr. Collins. She knew the lady was aunt to Mr. Darcy, mother to Mr. Darcy's late wife, and therefore, grandmother to Ellie.

"How nice she has come to visit Ellie," said Elizabeth seemingly unaware of the pervasive tension around her.

She looked at her daughter, and the little girl looked back at her with adoring eyes. "Come, Ellie, let's go see your grandmother," she said as she nestled the little girl in her arms.

As soon as she opened the door, the woman rose from her chair. "Good afternoon, Lady Catherine. I am Elizabeth Bennet. I am happy to finally make your acquaintance."

"Where have you been with my granddaughter? I have been waiting an hour at least!"

So much for civilities.

As the little girl eyed the woman, she clung tighter to Elizabeth's neck, hiding her face.

"I'm sorry, Lady Catherine; I was not informed that you would be visiting, or I would have made sure that Ellie was here upon your arrival."

"It had been my intention to pay a surprise visit to my granddaughter, but now that I have been informed of my nephew's abandonment of her, I see I shall have to take a more active role in her welfare. I shall take her back to Rosings where she can be properly looked after."

Elizabeth unconsciously held her daughter closer.

She did not want to be rude to Mr. Darcy's aunt, but she was not going to let Ellie leave the house with *anybody*. She tried to maintain a pleasant and polite demeanour.

"I assure you, Lady Catherine, she is being looked after quite competently right here. We are all only too happy to attend her needs."

"Yes, I'm sure she is being *well* attended but by whom? Servants? Obviously Fitzwilliam has things to attend that are more important than looking after my only grandchild. What kind of father abandons his daughter to go traipsing around London? I will take her to Rosings where she can be with family."

"I'm afraid I cannot allow that, your ladyship. Mr. Darcy has left his daughter in my care. I would be remiss in my responsibilities should I let you take her from here without his permission."

"I do not need permission, Miss Bennet; I am the child's grandmother! I am almost the nearest relative she has. You will hand her over this instant!"

Lady Catherine took a step forward. Elizabeth held her daughter tighter and took a step back.

She had no doubt that Mr. Darcy would be angry with her for not obeying his aunt's wishes, but something in the way that Ellie reacted to this woman's presence made Elizabeth most reluctant. Her motherly instincts rose to the forefront.

"I shall not."

"Miss Bennet, you ought to know I am not to be trifled with. Despite your sister's advantageous marriage, it is obvious that Mr. Darcy looks upon you as no more than a servant, and a servant knows her place. You will do as you are told."

Elizabeth reached for the bell pull. Within moments the study door opened, and Mrs. Hawkins entered.

"Ellie has had a long afternoon, Mrs. Hawkins; perhaps you should take her up for her nap."

Mrs. Hawkins froze momentarily, seemingly stuck in the gravitational pull of Lady Catherine's glare. With immense concentration, she forced her eyes away from that lady's most disapproving countenance and took the child from Elizabeth's arms, trying desperately to avoid any further eye contact with Lady Catherine. She was visibly shaking.

Lady Catherine took a step towards the child, but Elizabeth crossed her arms over her chest and countered with her own move, blocking Lady Catherine while Mrs. Hawkins rushed out of the study with Ellie in her arms.

Lady Catherine stared at Elizabeth with beady eyes. "Mr. Darcy will learn of your insolence. I am most seriously displeased, Miss Bennet. "

Elizabeth turned her back on the woman and waited for her to leave, her heart pounding loudly in her chest. As soon as she heard the study door slam shut, she found the nearest chair and collapsed into it.

CHAPTER FORTY-THREE

Mrs. Evanston entered the breakfast room and informed him of a gentleman awaiting his presence in the study. "The gentleman is most insistent," she advised, "and has stated he has important business to conduct." Darcy released a sigh of annoyance at the unwelcome intrusion but put down his coffee cup and headed for his study.

London was already beginning to wear on his patience. A dinner party the previous evening among the highest of society was little different than that of Lady Waverly's except that the young ladies who attended were less obvious in their intentions; their intentions being, of course, marriage. However, what *they* lacked in directness, their mothers more than made up for. This morning his tray was filled with invitations to dine.

As he reluctantly entered his study, he observed a stout gentleman with a very round face and equally round glasses seated in the chair across from his desk. He was dressed in dull brown, which seemed to suit him perfectly. An overstuffed pouch, which obviously contained many papers, was resting on his lap.

As Darcy approached, the man immediately rose from his seat, dropping the pouch to the floor. He seemed torn between greeting his host and picking up the papers that had escaped their confines but chose the latter.

When he had gathered everything, he straightened to offer his greeting.

"I beg your pardon; please excuse me, sir," he said.

Darcy nodded.

The young man cleared his throat. "I take it, sir, that you *are* Mr. Fitzwilliam Darcy of Pemberley in Derbyshire, married and recently a widower of Anne de Bourgh, and father to Anne Elizabeth Darcy?"

Darcy walked over and took the seat behind his desk. "That is correct. Do you have business to conduct with me?"

The man seemed to breathe a sigh of relief. "I do indeed, sir. I have been trying to contact you for some time."

"In regard to what, may I ask?"

"Oh, forgive me, sir. I am Walter Whittaker. I am employed at the law office of Jerome Fagan Associates. I have come to execute the final provisions of Sir Lewis de Bourgh's estate."

Darcy indicated that he should take a seat, his curiosity piqued.

Mr. Whittaker retook the chair across from Darcy and rested his pouch on the desk. He spent the next several minutes shuffling through the papers it contained.

"Ah, here we are. Yes, the last official business of the estate," he declared as he adjusted his glasses on his nose. "Sir Lewis de Bourgh had bequeathed to his daughter and sole heir a sum of ten thousand pounds to be paid to her upon attainment of her thirtieth birthday." He looked up briefly from his papers to catch the eye of his host.

His eyes then went back to his papers as he continued. "In the unhappy event that Anne de Bourgh should die before attaining the age of thirty, the bequest shall be passed down to be shared equally amongst her heirs."

As he finished, he looked up, waiting for a response from Mr. Darcy.

Darcy's response was one of surprise, and it was evident by the look upon his face. "So my daughter Ellie is to inherit the ten thousand pounds?"

"That is correct, sir. All I need you to do is sign these papers where I have indicated."

Darcy looked over the papers for several minutes as he was not going to sign anything that he had not read. After determining that the papers were in order, he attached his signature where required.

"That should conclude our business, Mr. Darcy. May I say how very sorry I am for your loss, sir?"

"Yes, thank you."

As Mr. Whittaker was placing the signed papers into his pouch, he touched his hand to his forehead. "I don't know what is wrong with me today. My head seems to be elsewhere except on my business."

He again opened his pouch and produced an envelope affixed with Sir Lewis's seal. "This envelope was to be given to Miss Anne de Bourgh on her thirtieth birthday, along with her inheritance. I shall leave it in your capable hands, sir."

~*~

The carriage stopped in front of the theatre, and Darcy withdrew and helped his sister down. They only had one more day in London, and Darcy could not be more relieved at the prospect of returning to Netherfield. However, both he and Georgiana had been looking forward to tonight's play, one of Georgiana's favourites, *Twelfth Night*.

As they entered the lobby of the theatre, Georgiana looked all around her with pleasure. She always felt like a princess whenever she attended such events. Everyone was so finely dressed, with their best behaviours and manners on full display. Her handsome brother, the attraction of many female theatre goers, escorted her gallantly to their private box. He ensured her comfort and offered the opera glasses for her use during the performance.

At intermission, they again made their way to the lobby to seek refreshments. As Darcy braved his way through the throng of people, he was encountered by Lord Westcott. "Ah, Darcy, what a most pleasant surprise!"

His daughter, Miss Westcott, was immediately by his side and expressed her delight as well. After the usual pleasantries were exchanged, Lord Westcott declared, "Now you must join us for dinner tomorrow evening, Darcy. My daughter and I insist; isn't that so, Arielle?"

The young woman blushed but quickly responded, "Oh, yes, you must!"

Even though he had no objection to spending a pleasant evening catching up with old friends, he was anxious to return to Netherfield, and this would delay their departure yet another day.

"That is very kind of you, Miss Westcott, but I'm afraid we leave for Netherfield tomorrow morning. I am here with Georgiana," Darcy said as he indicated her waiting near the stairway to their box. Gaining her attention, her face lit up upon recognizing the faces that accompanied him.

Georgiana made her way through the crowd and joined her brother. "We have just invited you and your brother to dine with us tomorrow evening, Georgiana," said Lord Westcott. "But he has indicated his intention of departing the city in the morning. Perhaps you can convince him to stay one more day."

"Brother? Is it imperative that we leave tomorrow? I would so much like to have a chance to visit the Westcotts. Lord Westcott always has such wonderful stories to tell about mother and father. Please, might we stay one more day?" she implored.

Not wishing to disappoint his sister, he acquiesced.

~*~

After the confrontation with Lady Catherine de Bourgh, Elizabeth had almost been tempted to sleep on the floor of Ellie's nursery. But with her room only two doors away, she convinced herself that she would hear if anything went amiss.

As she entered the nursery the next morning, Mrs. Hawkins turned to her with Ellie in her arms. The little girl's delight at seeing Elizabeth was immediately reflected in her smile.

"Tell me, Mrs. Hawkins, how long are you to remain in Mr. Darcy's employ?"

"Not too many more weeks," Mrs. Hawkins replied. "Ellie will soon no longer require my milk. I have been gradually weaning her off it. And I have already been contacted to work for another couple soon. The wife is expected to give birth within the next two months."

Elizabeth thought about this information for a few moments before asking, "Do you know if they have already engaged someone else to look after Ellie?"

"I believe Mrs. Reynolds is interviewing for the position right now."

"Mrs. Reynolds?" asked Elizabeth.

"Yes, Mr. Darcy's housekeeper. She has been like a member of their family for many years."

Elizabeth dismissed the subject for the moment. "Have you seen the new doll Georgiana was sewing for Ellie? I have been looking for it for days but cannot find it anywhere."

"I believe Miss Georgiana was putting some finishing touches on it. It is probably still in her room. You go and look for it while I finish dressing Ellie."

As Elizabeth entered Georgiana's room, she looked around for the doll. Retrieving it from the bed, she turned to leave but noticed some miniatures on the dresser. Closer inspection revealed one to be of Mr. Darcy, and she smiled at the likeness. She decided she would borrow the small oval painting with an idea in mind.

~*~

The morning of their departure was finally upon them, and Darcy was eager to return to Netherfield. Georgiana had impeded their departure when she requested an opportunity to browse a few of the shops of London. In the second shop they visited, Georgiana noticed her brother's impatience at her indecision and questioned him.

"What is it, Fitzwilliam? You are not concerned for Ellie, are you? I am sure Miss Elizabeth is being most attentive to her needs."

"No, I believe I could not have made a better choice than Miss Elizabeth in whom to entrust Ellie's care. I . . . I guess I am just anxious to see her again."

"Ellie or Miss Elizabeth?" asked Georgiana as she raised an eyebrow.

"Why, Ellie, of course," answered Darcy as he felt his complexion change colour.

"Are you sure, Brother?" she teased. "I could not help but notice your preference for Miss Elizabeth's company at the ball."

"Yes . . . I think very highly of her. She is a most interesting young woman. One cannot help but admire her. Do you not agree?" he asked.

"I like her very much, Fitzwilliam. I have come to value her friendship," replied his sister.

He smiled at his sister, and, in his most amiable voice he said, "I, too, have come to value her friendship. I am most happy to see that we share the same good opinion."

"Could we invite her to join us at Pemberley, Brother?"

"I was thinking the very same thing."

Georgiana gave him a big hug. "Thank you, Fitzwilliam."

As they departed the city, he concluded that he was no more susceptible to the ladies of the ton now than he had been on approaching his first season. If anything, he was less interested than ever in anything or anyone the ton had to offer.

Even if friendship was all Lizzy could offer him, he would rather spend time within the confines of friendship with her than in the unbounded liaisons so recently offered in London. He also knew that he would compare every woman he would meet to Lizzy, and every one of them he would find lacking.

CHAPTER FORTY-FOUR

As soon as she entered Bingley's study, he realized how much he had missed her.

"Good evening, Mr. Darcy. I have been anticipating your return. I have been most anxious to speak with you," she said as she walked towards him.

He rose to greet her and gestured towards the chair next to his, and they both sat. "How did you enjoy your time alone with Ellie?" he inquired.

"You hardly need ask, Mr. Darcy. It was all I had hoped for." *Except for practically throwing your aunt out of the house*, thought Elizabeth.

"I trust your trip to London went well."

"It may not have been all I had hoped for, but it definitely was all I had expected."

"Do you plan to stay on at Netherfield for a while, or must you now return to Pemberley?" asked Elizabeth.

"Georgiana wishes to stay a few days before we must travel again."

"Then I shall be glad to have her company for a few more days."

His two weeks in London had accomplished little in the way of lessening his feelings. His concentration was now rested on her mouth as she spoke, and he recalled the sweetness he had found there.

"I am anxious to hear what solution, if any, you were able to come up with regarding my seeing Ellie, Mr. Darcy. I admit it has constantly occupied my thoughts these past two weeks."

"I believe I have found an answer, Miss Bennet. As Georgiana has expressed a desire to form a closer friendship with you, I thought perhaps you could spend several weeks during the summer and some holidays at Pemberley as her guest. That certainly would allow ample time for you and Ellie to be together."

He was not sure just what she had expected him to suggest, but her face most definitely registered disappointment.

"You do not look pleased, Miss Bennet."

She hesitated but a moment. "While your offer is very generous, I must confess I was hoping we could find a more permanent solution." She swallowed hard before continuing. "You must try to understand, Mr. Darcy. It would be most difficult for me to leave her now that I have found her again. I do not want to spend a day without her."

He would not bring up the subject of their agreement. Surely too much had passed between them for that subject to ever come up again.

Unable to remain seated, she stood and walked towards the fireplace. When she felt a comfortable distance away from him, she turned to speak again. Composing herself, she endeavoured to sound business-like.

"I understand Mrs. Hawkins will soon leave your employ, sir."

He gave a brief nod of his head. He thought for a moment and then was struck with the implication of her question.

"Are you suggesting you would wish the position of Ellie's nanny? You would wish to be in my employ, Miss Bennet?"

"I wish to see my daughter every day. If that can be achieved by my employment with you, then yes, I wish to be in your employ, Mr. Darcy."

"But with your situation now changed, you no longer require employment. Surely Mr. Bingley has offered you an alternative. How would you explain such a decision?"

"I believe I have demonstrated my independent nature so convincingly in the past that both Jane and Mr. Bingley would not be too surprised at my making such a choice. I have never been comfortable with idleness, Mr. Darcy.

"In all honesty, I do not know what I would do with myself here every day at Netherfield; not being mistress of the house nor guest, simply a relative who will eventually overstay her welcome."

"But you will be giving up the opportunity to elevate your station. You could now return to the status you enjoyed before your father's death."

Elizabeth looked at him incredulously. "Mr. Darcy, if it meant seeing my daughter every day, I would take the position of cleaning chamber pots."

As he looked at her he saw the determination in her eyes. He had no doubt she would do just that if left with no other alternative.

He wanted nothing better than having the pleasure of her company every day at Pemberley, but once she was in his employ, their relationship would have to change. They could no longer maintain the friendly association they now enjoyed. He would be her employer and expected to maintain a professional relationship.

How could he suggest a walk in the gardens together or request her presence in the library or ride with her in the mornings if she were in his employ? How would he ever hope to pursue her?

And certainly he was not one of those gentlemen who imposed himself upon his servants as others in his position had done. He had heard the rumours years ago about Sir Lewis, and, even though he was not one to believe in idle gossip, his opinion on the matter was now fixed.

"Miss Bennet, I'm afraid we must come to some other resolution," he insisted.

After her confrontation with Lady Catherine, Lizzy was determined she must stay close to her daughter. What if Lady Catherine returned? What if she was successful in taking Ellie to live with her? Elizabeth knew if that were to happen, she would never see Ellie again. Those thoughts were making her more anxious. With her frustration and apprehension mounting, she felt an uncontrollable urge to strike out at him for not understanding her desperation.

"Perhaps if I were willing to lower myself even further, Mr. Darcy."

He looked at her in confusion. She raised her chin in defiance, a look he was now becoming very familiar with.

"If cleaning chamber pots is not demeaning enough, sir, perhaps the degradation of agreeing to be your mistress would grant me the privilege of seeing my daughter every day," she mocked as she boldly held his gaze.

He stared into her eyes, and she could see the hurt she had inflicted upon him. It seemed an eternity until he finally spoke.

"You have been gifted with a talent to express yourself most effectively, Miss Bennet.

"If you will excuse me," he said as he rose from the chair. He gave her a perfunctory bow as he left her company without so much as a backward glance.

~*~

Darcy rose from his bed early the next morning, unconvinced he had slept at all. He spent most of the day riding the boundaries of Netherfield Park, reflecting upon the previous evening's conversation with Elizabeth.

Thursday's Child

Her words had cut him like a knife. He had thought that day on Oakham Mount had brought them to an understanding, that she had forgiven him, but she had not.

He had wanted to know her feelings towards him . . . and now he knew. Had her amiability only been a ploy to ensure that she be allowed to see her daughter? Had he not succeeded in changing her opinion of him at all?

To be in her company and know they could never go beyond the boundaries of friendship was one thing, but to know she found him so abhorrently offensive was quite another. How had they come to this? It was difficult for him to acknowledge that, after all they had shared, she now held him in no particular regard. No, even that was being too generous. She held him in such low esteem as to declare cleaning chamber pots preferable to enduring his attentions.

~*~

Elizabeth spent most of the morning with Ellie, and, in the afternoon as Mrs. Hawkins took the child upstairs for her nap, she made her way towards the music room. She sat down at the pianoforte and mindlessly fingered the keys as her eyes once again filled with tears. Any attempt at an apology was thwarted by his avoidance of her company. Why had she spoken so imprudently? Would he forgive her for her hurtful words? Had she jeopardized her chances of being allowed her daughter's company?

In the hallway she heard Georgiana greet her brother and suggest that he have tea while she entertained him on the pianoforte with a new Mozart piece she had recently learned.

Elizabeth immediately wiped her eyes and did her best to put forward a pleasant countenance. As they entered the music room, Georgiana immediately brightened at the sight of her and greeted her most amiably. As Darcy eyed her, he stopped his progress into the room.

"I'm sorry, Georgiana; I have just remembered I have correspondence of some urgency to attend. The pleasure of hearing you play shall have to wait for another time. Pray forgive me."

"Of course, Brother. Do not concern yourself. Elizabeth and I shall find a lively duet to play. Shall we not, Elizabeth?"

Elizabeth's eyes barely reached those of her friend as she agreed to such a plan.

"I shall make every effort to complete my business by dinner," said Darcy as he made a slight bow to both women before departing.

~*~

An awkward silence prevailed during dinner. Georgiana did her best to engage both her companions in conversation, but each attempt produced little more than one word responses. Neither Elizabeth's nor Darcy's eyes travelled beyond the rims of their plates.

"I shall be happy to see Mr. and Mrs. Bingley return soon," said Elizabeth, hoping for some response from William. However, he remained silent and only Georgiana replied that she, too, was looking forward to the event.

As Darcy drained his wine glass of its contents, he rose from the table and, with little effort to disguise his impatience to depart company, gave a flimsy excuse regarding some inconsequential task.

Georgiana looked over to Elizabeth with embarrassment. "I don't know what has gotten into my brother, Elizabeth; please forgive his unsocial manner this evening."

"Perhaps he is just tired. He looks to have not have slept well."

"I have noticed the change in his behaviour since yesterday. He has been acting very strangely, Elizabeth."

She put her hand on Georgiana's and tried to reassure her that whatever was bothering her brother would most likely pass very soon.

Thursday's Child

Darcy did not make an appearance for the rest of the evening. At breakfast the next morning when asked, Mrs. Hawkins informed Elizabeth and Georgiana that Mr. Darcy had visited Ellie very early, but she had not seen him since.

By midday he still had not been seen. Elizabeth tried to conduct herself as usual; she played the pianoforte with Georgiana after breakfast and read to Ellie before her nap. A walk through the gardens after lunch did little to help ease her mind.

~*~

Darcy had spent the morning riding Marengo in contemplation. He carefully thought over his options. He could refuse her request, of course. But where would that leave them all? Lizzy would be denied her daughter's company, Ellie would be denied the love and attention that only a mother could bestow upon her child, and he would be denied the pleasure of having Lizzy in his life. He had pledged to keep her safe, and he would not break that pledge. She would be safe with him and Ellie. In his heart he knew he really had no options at all.

~*~

That evening, Elizabeth sat in the library, and, though she held a book in her hand, she had not read a complete sentence since she had opened it an hour before. Her mind could not focus on anything but the fact that she might lose her daughter's company by tomorrow.

As she heard the door open and footsteps enter the library, she tried to concentrate on the page before her. From the corner of her eye, she watched Mr. Darcy reach for a book from one of the higher shelves. A moment later he pulled out the chair across the table from hers and sat down. Silently he opened the book and proceeded to read.

They sat like that for more minutes than Elizabeth cared to count, each pretending to be engrossed in their book. She wanted to speak, to explain to him that she had not meant her offensive words, but she could not even force her gaze upwards to look at him.

Finally he closed his book and stood. As he slid the chair back under the table, he addressed her.

"I have written to Mrs. Reynolds informing her that the position of Ellie's nanny has been filled."

He did not wait for a reply but walked directly towards the door. Elizabeth was too stunned to speak. He turned as he took his leave, and their eyes met briefly before he was gone.

CHAPTER FORTY-FIVE

He entered the study and was debating his choice of tea or brandy, already knowing where his preference lay, when Bingley entered the room. "Darcy, how good to see you again! Had I known you were here, I would have come down sooner." Upon thinking of his and Jane's recent occupation in their bedchamber, Bingley mentally conceded maybe that was not entirely true.

"Bingley, you are looking well," said Darcy as the two men shook hands. "How was your tour of the lakes?"

"Well, I'm afraid we didn't get to see as much as we had hoped," said Bingley as a deep blush overtook his countenance.

"Really?" asked Darcy as he suppressed a smile.

"Ahem, well, yes . . . other interests managed to occupy our time," he said with a blatant grin.

"Come, pour yourself a drink, Bingley, and tell me all."

"I will join you in a drink, but a gentleman never divulges such information," said Bingley with a good natured laugh. "How was your trip to London?"

"You know how I hate these social activities, but I must keep up some appearances for Georgiana's sake. She will be out soon, and I must make sure she is seen at social affairs. I admit I did enjoy the theatre, and Georgie and I spent a most enjoyable evening in the company of Miss Westcott and Lord Westcott. His memories of our mother and father delight Georgiana so much. Since she has no memory of our mother at all and only vague remembrances of our father, she is desperate to hear the many stories he tells of them.

"But the dinner parties I attended proved to be intolerable. My status as a widower has once again made me the object of every matchmaking acquaintance in London. I will not feel completely safe until I am back home at Pemberley."

"Have you spoken with Miss Elizabeth since your return?" asked Bingley.

Surprised by the question, he answered slowly, "Yes . . . we spoke briefly on a few occasions."

Noticing his friend's strange demeanour he asked, "What exactly is on your mind, Bingley?"

Bingley glanced at the door to make sure it was closed before he spoke again. "Darcy, I know you have been reluctant to reveal any feelings you may have for Miss Elizabeth, but I have some information that might persuade you."

In light of his and Elizabeth's recent interactions, he was about to protest but decided to remain silent, allowing his friend to continue.

"Jane has informed me of a conversation she and Miss Elizabeth had the night of the ball."

"A conversation that involved me?" asked Darcy.

Bingley nodded.

"I have never known you to spread gossip, Bingley. Perhaps you should allow private conversations to remain so. I am sure Mrs. Bingley did not mean for you to relay such a conversation to me."

"Well, she did not say I should not, and I believe it is something you should know."

"Do you now also share *our* private conversations with your wife?"

"Well, not all our conversations," said Bingley slightly embarrassed. "But, I was explaining to Jane about the night I came to see you in London. You know, the night you opened my eyes to things."

"Yes, I recall the night you speak of Bingley, but please go on with your story," said Darcy, already knowing he would not be pleased.

"Anyway one thing led to another, and, before I knew it, I had disclosed to Jane that you might . . . well, that there was a possibility you had feelings for Miss Elizabeth."

"Bingley!"

"Come now, Darcy, you must admit you do have feelings for the woman," pleaded his friend. "And I did make Jane promise not to say anything to her sister."

Darcy shook his head. "Does this story have a point?"

"Yes, I was getting to that. Jane told me the most extraordinary thing! During their conversation, Jane got the distinct impression that Miss Elizabeth has feelings for you also, though she was most reluctant to make such an admission."

"I doubt very much Miss Bennet possesses any such feelings," said Darcy as he recalled that painful conversation with Elizabeth.

The sound of a light knock prompted them both to turn their eyes toward the door. "Enter," they both said simultaneously; Darcy forgetting it was Netherfield's study they occupied, not Pemberley's.

Mrs. Hawkins appeared in the doorway with Ellie. "Excuse me, Mr. Darcy; I must pick up something at the apothecary in Meryton, and Georgiana and Miss Bennet seem to be out at the moment. Since I do not trust leaving Ellie with anyone else after what happened the other day, I was hoping you could watch her for a little while."

"What do you mean, Mrs. Hawkins; what happened the other day?"

"Did Miss Bennet not mention it, sir?"

"No, she did not mention anything to me. Did something happen to Ellie?" he asked with concern in his voice.

Mrs. Hawkins looked at both gentlemen, from one to the other. "Well, no sir, not exactly. It was Lady Catherine, sir. She arrived in a most agitated state while Miss Bennet and Ellie were in one of the gardens. When they returned, she demanded that Miss Bennet relinquish Ellie over to her so she might take her back to Rosings."

Darcy startled. "And what did Miss Bennet do?"

"She flatly refused, sir, to Lady Catherine's great consternation. Her ladyship was most officious and quite angry. She expressed her displeasure and said she would inform you of Miss Bennet's insolence."

If Aunt Catherine had tried to abduct his daughter to Rosings, he would be the *last* person she would inform. She knew his feelings all too well on that subject. And knowing his aunt, he was sure Lizzy had suffered in her company. But…she had protected their daughter.

"Thank you, Mrs. Hawkins."

Darcy reached for Ellie as Mrs. Hawkins held the child out to him. Ellie lifted her arm and removing her small fingers from her mouth pointed them in his direction. "Papa," she said in a small voice. She then reached both arms out to him and said with more confidence, "Papa!"

Darcy momentarily startled as he heard Ellie call out to him. "My sweet Ellie," he said as he took his daughter in his arms, giving her a hug.

"Did you hear that?" he asked in delightful astonishment. "She called me Papa!" He looked over to Bingley to confirm that he had heard it also.

Bingley grinned and nodded his head.

Darcy then turned back to Mrs. Hawkins. "What . . . how . . . were those first words? How did this come about?"

"Miss Bennet, sir," said Mrs. Hawkins. "Every day she would show her Miss Darcy's miniature of you and repeat 'Papa' until Ellie said it back to her. She said she wanted to surprise you."

~*~

The following morning his departure to Pemberley was upon him. As Darcy approached the breakfast room, he saw Elizabeth seated at the table.

Of course, deep down in his heart he knew there was no one better suited to care for Ellie than Elizabeth. Who better to love and protect the child than her own mother? But knowing his feelings for her, it would be difficult to have her so near every day *and night*.

She had protected Ellie and stood up to Lady Catherine. And yet she had shown her sweet nature when she had taught their daughter to call him "Papa," even though she had no hope of ever hearing Ellie call her "Mama." Despite his own fears and misgivings, he knew there was no point in pretending anymore. He had completely lost his heart to her.

Though he was convinced that the information Bingley had related was far from true, he still could not help but cling to a small hope that he could still win Lizzy's affections.

"Good morning, Miss Bennet," he said, as he watched for her reaction.

"Good morning, Mr. Darcy."

It was the first time they had been alone together at breakfast, and they both felt the singularity of the occasion. Hoping they could return to the ease of their former understanding, Elizabeth endeavoured to make casual conversation.

"Will you be leaving for Pemberley soon?" she inquired.

"Yes, Mrs. Hawkins is helping with the last of the packing, and Georgiana and Ellie are almost ready to go. I have much to prepare for the guests who will be arriving next week."

"Will there be many?" she asked as she watched him pour a cup of coffee and take a seat across from her.

"Though it is not my customary habit to entertain such large gatherings, I'm afraid this is turning out to be one of those rare occasions. Much of my family will be visiting over the next two weeks. I am also expecting Lord Westcott and his daughter. They were kind enough to invite Georgiana and me to dinner during our recent stay in London, and I felt etiquette required I reciprocate by inviting them to Pemberley."

"They were at the ball, were they not?" Elizabeth's mind immediately recalled the attractive honey blonde haired woman with whom William had danced. *When did I start thinking of him as William again and not Mr. Darcy?*

"Yes," he said. "We met again last week while attending the theatre in London."

"Oh."

For an awkward moment they stared at each other until Darcy picked up his cup and took a sip of his coffee. Elizabeth withdrew her eyes from him and reached for the pot of jam. She had not considered having to watch him entertain beautiful young ladies as part of her upcoming duties, but that thought for some reason was now forming a disagreeable image in her mind.

"Mr. Darcy, I feel I must apologize . . ."

"Please, Miss Bennet," he interrupted, "I would wish to forget the entire episode."

Quickly changing the subject he said, "I see you are enjoying a book of poetry. It is Byron, is it not?"

"Yes, sir. I have lately received, somewhat mysteriously, a fine collection of his work, among others," she replied.

"I doubt that it is quite the mystery you profess it to be."

"I may have some idea as to the source, but the motive remains unknown to me."

"Perhaps it was meant as a peace offering, Miss Bennet. Some people are unable to articulate their feelings as readily as others. I, myself, find I suffer from such an affliction."

"Well, whoever it was, I would wish that they knew how much I am enjoying such a thoughtful gesture," she answered, still staring into the deep brown pools of his eyes.

"I would trust that they do, Miss Bennet."

Their colour increased in proportion to the length of their stare.

"Have you told your sister of your plans?"

"No, but I plan to do so today, if I can find a moment alone with her. I was surprised to see her absent from the breakfast table this morning as she is usually an early riser."

Darcy wanted to relate that it was not uncommon for newlyweds to arise late but decided not to offer such intelligence, thinking perhaps she would assume he was speaking from his own experience.

"Of course, you may do as you wish, but may I suggest you consider postponing that conversation for a short while?"

She looked at him questioningly. He had not changed his mind, had he?

"Mrs. Hawkins will still be in my employ for a few weeks, and I would like that your duties not begin until she has departed. Perhaps you could delay informing your sister and Charles until then.

"I . . . I would like you to see Pemberley for the first time as my guest, Miss Bennet, not as an employee."

Their eyes were again fixed on each other.

"Georgiana has expressly requested your company next week. I hope you will not disappoint her. She is looking forward to your joining our other guests. You could accompany Mr. and Mrs. Bingley, as they have been invited also."

"That is most kind of you, Mr. Darcy."

As he intently held her gaze, she found herself unable to look away. His hand reached across the table towards hers, but the next moment found the rest of Netherfield's inhabitants descending upon the breakfast room.

The time for departure came quickly, and Elizabeth watched with sadness as Georgiana, Mrs. Hawkins, and Ellie rode away in their carriage. Saying goodbye to Ellie for a second time had been a difficult task. But the thought that in one week she would again be in her company gave her great comfort. This was the last time she would ever be separated from her daughter again.

Darcy mounted Marengo and followed the path of the carriage. He turned around one last time to look back at Elizabeth. He would not give up hope yet.

CHAPTER FORTY-SIX

"Be careful with that!" As the footman placed Caroline's third trunk into the boot of the carriage, she sniffed the air. Mr. and Mrs. Hurst had been waiting impatiently for their sister to make her appearance; as she finally sat down in the coach, the feather on her bonnet brushed against the roof and bent slightly forward. "You really should consider purchasing a larger carriage, Mr. Hurst," she offered, her voice indicating her displeasure.

Caroline was most eager to once again be in Mr. Darcy's company. She was anticipation personified and quite determined that she would not let this opportunity slip away as she had during their recent stay at Netherfield. Convinced that whatever arts and allurements Miss Eliza had used to bewitch Mr. Darcy had by now lost their appeal, she was ready to spend the next few weeks exhibiting her charms without the hindrance of any competition.

Yes, Caroline reasoned, Mr. Darcy had allowed himself the indulgence of a brief diversion, but now she knew he would conform to the rules his society demanded and marry someone of equal station. And Caroline thought enough of herself to believe that she was such a woman.

Had not the London Gazette announced her name as being hostess to a ball attended by Lord Westcott? That little news item had benefited her with several prominent invitations into London society. Why, yes indeed, she was becoming a social sensation!

And now she was Mr. Darcy's particular guest at Pemberley, an invitation he would never extend to someone so unworthy as Miss Eliza Bennet. Certainly he now must concede that country chit's total lack of sophistication.

Really, men can be so easily influenced once their libido has been aroused, she thought. She had a momentary flash of guilt as she suddenly thought of Dr. Adams, but the moment was short lived as she immediately began planning her strategy to secure Mr. Darcy's affections.

~*~

Mr. Bingley's carriage rose over the ridge, and, for the first time, a full view of the estate that Elizabeth Bennet had heard so much about could be seen unobstructed. As she looked out the carriage window, her jaw unconsciously dropped. She turned her head back towards Mr. Bingley and gave him a look of astonished disbelief. She had imagined the estate to be larger and more lavish than Netherfield Park, but nothing she had heard could have prepared her for the sight now before her.

"Mr. Bingley, I had no idea that Pemberley was as grand as this," she stated.

Of all this, one day my child shall be mistress, she thought.

"Now that we are brother and sister, could we not be less formal? I would wish you to call me 'Charles,' Miss Bennet."

"Well, then you must return the favour and call me Elizabeth."

He nodded his head in concurrence.

When they reached the carriage house, Mr. Bingley alit first. He handed down the two ladies and escorted them to the entrance. Mr. Darcy was waiting to greet them as they approached the door.

"Welcome to Pemberley," he offered to his new guests with a slight bow.

Elizabeth could not help but smile at the sight of him standing so proud and regal before them. He offered his arm to her as he escorted them into the house.

Georgiana was immediately upon them and expressed her pleasure at seeing them all again. As she approached Elizabeth, she could not refrain from giving her an affectionate hug which was sincerely returned.

As they entered the parlour, there was only one other guest in attendance. Elizabeth was startled to see Ellie seated upon the lap of none other than Lady Catherine de Bourgh.

As soon as the child saw Elizabeth enter the room, she began to squirm to affect her escape from the woman's grasp. Unable to contain her any longer, Lady Catherine allowed the little girl to stand, though her stance was indeed somewhat wobbly.

Ellie reached out her arms and, as Elizabeth knelt to the floor several feet away, she, too, raised her arms, beckoning her daughter towards her. Without hesitation, Ellie lifted one chubby leg and placed it decidedly down in front of the other. She did this two more times until she could just reach Elizabeth's outstretched hands.

"You are walking!" she exclaimed as she pulled the child into her embrace. This little demonstration garnered everyone's attention. As they all watched in silent amazement, Darcy finally found his voice.

"I assure you, Miss Bennet, this is the first I have been witness to such. I believe those were her very first steps!"

Elizabeth quickly rose, lifting Ellie up with her as she stood. "My, what a clever girl you are, my sweet child," whispered Elizabeth in her daughter's ear. The little girl smiled brightly into her mother's eyes.

An awkward silence pervaded the room momentarily as everyone stared at Elizabeth holding the child in her arms. She immediately blushed from embarrassment, but Darcy quickly took command of the situation and offered introductions.

Lady Catherine, may I present Miss Elizabeth Bennet. I believe you made her acquaintance recently at Netherfield."

Elizabeth stiffened by his side.

Lady Catherine turned her beady eyes to Elizabeth. "Miss Bennet," was all the greeting she offered.

"It a pleasure to see you again, your ladyship," said Elizabeth.

"Perhaps your sister's fortuitous marriage has elevated your situation after all. To be invited to Pemberley must indeed be a great honour for you."

No longer surprised by Lady Catherine's directness, she smiled, replying only, "Indeed, it is," in response, then politely stood aside while Mr. and Mrs. Bingley were introduced.

Tea was offered to the new arrivals; afterwards, they were directed to their accommodations so that they might refresh before dinner, all agreeing to meet three hours hence in the main dining salon. Georgiana was helpfully leading them to their rooms when Mrs. Reynolds greeted them at the stairway.

As Georgiana introduced Mrs. Reynolds, Elizabeth recognized her immediately as the woman who had interviewed her, and she felt the colour begin to drain from her face. But then Elizabeth did as she always did when feeling intimidated, she raised her chin and met the woman's eyes.

"Good afternoon, Miss Bennet. I hope you don't mind, but with so many guests expected this week, we had to put you up in the west wing of the house near the family quarters."

"Not at all, Mrs. Reynolds, for I assure you, any room in this lovely home would be to my liking." She concluded her discourse with a most appreciative smile for the elder woman's kindness and discretion.

Mrs. Reynolds returned her smile, giving her a slight nod of her head. Their friendship was solidified in that brief moment of understanding.

Mr. Darcy had prepared Mrs. Reynolds for the arrival of Miss Bennet, and she had immediately sensed something in the air. She had never before seen her master behave as he had this entire week. One would have thought the queen was coming to visit.

"Miss Georgiana, why don't you show Mr. and Mrs. Bingley to their rooms while I show Miss Bennet to hers?"

"Of course, Mrs. Reynolds. I shall see you later, Elizabeth."

As they reached the top of the staircase, Georgiana, Jane, and Charles took the hallway to the right, while Mrs. Reynolds and Elizabeth turned to the left. As they reached the rooms assigned to Elizabeth, Mrs. Reynolds pointed out Mr. Darcy's suite of rooms a mere few doors from hers. Further down on the right were Miss Georgiana's rooms, and at the end of the hallway was the nursery.

"I just hope I shall be able to find my way back to the parlour," noted Elizabeth as she observed the vastness of her surroundings.

"If you have any trouble, I'm sure one of the servants will gladly direct you," assured Mrs. Reynolds with a smile.

CHAPTER FORTY-SEVEN

As Mrs. Reynolds departed, Elizabeth turned around slowly, staring in awe at the gracious accommodations of her rooms. Not only had she been provided with the most beautiful bedchamber she had ever seen, richly decorated with the finest brocades in light blues and yellows, but there was also a small sitting room furnished simply but tastefully off to the left and a dressing chamber with a bathing tub off to the right. As she moved the draperies to allow light in from the windows, she was delighted to see a balcony as well.

Certainly there must be some sort of mix up, thought Elizabeth. *This could not be intended for me.* A servant arrived shortly with her luggage, followed by a maid who asked where she would like to have her things laid out.

"Please do not bother to unpack my things as I am sure some mistake has been made as to my accommodations. I am sure these elegant rooms must be reserved for someone other than myself," said Elizabeth to the young girl.

"Oh, no, madam. Mr. Darcy was very clear as to where each guest was to be situated," replied the maid.

"Well," said Elizabeth with hesitation, "if you are sure . . . then please unpack the small bag first. I would like to bathe and change after such a long trip. And please call me Elizabeth."

"Very well, Miss Elizabeth. I am Dora," she said as she curtseyed. "I will see to your needs during your stay."

"I'm very pleased to make your acquaintance, Dora," said Elizabeth. "The first thing I shall need is a map, so that I may find my room each night."

The young girl grinned at her and explained, "There is a trick to it, Miss."

Elizabeth raised an eyebrow in question, and Dora continued. "We are located in the family wing, and, as Mr. Darcy favours blues and yellows, all the rugs and wall coverings are in those colours. So if you just follow the colours, you will find your way to your room."

"I see. Well, that is very helpful indeed, Dora. What colours occupy the walls and floors where Mr. and Mrs. Bingley are residing?"

"Let's see . . . that would be the east wing. Green and coral," said Dora with a smile. "Might I direct you anywhere else?"

"I have heard so much about the library at Pemberley that I would be remiss if I did not seek it out as soon as I may. Perhaps I could visit there before dinner."

After receiving directions to the library, Elizabeth went about readying herself. To her delight she discovered that Dora was also very adept at fixing her hair, and, as she departed her lovely suite of rooms, she felt herself quite in vogue with her surroundings.

While crossing the hallway, she heard the unmistakable voice of Caroline Bingley wafting across the expanse of the passages, admonishing some poor servant for the lack of light in her room.

"Why have I been relegated to a room facing full west? I can barely see my hand in front of my face! And do I not have a balcony? Where is Mrs. Reynolds? I demand to see her immediately!"

"Yes, Miss Bingley, I shall summon her right away."

Elizabeth quickly made her way down the stairs to avoid any contact with Caroline as she headed for the library.

This room, too, inspired awe. Never had she seen so many books! As she walked past each row, she noted the vast array of subjects, from botany to Greek mythology and everything in between. How her father would have loved this room! He would gladly have closed himself up here for days, requiring nothing more than a bottle of port and his reading glasses.

The leather furnishings and deep mahogany book cases and tables gave it so a strong masculine air that she could not help but imagine William here. She smiled when she thought of him.

She wondered what her life would be like here. How would they get on? She must admit she enjoyed his company. It would not be a burden to spend her days with him. She would be content to be his friend and live with him and Ellie in this beautiful place. Yes, she could picture such a life.

Just then the door opened, and he entered the library, scattering the thoughts she had just so neatly arranged. "Ah, Miss Bennet, I should have guessed you would seek out the library upon your arrival."

"It is most magnificent, Mr. Darcy. I should be quite content to spend many hours here surrounded by so much knowledge."

They shared a smile.

"And do you find your accommodations suitable?" he asked.

As soon as the words left his mouth, he recognized them as the ones he had spoken to her that first night in Scotland. Elizabeth, too, remembered those words, and as their eyes met, an embarrassing blush overtook her countenance. "I . . . I am honoured to be situated in such elegant quarters, sir.

"I know you have been informed of my meeting your aunt at Netherfield, Mr. Darcy. I am sincerely sorry that I treated her so poorly."

"I doubt it is your behaviour that requires an apology, Miss Bennet. I know my aunt all too well. That you survived her visit unscathed is remarkable."

"Well it did leave me a little shaken. But that still does not excuse my behaviour."

"My aunt is of the opinion that she would be better suited to care for Ellie. I have tried to dissuade her on several occasions, but she seems rather insistent upon it. Had I been there, Miss Bennet, I would have reacted in the same manner as you. From what I understand of the circumstances of that day, had it not been for you, my aunt would have taken Ellie with her to Rosings. So no apology is warranted, I am sure. On the contrary, I should be offering my thanks."

They held a gaze for a moment.

"Is Mrs. Reynolds aware that it is *I* whom you hired as Ellie's nanny?"

"Yes, she is the only one, however. Have you told your sister? "

"No, I have heeded your advice and will not tell her until it is time for Mrs. Hawkins to leave."

"Good," he answered, relieved that no one else would know of her impending employment. "Then you are Georgiana's and my guest until Mrs. Hawkins must depart.

"I would wish to thank you for allowing me this opportunity, Mr. Darcy. To be allowed to care for Ellie and watch her grow is my greatest desire. As long as she is happy, I will require nothing more. I will be content with my situation, and I shall make every effort to avoid your disapproval."

"I do not recall a time when you earned my disapproval, Miss Bennet."

"I believe in such cases, a good memory is unpardonable, Mr. Darcy. It is to my benefit that you do not possess one, sir." He could not help but smile at such a statement.

"Perhaps that could be said for the both of us."

~*~

Jane Bingley was unconsciously humming as she stood on the balcony of her lovely bedchamber when Elizabeth knocked on her door. Annie, one of the maids assigned to the east wing, greeted her on her way out.

"Oh, Lizzy, is this not the most beautiful place you have ever seen?" gushed her sister.

"Yes, but it is a little overwhelming," agreed Elizabeth, mentally noting that her own room was even grander than the one her sister occupied.

"Where is Charles? I thought we could all go down to dinner together. Amongst the three of us, I am sure we shall be able to locate the dining salon."

"He was summoned by Caroline, who seems to be having a problem with her accommodations," said Jane.

"Yes, I believe everyone in the house has been made aware of Miss Bingley's dissatisfaction."

Elizabeth took Jane's hand, and they sat together on the large bed. "It has been so long since we have been able to talk privately, Jane. You certainly look the happy bride."

"Oh, Lizzy, how I wish that you could know such happiness."

"I could never have your happiness until I have your goodness, Jane."

"Why do you speak so? Oh, Lizzy, you have so much goodness; anyone can see that. When you say such things, you puzzle me exceedingly."

"I do not wish to be a puzzle to you, dear sister. I am just saying that Charles could not help but fall in love with you. Your goodness and beauty captured his heart almost immediately."

"Well, he may have fallen in love with me, but if Mr. Darcy had not advised him, he never would have proposed."

"What? Are you saying that Mr. Darcy convinced Charles to propose to you?"

"Charles confessed on our honeymoon that he had been swayed by his sisters' opinions and that he was also under the impression that Mr. Darcy did not approve of me either. He said he was so miserable without me, Lizzy, that he decided to confront Mr. Darcy."

"That is most unbelievable, Jane," said Elizabeth. This did not correspond with what Caroline Bingley had intimated on the balcony that night. "What did Mr. Darcy say to him?"

"He advised Charles that he should act according to his own desires and not those of others. Charles said he had a very odd feeling that evening, as if Mr. Darcy was trying to tell him something of himself."

"Did Mr. Darcy reveal anything further about it?"

"I do not think he elaborated on the subject; at least Charles did not mention it."

"So Mr. Darcy actually encouraged his friend to propose to you! I am all astonishment!"

Now that she thought upon it, Miss Bingley had said she sought Mr. Darcy's help in separating Jane and Mr. Bingley; she did not say he had given it.

"Does Mr. Darcy continue his attentions to you, Lizzy?"

"Our relationship is precarious at best. But I feel we are making progress as to becoming good friends.

"Well, the two of you always seem to have so much to talk about."

"Yes, we speak on many subjects. We have discovered similar interests in books and philosophies, and we both enjoy riding."

And our similar interest in Ellie, thought Elizabeth. "Why do you ask so many questions regarding Mr. Darcy?"

"Oh, no reason. I was just wondering . . . well, since he was so very attentive to you at the ball, I was curious if perhaps he had . . . expressed any . . . any . . ."

"Any what? What are you trying to ask me, Jane?"

"Oh, Lizzy, do you not think Mr. Darcy might be partial to you?"

"He treats me as he would any relative to Mr. Bingley. Do you not remember that Miss Bingley has been invited to Pemberley also? What makes you think he holds me in any special regard?"

"I don't know. I thought I detected some preference on his part," said Jane as she looked down at her hands in her lap and blushed.

"My dear sister, you are the world's worst liar. I am thankful my life has never depended upon your convincing someone of an untruth." Lizzy raised an eyebrow at Jane. "Okay, out with it. What do you know?"

Jane's brow furrowed as she bit her lip. This was indeed most perplexing. To whom does one show their allegiance? To the sister she has loved dearly and confided in all her life? Or to the husband she had just agreed to love, honour, and obey?

CHAPTER FORTY-EIGHT

If looks could kill, Elizabeth knew she would never have survived the first course of dinner. Caroline Bingley stared at her from across the table, her displeasure clearly written on her face.

Caroline could not fathom how such a thing could possibly have come about. Certainly this was not by Mr. Darcy's design. Miss Eliza must have wheedled an invitation somehow, preying upon Georgiana's sweet nature perhaps or using her new brother to appeal to Mr. Darcy's generosity.

Yes, that must be it. Poor Mr. Darcy, to be put in such an awkward position—being forced to entertain someone so unworthy as Miss Eliza. Caroline could not help but demonstrate her superiority in front of her host.

"Thank you, Mr. Darcy, for rectifying the error in my accommodations," said Caroline sweetly. "I know it was not my place to reprimand your staff, sir, but such an obvious blunder had to be addressed."

Darcy had been seriously annoyed to learn of the abuse endured by those in his employ at the hands of Miss Bingley and repeatedly had to remind himself that it was for his best friend that he tolerate such behaviour. "I trust you are now situated to your liking, Miss Bingley?"

"Oh, quite, sir," replied Caroline as she batted her eyes in his direction. "The view from my balcony is breath-taking." She peered across the table and directed her next words towards her unworthy dinner companion. "It is a pity you do not have such a view, Miss Eliza."

"I am exceedingly pleased with my rooms, Miss Bingley. I could not want for anything finer," answered Elizabeth.

"Of course, it is all in what one is accustomed to," Caroline replied imperiously. "Certainly Pemberley must be beyond all your expectations. Naturally you would be exceedingly pleased with any situation you might find here."

Caroline turned her head in a dismissive manner and gave her full attention back to her host. "How is dear Ellie this evening?" she asked.

"She is exceedingly well. Now that she has taken her first steps, she is keeping Mrs. Hawkins quite busy. She is almost running after only one day." Darcy unconsciously looked over to Elizabeth and gave her a warm smile.

A voice from the opposite end of the table brought all eyes to Lady Catherine. "Miss Bennet, my granddaughter seems much attached to you. How do you account for this?"

Elizabeth looked over to Lady Catherine and nervously smiled. "Yes, your ladyship, as you know we spent much time together at Netherfield. She is a very bright and endearing child. I . . . I am very fond of her."

"As are we all, your ladyship," Caroline immediately interjected. "Have I not expressed the same sentiments on many occasions, Mr. Darcy?"

"It is so," was all the reply Darcy could muster.

Discourse continued as Bingley captured Darcy's ear regarding his planned improvements to Netherfield Park while Jane, Georgiana, and Elizabeth spoke of tomorrow's activities. Lady Catherine claimed fatigue and made an early departure to her rooms. Mr. Hurst said little as it would be impolite to speak with one's mouth full, while Caroline and Louisa spoke in hushed whispers between themselves.

That evening a new guest arrived rather late, one that Mr. Darcy had especially requested to join them for a day or two. A Mr. Thomas Gainsboro arrived, carrying with him only a small satchel, which he insisted on attending to himself.

The ladies were informed that as an entertainment the following day, miniatures would be painted of each of them. Mr. Gainsboro was touted to be an up and coming artist, and Darcy thought it would serve two purposes to invite the gentleman to Pemberley: a day's diversion for the ladies and a way to assist the young man in his artistry. Indeed, to be invited to paint miniatures at Pemberley was an affirmation of Mr. Gainesboro's talent, one that all good society would not ignore.

The men spent the next day shooting while the ladies each spent a little leisure time in the gardens awaiting their turn with Mr. Gainsboro. With their miniatures completed, Elizabeth, Jane, and Georgiana decided on a walk.

Upon their return to the garden, Mrs. Hawkins arrived with Ellie in tow. The little girl toddled steadily towards them while holding Mrs. Hawkins's hand. She had already become a very proficient walker, much like her mother. Delighted to see her daughter, Elizabeth almost ran to meet her.

With Caroline's miniature just completed, she entered the garden where the sight of Miss Eliza and Ellie seemed to annoy her greatly; the contemptuous look on her face revealed her distaste for the pair.

Caroline was more eager than ever to rid herself of this country chit's presence, especially after learning that she occupied chambers in the family quarters. *How had she manipulated that little feat?*

That evening, when dinner was over, they proceeded to the music room where a choice of tea, coffee or port was offered. Mrs. Hurst entertained at the pianoforte while the rest of the guests sat and indulged in conversation. By the time the evening ended, Elizabeth was exhausted as it was indeed quite late. She climbed the stairs, following the blue and yellow carpet to the west wing. She entered her bedchamber, and, upon noting that the time was well past midnight, she was struck with something that could not wait. Leaving her room, she continued to follow the blue and yellow carpet as she moved towards the nursery. As quietly as she could, she opened the door and saw her daughter asleep in her crib. She approached her and bent down to kiss her cheek.

"Happy birthday, my sweet child," she whispered.

As she stood there gently stroking Ellie's back, listening to the steady rhythm of her breathing, an overwhelming sense of contentment fell over her. Tears of happiness filled her eyes as she watched her sleeping child.

Yes, she could be content with this life. Having Ellie so close every day, watching her grow and knowing she was happy, knowing she was part of the reason for her daughter's happiness. She knew she owed William a debt of gratitude.

Just as she was about to turn to leave, she felt a hand on her shoulder. At first startled, the touch turned into a tender caress, arresting her fear. He stood so close that she could feel his breath on the back of her neck.

She could not help herself. She reached up and put her hand over his as they both stood there together, gazing down at their daughter. After several moments, he turned her towards him, and their eyes met. His hands secured her waist, and he pulled her closer. As his arms surrounded her, he lowered his head and placed a tender kiss upon her willing lips. His senses came alive with her lavender scent and the sweet taste of her lips as he deepened their kiss, enveloping her so tightly into his embrace that it was a wonder she could still breathe.

He drew back, and their eyes met briefly once again. A moment later he was gone, leaving Elizabeth to wonder if it had only been her imagination.

~*~

He had been as a schoolboy the entire week, anticipating her arrival, imagining her in every room of Pemberley. In the music room, he saw her playing the pianoforte; as he dined, he imagined her conversing next to him. He envisioned her in the nursery, tending their child, and nightly, he conjured her presence in his bedchamber.

It was perhaps unwise to have her rooms situated so close to his own, but knowing that she slept only two doors away from him was exquisite torture. Indeed, only a connecting sitting room separated their two bedchambers.

He had no sooner entered his room than he heard her pass his door and enter the nursery; he had no choice but to follow. As he witnessed the scene, his heart went out to her; a secret happy birthday to her daughter. For all the rest of the world Ellie's birthday would be in two days, the day she had first been brought to Pemberley, but today, he knew Elizabeth celebrated the day she had given birth to their child.

He did not know what possessed him to kiss her, but the temptation had been too great to resist. How could he ever hope to gain her good opinion if his behaviour was so improper? Once again he found that while in her presence, he had acted as he should not. What was it about her that made him do such things?

But it had always been that way with her, from the beginning. He had said and done and felt things with her that he had never said nor done nor felt with any other woman. He imagined it would always be so.

As he had stood behind her, gazing down at Ellie, he felt all was right with the world. After all, were they not, in every sense of the word, a family? What could be more natural than to celebrate their child's birthday with a kiss? Or perhaps more than a kiss? He felt his body react as he imagined taking her to his bed, kissing his way down her body, touching her intimately . . . Oh, bloody hell.

~*~

The following afternoon saw the arrival of Richard and his parents, Lord and Lady Matlock. Richard was not surprised to learn of Miss Bennet's presence at Pemberley and was quite anxious to see what developments might transpire during his visit.

At Darcy's insistence, Elizabeth selected a horse to be hers to ride whenever she wished. She chose a beautiful silver grey mare, Shayla. It was at the stables that Richard first encountered her.

"Miss Bennet, I am delighted to see you again."

"Colonel Fitzwilliam! I am delighted as well. Have you just arrived?" asked Elizabeth, now grateful she had accepted Georgiana's gracious lending of one of her riding outfits.

"A short while ago. My parents insisted that I have tea with them and our host before I headed for the stables. They know only too well that once I see Darcy's horses, I will not be seen for some time to come."

"I'm awaiting my mount, sir; would you care to join me?" asked Elizabeth.

"It is kind of your to offer. It shall be my pleasure to accompany you."

"Although I admit to having a generous nature, I must confess my motive may be more self-serving than kind. I fear if I ride alone, I may get lost and never find my way back to the house."

"I will gladly be your guide, Miss Bennet," said the colonel with a laugh.

The two rode for well over an hour as the colonel pointed out some of the delights of Pemberley's grounds. Elizabeth was enthralled with the beautiful woods and trails that surrounded the estate. They went on as far as the eye could see.

When they returned to the house, they entered together and were immediately informed that the rest of the party were enjoying refreshments on the veranda. Elizabeth expressed her desire to freshen up and departed to her rooms while the colonel headed towards the gathering of guests.

Darcy eyed his cousin with displeasure as he watched him approach the portico. Wishing to talk to him alone, he directed his long strides in his direction, reaching him just before he entered the veranda. "Might I have a word, Richard?" he asked as pleasantly as was possible, considering his ill mood.

Richard nodded, and they walked to the study. Once inside, Darcy poured out a drink for each of them. Knowing exactly what had triggered his cousin's disagreeable manner and look of disdain, Richard had a hard time keeping his countenance in check.

"I was just showing Miss Bennet some of your lovely woods and gardens," he offered, trying to get a rise out of his cousin.

Handing Richard his drink he responded, "How fortunate that you were available to give her a tour of my property while I was busy entertaining my other guests. Perhaps you would care to invite her to visit my private orangery tomorrow?" replied Darcy.

"An exceptional idea! But I promised Mr. Bingley I would join his shooting party tomorrow," replied Richard feigning ignorance of Darcy's sarcastic remark.

Darcy gave his cousin a look that would have rivalled any Miss Bingley had ever bestowed upon Elizabeth. "Be careful, Richard."

"Of what danger do you caution me, Darcy? Can a man not simply enjoy the company of a beautiful woman? She is not spoken for; at least, she has given no indication of a suitor."

"She has none," replied Darcy, immediately wishing he had not spoken with such conviction. "That is to say, I have no knowledge of her having a suitor," Darcy replied, endeavouring to hide his obvious irritation.

"And you have denied any partiality towards the young lady yourself. Or has that changed?" Richard waited a beat before continuing. "So I can see no impediments to my spending some time in her company; can you?"

"While Miss Bennet is under my roof, I have an obligation to protect her reputation," said Darcy as his breathing became more difficult to control.

"How very noble of you, Cousin. I shall bear that in mind. Before I act on an impulse which may cause damage to her reputation, I shall make certain I inform you first. However, I am of the opinion that the young lady may not be as innocent as you proclaim. I am anxious to test that theory."

As Darcy heard these words, he saw red; he had no control over his actions as he pulled back his fist and struck his cousin squarely on the jaw. Richard reeled backwards as he struggled to remain on his feet. As his shoulders hit the wall, he steadied himself and stared at Darcy for a long moment.

Darcy stood across from him, breathing heavily and taking a stance as to defend himself, if necessary.

Bringing his hand to his jaw, Richard rubbed it gingerly and then did the unexpected—he gave Darcy a wide grin.

"I believe that is only part of the information I was seeking," he said, the grin still not leaving his face.

"The other part is, do you *ever* plan to make your feelings known to Miss Bennet?"

CHAPTER FORTY-NINE

At seven o'clock that evening, an impressive carriage pulled up in front of Pemberley, and Lord Westcott and his daughter, Arielle, were announced. Darcy greeted the new arrivals with pleasure and escorted them into the parlour. All of Pemberley's guests were in attendance except for Elizabeth, who had wanted to spend as much time with Ellie as possible before she was obliged to join the others.

Lord Westcott once again held Darcy and Georgiana captive as he regaled them with stories of years gone by regarding their parents and his late wife. Arielle stood quietly next to Mr. Darcy, occasionally looking up shyly at his amused expression which displayed his enjoyment of all he heard. Charles, Mr. and Mrs. Hurst, and Caroline were playing a game of whist at one card table as Jane looked on while Lady Catherine, Lord and Lady Matlock, and Richard were seated at another.

Caroline was having difficulty concentrating on the cards in her hand. She silently cursed herself for having brought Miss Westcott into Mr. Darcy's life. Having to cope with the likes of Miss Eliza was one thing, but this woman possessed all the qualifications Mr. Darcy would require in a wife.

She was young and healthy, probably no more than twenty. And by the way Mr. Darcy had admired her at the ball, Caroline supposed the young woman could be considered attractive. Her father was titled, and it was rumoured that she had a vast fortune of her own, left to her by her late mother's estate. Caroline could not help stealing glances as Mr. Darcy bestowed his rare smiles upon the woman.

Caroline was not the only person in the room who was more than a little interested in the way Mr. Darcy attended his new guests with such amiability. Lady Matlock raised an eyebrow towards her husband, who in turn nodded his head to indicate he had been struck with a similar notion. While Caroline's objective was to separate the two as soon as possible, Lord and Lady Matlock's was quite the opposite.

When Elizabeth entered the parlour, William's eyes met hers. They had not spoken of the kiss that had occurred between them the night before. She tried to read his thoughts, but his countenance betrayed nothing. "Miss Bennet, please allow me to introduce you to Lord Westcott and his daughter."

She joined the foursome and graciously greeted them. Before they had conversed for very long, Lady Matlock also joined them. "Stanford, your daughter has grown into a lovely young woman," she stated,

"Yes, although it seems like only yesterday that Arielle was playing hopscotch with her friends," he replied.

The young woman blushed. "Papa, really! I have not played such childish games for years and years," she protested.

Darcy smiled at the young girl. Lady Matlock then asked, "Tell me, Miss Westcott, do you play the pianoforte?"

"Why, yes, it is one of my greatest pleasures."

"Well then, Darcy, you must show Miss Westcott the music room since she is so fond of playing. Go along with them, Georgiana, and show Miss Westcott your new pianoforte." Again the young woman blushed.

"It would be my pleasure, Miss Westcott," said Darcy as he extended his arm to guide her.

Lady Matlock beamed as she witnessed Darcy's attentiveness. "Let us leave the young people to their own diversions, Stanford. Come take my place at cards. Henry could use a partner with your cunning. My son has beaten us three games in a row."

Satisfied that she had arranged for Darcy to spend time with the very eligible Miss Westcott with only Georgiana as their chaperone, her face betrayed her disappointment as Darcy turned back and asked, "Miss Bennet, won't you join us?"

"I thank you, sir, but no."

"Do you not play, Miss Bennet?" asked Miss Westcott as she timidly rested her hand on Mr. Darcy's arm.

"A little, but very ill indeed," answered Elizabeth.

"That is not true, Elizabeth," protested Georgiana. "You play wonderfully. Please come with us."

At that moment Caroline Bingley made her way from the card table. "I'm afraid Mr. Hurst has undone us all," she proclaimed. "Mr. Darcy, were you about to seek entertainment in the music room? I would be most happy to play for you. Of course, you must agree to turn the pages for me," she cooed as she took his other arm.

Elizabeth took in the scene before her. She would not be part of this shameless vying for William's attentions. "I beg you would excuse me," she pleaded. "I fear a headache coming on. I think it would be wise to retire to my rooms." She bade everyone goodnight and ascended the stairs, following the now familiar blue and yellow carpeting.

Once in her room, Elizabeth knew it was too early to seek sleep. She had not ventured into the sitting room since her arrival and thought this would be a good opportunity. She changed into her nightclothes, picked up one of her books and opened the door that connected the two rooms.

Closing the door behind her, she chose the comfort of the oversized chair rather than that of the divan. But her mind was too busy to read just yet as she pictured William in the company of Miss Bingley and Miss Westcott. If you included Georgiana, the man was surrounded by woman who obviously adored him; he did not need her to add to his admirers.

She was beginning to believe she was not as immune to Mr. Darcy as she had pretended to be. He certainly had been his most charming while in her company. He had afforded her every courtesy and had treated her with the greatest respect. And most importantly, he had completely disregarded the terms of their agreement, allowing her complete access to her daughter.

As she thought upon it, she tried to think back to every interaction that had occurred between them since that fateful day she had fainted at the sight of him and Ellie. As she did this, she was all astonishment. In every instance she could bring to mind, he had been nothing but kind and generous. Had she allowed her shame to taint her judgment of him?

His kiss last night was not unwelcomed. Had she been secretly hoping he would kiss her? But she could think of nothing worse than discovering she was in love with him, only to find that he did not return her love.

Her last defence against her barricade of misgivings had been shattered when she had learned from Jane that Mr. Darcy had been instrumental in Charles's proposing. The other tidbit of information that Jane had inadvertently revealed only convinced her that Jane's innate nature made her convey her own optimism in regard to Mr. Darcy's affections rather than any he may have actually expressed.

She opened her book and began reading. After an hour or so, as interesting as the book was, she fell asleep. She awoke some time later unaware of how much time had elapsed. The candles she had brought in with her were now just pools of liquid wax. With only the light from the moon shining through the windows, she sought the door to her bedchamber. She entered the room, but did not recognize her surroundings. As she discerned she had obviously opened the wrong door, she turned to retreat, but something caught her eye.

She noted the décor and the exquisite furnishings. But what had drawn her attention was the painting above the bed. It was her painting. The painting she had bought in St. Andrews.

Elizabeth was drawn to it, and she moved towards it as though it held some power over her. It could not be the same painting. But as she approached it, she read the plaque on the frame and confirmed her suspicion. Yes, it was the very painting she had bought. The painting she had left behind at the cottage.

But how did it get there? And why did it merit such a prominent place?

Before she could gather her thoughts, he entered his bedchamber. Startled by the sight of her, but aware of the impropriety of her presence, he quickly shut the door to avoid discovery from others.

His eyes devoured her. She was modestly covered by her nightdress, but knowing that the thin material was the only obstacle to her lush body made his pulse quicken, not to mention its other effects.

"Miss Bennet," he acknowledged as he circled around her. Whatever reason had brought her to stand in the middle of his bedchamber, he cared not.

"Oh, Mr. Darcy! Please excuse me!" She hurriedly turned to walk back towards the door to the sitting room, her face red with embarrassment. But he caught her arm and brought her exceedingly close.

"I should not be in your bedchamber, sir. I opened the wrong door and entered your room by mistake. I . . . I saw the painting above your bed, and it drew my attention. It is my painting, is it not?"

"Yes."

They stared at each other, and Elizabeth suddenly felt out of breath.

"I should leave, Mr. Darcy." She again turned towards the sitting room door, but his voice stopped her just as she reached for the knob.

"I went to see you again at the cottage," he said abruptly, "but you had already gone. When I saw the painting, for the first time, I understood. To keep such a memento of our time together could only mean you had feelings for me. But your leaving it behind could only mean that you wished to forget me. Although I knew neither of us would ever forget, I thought it was best for both of us to at least try."

She turned from the door, and he was now standing directly before her. She looked up at him and met his gaze. "What would you have said to me had I not already left the cottage?" she softly asked.

"I have thought upon that often. I had nothing to offer you, but I wanted you to know . . . to understand that you had touched my heart as no other woman had before. He reached for her then, his hand securing her waist as he drew her towards him, his mouth now inches from hers. "Lizzy . . ."

As he said her name, she let out a small gasp. She had not heard him call her that since Scotland, and she could not deny her desire to relive the intimacy they had once shared.

"I must go," she said as she forced herself to leave his embrace. She exited his bedchamber and quickly closed the door behind her.

CHAPTER FIFTY

In the early morning hours of the next day, Darcy entered the breakfast room and was surprised to find Richard already seated with a cup of coffee before him. Darcy poured one for himself, and the two cousins sat across from each other.

"I am usually the only one up this early," stated Richard. "The military has trained me to rise before dawn. What has you up this early?"

"I could not sleep." confessed Darcy.

"Perhaps you have something on your mind that needs to be discussed?"

There were a few moments of silence.

"I don't believe I ever apologized for my poor behaviour yesterday. I don't know what came over me."

"Do you not?" asked Richard with a slightly bemused look.

With resignation in his voice, he answered, "I suppose I do."

He looked directly at his cousin. "I love her, Richard."

"I know."

"I have no idea if she returns my feelings."

"Darcy, don't you think it's about time you found out?"

"I am almost afraid to find out."

"Do you believe she has reason to reject you?" asked Richard.

"I have given her many. But that is not my greatest fear."

His cousin looked at him in question.

"My greatest fear is that she will accept me for reasons other than love. I have already experienced a union where an inequity of feelings existed. I could not bear it if we were to marry and she did not return my love."

"Do you fear how our family will react if she does return your affections?"

"It is obvious your parents wish for me to form an attachment to Miss Westcott. The poor girl has barely been here a day, and your mother is already scheming a match."

Richard smiled at his cousin. "My mother is always trying to match someone. The only reason she is not trying to match me with Miss Westcott is because I told her years ago that if she did not allow me to choose my own wife, I would not marry at all."

Darcy thought wistfully for a moment. "I have tried to imagine if my father were still alive, what his reaction would be to my intentions towards Miss Bennet. I know his expectations were for me to marry into a titled family as he had done. But I would like to believe that had he met Elizabeth, he would understand my decision."

"Anyone who has met Miss Bennet could not but approve, Darcy," replied Richard.

"I must ready myself," said Richard as he rose from the table. "I am accompanying Georgiana and my parents to Lambton this morning."

Before he left the room, he turned to his cousin once again.

"Would Georgiana not have had a happier childhood if not for the loss of her mother? Little girls need their mothers, Darcy."

~*~

A new dawn brought Elizabeth much anxiety. She was grateful that many of the inhabitants of Pemberley had their own agenda and her absence from their activities was not obviously noted.

Richard, Georgiana, and Lord and Lady Matlock had departed for Lambton earlier in the day while Mr. Darcy and the rest of the party took to various outdoor activities—the gentlemen fishing, while the ladies found themselves gathered on the lawn of the east gardens, excessively diverted with a newly introduced game called dominos.

Elizabeth kept to herself except for a morning walk with Ellie and Mrs. Hawkins.

In the afternoon she went to the stables and rode Shayla aimlessly until she came upon a copse of trees that afforded a fair amount of shade. She dismounted and sat upon a large rock.

She tried to ascertain William's feelings. Was he attracted to the young and pretty Miss Westcott? Did he support his aunt and uncle in their obvious campaign? They certainly made a pretty picture together; her light hair and complexion a dramatic contrast to his dark features.

But last night his words to her made her wonder if Jane's opinion had been correct, that it was possible that William truly had feelings for her. But if he did, why was he not telling her?

She knew her feelings for him were much more than she would admit. When he had called her "Lizzy," she wanted to remain in his arms and relive the memories they had shared in St. Andrews.

As much as she had tried to deny it, she now had to admit she was in love with the man. That realization did not bring her joy. What could be worse than unrequited love?

She had arrived back at the house in time to ready herself for dinner. She had not seen Jane the entire day and did not wish her to worry. She squared her shoulders as she approached the dining salon.

Of course, Elizabeth observed, Mr. Darcy was seated next to Miss Westcott as Lord and Lady Matlock again conspired to initiate a courtship between the two.

"John, will you and your daughter be staying long at Pemberley?" asked Lady Matlock.

"I'm afraid we leave for London the day after tomorrow," said Lord Westcott. "We have been invited to St. James as Arielle is to be presented at Court."

"How exciting!" cried Lady Matlock. "Darcy, is that not exceptional?"

"Indeed, it must be quite an honour, Miss Westcott," replied Darcy. The young girl beamed and blushed.

"Perhaps you could visit them in London, Darcy," suggested Lady Matlock.

"Perhaps," he said. "But I have no immediate plans to travel there soon."

Caroline Bingley could not have been more pleased than to hear that Miss Westcott would soon be leaving Pemberley. Now if she could only find a way to rid herself of Miss Eliza as well.

Darcy was relieved that Elizabeth had joined them for dinner. Since he had not seen her all day, he had been afraid that after their encounter last night, she was avoiding his company. He should have declared his intentions while he had had the chance. He should have told her then of his love for her.

When he returned his attention back to the discourse at tonight's dinner table, he found Elizabeth in discussion with Miss Westcott on the subject of Shakespeare. Though Miss Westcott endeavoured to further the conversation, her knowledge on the subject left much to be desired.

"Have you read many of his plays, Miss Bennet?" Darcy inquired

She turned her head from Miss Westcott and looked directly at him. "Yes, Mr. Darcy. I have read them all."

"And which do you prefer, comedy or tragedy?"

"While I admit a fondness for *Much Ado About Nothing* and *As You Like It*, I must confess I enjoy his tragedies more, sir," she replied.

He lifted his eyebrows as if to show his surprise at her answer. "And why is that, Miss Bennet?"

"Do not his tragedies more accurately describe the reality of the world around us? To believe that happy endings are the way of the world is to be foolish and naïve."

"You do not have to convince me of your convictions, Miss Bennet, for I heartily agree. I, too, seem more drawn to the tragedies than the comedies. Art often imitates life. As in many of Shakespeare's tragedies, often times unhappy endings are beyond our control."

"Perhaps, Mr. Darcy. But I believe most of Shakespeare's tragic endings reveal an ironic twist of fate. A more agreeable outcome was almost always within command; however, the realization of that fact would inevitably come too late."

There was an uneasy silence that pervaded the room as they stared long and hard at each other.

Was she trying to tell him something? Was she suggesting that they could have a happy ending if he just took command of the situation? Or was he just so desperate that he was reading his desires into her words.

"Really, Miss Eliza, you do go on. She is much opinionated, is she not, Mr. Darcy?" said Caroline, attempting to take Mr. Darcy's focus away from Elizabeth.

Darcy turned and smiled at her. "She is merely conveying her point of view, Miss Bingley. I have found Miss Bennet can be quite persuasive in expressing her beliefs. I admit she has altered my opinion on several occasions."

Again they held each other's gaze, as if they were trying to will each other to understand.

"I, myself, would find life rather tedious debating the merits of every opinion that popped into my head, Mr. Darcy. I possess a much more agreeable disposition, sir," cooed Caroline, displaying the demurest smile she could conjure.

Darcy then turned toward Georgiana. "Let us hear your opinion, Georgie, on the play we saw in London recently. For I know you love the comedies best."

Georgiana raised her brow with a stunned look, but he gave her a reassuring smile of encouragement, and she shyly described *The Twelfth Night* and how she had now seen it thrice and enjoyed it more with each subsequent viewing.

~*~

The next afternoon the entire party gathered for Ellie's "official" birthday. Elizabeth had a special gift for her daughter but did not wish to give it to her in front of the others. It was to be a keepsake, something for when she was older. She sought out Mr. Darcy so that she might present the gift to him.

She found him alone just outside the parlour and took the opportunity. "Mr. Darcy, I would like you to keep this gift for Ellie. She is too young to wear it now, but I wanted it to be her very first birthday present."

He took the small box from her hand as he tried to engage her eyes. Today, again, he had not been in her company all day, and he now was truly wondering if she was avoiding him. He opened the small box and inside, on a golden chain, was a delicate ruby cross, slightly smaller than the one Elizabeth always wore around her neck.

"It is beautiful, Miss Bennet," he said softly. "I am sure she will treasure it."

Elizabeth finally allowed her eyes to meet his. She could not help but offer him a small smile. She started towards the parlour, but his words stopped her.

"Have you been avoiding me, Miss Bennet? I was hoping you would indulge me once again with your discourse. I have missed our conversations."

At that moment Miss Westcott appeared in the doorway. "Oh, I beg your pardon, will you be long, Mr. Darcy?"

He turned his gaze from Elizabeth to Miss Westcott and pleasantly addressed her. "No, I shall join you in a few minutes." He waited to continue his conversation with Elizabeth until the young woman had turned and gone back to the parlour.

Elizabeth raised an eyebrow and inquired, "Do you not enjoy your conversations with Miss Westcott?"

"Miss Westcott does not converse, she blushes. I know my aunt and uncle wish me to form an alliance with her, but I cannot look upon her as anything more than a child. She is barely two years older than Georgiana."

They stood and stared at each other for a long moment. Finally Elizabeth relented as she smiled at him. "I guess it would be uncivil of me to remain in your home and not afford you the courtesy of conversation, Mr. Darcy."

~*~

Long after the rest of the inhabitants of Pemberley had gone to bed, Darcy and Lord Westcott remained in Darcy's study, enjoying a glass of brandy. "Arielle and I have enjoyed your hospitality, Darcy. I will be sorry to be leaving in the morning."

"It was my pleasure, Lord Westcott. Both Georgiana and I are always eager to hear stories about our parents."

"Your father would have been well proud of the man you've become, Darcy."

"I am not so sure he would approve of everything I have done. Or, for that matter, what I hope to do very soon."

Lord Westcott looked at him curiously. "Why would you say that?"

Darcy let out a long breath. He might as well confide in him. Since the gentleman had known his father so well, he might have some insight as to what his father would have thought of such a match.

"If the young woman will have me, I am about to enter into an alliance that I am sure my father would not have approved of. I believe my father would have considered the young lady unsuitable."

"Are you speaking of Miss Bennet?"

Darcy was startled that Lord Westcott had made such an observation.

"Have I been that obvious?" he asked.

Lord Westcott could not help but laugh. "I would say you have the same look about you when in her company that your father had when he first met Lady Anne."

Darcy smiled to himself at the thought.

"How could your father disapprove of such a match? He, of all people, would have understood."

Upon seeing Darcy's bewildered expression he declared, "Don't tell me you've never heard this story before?"

"I'm afraid you have me at a disadvantage, my lord."

"In that case, perhaps it is not my story to tell, Darcy. I had just assumed somewhere along the way . . ."

"I would be grateful to have knowledge of this story, if you would not mind indulging me, sir."

Lord Westcott studied the younger man's face. "Is it of some importance to you?"

"Yes."

Lord Westcott let out a deep breath. "Well, you know how I love to tell a good story. I can see no harm in my conveying to you the circumstance of your parents' marriage. It was common knowledge at the time. I can recall it as if it were yesterday."

Lord Westcott reached for the bottle of brandy and refilled both their glasses. He sat back in the comfortable chair and looked at Darcy as if he were about to reveal the meaning of life.

"Your father was a handsome devil, to be sure. He was wealthy and a prominent figure in London society. His lack of title was hardly a deterrent for any young lady of the ton. Your mother's family was indeed titled, her father being an Earl.

"However, after the Earl's wife died, his gaming habits and carousing soon became scripture for London gossip columns. Everyone knew he was living in a house of cards that was soon to collapse.

"George Darcy's family had high hopes for their son. They had arranged for a courtship between him and Lady Susan, the daughter of a wealthy Duke. Although she was a pleasant girl, the match was not well suited. But your father was willing to do what his family required of him and was prepared to marry her; that is until he met Lady Anne.

"Although I am not one to believe in love at first sight, I would have to say this was the exception. I was with your father when he first laid eyes on your mother. She was leaving a jeweller's shop in town as we were entering. He was smitten from the first. When he inquired to the shopkeeper as to her identity, he learned that she had been there to sell some of her late mother's jewellery. It seemed the Earl's excessive lifestyle had finally caught up with him, and the family was in dire need of funds. That would have been reason enough for any eligible gentleman to abandon interest in the young lady, but your father pursued her anyway.

"Of course, his family objected to such a match. They forbade him to see her and insisted he continue his courtship of Lady Susan. They even went so far as to have the banns read at the parish church in Lambton. But your father would have none of it. Even when they threatened to disinherit him, he would not back down."

Darcy kept his countenance blank. He felt as if he were listening to the events of lives wholly unconnected to himself.

Lord Westcott took a sip of his drink and continued. "George and Lady Anne married in a private ceremony with only Lady Westcott and myself as witnesses. It was quite a scandal at the time. But your father never regretted his decision to marry Lady Anne. He loved her dearly until the day he died."

"Did the marriage cause a breach in the family?" asked Darcy.

Eventually your grandparents and the rest of the family came around and reconciled themselves to the marriage. But your Aunt Catherine till this very day will never admit that her sister's marriage to your father had saved their family. Indeed, Sir Lewis would have never married Catherine had not your father restored the family's fortune and good name."

At the mention of Sir Lewis, Darcy's interest was piqued.

"Had your association with my parents brought you often in Sir Lewis's and Lady Catherine's company as well?"

"Certainly, on many occasions, although Sir Lewis was absent much of the time. We used to dine at their home regularly."

"Do you recall a servant in their home, a Margaret Harrigan?"

"I don't think . . . no, I believe the cook was a Kate Harrigan. Margaret could have been one of her daughters. I believe she had three, all young and lively girls as I recall. I remember Mrs. Harrigan was one damn fine cook. Just thinking about her stew is making my mouth water. What made you ask?"

"I recently came across the name, and it drew my curiosity. I suppose it's a common enough name," said Darcy.

When they had finished their drinks, the two gentlemen said goodnight, but Darcy lingered in his study.

He thought upon Lord Westcott's story. It was not his mother who had defied her family for love, it was his father. His father, who no doubt had been raised to follow all the rules his society imposed upon him, when faced with the moment of truth, had chosen love over propriety. His father had been willing to do anything to marry the woman he loved.

Would he be willing to do anything to marry Elizabeth? He knew the answer. Yes, he was even willing to risk another marriage of convenience.

CHAPTER FIFTY-ONE

The next day saw the departure of many of Pemberley's guests, with the exception of Mr. & Mrs. Bingley, Elizabeth, Richard and Caroline. Mr. and Mrs. Hurst were travelling to visit friends further north but would return in a se'ennight to bring Caroline back to London with them.

Dinners were much cosier and had the feeling of less formality now that the other guests had departed Pemberley. Darcy felt more relaxed not having to escape his aunt and uncle's matchmaking attempts.

To be honest, he wished all of his guests would depart so that he might be alone with Elizabeth. He needed to tell her of his feelings, no matter what the outcome. This not knowing was torture. He had to ascertain if she returned his affections.

He turned towards Elizabeth as she conversed with her sister, noting that her eyes often found his. He instinctively gave her a warm smile and was more than encouraged when she held his gaze for several moments, an attractive blush colouring her cheeks before returning her attention back to her sister.

It was time he confronted his greatest fear. He prayed he had gained her good opinion. He prayed she returned his love.

Now that the very young and pretty Miss Westcott was no longer in attendance, Caroline again found her voice of superiority and, as usual, directed her caustic comments towards Elizabeth.

Thursday's Child

"So Miss Eliza," she asked, "what are you planning next? Lady's companion? Book shop clerk or was it librarian? You seem to have a variety of employable talents."

"I have not made any immediate plans, Miss Bingley," replied Elizabeth. She would not reveal her upcoming employment.

Georgiana gave her brother a look of distress as she heard Miss Bingley's derogatory comments towards her friend. Although he knew Elizabeth would not be intimidated by Miss Bingley, he was desirous to change the topic of conversation.

"Miss Bennet, will you be riding tomorrow?" he asked.

"If the weather holds, I hope to ride in the afternoon," she replied.

"I would love to ride tomorrow also, Mr. Darcy," interrupted Caroline.

"Caroline, you have not ridden since you were a child," said her brother, "and even then, you were not very accomplished."

"Oh, I am sure it will all come back to me once I am upon a horse again," replied Caroline. "Will you not join us, Colonel Fitzwilliam?"

"I would like to see someone try to stop me. We could ride the south meadows. Might I invite you all to visit my cousin's private orangery?" he asked with a devilish grin in Darcy's direction.

~*~

A perfect afternoon for riding was upon them. Darcy, Elizabeth, Caroline, and Richard had agreed to meet at the stables after lunch. Darcy was the first to arrive. He hoped this outing would allow him time alone with Elizabeth, for he vowed he would not wait another day before telling her of his feelings.

He had no sooner approached the stables than Miss Bingley called to him. He immediately stiffened as he had no choice but to pause until she caught up with him.

"I am so looking forward to this, Mr. Darcy. I understand it is a privilege indeed to be escorted to your private orangery. I have heard rumours it can be quite an intimate setting." She batted her eyelashes and gave him her most engaging smile.

"I hope it is not your intention to take advantage of me, sir. But I trust that you are a gentleman. Perhaps we might go on ahead and let Miss Eliza and Colonel Fitzwilliam follow when they are ready."

As he was about to protest such a suggestion, he was relieved to see his cousin enter the stables.

Caroline let out a long sigh of frustration. She was running out of time. Mr. and Mrs. Hurst would be returning to take her back to London in a few days. She was determined to achieve her goal by then and, if necessary, would resort to whatever devious measures were required.

The colonel helped Miss Bingley choose a horse, one that was not too spirited, and helped her to mount.

"I see you have your own riding crop, Miss Bingley. For someone who has not ridden in so long a time, I am surprised to see you so well equipped."

"It is my brother's." As she spoke, her horse whinnied, and she quickly grabbed the reins tighter to keep from falling. Colonel Fitzwilliam calmed the horse and patted its nose. "Are you sure this horse has been trained properly?" Miss Bingley inquired indignantly.

"You are pulling too tightly on the reins, Miss Bingley," observed the colonel. "Relax your hold a little."

As Richard mounted his horse, he noted Darcy leading a tall silver grey mare, recognizing it as the one Elizabeth had ridden several days before. He observed with some humour as his cousin ran his hands down the length of each of the horse's legs and checked each hoof individually, making sure the animal was properly shod.

Thursday's Child

He then handed the reins to Billy, one of his young grooms, while he went to seek out Marengo.

Elizabeth had been hurrying towards the stables as she was late changing into her riding habit. She had just crossed the threshold of the stable door and was headed for the groom who was holding the reins to her horse, when she heard her name called. She turned to look back. There she observed Georgiana walking towards her with Ellie.

"Ellie wanted to see you off," said Georgiana.

The little girl started to run towards Elizabeth, letting go of Georgiana's hand. "Izabet," she called, her closest resemblance to Elizabeth's name.

Caroline observed the charming scene, and the intense look of loathing she cast upon Elizabeth was undeniable. Her predatory nature took over. She smiled as she saw her opportunity and without hesitation she acted upon it.

Elizabeth heard the horse, and an instant later she saw a black blur from the corner of her eye. Observing her daughter running towards her and seeing the inevitable path of the horse, Elizabeth ran the last few yards towards Ellie, and, with time to do little else, reached her arms out and pushed her as hard as she could out of harm's way as she herself reeled forward.

As the black horse approached Elizabeth, it reared up, causing one of its hooves to strike her head, knocking her to the ground.

"Miss Bingley! Pull up the reins!" yelled the colonel as he jumped to the ground and tried fiercely to grab the horse's bridle before its hoof could again strike Elizabeth.

As Darcy heard the commotion, he quickly made his way from Marengo's stall and ran to Elizabeth, dragging her body to safety while Richard struggled to get the horse under control.

"Lizzy!" he cried as he gathered her into his arms. He immediately noticed the blood on her forehead. He yelled over to Georgiana, who was now holding a crying Ellie in her arms. "Is Ellie injured?" he called to her.

"I do not think so, Fitzwilliam; I believe she is only frightened. She looks to be unharmed."

"Richard, take Georgiana and Ellie to the house and have Mrs. Reynolds send for the doctor immediately," he commanded. He then turned his eyes to Miss Bingley, who had dismounted the black horse and was now looking repentant.

The look he gave her sent chills throughout her entire being.

"Mr. Darcy, I don't know what happened! Honestly, I could not stop the horse. It would not respond to me."

He said nothing as he turned his attention back to Elizabeth's motionless body. He rested her head on his arm as he reached into his pocket and pulled out a handkerchief, placing it over the laceration on her temple, trying to stop the flow of blood. When it had sufficiently subsided, he lowered his head and pressed his face to her cheek, holding on to her as if his life depended upon it.

CHAPTER FIFTY-TWO

Dr. Chisholm looked at the four faces staring at him as he left Elizabeth's room upon completing his examination. Jane, Bingley, Colonel Fitzwilliam, and Darcy all watched him and waited for him to speak.

"Besides the laceration on her forehead, I cannot find any other injuries. "I have stitched the cut, but I cannot tell how seriously the damage will affect her. We will have to wait and see how she progresses. If she demonstrates any signs of mental impairment, if she does not remember things, or is confused, I should like to be informed right away. She will most likely be in and out of consciousness for the next day or two. Should she awaken and be in pain, I have left some medication for her."

Jane began to cry at the doctor's words; her husband put a comforting arm around her.

"Are you certain she will be all right?" asked Darcy.

"Mr. Darcy, I cannot guarantee anything at this early stage, but her injuries do not appear to be life threatening. She is young and healthy; I see no reason not to expect a full recovery. We will have to wait until she awakens to see if the blow to her head has caused any harm."

Darcy let out a tentative breath of relief. After the doctor had departed, Darcy went to the nursery to make sure Ellie was resting. The doctor had looked after her bruises and assured him her injuries were minor. She was lying in her crib when he entered, and she turned her sweet face towards him. "Papa."

He went to her and bent down to kiss her forehead. "My sweet, sweet Ellie." He did not want to pick her up, afraid to touch where she was bruised.

When the door again opened, she looked towards it and called "Izabet," but it was Georgiana who entered.

As soon as Georgie saw her brother, she rushed to his arms. They gave each other a comforting hug. "Georgiana, please do not be distressed. I know you are as worried for Miss Elizabeth as I . . . as we all are. We will do all we can to help her recover. And Dr. Chisholm has assured me that Ellie has suffered only bruises that will heal in time."

"It is not only that, Brother. It is my fault. I am the reason Elizabeth was injured."

"Georgie, you are not to blame. You could not have prevented it."

"I let go of Ellie's hand," she sobbed. "Had I not let go, she could not have run into the horse's path, and Elizabeth would not have had to save her."

"Come with me, dearest. Let's allow Ellie to rest."

He led her to her room and, once inside, he tried to comfort her.

"You cannot blame yourself for this, Georgie. You thought she would be safe going to Miss Bennet. I would have done nothing different."

"I should have been more cautious, Fitzwilliam."

"Did you see anything else? Anything you thought was unusual?" he asked.

"No, Brother; I am sorry. I was looking only at Ellie."

Thursday's Child

Darcy stayed with her for a while, trying to convince her that she was not the cause of this accident, but he left feeling he had not completely accomplished his task.

~*~

Jane Bingley could not be persuaded to leave Lizzy's side. Her husband had tried unsuccessfully to coax her to come away and rest in their bedchamber, but she was unmoved. Elizabeth's condition had not improved over the last several hours, and Jane refused to relinquish the care of her most beloved sister.

Darcy was growing more and more impatient. This waiting for some sign that Elizabeth was recovering tormented him. She still had not awakened. He needed to do something! Anything! He could not abide this helplessness. In the early morning light, he knocked lightly on Elizabeth's bedchamber, but there was no reply. Slowly he opened the door and observed an exhausted Jane sleeping soundly in the chair.

He quietly moved over to where Elizabeth lay and, without thought to propriety, sat on the bed beside her. He reached for her hand, holding it in his, stroking it lightly. Her breathing was shallow but steady. Bending slightly towards her face, he softly called to her. "Lizzy, you must wake up. You must try for Ellie's sake . . . and for me. Please try. I have so much to tell you, Lizzy. Please come back to me."

The only response he received was a slight twitching of her fingers, and, although he knew it most likely an automatic reflex, he preferred to believe that she had heard his plea. He brought her hand to his lips, kissing her fingers and then pressed it to his cheek as tears filled his eyes. As he heard Jane stir, he reluctantly relinquished her hand and stood. His grief turned to anger as he left Elizabeth's room and headed directly for the stables.

He conferred with Mr. Cassidy, his stable master, giving him instructions in regard to the black horse. He then had Marengo saddled and tried to ride off some of his frustrations. By the time he returned, there was much activity in the house he had left completely silent only two hours before.

He first encountered Mrs. Reynolds who immediately made him aware of the reason for all the commotion. "Miss Bennet awoke about an hour ago!" she exclaimed. As these words had a consoling affect upon him, he could not comprehend why his housekeeper's look exhibited distress.

As he began quickly climbing the stairs to Elizabeth's bedchamber he called down to her, "That is good news, is it not?"

As she looked up at him, he stopped his flight and demanded, "What are you not telling me, Mrs. Reynolds?"

Before she could speak, Darcy grabbed the banister and projected himself up the stairs, taking them two at a time until he reached Elizabeth's room.

When he opened the door, his eyes immediately fell upon Elizabeth, who still lay motionless with her eyes closed. He then observed Jane sitting on the bed. She was crying, her hands shaking as one held Elizabeth's while the other stroked her cheek. When she looked up, her eyes met his.

Startled by what he saw, Darcy could only think the worst. He felt the air leave his lungs as he stood there unable to move. Holding on to the doorway for support, he felt the tears welling in his eyes.

Then the most beautiful sound he had ever heard reached his ears as Elizabeth inhaled a shaky breath. He closed his eyes and silently thanked God.

He watched as Jane gently tucked Elizabeth's hand under the covers and rose to meet him by the door.

"Mr. Darcy." She allowed herself to breathe as she tried to keep her voice calm. "My sister awoke about an hour ago and in an extremely distressed state. The injury to her head must be grave indeed, for she was calling to Ellie, asking if her daughter was safe! When I tried to tell her that she had no daughter, that Ellie was not her child, she became even more agitated and tried to leave her bed. What are we to do, Mr. Darcy? She believes Ellie to be her daughter!

"I asked Mrs. Reynolds to send for Dr. Chisholm to make him aware of this delusional state Elizabeth is in, but she insisted that we wait for your return. But why should we wait, Mr. Darcy? The doctor asked to be informed immediately of any signs of mental impairment."

Darcy again looked over to Elizabeth. Her looks had altered but little since he had seen her earlier except her breathing appeared more erratic. "How did you calm her?" he inquired.

"I had to restrain her from leaving her bed, and she seems to have gone back into an unconsciousness state. Will you not send for Dr. Chisholm now? I do not think we should wait any longer. Please, Mr. Darcy."

At that moment Mrs. Reynolds appeared in the doorway. "Mrs. Reynolds, will you stay with Miss Bennet while I speak with Mrs. Bingley in private?"

Mrs. Reynolds nodded her head and proceeded into the room, taking the chair by the bed. She knew what their conversation would reveal, and she did not envy Mr. Darcy's plight.

~*~

Caroline Bingley had not ventured from her rooms since the "unfortunate incident." She sensed that both her brother and Mr. Darcy had been more than a little displeased with her, and she did not wish to face their wrath.

She would never have a better opportunity than now to achieve her goal of winning Mr. Darcy. With some satisfaction, she acknowledged there was no one left with whom she must compete for his attentions. She would have him all to herself for the next few days; this time, she would make sure of the outcome, even if she had to compromise herself to do it.

She decided to test the waters and make an appearance at the dinner table. Certainly she had been forgiven by now. Well, perhaps Jane might still hold some resentment towards her as she was such a devoted sister. But as far as her brother and Mr. Darcy were concerned, she was sure she would be able to convince them of her regret over the entire episode.

As she entered the dining salon, Colonel Fitzwilliam, Darcy, and Bingley all rose in a gentlemanly manner until she was seated. Jane was not in attendance, as she refused to leave Elizabeth's bedside, and Georgiana was still too distraught to leave her room.

"My, I certainly feel honoured to be surrounded by such charming gentlemen," she cooed.

Darcy could hardly contain his contempt as he did his best to keep the look of disgust off his face.

An uncomfortable silence ensued.

"Tell me, Colonel, are you expected back at your regiment soon?" she inquired, unaware of the unease that pervaded the room.

"I have no desire to depart while the situation is so unsettled, but I must away tomorrow at first light to make it back to my regiment on time."

"Unsettled? What is unsettled, sir?" she further asked.

He stared at her for a long moment. How could she not perceive the import of his words?

Another long silence filled the room.

"Perhaps we could play a game of cards after dinner," she suggested. All three gentlemen expressed their desire to attend personal matters.

As if it were a complete afterthought, she asked, "And how is Miss Eliza faring this evening?"

Darcy felt his ire build and could not even manage to look at her. Fortunately Bingley responded. "Her condition has not changed since this morning," he said as he looked over to Darcy and witnessed the anguish upon his friend's face.

"Oh, such a dreadful situation!" cried Caroline. "One cannot help but feel sympathy for the poor girl. Thank heavens Ellie was not seriously injured. That would have been far more grievous. Don't you agree, Mr. Darcy?"

Darcy took the napkin from his lap and wiped his mouth. He rose and, with conviction, threw it down on the table before heading for his study.

~*~

Darcy slept ill that night. As he heard the chirping of the birds greeting the early morning dawn, he rose from his bed. Approaching the breakfast room, he was relieved at the sight of his cousin seated at the table.

"I was afraid I had missed you," said Darcy.

"I've little time left before I must make my departure," replied Richard.

Darcy poured himself a cup of coffee and sat down.

Richard observed the look of grief in his cousin's eyes.

"I have never known another woman as strong willed as Elizabeth Bennet. I am sure she will recover soon, Darcy. The doctor said it might take a couple of days."

"I pray you are right, Cousin. She has now become a part of my life. I cannot imagine a day without her in it. Ellie and I have become dependent on her for our happiness."

"I have every faith that she will recover. She has already awakened once; she is finding her way back."

They both sat quietly for a moment.

"Do you remember the night of the ball; you asked me if I still put my family's expectations before my own happiness?"

Richard nodded.

"Elizabeth *is* my family. She is the woman I love and the mother of my child. I would gladly spend the rest of my life trying to live up to her expectations."

"And you will have the chance; you will see. I have seen many such injuries in my career. She will awaken as soon as she has a chance to heal.

Richard pulled his watch from his pocket and, observing the time, stood. "I'm afraid I must depart, but I will be anxious to hear of Miss Elizabeth's recovery. Write to me with any news."

~*~

Jane Bingley sat and watched her sister's uneasy sleep. Her head was still reeling from all she had discovered from yesterday's conversation with Mr. Darcy. How could all of that have happened unbeknownst to her? How could Elizabeth have kept so many secrets from her?

Jane shook her head in disbelief. *She* had always been considered the one with all the goodness, but that was not the truth. It was Elizabeth who had sacrificed everything to help her family. She had to recover. She just had to! "Please, Lizzy," she cried.

As if she had heard her sister's plea, Elizabeth slowly opened her eyes. Jane immediately grabbed her hand as the words gushed from her to quickly ease her sister's distress. "Ellie is well, Lizzy. She was unharmed. Do you hear me? Your daughter is well!"

Elizabeth stared back at her sister as tears formed. She managed to lightly squeeze Jane's hand to let her know she had heard her words before she again closed her eyes. However, this time Jane witnessed an easier rhythm to her sister's breathing as if she could now attend to her own wellbeing, knowing her daughter was safe.

~*~

Darcy paced the length of his study. For a man who had always been in control of everything in his world, he was finding this impotence impossible to tolerate.

There was a knock on the door. "Enter," he commanded as he took his seat behind his large desk.

Mr. Cassidy rarely sought him out. He had worked at Pemberley through two generations and knew his duties well. Whatever business took him from overseeing the large stable of horses on Pemberley's grounds must be of some importance. He was accompanied by Billy, one of several grooms employed on the estate. The young boy stood nervously next to Mr. Cassidy, fidgeting with the cap in his hands.

"Beggin' your pardon, Mr. Darcy," said Mr. Cassidy, "but Billy here seems to have somethin' to say 'bout the orders you gave me yesterday."

"Regarding my orders?" asked Darcy. "My orders are not to be questioned, Mr. Cassidy. I will not have that horse in my stables. It could have killed Ellie, and because of that horse, Liz . . . a guest in my home has been seriously injured. I cannot allow such a dangerous and mean-spirited animal to remain at Pemberley."

"He ain't mean-spirited!" responded the stable boy. "He's ain't! He's a good horse. I been tendin' him since he been born. No, sir! He ain't nothin' but a good horse."

The boy now looked down at his feet, fearing he would be punished for speaking to his master so disrespectfully.

Darcy eyed the young boy curiously. He obviously had a strong opinion on the matter.

"I tried explainin' the way things are to 'em, Mr. Darcy," said Mr. Cassidy, "but the boy insists what happened was not the horse's fault. He was so insistent that I thought it best he come speak his piece to you directly."

"Come here, boy," said Darcy. Billy cautiously took two steps closer to the large desk.

"Now, what is it you have to say in the horse's defence?"

"He done nothin' wrong, sir, is all I'm sayin'," said Billy, unable to look his master straight in the eye. "No reason to be puttin' 'em down."

"Why don't you tell me what happened and why you believe the horse should be spared," encouraged Darcy.

The young boy turned to look at Mr. Cassidy for support. "Go ahead, boy. Tell the master what you told me."

The young boy swallowed hard. As he unconsciously pulled at the button on his cap, he finally looked Darcy straight in the eyes.

"I . . . I saw the little girl, sir, Miss Ellie, I saw her runnin' towards that nice Miss Bennet lady. I was holdin' the reins to her horse thinkin' she was comin' to get it, but she turned 'round when Miss Georgiana called to her." Billy stopped to look back at Mr. Cassidy and then back again to his master. Both men were intent on his story.

"What else did you observe, Billy? Go on, I am very interested in what you have to say," assured Darcy.

"When Miss Ellie was runnin' to Miss Bennet, I saw that other lady, who I ain't never seen at the stables before . . ."

"Miss Bingley?" suggested Darcy.

"I guess so, sir. She had a real mean look on her face, but then I saw her smile. It was kinda . . . spooky. I mean . . . one minute she's lookin' real mean and the next she's smilin'. She was lookin' right at Miss Bennet."

"What happened next?" Darcy heard himself ask, hardly able to breathe.

"I saw her raise her ridin' crop and hit the horse real hard on the rump, and then she dug her heels into his flank. The horse din't mean to do it, sir. He was forced to! That lady *made* him do it. Please, please don't put the horse down. He's always been a good horse," cried Billy.

CHAPTER FIFTY-THREE

"Please, Jane. You must rest. You will be of no use to Elizabeth when she awakens if you do not get some sleep yourself. She will be in good hands with Mrs. Reynolds watching over her."

Jane knew her husband was right. She could hardly keep her eyes open, and her back was sore from the uncomfortable position in which she had slept the last two nights. But when Elizabeth had opened her eyes and squeezed her hand last night, she was sure her sister would soon regain full consciousness.

Dr. Chisholm, who had attended Elizabeth early that morning, assured everyone that it was a good sign that she slept so peacefully. "She is giving herself a chance to heal," he informed them all. "She will awaken when she is ready. In the meantime, continue your encouraging words to her."

No mention was made to the doctor regarding any mental impairment, as Jane now understood Elizabeth's mind was as sound as ever. It gave Jane much relief, knowing her sister was not some raving madwoman, claiming to be mother to the Master of Pemberley's only child, while they locked her away for the rest of her days.

As Darcy climbed the stairs, his downcast eyes looked up, and he saw Bingley help his wife from Elizabeth's room. He observed the exhaustion on her face and was relieved Bingley had finally removed her to sleep for a while in their bedchamber.

"I will stay with Elizabeth until you send for Mrs. Reynolds," said Darcy.

~*~

Darcy entered the room quietly, his eyes immediately fixing upon the woman who had completely consumed his every thought for the last two days, if not the better part of the last two years.

He sat beside her on the edge of the bed and took her hand in his, gently caressing it. He stared at her face, willing her to open her eyes, but she remained unmoved, seemingly unaware of his presence.

He cleared his throat, knowing his voice would sound hoarse and unsteady.

"I am not good at expressing my feelings, Elizabeth, but if I am ever to improve, now would seem the ideal time to start practicing. It seems the only time I am capable of telling you my feelings is when I am sure you cannot hear me. I have told you so often in my dreams."

He moved her hand between both of his, giving slight pressure.

"I love you, Lizzy. I imagine that I have always loved you. Perhaps even before it was proper to do so." A tear slowly rolled down his cheek.

"I wanted to tell you so many times, but I had not the courage. I was afraid you would accept me for Ellie's sake alone, without regard for me as a man who loved you. I was afraid you did not return my feelings…could not return them." He did his best to swallow the lump in his throat; his eyes never left her face.

"I desire nothing more than to have the chance to make up for all the heartache I have caused you. I do not want you to stay as Ellie's nanny. I wish you to stay as my wife; that is if you would be willing to bestow upon me such an honour. We will be a family, Lizzy, I promise you. And we will give Ellie brothers and sisters. When you awaken, Ellie and I will be waiting for you. I love you, my dearest Lizzy."

As he was about to release her hand, he felt the slight grasp of her fingers.

He looked down at her hand and watched as her fingers tightened around his. He then raised his eyes to her face and saw the subtle movement of her eyelashes. The next moment he was staring deep into the dark pools of her eyes.

"Lizzy," he sobbed as he hugged her body to his. "Oh, my Lizzy, I love you so much."

Mrs. Reynolds approached the door, and as she did, she tactfully coughed to announce her arrival and to give Mr. Darcy a chance to remove himself to a more discreet location in the room.

~*~

Caroline Bingley's hands trembled as she read the note that had been delivered by one of the maids. Even if it had not been signed, the distinctive script had told her it could be from no one other than Mr. Darcy. He was requesting her company for a private meeting in the library in half an hour. Her smile was triumphant. At last he had seen her for what she truly was. At last he had recognized her beauty and sophistication. At last he had made his move!

She quickly rifled through her gowns, deciding which one would be most appropriate for such a rendezvous. As she came across the tangerine organza, she hesitated. It certainly was her most revealing, the neckline barely covering enough skin to be considered decent. But after all, when a gentleman secretly summons a lady to a private meeting at midnight, seduction can be the only motive. And Caroline Bingley was clearly up to the challenge. If she was not about to be seduced, she was ready to take on the role of seducer.

She quietly approached the door to the library, but did not knock before she entered. As she peered into the dimly lit room, she saw him there, sitting by the fireplace. His eyes were closed, and his head was resting against the back of the chair. His cravat was untied, and she could see his exposed neck, the sight of which caused her to inhale a slight gasp. At first she thought him asleep, but she watched as he lifted the glass in his right hand to his mouth and took a long swig of its contents. With his eyes still closed, he returned the glass to the table beside him.

She furtively moved towards him and stared down at his resting form. Stealthily she reached for his shoulders and lowered her body to sit upon his lap. Startled by such a manoeuver, Darcy opened his eyes to find his face inches away from a pair of heaving breasts bursting forth from a very low bodice. From his vantage point, he could discern the nipples that hardened by means of his stare.

As his eyes moved up to the face that owned the exposed bosom, his first reaction was to stand, thus removing the objectionable visage that greeted him, but Caroline clung to the chair and held her position on his lap.

"There is no need to get up, Mr. Darcy. I am quite comfortable where I am," she cooed. She moved her lips towards his exposed neck. "I knew you would come to your senses sooner or later."

This was just too much! Using all his strength, he pushed forward to stand, promptly depositing Caroline on the floor.

"What game do you play, sir?" she demanded as she looked up from her embarrassing position. "Did you not summon me to a private rendezvous?"

"Yes, I did summon you, madam, but seduction was the furthest thought from my mind," he retaliated.

When he made no effort to assist in her rising, she had no choice but to awkwardly climb to a standing position. Pulling herself up to her full height, she indignantly asked, "For what purpose then have you sought my company?"

At that moment Charles Bingley entered the library.

"You are late, Charles."

"I say, Darcy, I got here as quickly as I could," replied Bingley. "What's this all about?"

"Yes, Mr. Darcy, what *is* this all about?" echoed Caroline.

"I have learned of your treachery, madam," said a barely contained Darcy.

"Of what do you speak?" asked Caroline, careful not to betray her alarm at his accusation.

"I have a witness as to your actions that day in the stables."

"I think you'd better explain yourself, Darcy. Are you suggesting that Caroline intended to injure Miss Bennet?" asked a wide-eyed Bingley.

"I'm afraid it is all too true, Bingley."

A quite disbelieving Bingley stood in awe at hearing these words. As he was about to come to his sister's defence, he turned to her and saw the flicker of fear that quickly passed over her face, a look that made him hold his tongue.

That fear quickly faded from Caroline's countenance and was replaced with her usual supercilious look of contempt.

"That is quite ridiculous, Mr. Darcy. Who would make such false accusations? Why, of course, it must be Miss Eliza. Has that little chit made claim against me? You can't possible believe a word she has said. She is most likely jealous of our close association, Mr. Darcy, and wishes to diminish your estimation of me. Why in heaven's name would I wish harm on that poor pathetic girl?"

"As to your reasons, I can only guess. Your jealousy and your disdain for Miss Bennet have been demonstrated at every turn. You could never even begin to understand a woman of such substance. Your thoughts are for no one but yourself.

"It was not Miss Bennet who witnessed your actions, Miss Bingley; it was one of my grooms, a person so wholly unconnected to you as to have no motive to accuse you falsely."

"A groom? Did you say a groom, Mr. Darcy?" Caroline visibly relaxed at this news. "What rubbish! How could you possibly take the word of a lowly groom over mine? It is to add insult to injury, sir. I must insist on an apology at once!"

"Hell will more likely freeze over, Madam, before you have heard an apology from me," declared Darcy.

"Brother, are you going to let Mr. Darcy speak to me this way? Will you not come to my defence?"

"Perhaps the boy was mistaken, Darcy. Can you not even entertain such a possibility?" asked Bingley with scant hope in his voice. "What did the boy lay witness to?"

"He observed your sister strike the horse on its backside with her crop and dig her heels into its flank, directing the horse towards Liz . . . Miss Bennet. Bingley, I do not wish this to cause a breach in our friendship, but the boy would have no reason to make up such a story. I believe he is telling the truth."

Bingley studied the ceiling for a moment and then let out a breath. "Caroline, go up to your room," he said calmly.

"You do not believe him, do you? You cannot possibly take a groom's word over that of your own sister."

"I said go up to your room, Caroline. I will speak to you later after Darcy and I have finished our discussion."

When she did not move, he stared into her eyes and said emphatically, "Now, Caroline!"

As tempted as she was to disregard such a command, something in his demeanour told her she should not. His glare followed her until she had closed the door behind her.

Bingley sat down in one of the large chairs before the fireplace. He combed his fingers through his hair, then rested his elbows on his knees, his head in his hands. "I cannot believe she would do such a thing! Louisa warned me, but I would not listen."

"What do you mean? Mrs. Hurst knew Caroline *planned* to harm Miss Bennet?" asked Darcy in dismay.

"She came to me after the ball and told me she worried that Caroline was becoming more and more obsessed with you; that she was talking some nonsense about Miss Bennet being a threat to her and how she was prepared to do whatever it took to remove her once and for all from your life. Louisa cautioned me she feared that Caroline would do whatever was necessary to see that Miss Bennet was no longer a temptation to you."

"How could you not warn me, Bingley? How could you let Miss Bennet be unwittingly exposed to harm?"

"I could not let myself believe that Caroline was capable of such things. She is my sister, Darcy. I wanted to believe there was some goodness in her. I have made excuses for her behaviour so many times over the years, thinking she would change. I could not reconcile myself to the truth that Caroline is of mean spirit, a fact that I must now acknowledge."

Darcy thought Bingley's words befitting as he recalled using the same words to describe the now exonerated black horse.

"I know you are within your rights to summon the magistrate, but I beg you to allow me to remove Caroline from here and send her away where she will be no threat to anyone."

Darcy's next words came out strained, as he was barely able to contain his anger towards Caroline Bingley, imagining the pleasure of his hands around her throat.

"I will trust that you will take care of this matter, Bingley; for if you do not, I will. In the meantime, I do not want to see her, as I might not be capable of controlling my actions. See that she stays in her rooms until you are able to remove her from Pemberley and my sight."

"I will take care of it immediately, Darcy. You have my word," said Bingley.

Thursday's Child

"You can thank God that Elizabeth is recovering, for I would not be so generous if she was not."

~*~

Elizabeth was reclining on the cushions of the divan in the sitting room off her bedchamber when she heard a knock on the door. The knock came from Mr. Darcy's room.

"Come in."

Darcy entered the sitting room, and their eyes met. "I beg your pardon; I thought your sister would be with you, Miss Bennet."

"She has gone to see about tea. She should be returning shortly," she said as she sat up straight on the divan, allowing him room to sit next to her.

"I would not wish to intrude on your privacy. Would you rather I leave?"

"Not at all, Mr. Darcy. I welcome your company. I have been made to do nothing for the last two days. I could use a little diversion."

He smiled a weak smile. "I. . . I would like to speak with you, Miss Bennet, about what happened the other night."

She watched as he rubbed his brow, looking a bit anxious. Then he clasped his hands behind his back and stared at her a moment before he started a slow pace.

She raised an eyebrow in his direction. "Please sit, Mr. Darcy; you are making me nervous."

He looked up and caught her gaze, then proceeded to take the seat next to her.

"I do not know if you recall that I was with you when you awoke from your injury. Your sister had just left your room, and I stayed with you until Mrs. Reynolds could be sent for."

Elizabeth smiled at him. "Yes, Mr. Darcy, I believe I do remember your being there when I awoke."

He cleared his throat. "As I saw you lying there, I thought perhaps if I spoke to you, you might awaken."

"That sounds very reasonable, Mr. Darcy. And what did you speak about?" she asked.

He again stood, unable to remain seated. As he paced before her, his expression was almost one of pain.

"I spoke of . . . my feelings, Miss Bennet." As he said these words, he turned to her and his eyes held hers.

"I see. And what did you tell me of your feelings?"

He stopped directly in front of her and reached for her hand. He held it tentatively between his own. "I told you that I love you, Miss Bennet."

They stared into each other's eyes, and there was a moment or two of silence while he waited for her reaction.

She looked up at him and, keeping him in suspense no longer, finally spoke.

"I believe your exact words were, 'I love you, *Lizzy,*'" she said as she gave him the most delicious smile.

"You . . . you heard me?"

"Yes, I'm afraid so, Mr. Darcy."

"All of it?"

"Yes, all of it, including your proposal. So if you are thinking that you can back out of it, I must advise you, sir, that I intend to hold you to it."

"Oh, Lizzy," he said as he pulled her up into his embrace. When he released his tight hold upon her, he lowered his mouth to hers and kissed her sweetly.

"Tell me you love me, Lizzy," he whispered.

"I love you, William, so very much."

CHAPTER FIFTY-FOUR

Mr. and Mrs. Hurst arrived at Pemberley, unaware of the situation that had developed during their absence. They were greeted by their brother who led them to Darcy's study where he informed them of the events that had taken place over the last several days.

The couple was shocked to learn of such news, but as Mrs. Hurst observed, "It was only a matter of time before Caroline's obsession with Mr. Darcy wrought havoc of some kind."

Caroline's ultimate fate was yet to be decided; however, Charles had already written to distant cousins in the Scottish Highlands requesting that she be allowed to live with them on their pig farm. He assured them that she would earn her room and board in whatever manner the running of such a farm might require of her.

Caroline Bingley did not take kindly to the fate to which she had been relegated, but, when offered the choice of Bedlam or a pig farm in the Scottish Highlands, she saw the wisdom of the second choice. Of course, she did not go quietly into that good night as she spewed out every abuse she could think of on her family, Mr. Darcy, and, of course, Miss Eliza, while she was being led away most reluctantly to Mr. Hurst's awaiting carriage.

~*~

Jane Bingley—sweet, compassionate, and caring Jane Bingley—was starting to weigh on her sister's patience.

"Jane, I assure you I am recovered enough to leave my bedchamber. At least let me go down to breakfast and perhaps sit on the veranda for some fresh air," stated Elizabeth as she tried to keep a pleasant demeanour.

As Jane finally acquiesced to her sister's plea, she allowed Elizabeth to go below stairs and breakfast with the rest of Pemberley's inhabitants.

Darcy stood as soon as she entered the room, and their eyes met. Georgiana was the first to greet her. "I am so happy to see you up and around, Elizabeth. You can never know my relief that you are so well recovered," said the young girl as tears filled her eyes. The two young women hugged, and Elizabeth assured her she was certainly not to blame for what had occurred.

Mr. Bingley offered his greeting also, almost afraid to meet her eyes, as he conceded some guilt in the matter. She gave him a reassuring smile. "It is your nature, Charles, just as it is Jane's, to look for the good in everyone. I cannot hold that against you, sir."

Darcy finally approached her. He reached for her hand and tucked it under his arm as he led her to the breakfast table. Elizabeth blushed but was pleased by his attendance. As they sat beside each other, he took hold of her hand and did not let it go.

There had hardly been a ripple of surprise when Darcy and Elizabeth informed Jane, Charles, and Georgiana of their engagement. Mrs. Reynolds seemed least surprised of all by the news and barely batted an eye. It seemed the happy couple were the only ones who had not been aware of the love they shared for each other.

Darcy leaned towards Elizabeth and whispered in her ear, "I am happy to see you have been given a reprieve, Elizabeth. Was it time off for good behaviour?" he asked with a smile. "I hope to change that very soon."

She blushed again, but she did not argue the point. Indeed, they had not been able to spend five minutes alone together, a situation they both found quite disagreeable.

Elizabeth assured her sister that she and Charles might return to Netherfield until the wedding. After all, they were newlyweds themselves and should be allowed some private time together in their own home.

"Georgiana will be here to chaperone us. Besides, you know I will not leave Ellie, so there is little point in trying to convince me to return with you to Netherfield."

Jane informed her they would yet stay two days before leaving, just to make sure that her recovery was complete.

~*~

The next day Elizabeth was allowed to venture as far as the veranda where, at least, she was able to watch Ellie play in the garden. However, she was prohibited from leaving the divan and had to content herself with sitting by Mr. Darcy's side while Jane looked on, observing them.

On the following day she practically had to demand that she be able to take a walk in the gardens. Darcy joined her immediately, carrying Ellie in his arms. He set the little girl carefully on her feet, as he tried to avoid touching the now black and blue remnants of the bruises she had incurred that horrible day. He knew those marks were nothing compared to the injuries that might have befallen the little girl if not for Lizzy's quick reaction. As Ellie's feet touched the ground, she immediately toddled towards Elizabeth, calling to her, "Izabet!" This caused a slight frown on Darcy's face.

Elizabeth looked up to him in question, but he simply shook his head and smiled at her to ease her concern. Elizabeth scooped her daughter up in her arms and kissed her face a dozen times or more, causing the little girl to giggle till she was breathless.

The three then set out on their walk, each holding one of Ellie's hands. When they reached a curve in the path, Darcy looked behind them, making sure they could not be seen from the veranda where they had left Jane's company.

Darcy lifted Ellie and, holding her in one arm, brought his other arm around Elizabeth's waist, drawing her near. "Do you think I might at least steal a kiss today, Elizabeth?"

"I do not think you will have to steal it, William, for I am more than willing to give it to you," she teased.

He bent towards her and placed his lips over hers. They kissed a long sweet kiss—until Ellie made it clear she was missing their attention.

"I hate to admit it," sighed Elizabeth, "but I will not be too sorry to see Jane and Charles leave tomorrow."

~*~

As Mr. and Mrs. Bingley seated themselves in their carriage, Jane enumerated the list of *do*s and *don't*s, which turned out having many *don't*s and very few *do*s, that Elizabeth was to follow. Elizabeth assured her sister she would take care and adhere to her advice.

The carriage had no more than driven out of sight when Darcy pulled Elizabeth into his arms. He stared down into her eyes for a moment before he kissed her, a kiss that told her how much he loved her.

"Shall we take a walk?" he suggested.

Elizabeth took his arm, and they strolled along a garden path. When they came upon a bench, he led her towards it.

Elizabeth sat down, but Darcy remained standing as she stared up at him with a look of curiosity on her face.

He raised her hand to his lips, kissing it gently, then caressing it between his own two hands.

"I believe you have been denied a proper proposal, Miss Bennet, one which you are fully conscious to receive," he said, a small smile playing on his lips. "And I have been denied the pleasure of hearing you accept me."

He moved to sit beside her on the bench. He did not raise his eyes to hers, but kept his focus steady on their joined hands.

He was quiet for a moment as if seeking the right words to say.

"I had searched for you for so many years, Elizabeth. Before we ever met, I had dreamed of you. But I believed you only existed in my imagination. Had I known you were real, I would never have stopped searching for you."

At last he raised his eyes to hers. "I love you with all my heart, Lizzy, and I regret the pain that you have suffered because of me, but I vow to you now that I will spend the rest of my life proving my love for you and for Ellie. I am sure I do not deserve you, Lizzy, but I am asking you to make my life complete and become my wife."

Elizabeth could not hide the tears that welled in her eyes as she heard his declaration.

"We should not regret what has brought us to this moment in our lives and to this love we now share. I would do it all again to have both you and Ellie in my life. I love you, William, and I cannot wait until we can start our life together. I am most happy at the prospect of being your wife."

He reached into his pocket and removed a small box. As he presented it before her, he opened it and withdrew the diamond and ruby ring that it contained.

He slipped the ring on her finger.

"This ring once belonged to my mother, Elizabeth. You are the only other woman to ever wear it." She met his eyes as he made this statement. "I wanted you to know that."

He then leaned over and gave her a kiss so sweet, she was sure she would swoon.

~*~

The following afternoon Darcy found Elizabeth and Georgiana in the music room at the pianoforte. He was carrying Ellie in one arm and a picnic basket in the other.

"I have come to invite both of you ladies on a picnic by the lake," he informed them.

Georgiana watched as her brother and Elizabeth looked at each other, their love clearly showing in their eyes.

"Oh, Brother, I cannot come with you. I promised Mrs. Reynolds I would help her with the menus for the week. Would you mind terribly going on without me?"

Georgiana knew her excuse was weak at best, but she hoped it might be accepted as the truth. She knew the newly engaged couple had not been able to spend any time alone together. Surely there were things that betrothed couples needed to talk about in private, she thought.

"Are you sure, Georgiana?" asked Elizabeth.

"Yes, you go with Ellie and Fitzwilliam. I shall see you later."

~*~

Ellie sat on her father's lap at the edge of the lake. He had just finished tying a rather large and repulsive looking fly to the end of his line, and Ellie made a face at him indicating her abhorrence.

Elizabeth was sitting under a tree a short distance away on a blanket as she watched William and their daughter fish.

"Have you written your family about the wedding yet, Elizabeth?"

"Not yet, but I must do it soon as the banns will shortly be announced at Meryton Church. I want this to be a small, simple wedding, William, and if I give my mother too much time to prepare, it will be anything but. I can't even imagine what her reaction will be to our marrying. "Have you written to yours?"

"I guess we are of the same mind, my dearest Lizzy. If I could whisk you off to Gretna Green tomorrow, I would. I will write to them in a few days."

He felt a tug on the end of his fishing line. As he reeled in the fish, Ellie squealed with delight. He took the fish in his hands and allowed Ellie to touch it as it flipped around, his large hands barely able to contain it. She watched it curiously for several moments.

When she was satisfied with her investigation of the creature, Darcy released the fish and Ellie clapped her hands as they watched it swim away.

After they had depleted the picnic basket, Ellie soon fell asleep while Elizabeth sat with her back against the tree. Darcy moved over to her and rested his head in her lap. She closed her eyes and let herself float in the perfection of the day.

"We have yet to find a new nanny for Ellie. Mrs. Hawkins will be leaving my employ next week," said Darcy

"I have already written to someone with regard to that very thing. I am hoping you will approve."

"Who?"

"Hannah," she said as she waited for his reaction. "Do you have any objections, William?"

He remembered the kind young woman who had first placed his daughter into his arms, the young woman who had been a friend to Lizzy during such a difficult time in her life.

"I have none at all. I think it a splendid idea. I would trust her with Ellie's care without question."

He lifted his head and gave her a kiss. That was all he had intended for it to be, just a quick little kiss. But as his lips moved over hers, he found himself unwilling to withdraw. Instead he moved beside her and put his arms around her and deepened the kiss. She responded with equal enthusiasm, moving her hands down his shoulders and over his chest.

He pulled her closer as his hands moved slowly over the edge of her bodice. He felt the satiny texture of her skin, and then his fingers delved into the fabric that had shielded her pert nipples. He kissed his way down her throat and moved his mouth towards . . .

Ellie awoke with a cry, but upon seeing Elizabeth and Darcy seated near her, she immediately brightened and sat up.

Darcy sighed but smiled at his daughter as he reached over and scooped her up, placing her happily between her mother and father.

~*~

The following evening Darcy, dressed in his most striking tailcoat and trousers, waited at the bottom of the stairs as Elizabeth and Georgiana descended. They were also dressed in their finest as they were about to be escorted to a concert in Lambton.

It was their first time out in public together, and Elizabeth found herself quite the envy of many young women, as Darcy was his most attentive. During the concert he sat between the two women while he held Lizzy's hand.

As the music swelled around them, Darcy stealthily undid the two buttons of her glove. He inched the garment down from her hand. When her palm was fully exposed, he brought it to his lips and kissed it provocatively.

Elizabeth found it most difficult to concentrate on the music. She was grateful that the room was so dimly lit, for she was sure her colour was high. She was also appreciative of the darkness that allowed him to continue his seemingly innocent, yet erotic, ministrations.

When they returned to Pemberley, Darcy gave Georgiana a kiss on the cheek at her chamber door, and then he stood with Elizabeth at hers. He enfolded her in his arms.

"We are finally alone for a few minutes, Elizabeth." As he was about to bring his lips to hers, he heard a door open.

Georgiana stepped from her room, and the two quickly stood apart. "I am just going to check on Ellie. Would you like to come with me, Elizabeth?" she said.

"Yes . . ." she said as she looked over to William, an apologetic look on her face. "Let me just say goodnight to William. I will be right there."

He bent down and gave her a quick kiss and whispered in her ear. "Meet me at the stables at first light." She raised an eyebrow but nodded her head in agreement.

CHAPTER FIFTH-FIVE

Darcy approached the stables as the dawn just hinted of its arrival. As he approached Shayla's stall, he heard a conversation in progress. Well, it was more of a one sided conversation.

"Wait a minute. Don't be so impatient!"

"There you go, girl. You like that, don't you?"

It was Elizabeth's voice. She was talking to her horse!

"Good, isn't it? Hey, just the apple, not my fingers!"

Darcy smiled to himself. *God, how I love this woman.*

He approached the stall where she stood, her back to him as she fed Shayla pieces of apple. He slipped his arms around her waist, kissing the back of her neck as he did.

Elizabeth let out a gasp but quickly identified her attacker. "William! What are you doing?"

"I was planning to kiss you, Lizzy, a plan that everyone at Pemberley seems determined to foil."

As if on cue, Darcy turned to see Billy, the stable boy, approaching and released his arms from Lizzy's waist.

"Beggin' your pardon, sir," said Billy as he approached his master. He timidly looked up at Darcy. "I . . .I wanted to thank ya, Mr. Darcy. For sparin' the horse, sir."

Darcy looked down at the boy and put his hand on his shoulder.

"You are the one who should be thanked, Billy. It took courage to come and tell me what you saw, to ask me to spare the horse. You did the right thing. You defended a poor helpless animal from my undeserved wrath." Darcy reached into his pocket and produced several silver half crowns. "Such courage should be rewarded," he said as he smiled at the young boy.

The young boy's eyes grew wide. As he received the silver coins, he looked up and gave Darcy a large grin before going on to perform his duties.

Elizabeth looked at Darcy with so much love she thought her heart would burst. He truly was the best of men.

Darcy had their horses saddled; as he gave her a leg up to mount Shayla, Elizabeth commented, "I believe this was on Jane's *don't* list," she teased. "Where are we going?"

"It is a surprise."

He returned the inquisitive look she gave him with a smile.

After they had ridden almost a half hour, they came upon a beautiful glass-domed building, looming up from the ground in the middle of the field like a mountain.

As he helped her dismount, he said, "I thought it was about time you saw the orangery."

"Oh, I have heard much of such a place. Is this where you take all your young ladies?"

"I assure you that you are the first," he said, then realizing the implication of his answer corrected himself. "I have no ladies other than you, Elizabeth."

"I am relieved to hear it, William," she teased.

He drew her into his arms. "The day of your injury, it was my plan to ride here. I was hoping I would be able to find a little time alone with you. I had intended to tell you that day that I loved you."

They stared deeply into each other's eyes. He kissed her sweetly and then took her hand, leading her towards the entrance. As he opened the door for her, he gave her a devilish grin. "While other places at Pemberley may rival its beauty, none other can rival its privacy."

They entered, and Elizabeth marvelled at the sight. It was an explosion of flowers. Since it was summer, the orange trees were not being housed inside; instead, every flower you could think of was blooming all around them.

Divans and tables were placed around the blooming rows of fragrant flowers for one to sit and take in the enjoyable view. They walked hand in hand past row after row of orchids and lilies and roses, and freesias and gardenias on and on and on.

They were enjoying the simple pleasure of being completely alone together in such a romantic and private setting with no one to interrupt them—no Jane, no Ellie, no Georgiana—just the two of them . . . alone.

As they reached the last row of flowers, he turned to her and put his arms around her shoulders. She snuggled close to him as she wrapped her arms around his waist. They stayed like that for several minutes.

He then withdrew his arms and tilted her face upwards to join him in a kiss. Her response was to meet him half way as their lips softly met.

"I am beginning to think you may have an ulterior motive for bringing me here, Mr. Darcy," she said teasingly as they broke from their kiss.

"Nothing of the kind," he said. "I believe my motives have been quite transparent; I have every intention of taking advantage of these few precious moments we have alone, Miss Bennet. I am reasonably sure that my intentions are honourable," he said with a grin.

Thursday's Child

She looked up at him and gave him a shy smile, but she had to admit his words held a certain amount of excitement. She, too, had been hoping they would have time alone.

She could not control the sigh that escaped her lips as he teasingly brushed his mouth across hers, trying to gauge what her response might be if he furthered his attentions. The thought of resisting his kisses had not even entered her mind, as she found herself anticipating the kiss to come. He did not disappoint, as he brought his mouth firmly down on hers.

How sweet to feel her lips against his own and to know all her experience at such an endeavour was due to him and no other. She was his and his alone. He moved his mouth over hers, and she granted him the access he sought as they deepened their kiss. They were both lost in the sensations that kiss created.

"Lizzy," he breathed, the sound of his voice thick with emotion. Trying to hold back the passion that he feared would be unleashed at any moment, he pulled away. As he looked down at her, her eyes remained closed, awaiting their next kiss. "We do not have to stay, Lizzy," he whispered. "We can leave if that is your wish."

She opened her eyes and stared into his, but made no attempt at escape. As he wrapped his arms around her tightly, they kissed again, both of them lost in the power of its intensity. His breath became ragged. "I feel my willpower weakening, Lizzy; you will have to stop me," he murmured between kisses.

She did not stop him. She did not want to leave the pleasure of his embrace yet. Just a few more kisses, she told herself.

The next kiss came without delay as he let his hands travel the length of her back, not ceasing until he cupped her bottom and brought her closer to the source of his need. She could feel the full measure of his passion pressed against her.

"Oh, Lizzy, how I love you so."

His kisses then trailed their way down the length of her throat, paying special attention to the spot just where her neck and shoulder met. He lingered there, feeling the rapid beat of her pulse. When his lips reached the top of her bodice, he hesitated, but then pushed the fabric off her shoulder as his tongue laved the exposed nipple. Elizabeth released a moan of pleasure as her hands raked through his hair, pulling him closer. She closed her eyes and relished the feel of his mouth upon her breast, the way his tongue washed over the tip, sending sensations throughout her entire body.

They were both breathless. "William . . ."

He lifted his head and peered into her eyes, love and desire clearly conveyed in his look. Yes, he wanted her; he wanted her so much it physically hurt.

He brought his forehead to hers, his breathing erratic. "Perhaps my motives are not as honourable as I had hoped, Lizzy."

"I am afraid I have done little to discourage you, William," she said, her voice shaky.

"I am going to try to do things in their proper order this time, Lizzy," he said as he helped her straighten her clothes.

"Oh, William, I wish our wedding were tomorrow," she sighed.

As he struggled to get his ardour under control, he confessed with a groan, "I wish it were yesterday."

CHAPTER FIFTY-SIX

A few subsequent early morning trips were made to the orangery in the following days, but they managed to maintain a certain amount of restraint. They did allow themselves *some* latitude, considering they were an engaged couple. Darcy was beginning to have great affection for the orangery.

Upon returning from one of these most delightful outings, they left the stables and entered Pemberley through the back entrance.

"I will go see to Ellie. I believe Georgiana was taking her for a walk this morning," said Elizabeth. Darcy pulled her one last time into his embrace to give her a quick kiss before she headed out to the gardens. Darcy headed for his study.

Soon they would be man and wife. That was all Darcy could think about. Of course, they could have anticipated their vows any number of times over the last two weeks, but because of their unusual beginning, he was trying to do everything right; he wanted her to have a proper courtship, as short as it was. He did not want their past relationship to have any bearing on how they now conducted themselves. Their wedding night would be special; they would consummate their love for the first time in two years.

He stood looking out the window of his study, and as the thought of making love to Lizzy brought a delightful smile to his countenance, the door to his study burst open and Lady Catherine de Bourgh entered, accompanied by a sombre looking gentleman.

His smile quickly faded.

Lady Catherine was carrying Ellie. The little girl had tears in her eyes; as she saw her father, she reached out to him, but Lady Catherine denied her the comfort of his arms.

Georgiana and Mrs. Reynolds rushed in behind them. "I tried to stop them, Mr. Darcy, but they pushed their way past me," explained Mrs. Reynolds. Georgiana looked pale as a ghost.

"It's all right, Mrs. Reynolds. I will see to them," he reassured her. "You and Georgiana should go upstairs while I attend to this matter." He looked over to his sister and nodded. "It will be all right, Georgie. Go with Mrs. Reynolds."

She reluctantly did as he asked, but turned back to look at him one last time, the look of worry still upon her face.

"What can I do for you, Aunt Catherine?"

"You can be at no loss to understand the reason for my journey."

"You are mistaken, Aunt, I am quite unable to account for it. If you are here to see Ellie, you know you are always welcome to visit. Of course, I would prefer a little advance notice next time."

At that moment Elizabeth rushed into the study about to tell him that Ellie was nowhere to be found, suddenly stopping when she took in the scene before her. Her eyes then went to William's.

"Miss Bennet, you will leave this study immediately. We are discussing a private family matter, a matter that is none of your concern," said Lady Catherine.

"Miss Bennet is my fiancée, Aunt, and she can stay wherever she wishes while in my home."

"Your fiancée? That is what comes from associating with tradesmen and servants! Are the shades of Pemberley to be thus polluted? Now I shall be twice as happy to remove my granddaughter from this house."

Elizabeth startled.

"I believe we have had this conversation before. Ellie is to remain with me, under my care and protection."

"That is your opinion. Now others shall make that determination."

Darcy walked over to his aunt. "You will hand over my daughter right now, Aunt. Do you understand? Right . . . *now*!"

"It will make little difference, Fitzwilliam. For tomorrow I will return with the magistrate, and I shall have the papers that will force you to relinquish Ellie's guardianship over to me."

"Do not make me ask you *again*," he said as he stared her down.

As she allowed him to remove the child from her arms, she again retorted, "I can wait one more day to claim her."

"You will never take Ellie from my care, Aunt Catherine; that I promise you." As he spoke, Ellie put her arms around his neck and hugged him tightly. He kissed her cheek and turned towards Elizabeth.

"Elizabeth, will you take her to the nursery and please tell Georgiana not to worry."

She took Ellie into her arms but did not move towards the door. She gave him that look, the defiant one, but he smiled at her reassuringly.

"It will be all right, Elizabeth."

She left the study with Ellie, happy to remove her daughter from Lady Catherine's view, but unhappy that she did not know what the woman was plotting.

"Now, what is all this about?" asked Darcy.

"I am sure you know why I am here, Nephew."

"I repeat, Aunt, I have no idea what has brought you to Pemberley this morning."

"Then let me enlighten you. I have come to take my granddaughter to live with me at Rosings."

"As long as I draw breath, that shall never happen."

"Let me be rightly understood, Nephew. I will have the law on my side this time! A report of an alarming nature reached me six days ago. I was informed that my granddaughter has been the victim of neglect and abuse!"

"I assure you that is not the case. As you saw, Ellie is perfectly safe."

"I do *not* think that is the case, nor does Dr. Smyth. Is that not so, Doctor?" she inquired of the grim looking gentleman beside her.

Dr. Smyth cleared his throat. "I have examined the girl and have found multiple bruises on both her arms and legs. Clearly, the child has been abused, and I will say so in my report to the magistrate."

"And I will petition to become the child's legal guardian; I am not in the habit of brooking disappointment. What do you have to say to that, Nephew?"

Darcy studied his aunt for a long moment. "I am sure the report you received also included the fact that Ellie's bruises were a result of an accident. Dr. Chisholm can verify this fact."

"Of course your doctor would lie to cover up your misdeeds. But I assure you, Dr. Smyth is a well-respected physician with connections in very high places, and his word shall prevail."

"Aunt Catherine, I believe it would be prudent that we continue our talk in private."

"Whatever you have to say to me can be said in front of Dr. Smyth," she countered.

"I am curious, Aunt; why are you so intent on having Ellie live with you? Is it so that you can bestow the same loving attention on her as you did Anne?"

"Of course, I would do no less for Ellie than I did for Anne. The child belongs with me, and I will see that it comes to pass."

He again gave his aunt a long studied look. He then reached down to the bottom drawer of his desk and withdrew a small box, secured by a lock. Producing a key from under his blotter, he unlocked the box and removed an envelope.

Lady Catherine watched intently as he did these things. As he placed the envelope on the desk, she noted the broken seal. She recognized it immediately as that of her late husband's. Her look of confidence was less apparent.

As Darcy watched his aunt eye the envelope, he said, "I will give you one last chance to discuss this matter in private."

She glared at her nephew. What was he up to? Until she found out, she would act on the side of caution.

"Perhaps my nephew is right. We have some family matters to discuss. Wait in the barouche, Dr. Smyth," she said, her eyes never leaving those of her nephew.

Dr. Smyth bowed as he left her company, and Darcy waited until he had closed the door behind him before he spoke.

"Have a seat, Aunt Catherine," he said as he walked around his desk and sat in his chair.

She did as he bade, but made her annoyance known as she harrumphed as she sat.

"I would suggest that you cease with this fallacy or, as much as it would grieve me, I shall have to make the contents of this envelope public knowledge."

"I am not so easily put off. I am sure whatever is contained in that envelope is of no concern to me."

"Perhaps you had better learn of its contents before you make such a determination, Aunt Catherine."

Darcy picked up the envelope and removed the official document from within.

"Well, if you are so intent upon my knowing what it contains, then tell me. What is it?"

He held up the document. "This is the registrar's certificate of Anne's birth," he said quite simply.

Darcy could see the colour drain from her face. "No such thing exists. You are bluffing, and I will not be intimidated."

He ignored her rebuff.

"I would have said it was the registrar's certificate of your daughter's birth, but we both know that is not the case, do we not, Aunt?"

She reached for the document, and he allowed her to look at it for a brief moment before he took it from her shaking hands.

"Be forewarned, Aunt; should you ever try to take guardianship of Ellie, I will not hesitate to make the contents of this document known to all."

"You would not dare."

"Are you willing to take that chance? I doubt that Anne would have objected to my revealing her true parentage if it meant saving Ellie from your grasp. Would you care for all of London to know of Sir Lewis's bastard child? To know you were neither Anne's mother, nor are you grandmother to the heir of Pemberley?"

"You would be harming your own reputation as well, Fitzwilliam, by revealing such a thing. Imagine the scandal that would erupt upon announcing to all good society that you married the daughter of a scullery maid!" The words spewed from her mouth with disdain.

"It would not concern me for a moment. Anne was one of the sweetest, most generous women of my acquaintance. For those reasons alone, I should have realized years ago that she could not have been of your blood. I will not hesitate to disclose her true parentage should you dare try anything like this again. Miss Bennet will be my wife in two weeks, and she will be the best of mothers to Ellie, and you will do nothing to interfere in our lives. If you think I am bluffing, Aunt, I would think again if I were you, for I assure you I am not."

Lady Catherine stood. She opened her mouth to speak, but, for once in her life, she was speechless. She turned and, without so much as a backward glance, left his study.

Darcy looked down at the document in his hand. His talk that night with Lord Westcott had confirmed his suspicions that Sir Lewis had fathered a child by their cook's eldest daughter, Margaret. Meg Harrigan. Anne had spoken of her once, of the affection she had received from the young girl with the copper hair and green eyes.

He refolded the document and placed it carefully back into the box.

CHAPTER FIFTY-SEVEN

Mr. Edward Gardiner stood at the rear of the small church in Meryton, his niece Elizabeth beside him. She took his arm as he proudly led her down the aisle towards the man who in moments would become her husband, her life's companion. Their pace was slow, for she was preceded by her sister Jane, her matron of honour, and Ellie, her flower girl.

Darcy waited patiently at the front of the church, Colonel Fitzwilliam standing beside him as his best man.

The church was filled to capacity as Mrs. Bennet had told as many people as she could in the short time she had, that her favourite daughter Lizzy was to be married to the Master of Pemberley. Mrs. Long, Sir William and Lady Lucas, and Mr. And Mrs. Philips were seated in the same pew as Mrs. Bennet. Kitty, Mary, Mrs. Gardiner, Maria, and Charlotte sat behind them.

Lydia did not make the trip as her confinement was nearing its end, and she would give birth at any time. She did, however, send a letter of congratulations. Well, at least it started out as such. She ended the note by saying that if Mr. Darcy was half as dull as her dear Wickie had described, she was sure Elizabeth would be most discontented.

Mr. Collins declined to attend the service, most likely advised by Lady Catherine that it would not meet with her approval.

Thursday's Child

Lord and Lady Matlock, Georgiana, Charles Bingley and Hannah sat across the aisle, along with Mr. and Mrs. Hurst, Lord Westcott and his daughter, Arielle.

As Ellie eyed her father at the end of the aisle, she moved more deliberately towards him. When she reached him, he took her hand, and she stood beside him, while Jane moved to the opposite side of the altar.

Mr. Gardiner kissed his niece on the cheek and relinquished Elizabeth to Mr. Darcy.

The couple looked into each other's eyes, and their exchanged looks conveyed all they needed to know. They turned and stood before the minister, their daughter between them. They spoke their vows and pledged their love to each other.

A breakfast wedding feast was held at Netherfield following the ceremony, after which the bride and groom, Ellie, and Hannah departed for Pemberley.

~*~

Elizabeth Darcy sat before her pier glass, draped in the beautiful pink silk dressing gown she had bought that day in St. Andrews. She remembered sitting in her room at the Fairmont Inn, wearing the same gown, thinking how she must look as a bride might on her wedding night, waiting for her husband to come to her. And now it was so. She was waiting for William to come to her.

She had declined his offer of a honeymoon trip, at least for now. She could not bring herself to leave Ellie just yet. Perhaps in a few months she would feel comfortable enough to do so. William had assured her she had nothing to fear; Ellie would never be taken from them.

He did not knock but entered from the sitting room. He was dressed in a dark blue silk robe, which emphasized his muscular form. He walked to where she sat and stood behind her as their eyes met in the pier glass. He let his fingers run through her hair, which was brushed out long and flowing over her shoulders. He bent down and moved it aside as he kissed her neck, while inhaling her lavender scent.

"You look beautiful, Lizzy," he said as their gazes met again in the pier glass.

She stood and turned towards him. "And you look devastatingly handsome in that robe, William." She let her hands run over the silk fabric as she caressed his shoulders.

She knew it was illogical to be nervous. Had they not already been intimate? Indeed, two years ago they had made love on their final night together in Scotland. But their recent trips to the orangery had revealed to Elizabeth that William had far more to teach her; there were more pleasures yet to discover.

He drew her into his embrace as her arms went around his neck, and they kissed; a slow, meticulous, lingering kiss that was meant to arouse all their senses. She took pleasure in the velvet of his tongue against hers as his hands unravelled the bow of her dressing gown.

He kissed along her jaw and down her neck while his hands traced over her body. He moved the material of her gown aside and slid his hands over her curves, cupping her breasts and running his thumbs over her nipples.

"Lizzy," he breathed out, "I know I am impatient, but I have been waiting for you for so long, imagining this night."

"I am just as impatient as you, William," she assured him.

He turned her towards the pier glass so that she could see their reflection. At first she was embarrassed at the mirror image looming so large in front of her, but, as she watched his hands caress her breasts, she let herself relax. The sight of watching themselves was arousing them both as their eyes stayed focused on the passion that was displayed before them. He slid the pink silk dressing gown from her shoulders, and she watched the reflection of it fall to the floor. Darcy stopped momentarily and stared at the bountiful beauty before him.

She was unknowingly holding her breath as his hands started moving slowly across her body, one resting lightly on the curve of her stomach while the other continued its journey towards what was now the centre of her universe. As his fingers mercifully reached their objective, she let out a sigh of pleasure. She turned in his arms, and they kissed again, while her hands searched for the tie of his robe. She moved her hands over his chest and was amazed to discover that he enjoyed much the same pleasures as she as her fingers traced the circle of his nipples. Her mouth was soon to follow, and her tongue flicked over a nipple. The sound he emitted confirmed his pleasure.

He brought her lips to his, and his kiss was so searing that she thought they might soon be enveloped in flames. Then, starting with her neck, he began to kiss her with torturously exquisite slowness, his lips making their way down her body until he was finally on his knees, worshiping her with his mouth.

When he felt her tremble, he rose and carried her to the bed, placing her on the pillows. He quickly ridded himself of his robe and lowered himself over her. She reached her arms up, drawing him closer. She revelled in the weight of him, the warmth of him, and the feel of his body over hers as he caressed her everywhere. Her only thoughts were of his next kiss, his next touch.

He could hold out no longer as he moved his body between her thighs and drew her to him, entering her on a sigh of pleasure. Their pace was quick as they reached the pinnacle of bliss which they had denied themselves for so long.

He nestled her in his arms. "I am afraid my love for you is equalled only by my desire for you, Lizzy. And you know I love you beyond measure," he said with some amusement.

"I guess it is a hardship I will have to endure as best I can, William," she responded with equal amusement.

They kissed again, and she snuggled against him.

"I love you, Lizzy."

"And I love you, William."

They were both asleep in minutes.

During the night, he moved against her, and his hands automatically drew her close, bringing her back to rest against his chest. As he felt the warmth of her body brush against his, he was immediately aroused. He reached around to cup her breasts and felt the nipples tighten with his touch. He was unsure if she would think him a beast to again indulge his passion for her, and her sigh of pleasure only served to increase his desires.

As his touches awoke her, she soon responded. She turned in his embrace, and they kissed. As each subsequent kiss was more intense than the last, it was evident that their hunger had not yet been fully satisfied. In the haze of sleep and the total darkness of the room, her boldness grew as she allowed her hands to explore his body. She circled his nipples with her fingers, and then kissed each one as she moved her mouth across his chest. He welcomed each touch, each caress. When he tried to bring her lips back to his, she resisted. She wanted to know more.

Her attention then made its way towards his hardened arousal, and she caressed him there, moving her hand down its length and then up again to encompass the tip. His breath became ragged. "Lizzy," he breathed out as he struggled to maintain control.

She moved her mouth down his body, and he closed his eyes as the pleasure engulfed him; he knew her destination. He also knew his restraint was on the verge of exhaustion. He forced her upwards and pulled her into his arms, then quickly rolled her onto her back.

"Do not worry, Lizzy," he whispered into the dark, "in time we shall experience all of it."

He entered her swiftly as they once again sought to relieve the insatiable need of their passion.

With their desires replete, Darcy acknowledged that he had yet to take his time with his new bride. But then again, they had the rest of their lives to become accustomed to such intimacies, a highly enjoyable prospect.

EPILOGUE

Elizabeth awoke the next morning and stretched her arms over her head. The smile on her face said it all. She reached for her husband, only to find him gone. For a brief moment she thought perchance he had he gone back to his own room during the night. Perhaps it was his intention for them to sleep in separate rooms. She knew many married couples did. But as she thought upon the night they had just enjoyed, she did not think it very likely.

Then the door to her chamber opened, and he appeared. "Oh, you are awake," he said as he removed his robe and slipped back into bed.

Her eyes grew wide, and she bit her lip, still unused to seeing her husband naked.

"Where had you gone?" she asked.

"There was a matter I needed to attend to," he responded as he drew her into his arms. As Elizabeth snuggled against him, he made his intentions quite clear, and Elizabeth was reassured that sleeping in separate rooms was definitely not in their future.

This time as they made love, it was not in a frenzied rush, but slowly, as they took their time enjoying each other, teaching and discovering each new pleasure that brought them once again to the height of passion.

As they rose for the day, Elizabeth immediately went to the nursery. Ellie was in her crib, and upon seeing Elizabeth, she stood up and raised her arms to be lifted out.

"Mama. Mama, up! Up!"

Elizabeth inhaled a sharp breath and stared at her daughter. Her precious child had just called her "Mama." She could feel the happy tears that welled in her eyes. She reached over and lifted Ellie from the crib and into her arms, embracing her tightly.

Darcy stood in the doorway, a look of satisfaction on his face. Right there; that was the image he would carry in his memory for the rest of his life.

She turned and saw him standing there, an endearing smile upon his face.

"You are not the only one who can make such use of miniatures, Lizzy," he said as he approached them.

"Will people not wonder at her calling me Mama?"

"Let them think what they will. We are a family, and the world will regard us as such. And those who do not, are of little concern to us."

He put his arms around his wife and daughter. Whatever adversities life might put in their path, they would face and conquer them all, together as a family, and he would never allow anything or anyone to harm them.

~*~

"Good morning, William," she said as he entered the stables. Elizabeth was already perched upon Shayla.

"I was surprised to awaken and find a note on your pillow instead of you, Lizzy. It was a poor substitute," he admitted as he looked up at her. "Why did you wish me to meet you here?"

"It has been so long since we have had one of our early morning rides, I thought we would take one this morning."

"Where do you have in mind," he asked.

Billy then appeared around the corner, leading Marengo from his stall to his master.

"Since we have not travelled there since before our wedding, I thought we might visit the orangery."

He raised his eyebrows in surprise. "Why there?" he asked as he took the reins from Billy and nodded his thanks to the young boy.

"Well, I have such fond memories of the time we spent there, William," she said as she gave him her most mischievous smile, "and I was always curious as to how we might have conducted ourselves . . . had we not any impediments to restrain our . . . activity."

Darcy looked up into her eyes, his desire aroused. How was he ever so fortunate as to have this woman as his wife?

"I am more than willing to help satisfy your curiosity, Lizzy," he said as he mounted Marengo.

She gave Shayla a slight tap of the reins to set the mare in motion and headed for the stable door.

He looked at her curiously. Was she only toying with him?

"Be careful, Lizzy, or I may just take you up on it."

"I am counting on it, sir," she replied.

As she passed the threshold, she turned back and just before she kicked Shayla into a full gallop, she said, "Of course, you will have to catch me first."

The End

Thursday's Child

IF YOU WOULD LIKE TO COMMENT ON THE BOOK YOU HAVE JUST READ, CONTACT
PAT SANTARSIERO
AT

pats.stories820@gmail.com

Visit Pat's Facebook Page

Thursday's Child – a pride and prejudice journey of love.

SHE WOULD LOVE TO HEAR FROM YOU!

Printed in Great Britain
by Amazon.co.uk, Ltd.,
Marston Gate.